Tasker

Tusker

Tasker

also by Bill Reed

BILL REED

Tasker
Tusker
Tasker

a novel

R

Published by Reed Independent, Melbourne, Australia 2018

Printed by Createspace, an Amazon company.

Available from Createspace.com, Amazon.com and most leading worldwide book retail outlets. Also available as an ebook via the major online retail outlets internationally.
paperback ISBN 9780994239907
ebook ISBN 9780994239914

Cover: 'Mind activating elephant red on green' by Jogdragoon courtesy of Child of Light, c/- FlamingText.com and Google Open Clipart. Glyph by Shutterstock.com.

National Library of Australia Cataloguing-in-publication data:
Author: Reed, Bill/ author.
Title: Tasker Tusker Tasker/ Bill Reed
ISBN: 9780994239907 (paperback)/ 9780994239914 (ebook)
Subjects: Australia Fiction/Sri Lanka Fiction/mystery
Dewey Number: A823.3

An elephant can't deny it never forgets.

For Evangeline.
Bless you.

But first...

One year to the day before Johnno started reading the dossier, some of the things that happened in Sydney were:

The earth-toned man was having a difficult time of it to muster the required energies, despite the woman's self-preserving efforts in the passageway of her own home.

He reached down and grabbed a handful of her hair and roughly pulled her mouth away from him. This time he did not slap her. In pain, in grief, she could only cow-eye up at him, since she was still being held in that cow-shed position by the other Tamil in heat behind her.

The earth-toned man dismissed his companion's brutish grunts that he wanted to carry on.

'We're running late,' he growled in Tamil. A command.

The distraught woman could understand the language. It was her own, her first still, despite the English.

Before the two men left her, so disgorged, there on her own hallway tiles, the earth-toned man plucked one of her ears upwards and roughly hissed:

'If your husband talks, we come back and the same thing happens to him, and we keep you and your children alive just long enough to watch.'

Yes, the language. Both the husband, the accountant who had been handling the books for the raided travel agency, and his wife understood.

And this also:

In one of the cells deep in Central Police Headquarters, one of the three Tamils being held there following the raid on the travel agency, looked up at the other two with a fierce and hawkish resolution. For a moment there, he had bodily squirmed in the struggle to come to the decision. Now he was ready. His sharp South Indian features gained, for a moment,

1

the pinched aristocracy of his ancestors before the scorn of youth for the other and older two reflected there in an instant of farewell to the craven.

He flipped his tongue to the top side of his mouth, dislodged the cyanide pill and unhesitatingly bit on it as other martyrs of the organisation had done so many times before. It had become the traditional form of defiance, and so was now the honour.

The other two watched him die very, very quickly. They had themselves to worry about. Yet, both of them could not help moving their tongues to the high reaches of their mouths. But there were no cyanide pills there as there should have been.

They would soon shyly smile at each other.

And this as well:

The Tamil passes over his forged passport, visa and first-class ticket to the Customs officer. His expression was genuinely languid. He could have been bored; he could have been tired. He knew there was no likelihood that the superb forgeries would be detected. He had done this so many times in many countries.

In only his late twenties, he was already a veteran of the organisation.

All so inevitable now.

He heard the dull thump of the enabling stamp, collected his documents with barely a nod and proceeded without anxiety through the Departures security systems.

When he strolled around the Departure lounge he was mildly curious about the number of his Tamil colleagues also leaving and also keeping themselves to themselves. So many at around much the same time was unusual. Some minor emergency no doubt, that wouldn't worry him, except that it somewhat offended his training sensibilities that he hadn't been able to finish the extortion procedure he had been flown in for a week earlier. But small irritations.

In the language of Tamil, he thought, it doesn't matter.

He was not to know that the hostilities had ended back in Sri Lanka and, like so many of his fellow fighters, he would soon be turning his attention to make money more comfortably as an out- and-out gangster, rather than as a petty looter of the spoils of civil war. Had he heard about the peace, he would have already known this: they might have negotiated the end to the fighting, but the real negotiations would have been about whom got carved which piece of the crime network that had financed the war. They just keep on popping heads off the battlefields, is all. Nobody on either side would ever cauterise the flow of easy money. There were some things as natural as the light of day, as sensible as the lining of pockets.

As well as this:

Johnno could tell that the intelligence reports on the man had been through too many hands. At the centre of it was the Interpol reports, but the dossier had become overloaded with file cuts from intelligence services in Europe, North America, Southeast Asia, South Asia, including a mishmash from Australia's own then ASIS and ASIO, infiltrated with further gleanings from a swag of State and Federal agencies.

The network the man had been either a large or small part of was huge and confusing but, to Johnno's practised eye, confusing not out of finely honed international planning, but out of an essentially uncoordinated enthusiasm of too many policing agencies and too many chums pitching in with their penny-worth from too many international perspectives.

The Tamils... Brenton D. Johns mused with that thankful objectivity of not having to care much anyway... who would have heard of them a few years ago?

Yet they were always there, working up networks all around the world, coercing, cajoling, blackmailing, killing to realise some supreme gratification of a Tamil home state somewhere in Sri Lanka or southern India. You would think they were just odd, slightly distasteful fifth-stringers, until someone whispers in your ear that there are nearly sixty million of them and it is they who make all the world's other fighting ethnic groups small beer by comparison.

They get their act together, rather than this seeming slopwork in this dossier, Brenton D. Johns thought naively, and they could be a fearful international force on any level.

Not that this Johnno was going to let his toes curl up over that prospect. The dropsy of his centre of gravity, wedged close to the earth beneath him by the shape of a roo's body -- and that itself seemingly held from bursting its sac by a leather lanyard he once purchased as a proud belt -- as plain to the fact that here was a man wedded only to the earth's crust that supported him.

Brenton D. Johns, the First Secretary of the Attorney-General's Department in Canberra, was a man of the hie and hoc, not the honk and tonk. Oh, he could use the distinguished grey furbelow to the jet-black crown of hair to carpet his concerns to faraway hypotheses whenever his position as one of the government's top lawyers had its diplomatic need.

At such times, he would let his portly-vicar appearance carry the pretence of his being occupied with what he had no earthly inclination of being occupied with. And this dossier before him now, even with its global implications, was going to be no exception.

He had only called for it, because it was not every day he had, until recently, on his staff an Assistant Attorney-General, a near Rhodes scholar it was said, who had allegedly been connected to some sort of trail of carnage across three countries.

Not that it was any great worry. Johnno, as he was easily called even to his face, had merely called for the file so that he could remain abreast of the lava flows of gossips in the department he ran, the Simon-pure of exemplary departmental

4

management, as he had apted it. He hadn't scoured the whole dossier, sheaf by sheaf, because anything in folders of any colour, including the pink Ministerials, no longer twanged even memories of curiosity in him, only suppressions of sudden lassitude.

What he could see was a veritable miscellany of international policing form-types and clerkships, all reduced to the yawn-hues of fax machines, and a whole landscape of English vernaculars from different countries that might, to the ill-humoured eye, constitute a far greater crime in themselves than anything the guy of the dossier might be alluding to.

Sighing with what might be that sort of humour, Johnno quickly winged it to a psychological assessment of the man with the alias of 'Tusker'. He did so because this comprised the last few pages of the whole wad and, therefore, was in the position from which he always began the reading of files because it seemed the commonsensical place to start because it simply was the quickest part from which to finish.

A psychological assessment was also something quite unusual in a police-style file. Here was one assessor, thought Johnno, who must have majored in the makings of sociopaths. Between the lines were effusions from lectures remembered, strung with mild iconoclasms of those lectures. You could see that in the heading: 'A Sociopath, No Two Ways About the Split'.

Johnno sighed and tried not to settle himself down too patiently and cause him to inadvertently do more than slide his glances over:

'It is not known when the man might have taken the alias of Tusker. This may have been something remembered from childhood or simply made up when the need for it became apparent to him.

'To assume an alias at all and then to live under it, such that its existence then becomes the raison d'être for criminal activities in itself, supposes some trauma along the way. Whether this trauma occurred before the perp [Johnno

5

shuddered at possibly the worst noun contagion, even before it would *not* go away, from across the Pacific] was allowed into Australia at around the age of nine would only be conjecture at this stage.

'Not that the perp didn't have all the criteria of entry into the country. He was born in the uplands of Sri Lanka of Eileen Mary Langhorn, an Australian national, and a Sri Lankan father, who might or might not have been an elephant trapper and trainer.

'Unless the records have been destroyed in the various commotions that have rocked that little country, it would seem that the perp's parents never married. That, of course, would have been shocking in then traditional Ceylon, especially in the more traditional upland tea estates.

'If, as a boy, he suffered anything like traumatically from this, we might never know. We do know, however, his father made an application to follow the mother and the boy out to Australia, but we do not know why the application was never followed through. There are some references to the reluctance of the Australian High Commissioner of the time to use his discretionary powers under the then guidelines of the White Australia policy. We might conclude that it could have been something to do with the father's colour tones, said to be "intense".

'The pattern we have of this "Tusker" is one of being neurotic, erratic and alienated, as well as hostile. He prefers living alone, and in isolated places. There is something childlike about him. A kind of placidity, a willingness to be moved about by events. You sense that he does not want to be the aggressor, but wants to be seen as a cheerful and a trusted 'mate'. Yet he is not subtle enough to be spontaneously witty. He loves to play "jolly" games on people and likes to be helpful. He'll lie very, very easily to get out of any trouble, however small. He has absolutely no interest in the world beyond what he is focused on.

'This subject comes across as a likeable, plausible person, and a natural imposter, until he loses interest, which is very quickly. Then he'll drop all pretence and move on. He is, yes, a liar, a thief, a brawler and ready to kill. That's why, as a sociopath – for he fits the classic mould -- he is so dangerous, because he can only fake normal feelings of fear, guilt, shame and anxiety. He doesn't feel these emotions; but he can surely and easily and readily fake them. To him, getting caught is far worse than the crime; that is why he can kill with such apparent easy facility. In fact, getting caught by his mother or father, or anything that represents that sort of authority, would be the one thing that would make him stay his hand, at least as a true-to-type.

'There are usually childhood manifestations behind these warps of character. Maybe his mother would have nothing to do with him, and he had to fake being halo happy in order to get thrown a few scraps of care and attention. But, beneath it all, it is most probable that he hated her, so maybe he puts rat poison in her food while he goes off to the movies, and enjoys the show with his "friends".

'The point is, he really will enjoy the show.

'As a sociopath, there is that very cold and strange entity that lives within him. It is the real he. What we observe as the man with the alias of Tusker is only the ventriloquist dummy, and that dummy is the human being you see who would, on the surface of it, bend over backwards to do anything for you. But the entity itself could never exist as a social human being.

'If we look at what this man has so appallingly done in the light of that duality ...'

Added to which...

Brenton D. Johns put the dossier aside because it was lunch and because he had read enough anyway to ward off any doubts someone might raise about him losing astuteness when it came to his staff. Someone else could call for the dossier now.

Nobody did. It stayed on his desk for months.

But then, Johnno would never have noticed, nor would have cared much even if he had.

Part One

First thing, I made up a list.

I've always made up lists. I can't think things through unless I've got a list to consult.

The first item I put down was 'Elephants'.

How, for example, were so many tuskers saved by a technology used in the next item I was about to put down: 'Tamil scams'?

The connection may be a bit loose but it had struck me a few days prior when I was running my eye over some contract CSIRO had wanted to sign with some chemical company for a new type of plastic that did something special like rot fast.

Somewhere in that woggly document, I discovered the connection was an American printer by the name of John Wesley Hyatt who, in 1870, turned his attention to the compound cellulose nitrate and camphor by the offer of a prize of a whacking USD 10,000 by Phelan & Collander, bless their non-synthetic cotton socks.

Hyatt threw in some ethanol and got up a solution with the camphor and then used it as a plasticiser, as the chemists say, for the cellulose nitrate. It worked so well the term celluloid was born. We call it plastic. And, you see, Phelan & Collander were makers of billiard balls and they were fast running out of ivory.

So old Hyatt came through for the African and Asian tuskers. One of the pioneer Conservationists. If only he knew.

I guess what you would call the father of plastics was not only the father of billiard balls that no longer cracked and turned as yellow as any old bull elephant's teeth do, but also the daddy of those plastic explosives my brother was smuggling.

So, there it is as I say: an action and its consequences direct from old John Wesley Hyatt to my second item, 'Tamil scams'.

And the third item I had written down for thinking through --'Family' -- as linked with the second item through the spirit of the elephant that must have imbruted the wild thing I have always imagined my father to have been. And John Wesley Hyatt in there somewhere too, because the less ivory Phelan & Collander used, the less bulls butchered and therefore just maybe a time not happening when my father got so enraged at the senseless 30/30 drilling of the forehead of some magnificent Ceylonese upland bull that he tried to intervene and might've got shot himself.

So perhaps John Wesley Hyatt also saved my father from an early extinction lasting for eternity, give or take a day. My father, yes. Item four.

Not that it would have mattered to us boys or to our mother. With his refusal to have anything to do with any of us, the old bastard deserved to be shot. Full bore, heavy calibre, plenty of shot shoved in, right in the middle of the forehead.

From this you'd have to say that perhaps John Wesley Hyatt also connects up with the fifth subject on the agenda I'm going to put down. But this one, 'Brother', this one so aggravates me that perhaps I shouldn't drag the worthy John Wesley Hyatt into it. He shouldn't have to be part of the slow oxygen burn I get when I think of brother 'Tusker'.

But there's no way out of thinking about my brother. This whole shemozzle, this unpretty pass I have come to, has broken up my life from my brother as suddenly and fractedly as the break of the triangle of John Wesley Hyatt-coated snooker balls.

Not that it's going to be possible not to think of my brother, this so-called 'Tusker'. As this guy's twin, I've always had an imperishable sense of what he was doing, thinking.

10

Oh, there were blurs. Yet these were mere mental fur balls. I had only to think what I would be thinking, to be able to tip what he was thinking. Then, his murderous schemes jagged at me with their shockingly sharp edges. I could *see* him as clearly as if he was in fact myself, and these images were full of drums and background clashings and clangings, full corybantic performances.

It's not that I ever tried to fine-hone this psychic ability. For most of our lives, I didn't care a hoot in hell-or-back where he was or what he was doing. He was a mere *feuilleton* to me, to my life. It's only been in the last year, though, that I've realised I hated the fact that he was around. Always around. The fact that he looked exactly like me, if you take away his embarrassing ebony colour. The fact that I should have ever been put in the position of having to fight in the womb with him for who was getting out of there first.

He *pipped* me there, too, and I've always hated that fact, too.

Can you possibly imagine how many billiard balls were made in the world in the ivory heyday of them?

How many billiard balls out of just one tusk; how many out of one magnificent tusker?

So, John Wesley Hyatt's cellulose also connects with the sixth item I'm going to put down, 'Sri Lanka Then', in that all I can really remember about the first nine years of my life was the elephants working around the estate under my father.

He was the vague darkened-silhouette figure atop them, shouting and prodding them. There was always the trumpeting at night—a bull on heat, a cow reciprocating—and I would lie in my bed and tremble at the sound of the weight of the beasts, frightened, for the walls of the house seemed so thin against what they could intend, always intended.

My brother was never around me then. I don't know where he was. He was so heavy-toned; he is so heavy-toned; and I am the billiard-ball creamy suede of my mother's skin. He might have been lurking out in the dark and smoky rooms of the servants' quarters; certainly, it is inconceivable that my gross grandparents would have let him remain inside the old estate house looking like he had emerged from some primordial inkwell.

Frankly, I didn't even know he existed then.

Okay, 'Australia Then' is the seventh item I'm putting down. I admit that. I've done so because I am Australian not Sri Lankan... let's get that right from the start... and don't go on all that charm-and-votive nonsense. All these years, for my brother though, I think Australia has just been an image in his head. Sri Lanka, too.

He has belonged to nothing, been destructive of everything. That's what I think, and I'm sure of it.

What I mean is, one of us was looking at Australia from the inside and one of us was looking at it from the outside. One of us saw Sri Lanka from the outside and the other saw it from the inside. And, when it all boils down to right and wrong, it is which one of us has been seeing what from where. It's always been like that with us, at least whenever we've connected. I know that so well that I added 'Australia' as a think-through agenda item, in order to anchor me from the madness I suspect possesses him.

There'll be nothing of John Wesley Hyatt here in the 'Australia' item. There'll be no billiards balls in there, no *bombes plastique*, and not even too many elephants. To go in there, there's really only my brother and me. And my mother of course.

'Why am I here?'

This is the last item I want to try to brainstorm through.

I only thought to add it recently, soon after I arrived back here in Sri Lanka in this now-time.

Here I am, back to the mountains of my childhood, in love with a beautiful forty-year-old lady who remains yet a virgin, helping out the good Father Thumbayaserni at the leprosarium here in Gampola, living with a family in a one-bedroom house, with one dunny that's a hole in the ground, and the parents and five little girls and their grandfather and grandmother and great-aunt and great-uncle. And me, the lodger, making up a round dozen.

The overt reason I've come back to my roots is simple.

It was my father who taught me how to track and trap.

I have come back to track and trap and kill my father.

'Tamil scams.'

I'm sitting at my desk, dossed down with a charge of slander against a couple of public servants up there in that wet tropics hotbed of northern Queensland, when Tilly comes up with a condemnatory yelp from across the room that some Inspector Ekanayake is still, she sneers, waiting out there, isn't he?

She might've got up off her bum from that blackjack game she pretends is a spreadsheet on her terminal to have told me he was there in the first place, but, no, not Tilly. She was supposed to service five of us lawyers in that office, but the only servicing she would have done would have been if she was pumped through a petrol hose. Bloody Tilly.

At first he turned out quite affable, this full-blooded Sri Lankan inspector of police, and his deference was only that which the so-called developing Other-World chums affect when visiting so-called first-order nations. Nevertheless, there was no hiding the essential dignity of the man, and I have to give him that. And tall with it, such that not even his crumpled suit (brown, brown, brown; why is brown so prevalent in the Subcontinent if it is not shameless to the hard bakes of its clays?) could shrink to less statesmanship.

I can even remember thinking then that, if this guy was your friend, you'd never be able to shake him off; he'd be the best.

As a copper back home, he would have been respected and obeyed down in his Galle. I had heard of the place professionally. Southern Sri Lanka. A Portuguese-and-Dutch-built real-live fort which was on the World Heritage List -- one of my boss Johnno-imposed legal specialties -- where, I'd heard, there was even a vestige of eccentric Australians hanging on after the civil war ended hoping to catch on to the economic miracle subsequently promised. I believe there was some trouble with them concerning the murder of the Australian High Commissioner recently. As I read it.

'Bloody fucking hell, sorry,' this Inspector Ekanayake came out with.

I begged his pardon.

Sorry, sorry, he repeated, too long with the Sydney CIB. He hadn't settled here, no, but a secondment for a few months. Liaison, it was written. And his long spatulate fingers dropped a batch of charge sheets, xeroxed-reduced, neat and crisp, and he had dropped them right on my desk, the cheeky bozo. As in, why pick on me?

There were seven of them. I glanced at the top one. Dense, almost-touching typed lines gave a look of concentrated confusion to what was on the page concerning some guy called Ramados, a surname I immediately recognised as Indian for some reason, then read to be Tamil. Wanted for extortion and embezzlement. I could see a Sydney address. I didn't bother with the rest. Hey, I was Environment (Legal), a government servant, not some creature with lingering twinges of curiosity.

So, I tried humour just to be a bit friendly, 'Extortion and embezzlement of the environment, Inspector?'

This Inspector Charles Ekanayake was puzzled. Obviously, the language instructor at the Sydney CIB where he had once been seconded hadn't got around to how to recognise a little Aussie joke, beyond conning him into

14

thinking bloody fucking hell was as socially-acceptable and socially-expected as 'cripes' if he was to pass local muster.

'Bloody fucking hell, *nae,* no. I would be wishing it was, isn't it?'

The thick Ceylonese tongue, heavy on the 'O's, rolling English into messing up a perfectly-good swear phrase made my teeth grate. I had spent a lifetime making sure I got my Aussie sounds right, and another lifetime avoiding coming within earshot of anybody who did not have them right. I've been told I was prissy with it. Well, okey-doke to that. But then, at office and not at play, I covered my distaste by mentally swinging my feet up onto my desk, the go-ahead=and-swear-all-you-like attitude, as it can come across. I was going:

'What can I do for you, Inspector?'

And got raised eyebrows and a question back, would you believe?:

'Been being here long, Mr Tasker?'

Bloody fucking hell.

'I have been here all my life, Inspector. What can I do for you?'

'That so?' he answered as though he would believe me in a million years and slid on to: 'Extradition, no?' His screwdriver of a finger was besmirching the character of this character, Ramados, of the charge sheet, as it was meant to before my very eyes.

'Back to India, going, are we?'

I wasn't going to make it easy. It had taken me years to become a full-blooded public servant.

'Back home to Sri Lanka.'

And if that was a nod, his flinted eyes still stayed very, very still in their grilling of me.

Obviously, this was an obstinate man, and I hadn't liked how he had emphasized home while peering at me. He had planted his feet and obviously wasn't going to move and obviously wasn't going to take a seat. Which was just as well

15

because I wasn't offering any relief to either state. He looked quite in fit with where he was anyway.

'Problems,' he was gravelling on, 'can you be telling me what might be any extradition problems my people might be facing, bloody fucking hell.'

His finger indicated I should look at the other sheets of paper beyond my first glance. I did so, though not with any better nature. Siddarththan, Subramaniam. Krishnamurthi. Aliases with each, sure, but these were the family-registered names.

'These are all Tamils, Inspector. Are we talking subversion, terrorism?'

'Yes, Mr Tasker, bloody fucking hell.'

'Tamil insurgency in Oz?' I tried to put a lot of scepticism into it.

'Never stopping for a moment all over the world, isn't it? North America, Europe, Middle East. Bloody Asia, bloody fucking hell.'

'Then you've got yourself a problem or two, Inspector, in the nature of belief, I guess. As to extradition, though, I don't see anything untoward, providing the due processes of law take place first. I'll have to let you know when I've checked a few things.'

It was after that that I did look it up. But it wasn't the statutes or regulations. My mind must have been flipping over what I might possibly know about extradition outside of refugees almost while my face was smiling, a la the public-service manual when you've got them on the leaving go as the Inspector was to my tiny dismissive wave, as near imperceptible as the manual would have it.

What was looked up and was looking back up was the bottom charge sheet. Somehow I had flipped through to it before I could realise what I was doing. Not a good sign again.

That sheet at the bottom had no photograph like the other sheets, only an Identikit drawing of who only Mother or I would have recognised.

Beneath the mug were no given names or surname.

'Mystery man, isn't it?' I heard Inspector Ekanayake comment from a height well above and near-the-door away from me. Way up and pouring it on down.

I was looking at the only identity they had of the fellow. Next to 'Alias(es)' was a single word:

Tusker.

And that's how all this got started.

Next item:

'Elephants.'

To be honest about it, Sturt Street in Adelaide wasn't the stuff of the Australian dream then. I don't know when Adelaide got conferred with the title of city, but it might have been about a century-and-a-half too early.

Beyond the ring of soursob-eyed parklands that surrounded the old town south of the River Torrens and upheight North Adelaide, there wasn't much else when we were living in Sturt Street.

There was nothing much more than workers' cottages south then, blocked together unprettily—lean clumps that broke away at the backs to give the space in the corrugated-iron enclosures they called backyards for washhouses, outhouses, chook runs and chopping blocks, vegetable plots and a lemon or orange tree or two. Corrugated-iron rusty sheets and chicken-coop wire. Bare and unshady. Adelaide. It was of then and maybe always will be of then.

To go to one more stage of being honest, too, I can't remember one tree there. Oh, there were the ancient ironbarks that sparsely haired the parklands, but they were full of bull ants and rounded by pervs who wanted to feel you up. The grey asphalt roads and footpaths always seemed to be bubbling hot pitch in the heat; I smelt of it; I always seemed

17

to have my nose being rubbed in it or pushing someone else's nose into it. Both states were too close for comfort.

And there I was, landed there, with the memory still of the lush swarms of Ceylon greens my mother had taken me from, and I couldn't understand why she had had to do that. How do you trade the estate of tea and elephants and the lusty hustle of people who were always kindly from their mud-and-thatch huts with this place that just seemed too large for itself?

The Adelaide sky; it was huge. It scared me to look up into the vast roamings of God's own backyard up there, His Eye fixed on you and burning you towards shelter so you couldn't be cheeky enough to keep looking up at Him. I wanted only the sullen moisture from the monsoon clouds, the condensations of the mountains and the jungle and the coconut palms that cooled the sky down. I only wanted to be hemmed in to a belonging, where my father was, again.

I don't think I even knew about countries then. I just wanted to go back home.

But we had one thing there in Adelaide, and I guess it's why I started thinking about my list's item of just-now, 'Elephants', and that was the ivory we had in the Adelaide house. I began to discover I could find the land of my father in most places I cared to look.

Then, there was the Sunday set of knives and forks we never ate with, especially on Sundays, or any other day, come to think of it. Ivory these, too. Hafted long for heavy yellowing handles.

I would open the drawer and just look down at them, trying to picture the size of my father's hands that surely would have been big enough to have gripped them by the fistful. I could see his hands around the great tusks as he stood for a moment waiting for the great grey beast to lift its front foot, so he could hoist himself from there to its knee to its neck, one hand whipping up the tusk to grasp its ear on the way.

I never heard my mother play the piano in Adelaide as she once had, but we had one. My loony Aunt Ethel played that sometimes when she came, and I never knew those keys were ivory too, until one day she invited me to sit down and 'tinkle the ivories' with her at 'Chopsticks'.

I got so I wouldn't dare play 'Snakes and Ladders'. I could not throw pieces of dice of my father's tusks around. I fancied I heard him grunt with shame and I fancy they became too heavy for me to lift, like the Sunday knives and forks.

On my mother's dressing table, I studied her comb and looking glass. When I realised they were ivory inlaid, I couldn't bring myself to touch them; the inlays looked irreverent, like the fillings in my own teeth, like extractions from my father.

At mealtimes in that workers' house in Sturt Street, Adelaide, I would sit with my back to the mantle-piece... to the carving of the man and woman from my father's land because I did not want to draw attention to the fact I couldn't keep my eyes off their ivory selves. Alone, though, I would trace their crowns, the jewels in ivory around their necks and ankles and loins and all over their many, many arms. They seemed to be dancing, she, naked, with full round breasts and full-humped nates, entwined and curling around each other for the joy of the tusk, yes, of my father's land.

Lord Siva and his Parvati meant nothing to me then, except they meant more than any names. They weren't strange to me. They were familiar. Not strange, no. What was strange was this open and dusty place my mother had brought me to. Too large, yes, for itself somehow, so how much did it hang in folds from little me?

This land of no elephants around where I now lived.

'Family.'

What family?

My mother must have been mid-thirties when she gave birth to us. Old, old for then. I can imagine the smut that must have gone around the tea estate about her swelling, then boiling over. In that land of ivories.

She would hold onto my ear when we walked alone those inner Adelaide streets, my head pressed to her thigh. That much I can remember about her.

I have loved no other human being. You know that. You come to know that in time, that being what it was.

I was in the Adelaide Children's Hospital -- lain in those wafts of ether in that ward that swooned me and made me heave into some old blue tin; gusts from time as old as graves -- when they told me my mother had sighed at home on the couch.

That she had sighed and died.

My mother.

Without me.

She had such a soft: voice and always seemed to be crying.

My aunts, those bags with crimson nail polish at the end of arthritic bones, once told me they used to send her home from the shoe factory in upper Sturt Street for crying about not being strong enough to carry on working.

Shoe seconds were the only things I didn't wear patched. So much for the rich *sudha*, as they used to call us whites in the estate village; the tea pickers and the mahouts under my father and all their families used to look at us with fierce but tolerating envy because my mother and me looked so rich there in Sri Lanka. Notice I did not say there my brother.

And my father was always coming, coming out to Australia to us.

'He'll be here soon,' my mother used to say to me. I think.

After my mother had sighed and died, he would surely come now.

Until those aunts sat me down to give me the glad tidings.

'You're a real little man now, Johnnie, so's we can tell you the truth rather than God getting our tongues if we don't, like.'

I watched one of their mouths, both alike and always the same-way gashed with thin rude welts of lipstick and sticky smudges on their front dentures and the pink pimples of rouge mud-sliding by perspiration at the corners of their lips, and the one going:

'That father of yours wrote to say he wasn't coming. You should be grateful your mother isn't here to hear it'.

And the other mouth. Of Aunt Eveline or Ethel, what did it matter?: 'Your father is a real dopey, but it's not for us to say'.

But 1 still wanted him not to be. Not to be a real dope. And I still wanted that he should come.

Where was he then?

Item: 'Father.'

My father. What I remember of him was he was as tall as a mountain to me, rising straight and as sure as the mountains around the tea estate. He seemed to stand higher than the tea factory itself.

I tried to make nervy contact with him some time after my mother had sighed and died, through a letter or two. After about a year or so, I got word back from him via Melbourne of all places that he was still in Sri Lanka and wanted nothing more to do with us.

Nothing more to do with us.

What was the 'more' bit? Some joke?

Item: 'Brother.'

21

My brother. He killed my mother.

My father wouldn't follow us 'out' as he had promised, but he sent my brother.

He came down the gangplank of the ship in Outer Harbour with one grey cardboard suitcase that was shockingly filthy, and he knew it was, and a big sign hanging around his neck.

'Tasker,' it said in rough large black letters.

'Tasker.' That was my name not his.

Four weeks slopping around the Indian Ocean to get to Adelaide. He was as sick as a dog, and he was a waif.

My mother cried out to him and, before the Customs could stop her, had broken through the barrier and had run and enfolded him. She tore past them and took him to her. And brought him home to Sturt Street.

That's what she told me, maybe. For me, he just appeared. One day I had not known about him; the next he was in my house using my name.

Four years, we'd been in Adelaide and I had forgotten all about him, if I ever remembered him.

Another six months, and the shock of him made my mother sigh and died.

He killed her, too.

And so sheened his skin was to dark.

Oh, dark somehow as if it emanated out from within him. He was like the Devil in those bible-class books I had to look at during Sunday school. He was like all the appearances you didn't ever want to be... the murky continent where white missionaries were killed in the colour plates. He was like the Aborigines who drank shoe polish with meths on our corners in Sturt Street, in rags and abused and abusive, not Australian as I was working so hard to be.

And I had to live in the same house as him. I had to sleep alongside him. I had to walk down the street in broad daylight with him. Go to school with the Devil that had taken my name

22

and address and could never, could never ever, look like he was related to me.

I resented that. I was Tasker.

What I'm saying is, he was almost like somebody I could see so clearly through but nobody else could, as if he was invisible.

Not even my mother, I think, in the little time she had left before the shock of him took her away from me.

Not even those dotty aunts who did their crazy best, I suppose, to bring us up after she sighed and died.

Until my brother Tasker killed them too.

If only someone could have seen what I could see, they might have seen how dangerous he was, even then.

Next item. 'Sri Lanka Then.'

Since I've been back here in Sri Lanka these last months tracking down my father to finish him off, I've only gone back to visit the old tea estate once. That might sound feeble, but it's stronger than that.

From where I am living now in Gampola up in the high country of Sri Lanka, it is up of the plateau that spreads itself northeastward towards the escarpments and valleys of east side of the island's uplands, never settling, always rising out of wakening dawns and sinking into the purpures of dusks, as though the time between the two was all waiting on the illusion, on the myths, on the mystiques.

I've given this sort of straining at the leash up by now, but the first time I went back to the estate I was still trying, painfully, not to stand out as a whitie, and being tapped on the shoulder by Inspector Charles Ekanayake or one of his coppers.

What would they say? 'The game's up, sir?' Quite probably. The British nineteenth century, they've managed to

23

stretch out to well into the twenty-first here. If the Poms realised that, they'd treat Sri Lanka with the respect for vintage it deserves, not with contempt for whatever it endeavours.

Not that I'd bother to expose myself that much by going back to the tea estate again.

At the mention of my father, the tea workers, the older ones, just went bone quiet on me.

The upland Indian Tamil has a way of smiling that is obstinate -- marks, perhaps, of some patient endurance his forefathers had to have when the British brought them over in drones from southern India to work under indenture the tea plantations more cheaply than the locals. That was over well over a century ago.

Anyway, from the peevy smiles-with-shrugs they gave me, I knew my father had long gone and they knew of him, but that was all they were going to give away to any foreigner.

At least I found out he was still alive and still creating mysteries. I just have to be patient.

This is the Sri Lankan way of the elephant.

The great house was still there. We had it for God knows how many years before Independence and a few years after, when they nationalised all the plantations.

Where my mother's parents ended up, I wouldn't know. Where they ended up, I couldn't care try as I might. From this, even I began to see that I didn't really belong there anymore.

What could I remember? I can only remember my mother's father as a shuffling moaning grey skeleton, and my mother's mother as a tobacco-y loose-jacketed bag of smells, but mainly homey ones and mainly striking camphor. And the tick-ticking of the grandfather clock during those afternoon siestas they insisted my mother and I had to endure. I hated the slow sunlessness of those forced siestas and that clock, while I knew my father was somewhere down by the river with his elephants, shouting his magic sounds to them, alive and loud, bronzed and sweating, while I pretended sleep in air that

24

was fetid to me while those heavy brocaded curtains kept closing in to smother me.

I cannot recollect one specific look or one single word from my mother's parents. I know they deliberately ignored my brother and me. The old man would shuffle out to do his rounds while the workers would have been waiting for the government to get around to turfing the old slave-driving Pom out. And she a moaning and bitching presence around the house all day, a shrill caitiff to the servants, even if she did smell nice and homely.

I don't know whether they actually refused to allow my father into the house, or he didn't deign to enter. All I'm sure of is I don't remember ever seeing him inside the great house.

At least the fire that almost destroyed the place is still visible to me mind. I put out the palm of my hand and some ash of some part of it, the great house, floated down gently and settled upon it. I'm sure I didn't dream that up.

I could still trace how it started from the new-fangled gas cylinders in the kitchen and wound its way around the front veranda corralling all the main bedrooms.

As long as it took that grandfather clock down to silent embers, I was happy.

They have expanded the tea plantings to the areas where my father had his elephants. There is no kraal there now, no stomping ground where he would train the young bulls and cows in the basics of lifting, balancing, pulling and shoving.

There are no huts where 1 thought my father's used to be where he lived with my Aunt Jayalitha. I have never forgotten her name. She would make sweet handfuls for me and take my cheeks in her leathery palms and sniff them, one after the other, in the way of their traditional kissing, and she would croon in my ear. She smelt of coconut and tamarind, but her silence towards me wasn't like the silence of those oldies of my mother who lived in the great house. It was like my Aunt Jayalitha and I were to share some sacred secret she was sure I was soon old enough to know.

25

So there wasn't much need to go back to the plantation. Too late, too late. My Aunt Jayalitha's line cottage was occupied by others. My father wasn't there. The great old house was gone.

I walked back past the charred splice lines of the fire on the old house.

I don't know what my brother thought about how my mother's parents treated us, but I know he lit that fire.

I think it led to the first heart attack that our grandfather had and to the nervous condition I think our mother's mother never got over from then on. Neither tried very much anymore from that time on

If for nothing else, the visit back there was worth it for remembering that. For the damage it did to those old people whom I never liked. I don't know why.

I'm sure they never let my father into the main house.

And also, the visit was worth it, because it brought back to me how 'Tusker' had lit it deliberately.

'Australia Then.'

Okay. Let it be next.

My country and my home. Until that Inspector Charles Ekanayake walked into my office area, you'd have to believe I was no more miserable than most, and a good deal more set up. I liked to blank a lot of it out, of course, but who doesn't. Go ask the Prime Minister's press secretary.

Sure, with a distinction from Melbourne Uni, I should have gone into private practice. But I went into government so that my twin could never again *pip* me.

Everything. Every little thing I wanted to do he made it a point to want to do better. It wasn't that he wanted to do it a lot better; it was that he wanted to do it only just a little better. *Pipping.* It used to drive me crazy.

26

I know what it was. It was his blackberry skin tone to my being able to pass for coming from somewhere around the Mediterranean.

I got distinctions in everything at uni, except business law. And so, would you believe, did he. So I asked for a reassessment, and what happens? They said that they found a double negative they misunderstood in his and tip him over in business law; in mine, they also say they find a double negative that they misunderstood too, but in the wrong way, so they left me under.

And, if you don't think it was like that for all those years through Melbourne High and Uni, you don't know what getting the constant shits is.

Dark-nightly Hanuman on my back, leering and *pipping*.

In the Olympic trials for Sydney, who was swimming through to take second place in the four hundred? But then, there he is on my shoulder, bloody refusing to go away and then driving me crazy by recording the same time, right down to the one-hundredth of a second, the best they could do then.

I know I'd beaten him, but they gave him the place in the national team, because of some count back of the lead-ups or something.

Then what does he do?

After waiting right up to the last moment, he pulls out.

I am not offered the vacant spot. I haven't been in training. You tell me how you can go on training when you've just been devastated.

What I'm saying is, none of my Australianism has come easily. I wasn't 'out' from Sri Lanka one day, and Australian the next. I had an accent to get over, colloquialisms to get through. I had to fight my way through the streets, through looking jihadist or something whatever it was in those days, and all the way through to being poor trash. You can laugh. But it's only been in recent times that acceptance has come easier for the likes of me.

Now it's the epicanths and the raggy head covers that give them all the trouble.

But I threw myself into being Australian and would have got that Rhodes scholarship if it hadn't been for his monkey on my back.

Oh, yes, he got it, and withdrew at the last minute again. He did that just to *pip* me again. What a prick.

That's why I decided on government not private practice. It was big enough to lose him, and you're surrounded by *pips* who've been *pipped* from pillar to post anyway. I knew he wouldn't follow. In those days, he would have known the public service wasn't too hot on heavy skin tones. Maybe a few adjustments of sitting next to somebody a bit woggy-looking were being made. If so, only just.

Anyway, I had been through the immigration process myself, so there was nothing they could ever throw at me that I wasn't expert on.

Until Inspector Charles bloody-fucking-hell Ekanayake.

'Sri Lanka Then',
again, and they would've just installed that gas cooking as an alternative to the wood stoves up at the estate house. It would have been propane in the cylinder and no plastic tubing then, only copper connection fittings.

It wasn't until I went back on that visit that I remembered seeing my brother tinkering with the couplings near the stove.

During that night I saw him doing that, the kitchen must have filled up like a bath tub with water until the gas reached the height of the pilot light, and that was that.

Bang and whoosh.

I only hope the trauma of burning down their home drove my mother's parents to early graves. God help me, but I have to say that. They never gave me a fig.

Nobody even thought that my brother might have done it.
At least my mother never mentioned it.
I know my father wouldn't have bothered.

'Australia Then',
again, and I'd like to be able to say that my first wife was doing some lucrative conveyancing for some leading private law firm or whatever, but she was just the cleaner, doing a temp.

She was American, but that might somehow make her seem she couldn't have worked as any cleaner even odd-job, but the office cleaner she was.

I spent nights wondering whether she would cry molestation after I had tried to tap her up one working-back night. I heard nothing. When I couldn't stand the suspense anymore, I stayed back again. I sat frozen at my desk when she got to cleaning up around my area. I felt giving her one rump a sneak glance would get her on screaming blue murder this time, because she'd know it wasn't an accident.

I was petrified. Yet, there was still the fall of her heavy breasts and the strong shallow concave of her back that narrowed so surely as to seem to brutally force her rump high, wide and handsome. A rump made for riding.

What could I say after the humiliation of quivering over her like a young tusker in musth?

I sat there detesting me, detesting her, detesting sex, and detesting the fact that I sat there detesting the fact that she was blithely ignoring me getting rubbing-want over her rump.

But she noticed all right. She said, using the Australian vernacular and just before moving off: 'I'm real ticked off, you know.'

Here it comes, I thought. The screeching for the powers-that-be.

'Why's that?' I heard myself squeak with meek innocence, and detesting that, too.

'Hey, do me a favour. I wear no knickers for you and all you do is sit there going all rubbery and dripping sweat.'

It took me a couple of long minutes to take in what she had said, tossing it around for a thousand bear-trap meanings, before I got up the nerve to get up and follow her into the female's toilet.

It took her about that long to leave her current husband, who had the cleaning contract, and move in with me, including getting married.

Her name was Neila.

Just like that. Neila. A man's name with a curt femininity tacked onto the end of it.

Everything about Neila was pretty much like that. She made decisions just like a man, with a bit of femininity tacked onto the end of it. She made love -- if the full-blown rortiness of that pretty disgusting act anywhere and anytime was love -- just like a guy would want it but with a tinge of femininity thrown in. She drank and smoked like a bloke, with just the faintest girlish hesitation thrown in at the end of them.

In all of what has happened, it is important for me to think of Neila, and now.

I can see now that what she did was to see me as another of her lost causes.

Neila couldn't resist lost causes, no way. So she was all female in that all right.

I was her fourth marriage by register. That was the other thing. She was honest and irascible, just like a man would tack that fact on and, having done so, would get all bullishly on the offend about it.

Her first had been a plain old American dog soldier who kept getting busted back to private for beating her up in public and who had to leave her because she wouldn't leave him while he was so screwed up. See, he became one of her causes. Having a wife like that must have been damaging to his career, if she had left him with one.

Another had been a con with whom she began as a penpal while he was doing time and whom she saw for the first time at the registry office the day he got out. He apparently had the lost cause of specialising in writing other people's cheques for them, including hers, until he had cleaned her out and sold her trailer-home from out under her, such that she had to dob him in herself. She carried on their correspondence where she had left it off because he had become a cause which she couldn't let go of completely.

But even then, she still wouldn't divorce him until she found out she had no need to; he'd been married all the time. Which made him, apparently, even more of a cause for her.

The third was the cleaning contractor. He was the first Australian. Him, she'd met at LA airport when he was being extradited back to Australia for no green card and no funds. She was on a flight to him one week later, just long enough for his telegram of proposal and hers of acceptance to complete the return crossing before her. He being thrown out of American so perfunctorily was the sealer of a cause for her.

Neila left me less than a year after we'd been married, to my immense relief. If I remember rightly, one of her many reasons was that she had found a new lost cause that needed her more than I did.

It turned out that number five stood only on one leg and could not understand how a compassionate God could keep him out of competing in the Bells Beach surfboard meet just because a shark had taken a fancy to his leg while he was an early teenager.

I admit I had to admit she had certainly found a worthier cause than I was ever able to drum up for her.

I'll say one thing for Neila; it took an American to introduce me to the cream of the Sri Lankan community in Canberra, my home town even if I could never admit it much.

31

That might sound strange, but I had assiduously avoided having anything to do with Sri Lankans, whether it was in Adelaide, Melbourne, Brisbane, Sydney or Perth. Toss in Cairns there too.

The way Neila set it up, I couldn't avoid it.

So that, in that aspect alone, Neila had as much to do with overturning my otherwise comfortable existence as that Inspector Charles bloody-fucking-hell Ekanayake had.

But I don't want to think about how she got involved with those hotshot Sri Lankans in Canberra just now.

Finally, I had to throw her out of the house.

It was because she made love to my brother.

So what, a lot of people might say.

Well... 'so what' came when she did it right smack on top of me?

It happened while I was three-parts asleep one night; at the minimum, I could only have been skirting the frontier of sleep and wake. I heard her moan in ecstasy, or thought I did, and then her hands seemed to be going everywhere. It was almost as if she was mounting *me*. Some hope. Yet, I just couldn't seem to wake up. I wanted to push her off, but couldn't move, couldn't speak.

Until I realised I was too far off for it to have been me.

It was like there was someone in between us. I just lay there inert, when, from far off, guttural and aggressively greedy, I heard her hunkering climaxing command: 'Come on, you big black beauty!'

My twin was nowhere to be seen when I woke up.

I knew I hadn't dreamt it. I demanded to know where she had hidden him. She swore he hadn't sneaked in.

Oh sure, Neila, pull this one.

'Weird, you know. You go weird sometimes.'

She ought to talk.

I threw her out. I knew. I knew.

That brother of mine had actually had the nerve to come crawling in in the dead of night and *pip* my wife in my own bed, lying right on top of me! In her words: you go figure.

If you think that's only brotherly love, you don't know what from what.

Yes, Neila.

She would have to be the only person I ever loved who didn't go and die on me.

The poor love died on someone else.

'Elephants.'

Second time around; why not?

What John Wesley Hyatt, with his new material plastic, would not have minded was the toenails and the tusks on our set of elephants we had at that Sturt Street home in Adelaide.

There is always a bit of innocent ivory floating around.

Tuskers don't live for ever. There are some myths about them living for 120 years or so, just like there's been stories that there's some hidden herds of pygmy elephants somewhere or other, still tucked away from man on the island of what was ye olde Ceylon.

Never you mind about the myths and the bits of truth thrown in. The average life expectancy is about fifty years. Another myth is that they go back to some one place to die, to turn their ivory chips in so to speak, so that there's some fabulous cache at the base of some inaccessible cliff where, among the mountain of bones of old bulls, there awaits a thesaurus of tusks only dreamt of by some pukka tusk hunter supplying the likes of Phelan & Collander, manufacturer of pre-Hyatt billiard balls in a world mad with its growing shortage of ivory and its growing amount of money to burn.

Nuh-huh. No ivory dice to that little hopeful thinking, either.

Elephants usually stay with the herd until the herd can't keep them propped up or wait for them any longer, or they have to wander away where the victuals are nice and soft and mushy, like around the agricultures of humans, where they can create a weeny bit of final mayhem, before Nature or the shot or bullet puts them out of their misery.

Either way, they fall where Fate has X-marked the spot. There is no grand and noble shuffling off to the ancestral burial ground, a route supposedly only once trodden by the footsteps of elephantine memories that never forget oneirocritical lessons. More's the pity.

At such times, there is ivory lying across your paddy field or amongst the wreckage of this year's some-other staple crop. You're supposed to notify the authorities, but who does? There's still good money in those two ancient and careworn teeth, and ever will be. As a villager, you still live off the land; nobody is going to come handing out a living. So, you cut them out of that gravitous head and you go selling. Tusks; nothing comes more tusky. Fine.

And I just know that's where the ivory would have come from for our set of mantelpiece elephants at home in Sturt Street in Adelaide.

Never mind those ivory dice, the Sunday knives and forks, my mother's comb and mirror; it seems for all my life those elephants strode forward in a row above me, almost out of reach, on that mantelpiece up there. In winter, we would sit around the fire listening to the early voices of the early television we couldn't afford come from next door, and would sit staring up at them, putting them centre stage in our oldtime weekly radio serials, like 'Dossier on Demitrius' or 'Twenty-six Hours', as though those elephants in a row of tall-to-shorty were the sounding pieces of all the world outside.

It was a set of eight of them. From, yes, the smallest up to the about the sixth, I could lift when my mother wasn't around to catch me. The biggest, the great bull tusker, stood a foot high, perhaps even higher, huge and ebony and shiny, leading his herd off to where?, the bathing hole perhaps, or the talipot palm stands, or to the next valley away from the tea planters and their hunter guests. Each of them, even down to the tiniest, had their ivory tusks and little ivory toenails. And each, too, as black as polished ebony, because my mother kept them polished and because they were made of what to me then was material from out of space.

How my mother got them home, when we hardly had a set of clothing between us to stand up in, I don't know.

I want my father to have carved and ivoried them out for her when she was living in the big plantation house and he had to keep down by the river with his elephants. I want him to have shown her what he had made for his family, for its journey away from him, for its forever journey away from him. I want him to have kissed her, kissed her hard, loved her down by where he had his beasts corralled, under a bursting moon, a *poson* night full of incense and candles bright and the siren chantings of the Buddhist monks from the temple across the valley.

I want that he should have lifted me high, high up in his arms, and held me tight and strong, man to little man. My son. You will come back. I will come to you. I will follow you to Australia.

I want for that he should have packed them for her himself and carried them himself in one of the old red buses following in the wake of my grandparents' car they wouldn't have dreamt of letting him in to. 1 want him to have arrived just in time, just before the ship departed, well after they had had the car doors open and had us deposited on the tarred logs of that lonely wharf with our few suit-cases and the hot sun of the shame of it. And I want it that he arrived just in time to carry me up the gangplank, with the box of our elephants in one hand, until a sailor took it from him with a grunt, so my father was free to turn and give his hand to my mother. He could only hold me. He could not hold her. That could not be done. Not in public. He was burnt-brown and we were white. If she touched, she was whore. If he touched, he was not true man.

They would not let him step off the top step of the gangplank to go on board. He was deep brown, yes. He was more shade-of than his elephants. There, on the tip of the gangplank, while the other passengers were all pushing rudely past us, my father and my mother stood as close as they could, touching furtively, trying to stand as far apart as they could for decency's sake, and we take our leave. Our eyes so bright, large, stunned and unblinking about what life was doing to us, where it was making us go. Where it was making *me* go.

It is how I wanted it, that way.

Alone in that Adelaide worker's cottage in Sturt Street, I would try to lift them one by one, those ebony-and-ivory elephants, wondering whether my father could lift the great bull with one hand while holding me in the crook of his other arm, or would it have had to be with his two having had to put me down?

Perhaps my father had fashioned the great tusker after the one on which I had taken that ride when I was only so young. Maybe he thought it would be a good thing for me not to forget that ride.

I would never forget it; how could he think that?

It was dark that terrifying time before he found me and could pull me off. They had set me up there on that beast before I had had breakfast. My stomach rumbling. These things you remember as a child. It must have been ten hours before my father got to halt the animal, to coax him to stop swaying from one leg to the other. I can still hear at the start of it all the mahout grunt, feel him bump against me as he half fell to the ground, and started screaming something. By the time my father got to me, my little hands were torn bloody, and I can still hear him crooning as he prised them off the beast's neck chain.

When I looked I didn't have all my fingers.

36

How could he have carved our mantelpiece herd in order for me to remind me of that? Unless it shows what kind of man he was, is.

Oh yes, the Sturt-Street mantelpiece of our Adelaide home.

And don't think I don't know it was that twin brother of mine who eventually prised off those ivory toenails of our fireplace herd and plucked out their ivory eyes with their black dots.

It was he who worried the tusks until they fell out, even from the great bull that had gone berserk with little me on its monstrous back.

And he did this slowly over time, drop-line vandalism, until the elephants stood up there on the mantelpiece abominated for their gone ivory, like the real things.

Dead.

Until one day, and this was in those crazy aunts' place, not my mother's Sturt-Street house, they weren't there anymore. My elephant herd was gone.

As sure as all those poachers' heavy-bore elephant rifles, he had made them, and my memories of my precious island time, extinct.

Everything, everything thanks to my brother. He couldn't, wouldn't, help himself. The *pipping*.

In many ways, he was just as bad as our father.

Next item.

'Tamil scams.'

I played cool about them in front of Inspector Charles bloody-fucking-hell Ekanayake.

I didn't even find it hard to keep up the professional public servant's detachment when, as I said, I came to the sheet which had my brother's name 'Tusker' on it in the box set aside for Alias(es)'.

I would, yes, look into any extradition snags that Colombo might have to be made aware of. Should be easy enough to plug into the extractions on international law for a generalised hypothetical or two.

I waved the charge sheets in front of him, knew it was a mistake of protocol but just couldn't help myself: 'Who's running all this, Inspector?'

'Bloody fucking hell, sorry, I am trying to find out myself still, isn't it? Here in Australia itself, there is being the New South Wales CIB, the Victorian Frauds Squad, the Federal Police, the National Crimes Authority, the ASIO, the ASIS, and others being. *Bohomer amarui*, very difficult, *nae*?'

He shrugged what-to-do and his appalling suit jacket seemed to jerk on his frame, as though don't talk to it about difficulty; difficulty it knew all about.

I sighed professionally, like a public servant should who is facing his own difficulty: 'To get all those guys to cooperate with one another, you're not kidding about difficult.'

Concurrence made him even more mournful; it was as slow a nod as I have ever seen:

'And there are also being having Immigration, Customs, insurance investigators. And you are having the same in my country and India, and then there is Canada, Germany, England, Hong Kong, America. And we are being only at the small beginning of the Tamil thing, *nae*?'

'Small beginnings?', and I saw I was waving the charge sheets again and getting annoyed at myself for showing quirk, and having to listen to:

'This is just travel, forgery rackets, isn't it? The end of many other rackets like them is being the shipment of arms to my country, bloody fucking hell sorry.'

I leant forward. I could now pretend to be engrossed by the larger picture, rather than just the bottom charge sheet. Alias(es). Tusker.

'Unless I'm getting stupid, Inspector, we're talking about worldwide here? Across-the-borders cartels, self-sealing national organisations, right? If so, I concur no one agency, anywhere, is ever going to be able to pull it all together.'

'When we are seeing a jugular,' his own was swelling with the passion of the hunter, 'we have to be keeping chipping away, Mr Tasker. My people are being good at that.'

I thought of what my damn brother had done to my set of elephants and the chipping of them: 'Yes, you are. Chipping away.'

All I was trying to get from him, of course, was what he might have on my brother, besides the alias.

I still hadn't got the opening I needed and the tall, thin policeman was already starting to leave in his whippetty way. I felt myself pull a little anxiously on the handshake, but he pulled away abruptly.

This was a man, this Inspector Charles Ekanayake, who did not like touching much. It was in the alacrity with which he drew his hand back to himself.

My opening came as an afterthought, just as he was about to escape. He had acknowledged bloody Tilly's pathetically-secretarial venatic look that said as much as she was sorry he had to go through trying to talk sense into me -- she really is a piss ant -- and was about to leave the legal area when he ran smack into my boss Johnno, who happened to be striding from one place of vacuity to another place of vacuity with his usual pomposity that was supposed to cover the vacuities.

In order to inquire whether one of his officers had given satisfaction, they had to look back towards me. Johnno did not notice that Tilly was shaking her head no-he-didn't. I quickly moved around my desk and went over to join them, all vacuities aside.

'By the way, Inspector,' I spoke, attempting to know, to a nodding Johnno, rather than the man himself, 'what you've got on these men beyond the charge sheets would help me what to advise.'

The Inspector was taken by surprise by the sudden offer of cooperation and would not have felt easier by Johnno's back-patting of him, as though this suggestion was clear evidence that his staff was on top of things and, led so well, intended to stay so.

Another fiction of his -- efficiency -- had Johnno actually answer for the Inspector, but looking at the Inspector not me: 'We'll have all we know on your desk tomorrow morning, Tasker.'

The Inspector had to laugh very briefly -- it was like a lightning strike -- because Johnno was laughing as he always did when he realised he had promised something he had no idea about.

For hospitality's sake, I had to demur for the Inspector: 'All right, Inspector?'

'Of course it's a-ok all right!' exclaimed Johnno with huge magnanimity on behalf of the crime and intelligence agencies of at least ten countries.

'Thank you,' I demurred, this time for myself, at the Inspector for giving his word.

I could have been demurring to a brick wall that some cartoonist had got to smile tightly back.

'Family.'

Some family. Some item.

Alone after my mother had sighed and died away from me, I imagined the one great Australian family of mateships would come and pitch in a little for me.

Where were the sods when I needed them?

I got stuck with my aunts.

I got stuck with the old bags.

For all of those embarrassing times I can remember having to suffer then, came, like a chorus those two carried around with them as tinny echoes of themselves, the catcalling, the mocking wolf whistles.

They loved it. Those aunts breezed past it all, tottering manically on their ridiculous high heels. Old, old. They must have both been pushing sixty, seventy. They could have been a drag queen version of Helena Rubinstein how much gunk the human body could carry above the neck without the head breaking off like a dried mud mould.

Bandy legs, both, and interchanging cotton frocks with large floral patterns and plunging necklines over skin, scaled like a sunburnt lizard, before the first button. They would sometimes be wearing those wide black elastic belts, but mainly they let their necklines sag down to the beginnings of their handkerchief-padded bras. There were always strings of pearls; maybe these were real.

I know the fox stoles were the real McCoys. They would fling these around their necks every Saturday afternoon when, at two-thirty sharp, they went down to the Royal lounge to booze the afternoon away. At one end, they had leather snouts and auburn glass eyes; at the other, motley tails and black paws. I'm talking about the fox, not the aunts. They differed by having *hooked* snouts.

At the Royal, they would listen to the races, get bets laid with the bookie in the lane outside, drink shandies, then go on to then's Purple Para, then start singing when someone got coaxed to the piano, and then stagger out to me at half-past eight.

I cringed having to wait out there, and I cringed when they took my arms and weaved off with me between them.

How classy they were was like this: every Saturday night, passing the fish-and-chip shop one of them would loudly sniff the air crudely and scream out raucously as though the entire world was not only listening but waiting to hear, 'Goodnight, girls!'

I was just a kid. How were they to know I didn't know what they meant? What did they care?

41

The other days of the week, they would hardly speak to me. Gone was my sounding shell: my mother. They served me my food last like I was their dog. They'd just get up from the table and go to their still black-and-white television which I wasn't allowed to watch and leave me the scraps—and the dishes.

I washed up under the eternal precipitation of their face powders.

I had to wash my own clothes, even though they got in a woman for theirs one morning a week. I was always going to school in half-washed, never-ironed deck-outs.

At least I was being left to myself.

But soon even I was beginning to cop the public ridicule along the streets for just being the kid who lived with the two crazies.

'They diddling your willy, idiot?'

I had become infected.

I can't say I was sorry when my brother had had enough and burnt their house down to the ground too, and putting them both in hospital with broken hips they would never recover from.

Good on him.

'Sri Lanka Then.'

I remember this: Around the elephants, my father used to wear the same as his men. And they?... well, they wore their sarongs doubled up so that they reached only down to their mid-thighs.

Those men were all deep brown, and the sun made their bodies almost sparkle as they sweated at work. But my father was different in that. One time, I looked up, way up, to him mounted on Maha, the biggest of the tuskers. In the high light, his body shone with a bluish tinge. It was a sheen. A smalt. As

42

though he was forged by fire and would never cool, never dull down.

My burnished father.

He spoke English. He spoke Sinhala. He spoke Tamil. To my mother, it would have had to be the English. To his mahouts, Sinhala. To the Tamil tea workers, Tamil, for they were apparently fierce even then about their South Indian origins.

As for him, I have learnt in my hunting of him that he was Singhalese on his father's side, Tamil on his mother's side.

The staffs and the distaffs of these lines of me I've never been allowed to know.

It seems that all of us in my family are neither one thing nor another. Here in Gampola, in this now-time, in the hunting down of my father, I don't know whether I am Australian or was never able to be anything other than Sri Lankan.

My brother seemed to be able to take easily to the Tamil side.

I hate it to think he could just make a decision like that and be able to stick by it.

Pipping me still.

I hate it.

And my mother? Australian, but did she want to be? Did she sigh to be as one with my father before she sighed and died, leaving me?

And my father, now, neither Singhalese nor Tamil, but the rogue hunted by both. And by me.

The rogue elephant, my father.

Perhaps, after all, there is only the trumpeting.

Each day -- I am absolutely certain of it—we ate as a family.

This was never in the big house with my mother's sour parents. It was in my father's mud hut, thatched with the

43

woven palm leaves, cool and vegetable. Always the rice and curry, my mother and I with the two spoons they would have kept there just for us, and my father naturally eating with his fingers, his hand lifting the food to his mouth like a bunched lotus.

His sister, my aunt, my real Aunt Jayalitha, always served us with slow care. She moved about in that dark and cool place to tender to us silently, her fingers, too, opening and closing like lotuses.

Three other things I have from that then-time: my feet bare and the cool roughness of the concrete floor tickling my soles. The smoke of the bamboo cooking fire like the secret incense of my father's temple.

And my father's little sister, younger even than I was.

Than we were. I keep hating to admit that my twin brother might have sometimes been with us.

Yes, back in my father's country, an aunt who was younger than I was.

Her name was Virathni.

I remember it still because I thought it sounded wonderful, that name. I have to admit I still do. Virathni. And she always stood silently ogled-eyed at our colour, away in the corner, while we ate. She was as dark too as the inside of the hut as my father was, yet her eyes shone silver and her small buckteeth were so dazzling white.

This was my aunt. I felt immensely old.

None of this is watching my father working his elephants. I was never allowed in the kraal where he kept the ones that were in training. And never near the copse where the herd was basically tied up for the night. But, for everything else, he let me trail along on the trapping, the taming, the training.

Only he would handle the tuskers. Maha was one, as I have good reason to remember. There were also the cows and calves. All of them had been trapped by him, so he must have brought a small fortune into the estate just by that in the older days.

But trapped as he said a man should trap, not laying snares on known tracks and certainly not using beaters to drive the poor panicked herd into crude, makeshift corrals, where they thrash around trying to escape and suffer terrible injuries.

I am sure I was with my father one time watching one of these drives. The elephants were not trumpeting in rage but screaming, an awful sound. Despite what he had said about treating his elephants it the old and 'good' way, the bulls were crashing around among the cows and the calves, just crashing through them. If they were not badly injuring each other, they were getting hurt crashing against the stockade itself or having their skins torn by the bamboo lances of the beaters trying to drive them back from the sides of the stockade, back to cannoning into the cows and calves again.

I saw blood, blood.

I saw a small calf roll over and give up.

I saw my father shaking his head with rage.

He crashed our way away from there, like an enraged bull himself.

But there were also some good times. The trick he had Maha do, curving its trunk for me to swing on. The soft moist pink and quivering touch of its snout as I held on there for dear life. The harsh leathery skin of that massive trunk with all those prickly hairs. And listening, while I was swinging back and forth there, to the crooning of my father's secret language: 'Hida, aliya: hida, Maha.'

I never once saw him use his ankus.

I also knew what he didn't seem to know: that his mahouts used these poles with their vicious iron hooks all the time while they worked the animals at the edge of the forest, clearing for tea.

How the elephants feared those hooks being jagged into their trunks and being heaved upwards, or hooked into their legs.

But not my father. He relied on the secret language and the reward of food. What he did to show his elephants his disapproval, I cannot remember. But he let me watch so I would learn and always allowed me, as the sun came down to soap the river gold, to enter the water and to scrub the ears of the herds wallowing in the shallows.

Maybe I should never have lived past Jonathan Swift; in the water there they seemed so large that I felt Lilliputian.

I can still feel that feeling.

This secretive load that I have shuffled along with. That I have not lived past lilliputting it down.

Okay, extradition.

Extradition was possible but fraught, was what I came up with for the good Inspector Ekanayake without overtaxing my public-service load too much.

What did we have there? We had a concept in extradition arising from a principle that was introduced in Belgium in 1833 and by Britain in 1879 by the Tour Villa case in which a Brit murdered his wife in Dyral in Austria and was extradited to stand trial.

Between Commonwealth countries, no matter whether they have separate extradition treaties or not, the principle is enshrined in the Commonwealth Law Arrangement signed in London and endorsed in Colombo in 1983.

This is usually called the Commonwealth Arrangements, and was as far as I bothered to go research-wise.

The core pertinent question that arises under the Commonwealth Arrangements is whether a crime is political in nature -- beyond the twenty-eight offences listed as extraditable, such as murder, rape, arson, blackmail, kidnapping, and for which you've got a good chance of getting back your man.

But terrorism wasn't yet one of those offences laid down by those wise Commonwealth law ministers and, in my opinion, there might have been a sticking point as to whether these Tamil scams, while crimes that would be arraignable in courts in Australia, might be adjudged political in the context that they were a hangover of influence from the once 'legitimate' fighting in the north and northeast of Sri Lanka during its terrible civil war.

If this were so, then Inspector Ekanayake's merry band of charge- sheeted rogues might well avoid extradition by claiming they would not receive fair trails if they were booted back to Sri Lanka.

They'd be mugs if they didn't.

My advice therefore boiled down to saying you've got a good show, Inspector, but you'll have to take a punt on whether the Australian Attorney-General, and the Australian courts if the Attorney-General's decision was challenged, viewed these guys' criminal activities as part of a habit inhumanly hard to shake of a once legitimate democratic struggle.

It wouldn't exactly constitute a ray of sunshine for the Inspector, but my skimming research produced a ray of sunshine for me.

This was that any extradition request had to be in the form of an arrest warrant not only specifying the crimes and the evidence and the specific law applicable, but had to be *complete*. And *complete* meant complete right down to the most mundane detail -- the spelling of the name, getting the right name even, putting down the specific residential address, and so forth.

And all that last charge sheet had was an alias of Tusker.

No name and no address.

Other than 'Tusker', only blank spaces.

I didn't know what the Inspector was keeping up his sleeve, but at least this would buy me time to warn my brother.

That much I owed him.

But first I had to find him.

As it turned out, I really shouldn't have lived past Dashiell Hammett.

The spokes on the wheel of my life are now starting to come around in nice comprehensible circles.

A few weeks ago, I even found myself back at the tea plantation and the fire rings still there scarring the old plantation's great house. I wasn't expecting anything and wasn't surprised that my father had disappeared from there years ago.

If the police find him first, I wonder whether they'll bother to take him in or just shoot him on sight.

I won't.

Not on sight, anyway.

He probably won't care one way or the other. He must know by now that his precious upland elephants have become so reduced in numbers up here that they'll undoubtedly be extinct give a few more years.

And if they're no more, I know he wouldn't want to be any more.

If for nothing else, he could thank the once-irrepressible king of Ceylonese 'sportsmen' for that. About the time John Wesley Hyatt was doing his bit for billiard balls, yet another pride of the British Empire was doing his level, heavy-gauge best to ensure that Phelan & Collander's $10,000 reward for an ivory substitute was a waste of good money.

Major T. W. Rogers was this scallywag's name. No finer sportsman had the British Empire sun ever rose upon. There was no finer shot, no bigger elephant bagger, none more honoured for advancing the cause of elephant extinction, when a bolt of lightning struck him down in his deadly prime while he was sitting on the veranda of the Haputale Rest House in olde Ceylon, with his boots on, taking tea, resting from his day's labours making the tea pickers labour, perhaps mulling over a few of his new district administrator's problems, perhaps reflecting on a long colonial life of wresting ivory from beasts which did not appreciate what God had given them, and was now giving him.

Major T. W. Rogers was such a sporty class apart that, had he lived, he might well have single-handedly wiped out the entire population of the once great upland herds, which might have saved Phelan & Collander their money for a few years longer by delaying the need for the quick invention of the tusk-substitute cellulose for billiard balls by John Wesley Hyatt. In that case, John Wesley Hyatt might have even lost interest, gone back to his printing, and never invented cellulose at all.

The dead-eyed major would have, therefore, made my father extinct long before I am going to, and therefore my mother's parents' contretemps with my father nonexistent, and therefore my own existence extinguished, since there might have been no excuse for my mother to secretly yearn for a man her parents violently disapproved of.

I can therefore claim my heart to be John Wesley Hyatt's but my earthly body to be Major T. W. Rogers's, whose prowess allowed him to blast the brains out of not less than one thousand and four hundred upland elephants before going down to a bolt of lightning, probably ordered by the half-elephant god Ganesh, near what is appropriately called World's End.

My father would have had Major T. W. Rogers's guts for garters.

'Australia'

and its Sri Lankans, then, okay. Well, I didn't find out until she left me after a year of marital glissade that Neila had known my brother, in the Old Testament way, before she allowed me to know her.

She saw him in me, she said.

Some compliment of a lost cause.

I shouldn't have lived past Martin Luther King.

She told me this when she took me along, as her ex-husband, a week after I had blessedly got my place back to myself again by throwing her out, to a Sunday 'outing'.

They were all Sri Lankan migrants there and they pocked the sands just north of Durras North like awkward watchers on the shore waiting for some royal barge to go across the horizon.

What they were doing spending a Sunday on the coast, and one so out-of-the-way, when they looked uncomfortable not being on something man-made like so many migrants from the older nations of the old world, I had not a clue.

Neila did, though, and knew them all with a familiarity that seemed to disconcert them, one by one. It wasn't just her American bluster, those hands groping for something fleshily tactile, either. Sri Lankan are reserved people; the extroverts amongst them don't even scare flies, so they're welcoming of her and the reception they gave me seemed strain-high, somehow paid for. In fact, they greeted me like they already knew me to be one of their number, high-hocked in their group, but were frightened of me.

Not that I was the life of the party.

I sat apart, glum and sullen, and couldn't help making a shag of myself. There was a reason and a principle for that.

The reason was that tonguing dingos at Ayers Rock would have been more acceptable to me, and the reason for that was the principle. I had always avoided going the social rounds with anybody to do with Sri Lanka. Sure, this was a taint and immature. But I was the one who had to two-step in life with that twin of mine.

That was Sri Lankan enough.

That was dark-dug enough, deep enough, rubbing up old ties enough.

So, spending a Sunday with some guys from some Sri Lankan cultural association wasn't my idea of a picnic on the beach. They called themselves the Serendip Lankan Association. SLA they might have been, but the Surf Lifesaving Association they weren't. They remained stately there, as though they had truly been beached and still hadn't got over the shock of being off-loaded on Australian shores, rather than where they had expected. Their knobbly elbows and spindly knees, once full and melting brown in their own country, now looked pasty in the Australian open sand dunes, imagine plains.

Their women, nationally maybe the most striking in the world, wore their sleeveless, long and shapeless frocks as if they were there to audition for Pollyanna parts.

The few grandchildren they had brought along, played and sprayed apart, berries of this country, totally at ease and so worlds apart.

As a whole though, they were so out of place there I noticed they even brought sandwiches in picnic hampers. Weirdness is being so organised on an Australian beach; foreign-ness is trying to keep it up despite the weirdness.

Not that I didn't know all those guys.

In their places around Canberra, these were the avatars that made the Sri Lankan migrants so fine, so respectable, so good for the country. There was the Associate Professor of Law at the Australian National University, P. E. Josephs; his stooped lankiness and nose-as-beak making him looked cloned for the job. There was probably the leading otorhinolaryngologist in the country, Dr Shankar Rajee, who had the delicious humour to insist on being called just that rather than plain old ENT. Yogarathnam Yogi, one of the most successful software developers in the world was trying sand castles. The head chef at the Prime Minister's Yarralumla

Lodge (but pate de foie gras on biccies on a windy beach?).
The creator of the biggest jewellery chain of stores in the
country. J. R. Nehru, famous for breaking the back of the
Australian unions in the freighting business and now starting
to top it out internationally.

But what struck me more, as I watched them in noli me
tangere, was that they were all Tamils, mostly first-generation
migrants of Sri Lankan Tamils.

What Neila was doing knocking around with this group
had me beat. During the day, she cornered each one of them
away from their wives and, looking for all the world, with her
hurried whispers and their furtive glances, that she was putting
all of them on promises.

Knowing Neila, she could well have been.

Another surprise, too. At some stage or other, each of
these high- powered gents sidled up to me and sort of muttered
much the same thing, like: 'Tusker, we've got to talk.'

The cheeky sods had me mixed up with my brother!

Bugger them. I didn't want to talk and I wasn't going to
talk.

Later, making me drive her back home to her new
boyfriend who was soon to be that number five hubby,
depending on when you started counting I guess, and too girth-
broad for her bikini which she couldn't cover up, or wouldn't
precisely because she knew she was oozing sexuality precisely
because she was oozing, Neila said something that struck me
as strange at the time:

'Well, that sure put the cat among the pigeon, you black-
hearted villain of a jerk, you.'

I had no idea what she was referring to.

But something started to dawn on me when Inspector
Charles Ekanayake came into my office area again and came

through with the backgrounds to those charge-sheet guys, including my own twin brother.

I skimmed through the resume stuff Johnno had virtually coerced the Inspector into supplying.

Inspector Charles sat there across my desk those few days later with his long patrician face looking fuller. I could see why. He was so unhappy about all of this that he had his jaws clamped tight and instead of sinking him in sullenness it seemed to push him higher.

I was really skimming to see if he or they had the real name for 'Tusker', but thankfully the alias seemed to be all they had.

Boiled down, the Australian operation was simple enough. It was basically a four-step scam. Sri Lankan businessmen arrive in Australia from the United States via Germany. They get the ill- gotten wherewithal from various local crimes and then send this to Swiss or German numbered bank accounts. They then fly off to the Middle East or Eastern Europe to chat up an arms dealer or two.

The weapons they purchase are shipped wherever they can be sold through the old networks so etched out when the cause of Tamil Eelam, or separate homeland for Tamils in Sri Lanka, was all the killing rage.

On the more-detailed scale it seemed to go something like this: die-hard Tamil activists continue to centre themselves in the city of Chennai or old Madras in the southern India state of Tamil Nadu. There, according to the Indian CBI, they keep up the tried-and-proven industry in forgery they set up during the 'vintage' civil-war generation of years -- faking up impeccable passports and visas, traveller's cheques and airline tickets, but now mainly for other international crooks or terrorists. Chennai also remains their main centre for making the film to print any number of currencies.

There, for example, the Ekanayake papers inform me, films for making the printing plates are 'supplied' essentially to the local Tamil organisation in any country, complete with printing instructions: ink mixes and sequences, prototype for minimum quality standard, paper types, faking up watermarks and other security measures, their local suppliers, and so forth.

The Open University of forgery, yet.

But the real specialty of the Chennai operation is supplying the nuts-and-bolts personnel to carry out any 'job' anywhere in the world, providing it's provably for some Tamil diaspora cause. If this option is taken up by the client, these Chennai ex-LTTE-trained 'troops' pick up their impeccably forged papers and are despatched on their 'missions' to do the dirty work for the local client without any traceable personal connection. It could be to Europe or North America, the Middle East, Southeast Asia or the Pacific. Even Australia gets a guernsey. If you like, especially Australia.

Wherever, these standover troubadours might pay just a flying visit, or they might go to ground and made to stay to organise for long-term targets.

If it was just a short visit, they were undoubtedly there to do physical harm and then get out before anything can be traced to them. It worked like this. The local Tamil boss cocky might complain to whoever he was dealing with in Chennai that he's got some trouble on his home patch with some important local Tamil 'civilian' not paying the usual obligation of ten or fifteen per cent of his income to the cause that was or the cause that is or the cause to come.

Unless he desired to in order to boost his reputation, and few did apparently, the local boss cocky wouldn't need to dirty his hands by lowering himself to carry out the threats, let alone muddy them by carrying out those threats. He's too easily traced and, if he gets nabbed, Chennai would feel more endangered than there was any need for, just for the sake of a few days' trooper wages. So the flying goons get flown in for him. They might break a few legs, might do some pushing

54

when the subway train is rolling in. They might just put a half cat in one of your kids' schoolbags and make you a phone call, so that you, the blackmailee, would undoubtedly lie awake at night wondering whether you'll be able to get to the bank tomorrow before they tear your life apart because you know they will without hesitation.

Oh yes, you go to the bank, all right. From the word of mouth of experience, you know that the local boss cocky will have all the alibis in the world and that the 'cousin' who has visited or phoned you cannot be proved to be even suspicion... at least not before he or she has already left the country after breaking your legs or whatever on his or her impeccably-forged passport.

Only you can lose.

If you're a Tamil anywhere in the world, you've heard from 'them' in some way even if it's a small percentage of your income for the genetic cause, and you know all this.

Europe is essentially the counting house. Britain, Germany, Switzerland, France ... here are where the money markets are set up for the laundering of the worldwide income from all the rackets and robberies, including maybe that portion of your pay packet. All is lovingly handled no matter how small. The USA and Canada provide the major cash flow from base resources. 'Base resources' means you and others civvies like you.

In the Middle East and Eastern Europe, or Southeast Asia and South America, are the branches for the keeping of the drug purchases and the husbanding the goods around the world, so they can get to where they can be paid for and so, in one sense, start the whole cycle again.

And, in all of the individual countries, there are the sinews to be nurtured of organised crime, embezzlement and extortion, the thousand and one bread-and-butter rackets, all flexed for the single- most world economy: drugs. Means money to buy arms. Means selling arms lucratively to whomsoever do, or rather would have, understood about the ongoing need for a Tamil homeland, even if it's put on hold just for a bit.

'Fifty-seven million Tamils around the world means a lot of clout, right?', I muttered fatuously to the muteness of the eternal glib that was the unjolly Inspector sitting opposite me.

I wasn't surprised when he obviously didn't think it rated a reply.

Where good old Australia fitted into this incredible organisation, I could see, but not treat seriously.

Oh, sure, my brother with the apparent alias of Tusker would treat it seriously.

But then you can always throw up fanatics to any cause.

Anyway, I wasn't thinking about my brother. I was thinking how on earth my ex-wife Neila had got mixed up in all of this.

Next separate item: the crazy aunts again.

So the crazy aunts had become my family.

Ethel and Eveline. Good Christ Almighty.

They were always high on the sexual display on those Saturday late arvos running into early nights, oh yes. But, come a birthday or Christmas, they'd bring back some of their sodden mates from the Royal for one of their 'little shindig'.

They'd load in a crate of beer and bottle of sweet sherry. On an intended high old time, it could be two bottles of sweet sherry. They flooded the parlour with smoke grog fumes and the body of odours of old people.

But that wasn't the worst. Come midnight and somebody would call for 'Knees Up Mother Brown' and my two old loony relatives would leap up, hoick up their dresses on their varicose-doughy, colourless moon-landscape legs that made me want to heave and then, holding each other on the shoulder, would jig sort of up and down, drunkenly kind of supporting each other, attempting high kicks to the music from that old phonograph. What that phonograph had seen!

God forgive me, they would always do this unashamedly, flaunting the porridges of their inner thighs and the loose cotton gussies around their crutches that to me, then, seemed great snatches of black and matted hair. Not the most virginal sight up there, after an afternoon and half the night on the bladder irritants of sweet sherries, shandies and Purple Para port. And the screeches of hilarity.

High on the hog was right. They were pigs.

The worst happened on the first New Year's night after my mother had sighed and died and left me. They dragged me up to join them before I could say no. I tried to hop and kick and I tried to hold my vomit down. I was trying my best. Hell, 1 was only a kid. Yet some drunken bum shouted at me as though it was the biggest joke of the century: 'Kick dem dere legs, Sambo!'

Sambo.

I could see, in my mind's eye, my brother stop in absolute fury. I sensed him. I heard him.

I heard, just like a voice talking quite plainly to me, that he hated these aunts and that he would do it.

He would do it, all right.

On the next Saturday, when they grabbed his arms for him to stagger them home, he did it.

There were five steep concrete steps from the lounge of the Royal to the footpath. At the top one, he gripped their hands hard into his sides and he deliberately tumbled down those steps taking them with him.

They each broke a hip.

They did, like the sad jokes they were: crazy Ethel's right, and crazy Evaline's left.

They were in hospital for six weeks. They lay in adjoining beds with their whole lower sides in plaster, left and right respectively, making a neat symmetry that they might've have done for many, many years if they'd tried a bit harder.

57

They lay there with their faces painted like celluloid dolls that had faded in the sun. I don't even think John Wesley Hyatt would have appreciated that sight of the possible uses of his beloved cellulose.

They were never to leave their bed again. Not figuratively anyway.

They left hospital in a single ambulance and they were carried into the parlour where someone had put up the double bed for them down there.

They certainly never left *that* bed.

If they had lived longer than the Norwegian Inge Widar Svingen, they might have broken his record of lying on a bed of nails for 274 hours. That was in November (the third) 1984, and they were sharp six-inch nails set two inches or something centimetres apart. But I doubt whether they would have beaten the fakir who called himself Silki who tacked himself on a bed of nails for 111 days in Sao Paulo in Brazil. That date was August (the twenty-fourth) 1969.

It became, that bed of those aunts, their bed of nails, too.

'My father.'

Okay.

There was the one-eyed bull he captured after it had killed some villager near the estate.

Normally, they'd shoot a rogue that had lost its fear of man, but I think my father couldn't stand the thought of the death of any elephant.

He called this one Rajah.

Half the elephants in Sri Lanka must be called Rajah. Well, he tamed it and it must be because it was one-eyed that I particularly remember how he did so.

First of all, he tied it front and back to trees. The ropes were thick and oily, made of leather, and I know he had his men take exceptional care of them. So, he tied this one-eyed

58

Rajah's left front leg forwards and right back leg backwards to those trees. This kept it from pitching over in its frenzy and actually killing itself in a three-tonne-or-something fall.

He then had his mahouts light fires around it. I now know this was to prevent other elephants trying to come to its rescue. They do that. It must be the frantic and outraged trumpeting. The abuse of it. The pain in it. The fires weren't only to protect us from other wild elephants; they were also to protect old Rajah. Elephants trying to free other elephants often crash about and inflict even worse injury to the one in trouble.

So much for legendary intelligence.

Maybe the fires were additionally so Rajah couldn't sleep, because my father just refused to let it sleep. All through the day and night, he and his men took turns shouting at it and banging tin cans.

Nor did he allow it anything to eat or drink for two or three days.

After the first day, he and the other men started walking around it. At first, they circled in wide arcs, but gradually they closed in. After two days of this, old one-eyed had got used to humans being near.

Gradually, they got to start touching its flanks or trunk, its tail, its legs; brush first twigs, then their fingers past its ears.

It was only when it got used to the fluster of hands on it that my father allowed it some water and something to eat.

But even then it had to reach for the food or drink, strain outwards with its trunk and against the tree at the back. And even then it only got what it wanted if those humans gave in and allowed it. It had to get to know that.

Then the water drum was allowed closer. Then the food, the great kittul leaves, closer. The touching and the handling more insistent. Patting 'good, good'; punching, and really punching hard, for 'bad'.

Within eight days, one-eyed Rajah was sufficiently tamed to human beings that my father could begin proper work on it.

In two days after that, he mounted it for the first time. In three months, it was completely trained.

One-eyed Rajah had become a lifer.

A rogue no longer.

Or shouldn't have been.

Training and work? Well, first it has to get used to carrying light loads, then to lift and roll heavier and heavier logs until it could work a tonne's weight and not cry out for the prison chaplain.

It learns to tug in chain harness. It learns to push—it could be a whole village hut in worse circumstances -- by steadily increasing pressure with its forehead and nasal bump.

It doesn't have to slog all day long, though. It is allowed to work quite leisurely, really. At midday there's a full-course meal, including something sweet like jaggery and something fruity and juicy like mango. Mud? It can break off and wallow in it. Bath-time, in the evening, it just lies in the shallows like King Tut while my father scrubs it down deliciously hard, even behind the ears and other areas of erotica.

Old one-eyed Raj. Well, they thought he was rogue no more.

I remember now, about six months after that, it was being walked along the dirt track that ran by the estate, when apparently one of those ancient public buses that are still running up here and which would scare the crap out of any Lomotil junkie, came careering down the hill faster than its manufacturer could have ever dreamt possible. That is an honourable state of things for Sri Lankan bus drivers and would have been even then.

Of course, all this happened on one-eyed Rajah's blind side. Does it ever happen anywhere else?

In fright, One-eye swung its trunk at the shrieking object and, as luck would have it, neatly swept up its mahout who was walking it.

To find a human in its grasp suddenly didn't help its state of shock, either. It tried one, two, three flicks to rid its trunk of this apostatic evidence, then threw its head back and flung the poor mahout as mightily as it could.

I remember my grandfather gruffing out uncaringly that the fellow died of a heart attack before he even struck the rocks across the other side of the road.

He wouldn't have been kidding there.

I'm mulling over what happened to old two-time loser Rajah because I guess it says something about my father. Another trainer would have felt obliged to have the man killer put down.

Instead, what my father did was to sit by it all that night.

He sat with it, yes, and he crooned to it gently, softly, gently and soothingly. And he not only did it in his own voice, but he also imitated the voice of One-eye's victim as well.

I don't know whether he managed to convince it that it hadn't broken vital bones after all, or even whether Rajah stayed on the straight and narrow after that.

The most important thing is, I have remembered it after all these years.

It's a true story, too.

As they say, I know because I was there.

Item: my brother and one-eyed Rajah. Two of a kind.

Natural-born killers.

They had something else in common, too.

They were both bloody lucky.

Nobody even suspected my brother might have rolled those two old ladies down those steps of the Royal lounge deliberately.

Nor what he did to them later.

It was about this time that I first began to feel he was trying to *pip* me in order to get in first with anything I was thinking of doing myself.

I was beginning to think that I knew what he would do.

I even began to think about what I thought I would hope he would do.

Sri Lanka in the now-time, yes.

For a house with only one small and smelly bedroom and, at this time of night, twelve human beings sprawled out over its floors like some post-nuclear survival drill, there is very little snoring.

I do the snoring, and I'm awake.

That might explain why everyone else is asleep.

These kind people who've boarded me, who never ask questions, have six daughters, no sons. That's a lot of children for Lankans of today. It's certainly a lot of daughters on the trot. They must have given up on trying for the son before their desperation became too obvious.

Even in my own boyhood days here, the Indian Tamil estate workers didn't have huge families, comparative. I think that must have been because, if you are brought-in labour and your real home is only a few hundred kilometres or so back across the Palk Strait in India, you keep the feeling of impermanence on a loose halter. So you'd keep the pitter-patter of tiny feet down as much as you could, in case things didn't work out and you wanted to hump the bluey back home again.

Very few ever did.

I grew up in their self-contained community. Around the tea estate, they had their community hall, their Hindu temple, the little school, the dorms for the single men, the 'lines' of mud or wooden huts for the families. They shopped at the estate stores. Mother, father, son and daughter all worked on the plantation, either in the fields picking or in the mill or around the estate, as with the elephants and my father.

Hardly any of them ever left the estate, even on their half day off a week. They didn't seem to mind in the least that the estate management worked them, paid them, sold to them and so received much of what they paid them back from them. They were happy in a closed, almost inbred community, and they still almost are today. They were happy living in a circle.

They weren't too different from the narrow-mindedness of my own snooty grandparents.

But they made a nice change from them.

And thinking about Australia, which I see by the next item in the faint candle light I'm down to think about now, I just wasn't able to believe Neila could have dragged me along to that Sri Lankan shindig at Durras North beach that time.

Driving her back after it, I asked her how she could possibly think I was interested in meeting those people.

She looked at me as though I had said something absolutely screwy.

'You're weird, you know,' she repeated by way of something screwy in itself. 'Sometimes, it's like you've got amnesia.'

'Like forgetting you and I are married?'

'That's positive, not amnesia. I got guilty, anyway. I was unfaithful to you too many times.'

'In one year?'

'You can't imagine how you were cramping my style.'

I tried not to, but I remembered back at the beach and the awkward way in which all these topshot Sri Lankans greeted her when she edged up nearer. Hands instinctively going to cover their genitals as though she had a pair of scissors aimed low. And turning, so that they got themselves between her and their wives so the missuses presumably couldn't see their

63

faces. The flurry of the too-obviously furtive exchanges, even if it's difficult to notice a Sri Lankan blush.

What did she have on them? What were these eminent men afraid of? Neila? An ex-scrubber who was just scrubbing off her fourth husband for a one-legged fifth, if you counted the questionable legitimacy of the first being actually the first one?

I had to ask.

'You call me weird. You don't find it weird that the Serendip Lankan Association is all Tamil?'

What was I saying? She probably had no idea there was such a thing called a Singhalese and a thing called a Tamil. A place called Sri Lanka? Neila? Forget it. But she was surprising me:

'I hope they're all Tamil, guy, after all the brain bashing you've given me.'

The woman never could carry any sort of conversation that made sense.

I discovered I was taking her to one of the better streets in most excellent Belconnen where longing daydreams across public-service desks are no longer needed. There, leaning against an impressive stuccoed stone wall that covered up the layered house beyond, was a fellow in his late twenties, I'd say, and certainly only on one leg.

I could have picked him a mile off as being a candidate for one of Neila's lost causes.

He was standing there in garish surfboard shorts. For a one- legged guy, that was bunting for a lost cause.

Ardent to take my wife off my hands, there was no two ways about that even if her fifth was still tagging along. Board-shorts was actually tapping the face of his watch at her as I pulled up. Neila waved him off; she hadn't quite finished with me yet, going:

'So, when?'

'When what?'

'When, when, when next, dummy?'

I had no idea what she was talking about and now the one-legged board shorts guy was tapping his watch at my window side: your marriage time's up, mate.

I took a desperate stab at an answer.

'I'll be in touch.'

Blessedly, it seemed the right response. Neila finally started to get out of the car, while, on my side, the other guy seemed hell-bent in getting in without waiting for her fifth to get out. But still she hesitated and turned back.

I had a panicky moment that I wasn't going to get rid of her, after all.

'Oh, hon, I need some of that money soon. Tomorrow too soon?'

Wouldn't you nod, if it got Neila out of the door and out of your life?

I nodded.

Thankfully it too had the right effect. I didn't bother to watch her go to her new life.

When, money. Money, when. And she had had the gall to call me weird, when all she kept doing was sprog plain gibberish to me.

Two weeks later, she had the weird gall to introduce me to my second wife.

If only for that, maybe I shouldn't have lived past the impulse I had of throttling her then and there.

'Tamil scams.'

Scams wasn't the word for it, even if it's an item come around again.

By the time, I was reading the background of the Australian side of the Tamil scams handed over to me by Inspector bloody-fucking-hell Ekanayake, they, the dudes on the bottom charge-sheets, should have already been scramming.

Hopefully, my brother whom I recognised with the alias there of 'Tusker' was the head scammer of the five of them.

No way, even at that early stage of knowing the fellow, would I have liked the prospect of Inspector Charles Ekanayake's hot breath on the hairs at the back of my neck. He might have been long and cartoon thin and temporarily out of his waters, but a water snake like that would never let go once it got its fangs into you, for sure.

Back home in Sri Lanka, I could see that he would be absolutely single-minded, yet street-smart, risen up through the ranks with a solemnity that would let nothing ever go passed over.

I could tell he was starting to feel more at home because he passed the torturous Tilly's acid test with aplomb and a healthy natural impatience that few had ever shown in her long drag of a secretary's life.

She had brought us—that is, the two of us—one cup of tea. She put it on the desk exactly between the two of us.

'Tilly, there's two of us.' I tried smiling away. Bloody Tilly.

'I'm not the tea lady,' and then at the good Inspector about me: 'He must have a broken leg that's never mended.'

She knew he would have to say no to the brew and therefore I would have to say no to the brew, even though he and I were both public servants and desperately in need of its bitter comforts. Well, the Inspector didn't know it would have been a bitter comfort because Tilly would have deliberately left the sugar out. So, she enthinned her thin lips into a nasty glee, took the cup back to her desk and gloated over having an extra cuppa for herself. Sugar at the ready.

I had to get out of there, and took the Inspector to the only Sri Lankan restaurant in town, Jaya's at Civic.

66

Tilly would have to sign the docket later and it would throw her into a bout of jealous surliness. A small revenge, but a revenge nonetheless.

Freddie Jayasinghe was the Asiatic Paul Newman of Australia. He had begun importing Sri Lanka chutneys until he realised he could make and market his own recipe. Another successful Sri Lanka entrepreneur. A few higher business steps on and he'd maybe qualify for membership to the Serendip Lankan Association and waste the occasional Sunday on some beach when, apparently, my ex-wife Neila snapped her fingers.

Stretched out in Jaya's, the Inspector's face positively lit up with pleasure; there was actually saliva at the corner of his mouth. He and Freddie rattled on about Colombo and Galle in their native Sinhala, while I watched and remembered the comforting ease of that language's sibilants plying together.

How they can talk, the Sri Lankans! They can stand in the sun for hours and yabber away. Unlike us, they love standing there in long silences, relishing the wait for one of them to start up again. It's not over-politeness waiting for the other to start up again; the longer they wait the more pleasure it seems they get rudely interrupting what the other's trying to say.

Special parippu soup, kakuluwo and sambol and brinjal moju with a cashew'd chicken curry, followed by a savoury kiribath. Rice and roti.

It might just have been his relief at being able to eat with his fingers again, but the food broke some of the Inspector's wariness just as surely as its spices cut through my phlegm. I had the sense we could talk now, a bit of prandial cross-examining while eating into my boss Johnno's entertainment budget. The Inspector wouldn't have known I was mainly thinking about the alias of 'Tusker' when:

'Those backgrounds. All very interesting, Inspector, but too general. What else you hiding up your sleeve?'

He became almost gregarious through a series of toothpicks: 'Some things are taking time, nae? We intercepted a shipment of arms carried on a freighter registered in Suva, but knowing it to be Australia. What we were finding out, with a little, persuasion that it was coming from Syria with Israeli consignments. Let me not be bothering you with details. The funds for the buy is coming from Australia bloody fucking hell sorry via Switzerland.'

'Drugs?'

He shrugged his shoulders. 'Drugs. Not much being drugs. But always drugs for the street in there somewhere, nae? It's the real currency, not money. Money is old ...'

'Hat?'

'... mush, bloody fucking hell sorry. I am being sent to see if we can landmine this path, among many others. Who doesn't know your Australian authorities are not being expected to know what is going on around the world. Here, the picture is being this: Premachandra and Ponnambalam,' and I recognised their names from the sheets he'd shown me, 'set up two travel agencies, isn't it?, in Sydney called True Holidays. They are being experienced in this business from Jaffna. They show forged IATA licences to operate here in Sydney and Melbourne and, within six months of Australian Eastern Standard Time, they are having defrauded major airlines of millions of dollars, not to mention from thousands of travellers, isn't it?'

'How did they do that?'

Printing, at the bottom of it, *nae*? Back in Chennai, they had printed, we are estimating, 800,000 fake National Australia Bank and American Express traveller's cheques, which they are selling to customers for real money and are issuing on behalf of the airline for the package tours they are offering. In six months they can hold off many payments to the airlines for the tickets they sold, isn't it? These two, the Australian Fraud Squad take off the plane as they are quitting for India. Fake Australian passports. I can see they are being printing in Chennai too. Chennai is Madras, don't you know, bloody fucking hell sorry.'

68

'Madras is Chennai', I had to correct, caught up in his pedantic way of English without the bloody-fucking-hell flaw at the end, and 'Travel agencies and printing. What else?'

'There are being gems smuggled from here to Thailand for drugs and sold back here for money to go on to Germany or Switzerland. Export Gems Pty Ltd is set up in Sydney with another two of these men—Ramados and Siddarththan—one of who is having a well- known jeweller in Colombo as a brother.'

'What's that mean?'

'Bloody fucking hell sorry, with what you Australians have basically been throwing away. You are taking out of the ground the blue sapphires, isn't it?, but there is another kind of corundum, sir, what you just let waste a lot and that can be being turned into sapphires by crafty Thai and, bloody fucking hell sorry, Sri Lankan men. They are being called geudas to us. Not the men, the you-know.'

'Who'd throw away anything like that?'

'Well, to be getting technical, some corundum is having the right impurities of iron and titanium to make the blue sapphires. In geudas, there is too much of iron, isn't it?, and these rocks have a yellow colour that is almost being worthless. If you are having the know-how, you can fire these stones in furnaces, drive off the unwanted iron and, *aeii*, blue sapphires out of the slag heaps, *nae*? Sounds easy, isn't it? It is not. Only a few handfuls of men in Thailand and my country are having the knowledge of this and they are guarding this very very carefully, bloody fucking hell sorry. They say they can look at geudas and know which of five broad categories they are being -- diesel, milky, silky, dun, and what they are calling 'ottu'—and the heat treatment to be applying in each case.'

'Alchemy! In this day and age?'

'*Oh*. And *bohomer*, very, valuable, *hari*. The last figures we are having is that Thailand exports in one year around 100 million dollars of converted geudas to sapphires. That is good

English pounds, bloody fucking hell sorry, not the smaller American dollars.'

'A lot of this miracle stuff from Australia?'

Inspector Ekanayake shrugged, with the exaggeration of a man who knows he is telling a good story, giving good earfuls: 'They are mainly getting it from Myanmar, India, Brazil, the United States bloody fucking hell sorry, Australia even ...'

Damn. I felt let down. Australia still small beer.

'... Turkey, but you are having to know what you are doing, *nae*?' '

'And I take it these two guys Ramados and ...'

'Siddarththan are known experts, *hora*, rogues? *Oh*, yes.'

'You have them?'

'Sydney CIB are having them, isn't it?, but,' he added ominously on the long, long lounge bodily, 'with your help with extradition we should be having them soon and then there will be answers.'

He was going to run out of toothpicks soon, and it was getting distracting. A whole forest for the sake of a bit of dental floss. So while he was at wood-chipping, I went fishing:

'Nar, all this doesn't gel. It's got to be more than your couple of rogues, Ramados and blah-blah. There's consigning, shipping, offloading, marketing and distribution. You're talking big business here, industries. The international travel business, big-time gem trafficking, wholesale printing, the up-tops of the drug bizzo. You don't just fly in "experts" like your two to run those. You need principals, not these back-alley small-timers you've got on a charge sheet. Any extradition advice I can give needs the whole picture, Inspector, you know that.'

I don't know if he knew I was still fishing for what more he knew about the alias of 'Tusker'. To all of that mouthful of mine and more tooth picks to his mouth, he only returned that shrug again, but not flamboyantly Italian at table, more

70

Russian at maudlin vodka philosophy. At least he was going past chewing wood:

'We are certainly not being finished, Mr Tasker, with travel agencies and gemmologies. We can only be concentrating on their weaknesses, isn't it?, and that is the freighting. In the air or on the open sea, that's when the racket is being vulnerable, bloody fucking hell sorry, *nae*?'

I understood what he was getting at.

'The fifth and sixth guys on your charge sheets, right?'

'Kanakraja and Rajapakse, bloody fucking hell yes, sorry, they have being worked for very large freight forwarders on the Subcontinent. Well-connected. Managers.'

'But not bosses, not principals. Still hired hands, sent out to do the dirty work.'

'*Nae*,' and this was as near an admission he would give that I could be right: 'The bosses, these principals as you are saying, must be living here. Locals, *oh*.'

I had cornered him as far as I felt safe to do. Now was the time to throw my fishing line into the muddy waters again; and I did it with a slow and low huskiness I couldn't disguise:

'There's one of your aliases you haven't mentioned.'

He was back to nodding again, but the movement reminded me suddenly of how my father's mahout would use their ankuses on their elephants. I heard him say from what seemed to be the distance of maybe a whole football field in an empty stadium -- and it was a low and slow huskiness of suspicion to match my own:

'The one who looks like you?'

That shrewd squint in those oily eyes stop-watching me.

'The one who looked like me.'

Only as much as a twin might.

'He could look like Joan of Arc with that charcoal sketch.'

To that Ekanayake only nodded tightly and then purled and carried one: 'You were mentioning the involvement of local principals, bosses, isn't it? The man with the alias of Tusker—Tusker, Tasker ...' He rolled the euphony around his mouth like a tantalising mouthful of Jaya's food while I tried to hold his eyes without showing how much I was flinching under his stare, 'is the only real principal we keep hearing about, but we can't seem to be closing in on him, bloody fucking hell.'

I felt a jab of exhilaration, but unhelpfully the Singhalese Paul Newman of Australia finally emerged again from his famous chutney kitchen. He only had a busy proprietor's time to stand by the table and continue the usual Sri Lankan chatter: how's old Paradise these days, kick the buggers up north back to India, might return to live and show 'em what real wealth-making is one day. The conversation and the food were bringing nostalgic tears to the Inspector's eyes. Noticing that sentimentality, I did as I felt my brother would do: put the squint back on him.

In their flushes of bonhomie, I finally pulled the squint away from Ekanayake and gave Freddie Jayasinghe the once over. He looked more Teutonic than Sri Lankan. Skin so fair that not even the European sun might have ever wanted to kiss it; a large corpulent body, with an enrichening embonpoint, balanced more like a northern oak on massive Black Forest legs. A big man with a white florid face from gourmandy.

'You know, Freddie,' I chipped in with a determined outsider's loudness, 'you look more and more like you should be running a Kraut restaurant, not a Sri Lankan one.'

'Oh, yeah?' he boomed through otiose cheeks, 'where does that leave you practising law? In darkest Africa?'

A great kidder, Freddie Jayasinghe.

He shouldn't have lived past Greta Garbo, that other Swede or Teuton with about the same-size tits.

I can't help it. I have to take this out of sequence. I just hope don't mentally throw myself into chaos, is all. Still, let it be an item.

'Brother.'

Brother, brother. Twin, twin. Him, him. What does that mean? I can only think about what it's never meant. All he's ever been in substance for me is some sort of heavy shading that falls across the corner of my eye. I've never been able to conceive him as a real human being. I've never been able to accord him those transports of emotion you're supposed to be able to give other humans, let alone of your own stock.

Mind you, this, my brother, doesn't even deserve being called human. If I'm missing a few ladles of consideration towards those irritants out there called fellow human beings, then he's been doubly scooped out.

This was precisely what I was thinking about when I got home after that lunch with Inspector Charles.

There was rain on the tin roof of my place that night, I remember that clearly.

If I ever get back to Canberra, I might even try to do the place up again. I'll never get rid of the port-a-loo because it saved my life. But I might get in a generator, instead of using the candles, and replace the camping stove I was always more than happy with. Gas bottles, as the song could go, have followed me all the days of my life. I might put a few tiles on the concrete floor or maybe even paint it, clad the iron-sheet walls, put gutters around the roof.

That is, I might, if I ever get around to having the roof and the concrete floor and the walls put back again.

But I'd never get rid of a tin roof, even mentally. For the rain on it, never.

Maybe I might even get a refrigerator to replace the water bag and the meat safe I used to have hanging on the Moreton Bay Fig the bulldozer missed.

Yes, what I had been talking about at Jaya's with the Inspector: Principals.

The principals that would have to be needed to run such operations here. You don't go just setting up travel-agency scams, high-level corporate forging, gem smuggling, money-laundering, drugs networks, then international freighting, without boardroom-type planning. You need principals to do that. And, apart from the guy with the alias of Tusker, all those charge-sheet villains were just middle-managers. The flown-in doers. Not bosses.

Bosses. And what did we have at the little Serendip Lankan Association's outing by the Dorras North beach? If that wasn't a mob of principals, not even Cabinet meetings were a mob of bosses.

You want shipment, we had there J.R. Nehru, the top shipper and air freighter in the country. Go on to a small matter of knowing a geuda from a sapphire, who better than N. A. Selverajah, Rajah's Fine Jewellery, getting badly sunburnt on the back of the neck while I watched him squirming besides my Neila?

The financial complications of travel scams? Why, Dr Yogendra Nath, head of the National Travel Insurance Fund, the trouble-shooter for the whole travel industry; what wouldn't he know about juggling interest-timings? Printing a million or so airline tickets, traveller cheques... why wouldn't you want to go to the owner of ten South Indian newspapers in Australasia and Southeast Asia, Mahinder Duraiswamy?

Take a few more of them getting sand all over themselves there trying not to look Neila's way: like Yogi with his computers. Like Professor Josephs with his hieratics of international law; speciality? Why, international banking, of course; the movement of monies.

For whatever you wanted, compared to these SLA cobbers, the Melbourne bourses could be called Marshmallow Fields.

Yet there was no way any of these cobbers could be called criminal types.

Unless they had no choice.

74

After all, nobody with any choice would trot along to that Sunday beach bash and endure such a miserable time of it.

So they had to go.

A meeting of some sort, with wifies and kiddiwinks trotted along for the 'ordinary' look of things?

If that was so, who ordered them, these high-shot cobbers, that they had to be there? I mean, really, forget Neila for that. Who had the clout to say you'll front up when told and you'll look like you're enjoying yourselves when told?

My brother Tasker. That's who.

I felt it in my bones.

What was the sticking point, though? Surely not simple travel scams, no matter how lucrative they were if you kept on the move.

How the hangover of terrorists and real horror-makers are doing all over the world, of course: blackmail, threats, extortion.

My brother?

Okay; then how did he ever get that sort of clout?

And Neila.

For sure, in there somewhere.

A yank of lost causes?

I didn't finish my cold can of Tom Piper's Irish Stew (whose resistance to the can opener should have been a warning to my stomach). I just sat there under the rain on the bit of the roof left, and began to realise I would have to go after this twin brother of mine.

I couldn't go after him to pull him down.

That would pull me down too, because I was already criminal in concealing from the Inspector material evidence.

I had to catch up with him before the Inspector did, so I could convince him to disappear pronto the donto.

He had to start covering our tracks with large, large chunks of track covering, and now, not later.

And after I had done that, I knew what I had to do.

It was then that the logic of it struck me for the very first time.

I had to go after my father.

All this was his fault.

What was it? The White Australia Policy of those days? The little embarrassment he might have had to go through Customs with, just because of his colouring? Not thinking he knew enough Aussie slang?

And because of that... one of those *nothings*, we had to fend for ourselves? My mother had to sigh and die and leave me? My brother had to be on the run from the law? And me, a lawyer with what was a bright future, I had to ruin my career by perjuring myself to protect the family?

Just because of him? My father's some little embarrassment he didn't want to go through?

I shouldn't have lived past my mother.

And that goes double for him.

'Elephants.'

Major T. W. Rogers, our great 'sportsman', would not have shot any of his fourteen hundred bags from any more than ten metres away. Ninety-nine per cent of them would have been either trotting along at a leisurely pace from the little aggravation of his beaters. There, old T.W. would be waiting in hiding with a couple of gun bearers ready to hike it up the nearest tree; they would be carrying his second, third or fourth 16-gauge, heavy-shot, two-bore Packards or Remingtons or whatever he put his murderous faith in. Or his 'game' would be standing peacefully, groping at second-height branches or lazily rubbing itself against a favourite rubbing tree, all keen sense, except for its terribly poor sight.

So, all the Major and his kind had to do was to not stomp too hard on breakable twigs with their hunting boots, keep down wind, get virtually under the nose of the next trophy tusk or ear, aim for the frontal ridge at the right angle and bam.

You tell me how you can miss the brain of an elephant from two metres away, when it's standing placidly there larger than any life? Sport? Maybe one or two the intrepid Major might have had to bring down on the charge. Let's allow the sod the sporting possibility of that.

There's no denying that then they must have been terrifying moments for him. But, even then, if you missed everything vital with those high specific-gravity shots spraying everywhere, you'd have to be no-armed and firing from your teeth. If you hit something as you'd be sure to if you stood your ground, the animal would vie off in shock anyway another ninety-nine per cent of the time.

It is actually hard to imagine how anyone ever missed.

Even if it didn't veer off or you missed the backside of its barn from two paces, you'd have to have two broken legs and be tied to the good earth if you couldn't leap or roll out of the way and get a winning head start scooting off at right angles. They're not the greatest spinners on five-cent pieces, are elephants.

I don't know whether the great plasticiser John Wesley Hyatt would have felt much about all this. Since he got his $10,000 reward from Phelan & Collander, it has to be speculated that he might even have thanked his lucky stars for Major T. W. Rogers. Had he ever heard of the mug? He might even have thanked all those other nineteenth- and twentieth-century 'sportsmen' in ye olde Ceylon, Africa, Burma, ye olde Siam, India, as well.

One of Britain's finest in the form of the youthful and heat-flushed Major Forbes, with a party of three other Europeans, sent 106 Ceylon elephants to a happier existence in just three days. That was in 1837.

They tell me, in these now-times, there might be twenty elephants left in the uplands here today. That's in the wild.

Thank you all, you wonderful pot shots.

Has it stopped? You bet it hasn't. They're still cutting out the great teeth. A third of a tusk's length goes back into the gum, so the bloody gouging to get the best and thickest part is worth the pestilence of the flies and ants.

On an average, they're going to get a set of about two metres plus long, weighing maybe thirty-six kilograms.

If you want to leap into the *Guinness Book of Records*, you're going to have to gouge out more than the set of eleven-and-a-half feet that was once lodged, where else insisting on the Imperial measurement?, in the National Collection of Heads and Horns in the New York Zoological Society.

At another time in 1897, using just a muzzle-loader, for chrissakes, some unnamed Arab got lucky and secured a hotshot pair of tusks weighing 240 and 225 pounds each. I can't remember reading which was the left and which was the right. That's near seven kilograms difference; the poor beast must have been walking around lopsided in circles. No wonder it succumbed to a muzzle-loader. Our Arab missed, it would come around again in time for him to add another load of wadding and be ready for another pot shot.

And yes, for the want of repeating myself, I've heard there might be a whole twenty or so true upland elephants left around here.

Of course, it would be less now. And of course that would be in the wild, like.

Somewhere up in those ergodic mountains, the everchanging, is my father.

The last tusker of them all

'Family.'

Okay, but the gungho types like the Majors Rogers and Forbes and even that fluky Arab with the muzzle-loader could have used their talents on aunts not elephants.

Aunts.

My life's autografts.

I get left by my father with my mother. I get left by my mother with my aunts. I got left by these aunts and at least thank God for that.

They weren't even aunts. Only ex-workmates at the shoe factory.

I get left by my mother with strangers from a shoe factory.

My berserker brother leaves my cacodaemonic aunts bedridden with matching hips in plaster, landed in the one double bed, yes, someone has rigged up for them downstairs in the parlour.

That means I couldn't go or come without their shrieking at me. Have I done this? Did I do that? Get this. Get that.

Painted harpies hunkered down, and greater harpies because they were hunkered down.

Now they do take notice of me and I wish they ignored me as they used to. I am just the bringer of soups and toasts and magazines and water for their gorgefuls of pills. Their brown bottles of what must have been almost pure morphine.

On their table-sides, they had bottles and jars and tubes and glasses accreted in a bed of damp face powders and rouges. They smelt of female. They smelt of fogs of Vicks Vapour Rub. They glistened with glycerines of Vaseline. There was something like dental cement mixed in with the odours, but I could never figure that one out.

They were crappy and crabby with one another. They were more especially crappy and crabby with me.

They kept developing these colds. There were snotty handkerchiefs crushed into gluey balls on the bed, all over the floor. I had to pick them up.

Before flopping off to school I had to get up to make their sickly teas and pieces of toast with the Marmite thick for Ethel and smeared lightly for Eveline. Maybe it was the other way around. Who cares? They did. After school, the mudded teas, the cleaning up of the snot rags and washing them, the

79

scrapping at the domestic gunk, the emptying of the chamber pot, the fluffing up of the pillows, while all the time they whined at me.

The worst were the body baths. They didn't have to ask me to do it; I was told I had to do it to prevent bed sores by some doctor who at least showed me roughly how to go about it. The silly old crones giggled and fluttered their eyelids at him. He patted them playfully on the tooshies and then got out of there.

It was all right for him.

With the basin of warm water and the flannel and soap, I tried to get them to wash each other, but they weren't having any of that. The half bums I had to wipe down -- Ethel's right cheek; Evaline's left; and then having to swop over -- surprised me a little for they were quite neat. I suppose they were the source of their ludicrous wriggles as they walked. But they were pitted like a child had poked around in their putties, and their backs were loose and wedgy; it was elephant underbelly skin, blotched and freckled and cape-ing the bones like loose rubber sheets.

I used to almost gag.

If that wasn't bad enough, when I had to do their back of necks and armpits, I also had to sponge their pectorals, or where their pectorals should have been, or, rather where their boobies might have once risen. Now those features, if they had ever been features, lay with deflated guesswork, black-veined and crapulous. But still they lowed with girlish moans of delight while I did so, egging each other on, and even came to hold me in the small of my back as I washed.

You see that was actually happening, don't you? They were laughing at me.

I had had to fight my way down the streets because of all the ridicule I got by having to live with them. Now the crazy reasons for all the ridicule outside had the nerve to be giving it to me inside.

80

Good God, I was only a boy. How could I help it if, at such times, I felt my cheeks were dripping with musth?

It was one night when it was raining and August chilly.

I woke up to hear the choral whine for me. I was so tired I could hardly force myself out of the cot. By the time I staggered in to them, I swear I was falling asleep on my feet.

They wanted a blanket that had fallen off or something. It was only Ethel, or the other one, who was somewhat awake; she was mumbling something and the other had gone back to snoring. I put the blanket back over her. The mumbler kicked it off. I just couldn't raise the energy to make out what she was on about, so I just crawled between them to hear her better and that was that.

I can remember the dream still. I was some sort of slug, or creature lying straight out on my back and helpless. I looked down and from the waist down I was sheathed in a blue fat cocoon of jelly. But the sensation was honeyed; it was warm and oozing. There seemed to be lullabies all around me. High-up voices crooning soft, loving things. They seem to be saying 'welcome, welcome' and I gave myself up sweetly into their warm hands.

When I woke, I woke up in a putrescent coffin, of which those two old ladies formed the sides. I literally thought I was in death, buried with them.

I was naked, cold, but still semi-tumescent.

It pains me to remember this. It will always be disgusting.

They were licking their fingers. Arthritic claws, licking them like bear cubs. Then they rubbed my sticky wetness into my chest and swirled their dried bones towards my cods, my disgrace.

Slowly, slowly, I worked my way towards the end of the bed. When I got my knees over the bed board, I stood up and fled.

I fled to their cackles.

I can't remember where my brother was all through this time but he wasn't too far away. I felt once again that entwining energy we must have had because we were twins. There is no description for it, except a type of extra fullness in and of your mind, some additional use of my thoughts and feelings, he makes use of to *pip* me.

I'm not saying he and I mentally spoke to each other, not literally. But we could certainly spook each other. A reading. Yes, a reading. Perhaps he was able to read my mind more than I could his. Even then, he just seemed to do what I would have done if I wasn't me.

I forced myself to go on washing them, even though he ordered me not to. I fed them their mud lakes of tea and toast; I cleaned up around and under their skeletons. I forced blandness. I pretended I did not know what had happened. In the meantime, my brother and I started to go to school together. It was as though he wanted us to be seen together, something we had always avoided.

At the week's end, the house went up while we were at school.

They diagnosed it as a loose gas fitting, the kitchen filling up like a gas bath, just like at my grandparents' estate lodge. My loony aunts screaming when, apparently, they began to smell the smoke but nobody was coming.

Oh, they got them out. I don't know what all their screaming was about.

By the time I arrived back from school they were already back in hospital with hips rudely broken again with all their frantic writhing.

They went, I heard, from the hospital to some old people's home, and were never able to wriggle those tooshies again.

In fact, I hear tell they had thrown their last snotty hankies over the side of the bed for the last time.

Us? My brother and I? We went from there almost straight to Our Boys Home in Henley Beach, where he started right in on kicking tooshies, male or female, from the word go. He would, wouldn't he?

I tell you, I had had it with my father who'd put us in for all this.

My brother, the so-called alias'd Tusker, got away with it again.

I think he thinks all you have to do is smile innocently and you can get away with murder.

He's proved that right.

I felt like I had done it. He had only done what I was thinking about, so what did that make me?

But apart from that, at some stage or other, whatever he turned out to be, my father must have thought of me more than just some young nuisance dogging his heels.

Maybe he had grown up around elephants so much that he couldn't resist any creature that was kept in a kraal.

At forty-something, you couldn't say, with her type of rotten up-themselves parents, my mother wasn't that.

How my father and my mother ever managed to get going you can only imagine. Probably the looks first. The hesitations before passing. I can't see him paying any sort of court, and, as sure as shootin', those grandparents of mine would never have allowed that, but I am sure he volunteered immediately to do the honourable thing having done the dastardly act on her and, dressed as well as he could, a borrowed suit perhaps, and with his sister, my Aunt Jayalitha, of course, would have visited the house to ask suit.

Nobody could envy him that.

Those pretend-Pommy snoots of parents of hers obviously gave him short shrift. They would have been too pukka to have evicted him on the spot. Those English colonials lived by the rules even if they had set them. There wouldn't have been tea, I suspect, but there would have been a sitting down in the parlour of the great plantation house and a formal hearing. Maybe the conversation ended before the maid had time to bring the tea, in which case they would have sipped it in stony silence and said no more. This dark-eyed man of the local earth man and their so-fair daughter.

What effect would a disgrace like that have?

Did my father-to-be smell of elephants? Can you smell of elephants?

No, if I remember correctly. I'm pretty sure they have baby-type smells. I think it was the only one little bull calf that my father managed to breed up during the time I was there. It would have been an amazing and rare event in those days and proof of his prowess.

But he still gave it to me.

I was the one he gave it to. Not my brother.

He called it Little Majah. I can remember that because I thought he was saying Little 'Major' like my grandfather pukka-type would.

Major.

Major T. W. Rogers would have blasted it off the face of the earth.

Little Majah didn't turn out to be a tusker. I wanted it badly to be an *aetha aliya*, as they call a tusker here, because my father had given it to me. But it wasn't to be, I guess.

It had a trunk like a lithe plastic hose that John Wesley Hyatt would have been pleased as Punch about. My mother was clapping her hands with delight on one side of me. My father had his hand on my shoulder when they took that running-to-yellow photograph.

Then I couldn't understand why he was letting one of the mahouts' sons go near *my* little elephant, but not me.

The next day, Little Majah wasn't there.

I was told they had taken it away to be trained by that boy's father for his son.

My father had given it to me.

He had given it all right, then taken it away.

Why would anyone do a thing like that to his own son?

'Australia then.'

Our Boys Home in Henley Beach South, at a time when the marshland belt ran behind the sand-hill dunes all along the coast to Glenelg North. Then. A viaduct had to get the trams from Lockleys to Henley Beach across what would have had to been once a tidal flat.

West Beach? You wouldn't know it now. Then, it was a wasteland of sand, thick and white and stinking hot. Where a few invisible Italians would grow their melons illegally on government sand land and hardly ever get caught. Mugs if they worried about it anyway. Where a handful of just-as-invisible hermits hid themselves away in sand clefts covered by rusted corrugated-iron sheets. No airport. No housing estates that have brought these once truly amazing swales under lawn and asphalt, that unbogged the marshes.

From my Sri Lankan uplands where the great leaves of the palm and the climbers fanned and chilled me and where even a boy had to stop and wonder at the crags teasing the monsoons, I had first been stepped down to the bubbling asphalts of gum-thin Adelaide. Now I was deposed to a desert wasteland where, to get shade, was to crawl under some shrub like a snake. Out Lockleys and Henley Beach way.

There was heat in my head, pricking heat, fly-crawling against the stickiness of my whole body, heat from the very earth I walked on by way of singeing sand hills. The whisked-up beards of the marram grass tufts making you think of dying of thirst. There was no longer the velvet of the earth cool and silky to my bare feet. Now there were the chalky dusts and the shell gravels, lifeless-bleached, as though the world had shattered here with frustrated fury, hot and stinking to the shoes and had wilted before each of your steps.

Now, I felt as chalk. Everything was weary.

I felt that the punishment decided for me was somehow a removal of the tones of all the world and the leaving in their place the bloodlessness, the anaemic, the albino, salted-sun crushed.

For my sins, I felt I had been flame-flared to bone.

What had I done to be despatched to Purgatory out of my Lanka?

And the dunes—a couple of kilometres in any direction at least— were nothing more to me than the desert of Armageddon of my mother's pictorial Bible, and I to wander across its deathly plains as one of the death soldiers of Satan; the melons of the invisible Italians lay on the sands like rows of heads lopped off in the final battle. I walked among them like the last survivor, scuffing the tortuous waveforms of the snake and lizard trails, and looking for the finish.

The only lost souls occasionally passing distantly by were those few hermits, shuffling and shouting in their deserted brain storms, blackened from the unlife bleaching only by the soiled, disgusting rags they wore ... stepping up, I fancied, from the nether world to beg alms of the living, and then to return back to the world of white fires after getting into my head and tormenting me.

The hell of it.

There must have been thirty kids confined to Our Boys Home in Lockleys South, a verge to the sand hills, from the ages of five or six up to the mid-teens, when they could be turfed out to do some labouring or whatever to pay for their keep. The Home would have been swallowed up by Adelaide airport a few years later. If it hadn't consumed it, the cockroaches would have. I had one old iron bed with missing springs and one plywood cupboard that collapsed in on me one night like a pack of cards. My brother was somewhere in one of those other corrugated-iron dormitories.

The only neighbours we had were from the Migrant Camp down West Beach Road as it was even called then -- a thin, crumbling two-way strip of tar-muck laid on sand full of great potholes we encouraged.

There must have been two thousand people somehow surviving in the Promised Land in those nissen huts, which Major Peter Norman Nissen of the 29th Company Royal Engineers of the British Army was said to have designed around April of 1916, such things needing to be asked and explained. They, being us living in the huts evolving from Major Peter Norman nissen's original concept, were supposed to be there only temporarily -- for six months actually, maximum, after which, according to the boffins of the South Australian Housing Trust of the time, we were then theoretically evolved to be prepared for the life, jobs, schools, networks outside in the town-sized city of Adelaide.

They, meaning us, were being nothing more than culturally quarantined.

Few of them ever got out, and even fewer of us ever escaped the welfare trap. Caught in the Lockleys South sand pitfalls.

It was a hard place. The Adelaideans could speak of it with no more horror than that it was a place of *knives* -- meaning foreign and *migrant* -- you avoided like the plague. These were not people in there; we were somehow other things from the barbarian depths of Europe, and southern Europe, to boot. So, they/we had to believe in barbarianisms they had the gall to call religions: strange Christian sects, Greek Orthodox, Russian Orthodox, Coptic; then Muslims, Jews, Hindus. There were Croatians, Serbs, Latvians, Ukrainians, Maltese, Sikhs, Chinese from countries you wouldn't credit they'd recruit from. There were Balts, gypsies, the poor Pommies from the mill counties, Lebanese, Persians. You could tell. They carried flick knives, see. And you could dig for years in those sand hills and not find a Methodist.

In Australia, they/we had to learn one didn't have flick knives. Not flick knives that flick, not flick knives you carried.

The Adelaideans were right too. There were always flick-knife fights. You cage together families that cannot even speak the same language under the same fast-evaporating dream of the good life; you cage within one compound the volatile suspicions of religions that have feared and hated each other for all- time; you coagulate the most fearsome of frustrations; and you have the self-fulfilling prophesies of the old flick knife-wieldings, the from-abroad gang fights, the hideous family bun fights turning southern-European murderous, infidelities along the lines of what non-Methodists do, and the breakdown of traditional structures, even before they or we get a chance to get on their and our feet and take any sort of step on the Australian gravy train.

Even to go anywhere was a barren trek across a baked-hard earth that tolerated animal scuffs, but not human footprints. There might have been one swaying bus pass there every three hours on a road that had one narrow way up and one narrow way down. How could they get anywhere? How could even we? Not too many of even the Adelaide set had cars in those days. Lots of treadlies then; lots of donkeying.

My twin brother loved the violence.

He lived in that camp next door more than he did in the Home. There was no one to mind; no authority in that lost world.

At first, we were maybe the only ones from the Subcontinent. Always there was the 'Fuck off, wog bastard'. It was the leader of the hot'n'flushed English mob mainly. An older guy, thin, red and freckled, with hair like the flames of this hell adapted, swept back greasily into a duck tail.

They found him one morning lying in the scrub at the back boundary of the camp badly beaten by a two-by-four.

I knew it was my brother, because that was precisely the fantasy of revenge on him I was having, I thought, all to myself.

One of his legs was badly burnt around the ankle; there had been an attempt to set him on fire.

Even in hell, human flesh burns with difficulty. On the verge of sand hills, you learn you don't get far with fire.

For six months, however, we weren't the only ones from the Subcontinent, I found out. The mother wore her saree defiantly and must have insisted her daughter wore one too. It made the family of two boys and the daughter stand out like sore thumbs, despite the fact that they were of lighter skin than you usually get from Tamil Nadu.

Their name was Ramaswarmy, which, of course, got them the chuck name of The Smarmies. The daughter's name was Rehana, and how could I ever come to forget it.

The Smarmy brothers I did not know, nor wanted to. I kept away from them, but my twin got to know them well. It was as it would turn out to be. My brother seemed genetically Tamil, where I seemed genetically English. That was starting to dawn on me as early as even then.

He had acquired an army survival knife, a real switch-blade, a beauty of a flip-flickie, but with other hole-punchers and corkscrews, and this he would hold, with all these open, in the palm of his hand, so that it looked like he had on a gladiator's gauntlet. Really vicious.

I have no idea why the gangs suffered my brother, this dark outsider. Perhaps he looked so sun basted, out of the natural lie of things there. I did come to learn he let it be known that he had no family ties, no race, no religion, only colour. And I know he boasted he would kill anyone who minded the colour; and I know they believed him.

Anyway and strangely, he became friendlier with the Ramaswarmys than I have ever heard him do with anyone, even since. It must have been the girl Rehana, with whom he started to tolerate good-hearted ribbing by the camp's rouseabouts, even the ruddy and silly-looking English ones. I mean, he was actually being seen with her and not minding it in the least.

Most of the Tamil migrants that started to come later, I learnt, were in Melbourne or Sydney. The father, Papa

89

Ramaswarmy must have thought he could make it on his own. He must have thought that until he took one look at the camp and, probably more to the point, one look at Adelaide.

Adelaide had done that to people more than once. You know, spike the bubble of the quieter hopeful moment.

Not that the Ramaswarmys seemed to belong in the camp. They had money, means. This was shown when one day a large black DeSoto, followed by a smaller Vauxhall for their luggage, pulled up to absorb Papa Ramaswarmy and wife and sons and particularly Rehana.

The cars had Victorian number plates and were obviously heading by way of luxury back to Melbourne.

After that, my brother got really wild. At least I was working in a hamburger joint right opposite the so-new Henley High, but he just stopped going to class altogether and I watched him from afar, as though he was at the end of a long kaleidoscope sliding off with the prisms so slitheringly that I could only see glimpses of him in my mind's eye. Which was all that I wanted.

Now my memory of him comes across like a print-form write-up about the alienation of today's urban poor. His dream of a migration to the good life no longer holds. He sees himself caught in a laid trap of suppression, alienation and poverty. And all that. Hey, and he wasn't even Muslim!

I am remembering him more in the present than in that past now. He becomes identified with the camp's hard Croatian gang, whose fathers had been fighting back in Yugoslavia with the Utashi, the anti-Tito movement that became so large in Australia during the sixties and seventies. They must have been hard hangovers of all that; because surely this is the late seventies.

Now, there are starting to come more and more, the carloads of outside native-born or -claimed Australian youths. They are beginning to drive past the camp, throw empty beer bottles over the cyclone fence, jeer at the wogs playing the woggy game of soccer on the baked ridges of the open camp square -- *go back to your own home, wogs!* -- on the bare and hard chalk.

'Dago wops!'

Again. We, as my brother and I, are hearing the ridicule again. But this time it is coming from outside, just how it had started to come because of those loony aunts who infected us. This is from a society that is supposed to be waiting out there with open arms for us to help develop it, to bring our skills to.

They let me go at the hamburger joint. Somebody has complained of having to eat a hamburger made by my dirty Indian hands.

My brother starts to hang out with the Croatian gang and on the outside of the Home and camp. They have somehow scraped up the money to get an old bomb, an Oldsmobile right out of the Chicago mobster days. They set off after the car loads of those Aussie youths yelling their abuses and out come the knives. Yes, the flick knives. Another search by the police of the camp. More beatings by the police behind the Nissen huts, don't you worry about that.

My brother takes these beatings. They are all right after a few times, he says. You get to learn how to roll, absorb things.

Drugs, the morphines, are coming in. They know where to get them along Glenelg Road. Honeysuckers, they call them. These are antimalarial prescriptions you can buy from any chemist, but fired down, concentrated and then syruped up again. Australian grannies have been hooked on these for a hundred years. They say anyway.

Yes, the gang also knows how to rob and get the money to buy honeysuckers.

They are playing the Beach Boys on the radio at the Glenelg Road Shell service station when the police shoot my brother's mate Michael in the head.

My brother escapes by actually rolling under the Oldsmobile, more to stay with his mate Michael than to hide or escape, until the cops give chase to the other Croatian gang members. Michael's drops of blood keep hitting the driveway right by his face before he gets to move again.

He gets back to the Home and stays indoors for the first time in months. They give him his alibi, because they have not even known he had been missing for those months.

Indifference saves my brother again. It looks like indifference anyway.

There had been ten in the Croatian gang. Within six months of venturing outside, my brother is the only one left. A Sri Lankan, the last representative of the Croatian Beaters.

Nevertheless, Michael's family, the Kushzinskys, give him the old Oldsmobile because none are left who can drive.

It is the rolling, and the totalling, of that old Kushzinsky Olds that gives the turn to our lives. The fine my brother gets for dangerous driving, driving without a licence and trying to bribe his way out of it takes all the money we have, or could beg, borrow or, yes, steal. It gets him before a magistrate but what of that?

I suppose it helps him to have seen the poverty in Sri Lanka more than I had. For my part I couldn't help him with any decision, because I had always kept to my father and his elephants when I could or was being held by my mother in the great plantation house. But he never had or was. He was always in the huts of the estate workers, washing himself at their communal well, eating off palm leaves as plates with them, squatting on their bare earth floors. In his eyes were the dim tallow candles of their nights and their resourcefulness of having to make do with what little they ever got to keep by way of hoarding.

He went, yes, to the Kushzinskys, but all they could give was a parcel of dry rations for our journey. Him being so dark skin-toned and standout foreign, it was just a gall trying to hitchhike. But he got lucky again. He was picked up by a carful of Aborigines who thought he was one of them, and then was amazed he wasn't, and then bitter for and with him because they knew well what he had been going through.

And they were going all the way to Melbourne.

A small thing, but it is enough to raise our hopes.

Within a few days, I see how my brother has tracked down the Ramaswarmy family. He has stood on their doorstep, a miserable and near-starving young man. The girl, Rehana, has answered the door and, seeing him, has stepped away to weep.

Her father comes out and leads him in.

That night my brother and Papa Ramaswarmy talk man to man. We are Tamils. We are all Tamils together. We will all always be Tamils, and we must never forget that. It is our duty to our great civilisation to ensure that they are forced, if need be, to grant us Tamils our own homeland somewhere. It does not even matter if it is in the Subcontinent or the Pacific, where the Tamil from seafarers on have always been.

All that night, yes, that thickset Papa Ramaswarmy talked to my brother now put down as 'Tusker' on an alias sheet, and there was put forward and agreed upon an ever-binding obligation to the Tamil cause, in return for financial assistance to us.

That night, without my knowledge, my own twin accepted that assistance and the obligation that went with it.

Whatever that was. I still don't like to think on it.

It is the night my brother is confirmed as always-fiercely Tamil.

Yes, and what else but all history?

After that I don't see how we had much to do with each other. As the years went by, I hardly heard from him, except the constant *pipping*. University. Sport and always pushing me into second. The taking of law, finally.

These things fell into place for us. I have to admit it, even despite the *pipping*. I have to admit too that all that wasn't by sheer accident. It was that pact... somehow the money to get through always falling into place.

Care of the Ramaswarmys. And I still don't know if there should be a question mark there. My brother would, I bet.

Besides, who cared? 1 had been given the Australian dream again, and the days did not burst it.

God forgive me, that dream is still with me. Australia. Past the mistake of me being born; past the evil eyes of my rotten grandparents; past the ever lack of duty by my father.

And past the sighing and the dying, and the things that just seemed to keep walking out and leaving me.

I shouldn't have lived past St Simeon the Elder. From AD 422, he spent the last thirty-seven years of his life sitting on a stone pillar up there on the Hill of Wonders in old Syria. Call him the grand tusker of all the stylites. He lived until he was nearly seventy, and nobody can tell me that wasn't good in those days, even for a tusker. Especially perched on a pole. You know how you get uncomfortable even sitting on a cushion?

That St. Simeon the Elder must have dreamt a lot of indelible dreams that stayed with him to have him last out that long.

Besides, up there, pole'd, nobody got to sap any of his life's energies by just being in the world with him.

He was lucky.

Maybe that's precisely why he went up there in the first place, and precisely why he never bothered to come down in a hurry.

There's this thing about leprosy and the 1870s, and there's this thing about the 1870s, even if you forget about the leprosy.

I'm talking about the early 1870s, 1873, just about the time John Wesley Hyatt was starting to enjoy, hopefully, the fruits of his $10,000 from Phelan & Collander and when Major T. W. Rogers was edentating and de-lugging number whatever of his fourteen hundred butchered elephants.

At this time Dr Armauer Hansen of Norway nailed the germs that had scourged the world for about two-and-a-half thousand years, give or take a day or two.

It had taken the little buggers that time to get christened. I'm talking of his germs. The moniker Dr Armauer Hansen gave them was *mycobacterium leprae*, when he really meant scaly, fungus-faced, scrawny little turds.

Dr Hansen wouldn't have shot elephants. No way. He would have been in the audience applauding away if they had ever given John Wesley Hyatt the Nobel Prize, which they should have prophetically done for contribution to the earth's biodiversity and for modern supermarket profitabilities.

I looked the good doctor up the other day because I found out that the home I'm currently helping Father Thumbayaserni with used to be called Hansen House, and I wanted to know who this British gentleman of this old mansion of colonial Ceylon was.

He wasn't. He was Norwegian, which you wouldn't put past him. The house was named for what it originally was -- a leprosarium, as now, or a hostel for the sufferers of Hansen's Disease or, you guessed it, leprosy.

It isn't fully a hostel just for that these days. About ten years ago, as I gather, the Daya Nivasa nuns took it over in the name of Mother Teresa, or Agnes Gonxha Bojaxhui, if you would prefer. Mother Teresa was born 37 years after Dr Armauer Hansen got introduced to his germs and pretty far away from being Norwegian, since she was basically Albanian. But we can't have everything.

Anyway, such wonderful Subcontinental ladies of hard and preoccupied eyes under workaday half-wimples of the Missionaries of Charity organisation were her nun-descendants. They converted part of Hansen House and sheds for the sick and destitute of Gampola and left the remaining front half (the hall, parlour, sitting room and two bow-windowed bedroom type dorms) for the local lepers.

I had followed Father Thumbayaserni from church after mass one Wednesday evening because I wanted to corner him in private to ask, as a lapsed Catholic and really one who had only come back into the fold because the Church was the only social outing going in Gampola, even now I hear, whether being divorced twice made any difference anymore if I wanted to get married before his altar. How were things at being swept under the carpet these days in the Catholic Church?, kind of thing. You don't ask; you never know, right?

I thought being Australian might be some help there. They are known not to hold back from the first thing that comes into their minds.

Now, leprosy isn't any longer the revolting slow killer it used to be, though the hairs on the back of my neck still hackled when I saw where he was leading me. Pus and scabs were more my brother's things. Anyway, if the leprosy's not caught early enough, and if it's the infectious strain of those scaly, fungus-faced, scrawny little turds of germs of the good doctor Armauer Hansen, then leprosy can still eat away your flesh. So squeamish is squeamish, and I had ever right to be.

God help me, then, when I edged in through the front double doors that were wide open, if I wasn't confronted by a stinking mass of man or woman with half its face eaten away, the suppurated rag that presumably should have been covering this monstrous sight looping down around its neck like the oldtimers' cowboy Tom Mix's of the silver screen (see my favourite 'The Texan' from 1920), and two bloody ulcerated lumps of mitts that I took to have once been hands held up in supplication to me. No, not to Fr Thumbayaserni, but to *me*.

The person gurgled, and seemed to cry out nearly as loudly as I clearly remember now I was doing at the time too. It, if I can use the term it... it was an it to me just then, believe me... held those hand-things up in prayer to me, would you believe, then shook in a way that made me swear later that pieces of its lower jaw went flying off, then, just

fell

at
my
feet.

'That,' Father Thumbayaserni said, after I managed to open my eyes on such a world again, 'is a Sign from Heaven.'

Sister Lima was making the Sign of the Cross as though the Father had called for instant sacrament.

I looked to where he then pointed and was nodding piously.

I couldn't believe those were my hands and they were lifting the bandage stickily back onto the poor creature's face, adjusting it, and in the process of patting it firmly onto the scabs and the suppurations. They were ministering hands; kind and gentle hands. They were my hands. It's hard to believe they were, even now.

And the butchered meat that was certainly what was left of the hands of that gutted human being there were stroking these, my hands, and stroking them with reverence, in soft putty gratitude.

And still I couldn't control what these, my hands, were doing. I watched them lifting the person from the ground. He trembled within the crook of my arm. I glanced at Father Thumbayaserni who, with his eyes, alternated between heaven and showing the way to the poor creature's leprous bed, as I still can only think of it being.

I tottered towards it with the man, this old scabrous man. He was weeping, bandage muffled. I was weeping. They were my eyes weeping. For what? What for? I got him to that filthy corner and I lay him down. Where I let him raise these, my hands with his own clumps and place them against his revolting once-lips.

Through the rag I could feel the hard ridges of gum bone. No fat of lips.

And I sat by him and wiped his forehead with the tissues I had in my pocket.

And, would you believe it?, he went to sleep right beneath those things I was watching that were supposed to be my hands.

Father Thumbayaserni and Sister Lima remained in the doorway, looking priestly and sisterly, as you could guess. I have no idea whether their expressions were also ones of being stunned but 1 do know this: before she left to go back to tending to the sick and destitute, as against the leprous and the destitute, Sister Lima made the sign of the cross at me, and smiled beatifically.

It would have been only slightly better if Mother Teresa herself had done it.

There was, in fact, none other there nearly as Edgar Allan Poe as my old leper there was. While I sat with him, I watched Father T. move around the other lepers in company with another Sister from the Missionaries of Charity. This one was a dumpling, her face a rubbery ball that looked like it had been on the receiving end of the poverty racket for too long. She was plainly down-at-heel herself, heavy with overwork. She has become one of my favourites. Sister Margaret, a crazy name for a Punjabi.

Sister Margaret rolled along by the Father's side like a ball-bearing attached by friction.

They were doing the rounds of the eight men and six women there in those two dormitories. Each leper sat on his or her leftover Victorian steel cot without energy or hope or conversation and took the medicine or the admonition.

When they got around to my old man's cot, Sister Margaret handed me the needle. No way was I going to plunge anything into someone who had held me as though I was his last hope. But she only patted me on the shoulder, and disturbed the air with a faint scent of cheap underarm deodorant, which could well have been disinfectant, to lean over me to get to his stewed fig of a bum.

Giving needles wasn't my job, and still isn't. My job, I knew even then, would be to do the menial things around the place. I would do the sweeping and the scrubbing, the body washes and the bandages. I had done it with those two gunk-headed aunts and I could do it here. I would take and bring the bed pans. If they overlooked the pans, I would wipe and wash them down, and I'd change those rag sheets and wash them all over with these things I still yet watch: my own hands.

Sure, and I would blow their noses and wipe their noses and I would wash those snot rags by hand, too.

It wasn't even a relief to read later about Dr Armauer Hansen's scaly, fungus-faced, scrawny little turds of germs and how they're all bluff, really. As germs go, they're all puff and wind basically. They just got centuries of good publicity for shit-faced germs like they are, centuries of sensationalising propaganda for the human race. Basically, you just ignore the little turds and keep washing and wiping-down instead. Just don't you go sucking on any nose drips they cause. Okay, I could live with that. Who couldn't? And put oil on your feet after soaking them in water when you're padding around the leprosarium. I could live with that, too.

I had survived Adelaide; I could survive Dr Armauer Hansen's shit-faced germs even if they have a fancy name.

I suppose it was dangerous for me to blow my cover, what with Inspector Charles Bloody-fucking-hell Ekanayake now in town looking for my father or for me, whichever.

But I took the chance and was able, within a week, to hand Father Thumbayaserni some money I had telegraphically transferred from Canberra.

He took it with as much surprise as handing a communion wafer. Priests. I was bleeding the hard-earned and there he was just nodding and folding his big mitt around it.

It was for new linen, more drugs, clean sheets, new bandages, brooms that had some fibres left to broom, pans and buckets without holes, an incinerator, a steriliser, some dry-cleaned hand- me-downs, and the things that females need (perhaps even the good Sisters, perish the thought).

It was also for buying things for me: stuff so I could rub, scrub, clean teeth, wipe bums.

It is hard to think now it was really buying things to make me, myself, feel good.

I actually started the morning after I met my poor old leper. It was six o'clock, time to get them up and cleaned before breakie. From then on, I stayed the mornings and returned in the evenings to reverse the whole thing.

On Sundays, I got to rounding them up and marching them off to Mass in the Tamil language, which I don't understand and nor deep down do they, being all, but one, Buddhists and Sinhala-speaking. At least it got them out of the house. There, in church, blessedly, we are segregated like in the bad old medieval days; no matter how crowded the service is, there are still lots of empty seats around us.

You have to give it to the scaly, fungus- faced, scrawny little turds of

Dr Hansen's germs. They have written themselves into a lot of scary books.

That much literature obviously carries with it a lot of respect when it comes to wide berths.

Anyway, on the first day he greeted me, my old leper man could have had no idea I was going to turn up for 'work' that next morning. I hadn't even mentioned it to Father Thumbayaserni or any of the Sisters. Yet there the poor old boy was, his bandages dripping again and fallen off suppurations, waiting in the doorway of those incredible mahogany double doors. And, when he saw me walk through the wire gate, he dropped to his knees again. I couldn't help it. I felt the same clutch at my senses, the same rush of love for him, for them all, as I had had the day before.

I took those pulps he was holding up in supplication again, led him back to bed and, would you know?, he went back to sleep instantly, again, even though he must have just woken up.

100

The crazy thing is that neither the Father nor any of the Sisters know all of their names. Not really. Certainly not without having to go to some metal cabinet and look them up and even then they'd be lucky. They had either come in off the street or been carried in off the street. Most of them have no idea of their proper names or how old they were or where they might have been born, or how the paths went that they had got there by.

Certainly, they didn't know the real name of my old leper man. So I called him Hansen.

In a real sense, he was lucky he lived past Dr Armauer Hansen of Norway. I guess he had Dr Armauer Hansen himself to thank for that.

The other crazy thing was that, when I cleaned him up, when I stroked off the dried blood and dried up the pus weepings from his face, and combed his hair and got him confident enough to look directly at me, I saw that he wasn't an old man at all.

In fact, he could be younger than I am, perhaps in mid-to-late thirties.

Young Hansen, really.

But let it stay Hansen. As maybe it always did from then on.

My work in the leprosarium had set me up as one of Father Thumbayaserni's most trusted parishioners, so, when I thought the time was auspicious, I broached the subject about which I had originally followed him to Hansen House for.

Marriage. In his church.

Because my fiancée wanted it and her family would expect it.

And they being strong pillars of his parish, and all that.

Shouldn't be much of a problem as far as I could see. We were sitting in his parish office which smelt of moth balls, as though the Catholic Church of the outside world was insinuating itself into Sri Lanka. A divorce here and there, I admitted to. A lapse of church- going for a decade, maybe two, I could freely own up to. A bit of a problem with the concept of the Immaculate Conception and the infallibility of the Pope and the concept of communion with a whole bunch of other people... well, who doesn't doubt in this day and age, Father?

'I don't,' he replied and blew a pipe smoke ring my way. He can open wider his chihuahua eyes than you would have thought possible, given all that bulldog skin folds around them, as though he was constantly seeing the light, or what lurked in the darkness beyond it. But ever sage. He remained there sage and listened sagely and even nodded sagely when I threw in my ace-in-the-pack.

'And, of course, I am Australian.'

I waited for his deliberation, as demurely as a man who knew it was in the bag but didn't want to hurt feelings of the other person's relevance. Finally, he gave out in a very altar voice, really:

'Jonathan, have you ever been to confession?'

'They don't go much on that in Australia, Father,' I lied like a dog. Then again, I *could* have been right.

'Jonathan, have you ever had confirmation?'

'I got a brother. He might have. Come to think of it, I'm sure he did. But he's a sort of Hindu or Buddhist, but I'm not sure because he likes nothing better than hanging on fences.'

'Jonathan, could you recite for me the Profession of Faith?'

'I see you sell that book in your charity shop, Father. I'll pick it up on the way out.'

'Jonathan, the Hail Mary?'

'I've seen that in that book, too, Father. A bit flip shoddy, but.'

'Jonathan, I would think you would know what a Novena is, *nae*?'

'Father, we don't go much on those in Australia either.'

'Listen, Jonathan, did you ever go to Mass in Australia?'

'You see, Father, there was always that inconsiderate time clash with the Canberra Raiders games.'

'Jonathan, are you really Roman Catholic?'

'I'm pretty sure my brother was before he got into that other stuff.'

'Marry you in church? Jonathan, just go away.'

It was a bit of a shock to get the knockback. A bit unfair, I think. And hurtful to an innocent. After all, it wasn't me who had to go and tell my fiancée's family I wasn't suitable; she had to.

I'm still working on the Father, though, even today. The lady I want to marry is only a few years younger than me, yet she says she is still a virgin. I believe her implicitly.

I believe her when she says it is her gift for me.

Her name is Virathni.

She had once been the tiny figure standing in the corner of my father's line cottage back at the tea estate, watching while my mother and I took our lunches there.

Virathni.

Who, when we were children here in Gampola, always intrigued me for being younger than me, while being my aunt.

I wanted to marry my younger aunt.

I've kept that one back from Father Thumbayaserni for the time being. He's got enough to pro and con with.

Part Two

Scam or no scam. If I was to try to cover my brother's tracks and so conceal my own, it was obvious I had to take leave from the Department.

I only had the suspicions that Inspector Charles's principals came from that strange agglomeration of high achievers that had somehow coagulated into that Serendip Lankan Association or SLA I mentioned with my weird Neila on Dorras North beach.

But when it comes to my twin brother, there are suspicions and suspicions, just as there were times when he seemed to do what I had been thinking of doing.

This mind-in-union had got a lot of people hurt over the years, but that wasn't my fault, unless thinking is a crime. He was that type of violent person and, I suppose, in some twisted way, that wasn't his fault either. If we hadn't been so physically un-alike, yet mentally so in hum, I might have been able to distance myself from his actions far better.

If I had, I wouldn't have had to cope with this deep feeling of guilt as what he did subsequently if I didn't perceive what his state of mind was at this or that time. How is there any knowing about twins? And I'm speaking from one side of them. Who could guess that he and I were really like spiritual Siamese twins if you put two imaginations together in the womb?

They should've had an exorcist come along and separate us at birth. After that they were too late.

The crimes he had done, the things I was suspicious about him for... all I had to do was close my eyes and see him carry them out, if I wanted to. Not that I wanted to. Frankly, I had never wanted to. I had enough troubles of my own.

I had the leave coming, after all. After twelve years, there were the long-service accruements. But how to get it pushed through without raising the possibility with Inspector Bloody-fucking-hell Charles that I was panicking?

You see, after the Jaya's lunch and him eating with his fingers in such a comfortable way, I had no doubt that he was somehow letting show some suspicion he had of me, even if it was probably only on the paranoid basis that I was Sri Lankan and had chosen to leave the place.

So, in the face of being in his face, what I did was to go to work and finish the report on the extradition this'n'that, took it into my boss Johnno's office, sat down angelically in front of him, and simply became catatonic.

Catatonia is the easiest mental breakdown to have. I recommend it. You don't have to go screaming around abusing people (although, when it came to Tilly, being catatonic without doing that was no way on the cards) just to prove you're busted a boiler, nor do you have to indulge in any of the things Stanislavsky, especially in the 1890s in Moscow as I read it, might demand for staging broken nerve strings. Frothing at the mouth, weeping, shaking all over, terribly slurred words; that sort of thing of keep-questioning.

That behaviour, anyway, is just below the surface of any public servant Canberra-bound and would get about as much attention as a yak's cough in the Gobi Desert. But with catatonia all I had to do was just go stiff-still in Johnno's office and keep staring glue-eyed at his name plate Brenton D. Johns, that's all.

You can even roll your eyes around for a bit of relief; nystagmus is a possible symptom of catatonia anyway.

The occupational nurse didn't want to move me without medical advice, and Johnno looked like he would have his own onset if someone didn't move this mental case from his office, where it might rub off, to some other office, where it didn't matter if it rubbed off. It looking like, by the everyday look of things, that it already had long ago.

On top of the extradition report I had placed on his desk, I had placed a catatonia-dispensing long-service leave request, all filled in, except the requested date of commencement. This normally takes a couple of months to come through.

Through my twitching eyes, I could see how his eyes alighting on that leave request saved the man from his own paroxysm. An evil thought lit him up. He took advantage of it when the departmental nurse sauntered in picking her teeth:

'No, no, sister. You do not get it, you see. I had just signed him out on long-service leave a few minutes before he went funny all over my carpet. Lucky for the Auditor-General; stiff for him, huh? He's on leave right now. So get his slack quoit out of here, will you?'

They wheeled me through the office on the way to the ambulance to take me home, when I spotted bloody Tilly running around from desk to desk in an absolute fury, squawking and going like a parody of her real self:

'He's going on leave; he's going on leave!'

She looked so green with envy she could have been in line for her own seizure. She'd have to have a few ball bearings in that head to achieve that, and unfortunately she hasn't. I can vouch for that. There is perpetual motion in there.

The first thing on my long-service leave was to invade Neila.

It had been a year, and one marriage for both of us, since that weird beach outing with the rich shitty Sri Lankans so-called 'New Arrivals' and dropping her off with her new husband-to-be and then having to meet her one-legged new 'other' guy in the two-legged board shorts.

Guy? That 'guy' only turned out himself to be the scion of one of the longtime famous families of Australia, the Camefors, who had long ago conquered west of the Great Divide and had, for the family's twentieth-century goal, set out to conquer east of the Great Divide where the real populations were, using the only talents they had left—intrigue and nepotism.

Which left them only politics, of course.

Even the Camefors could see that.

Neila had hitched up to the one-legged scion after marrying and getting rid of her next husband after me. I can only guess she did so because she could see the window of opportunity for the ultimate lost cause in a one-legged man desperate to hang ten, whose father had once been a two-legged ex-Olympian in cycling, and then a high-profile Minister of Sports Achievement. I am guessing that for Neila it wasn't so straightforwardly crude opportunism as that but rather more along the lines that the silver spoon in the fellow's mouth would have just seemed a symbol of his hopelessness, much like the condition of his board shorts. She would have been a push-over for that.

Her new father-in-law, in that year since that weird SLA outing, had become the patronymic Minister of Foreign Affairs and, a month before catatonia overcame me, had been invited to be Australia's next Governor-General. He had a famous enigmatic smile when money, intrigue and nepotism came into things.

Anyway, at the time I was about to invade her space again, Neila's poppa- in-law was still only Governor-General Elect, but the fact of the matter was he was a confirmed widower with a one-legged scion as his only child.

Which meant the doyenne of lost causes which was my Neila was to become the consort of the Governor-General of Australia. This bint from El Paso, USA.

There could be no money, intrigue or nepotism to bring that into being!

She was now living behind plain-clothed minders and a Doberman in a house you could not see from the road because of its surrounding wall or because you didn't see so far, designed by some architect who specialised in taking landscapes way beyond landscapes.

They, mainly the bossy dog, finally let me into the grounds that lawned you towards a 1930s house of English elegance with its resurgences of stain-glass glories in doors and windows. Even its wrought-iron filigree had been impeccably picked out in gentle red for highlighting against the best of Dulux's white exterior glosses.

Neila matched all this. She greeted me with lipstick that echoed the wrought iron and her skin had become so English-pasty that it looked like she had been recently prepared for a coat of Dulux's finest white interior glosses but far harder and weatherproof.

Her face had become finer; in a few years of devolution I could imagine her as an exquisitely carved ivory doll on the mantelpiece beside where my set of ivory-and-ebony elephants might be. The trouble was that she had become great in haunch, as though those haunches had finally been let off the leash to swing no joke. It gave to her quoin region the look of being a helicopter landing pad that was trying to make its own horizontality. If not, Darwin would have been impressed. But for another time, she might have been indexable somewhere within the 502 pages of the *Origin of the Species* which as you know was written over a year or so before its publication as long ago as November 1859. Showing you how impressive Neila's new nurtured haunches were, although maybe not saying much about how selective Nature is wont to be.

At two in the afternoon, even so, she was still in a housecoat. It was an exquisite one in *couleur de rose*, definitely customed and of course sewn by hand, not racked-up on, in order to hug those haunches so lovingly. The lot that falls to some mere pieces of cloth! But it was still my Neila; who else would be so openly proud of wearing a housecoat at that time of day and making it still look as sloppy?

Neila was not happy to see me, even though her new duties of being the Governor-General's consort required her to be happy to see anyone.

I reminded her of that, as she sat me down in a terribly English living room that was for furniture and soggy memories rather than for people who had dirtying feet of clay. Out through the french windows, by the swimming pool, I could see the newish Mr Neila. He sat forlornly by an exercise bike, as a Camefors should, and that is nobly. Did those exercise bikes work on one leg or did they get up lateral spins? Anyway, there he sat in his surfboard shorts.

I noticed there was a surfboard floating in the swimming pool.

'I have to go out.' Her voice was still excitingly throaty from the cigarettes she would surely soon be obliged to give up.

I pointed to the housecoat.

'In that?'

'I am expecting someone important.'

I pointed to the housecoat again. 'In that?'

She giggled. She hadn't changed. She's probably still the same sisyphean Neila, rolling lost causes up heavenly clouds and having them fall through back down to earth again.

'With him,' I was nodding towards Mr Neila by the exercise bike, 'out there?'

She giggled even more.

'His father.'

'There're going to tar and feather you, Neila.'

'They'll have to find some place where the flies haven't been yet.'

'You're doing well, Neila.'

'I won't be if you keep coming around.'

'Hey, first time.'

She looked at me with one of those lost-cause looks again that says I might not be the full dollar but you're one empty pocket.

'Weird. I told you you were going weird. Just don't go getting bad on me, Johnnie. I'm in a different league now.'

'So help me. I'm just trying to find my brother.'

'Your what?'

'Jesus, Neila.'

'Okay, but just don't go getting so weird on me. Look, Johnnie, all those prints, those hard drive stuff through the photo lens, huh, you've got to give them back to me.'

I thought it was best to wait, since I had no idea what she was talking about again.

Or did I?

That's a genuine question. I'm sure I had no idea but then, as soon as I thought that, I wasn't so sure. The sudden doubt had the tinge, the flavour, of my brother's doing again. *Pipping.* Something doing.

In the silence while she fidgeted with the tormenting image of a cigarette, I felt the physical presence of my brother's mind moving back into me, as it had done a few nights before after my lunch with Inspector Charles.

That something-to-do-with was for sure something to do with the Serendip Lankan Association and my brother.

That was easy.

But how was any twin of mine controlling the boss boys who comprised the SLA, maybe even as the 'principals' of the so-called Tamil scams the Inspector had the posse out for and me in its path? And I remember thinking, as if my brother was whispering to me:

'Neila. For sure, in there somewhere'.

It would have to explain why she was so suddenly worried for her new bright and glossy-fold future because of 'those prints, those hard drive stuffs'. Two plus two arithmetic meaning the modern equivalent to the old photographic negatives. I knew what she was referring to. But, as if, I would have been the only one with a logged-in gallery of Neila in comprising positions not fit for a Governor-General's escort. If she was going to mop them all up, she'd need an ocean-going dredge. If she was going to white-wash her past, she'd need a fleet of them working around many clocks.

All I could do was repeat: 'Jesus, Neila.'

The Camefors must have been training her up by a pretty good dredge, though. She appeared only for a fraction of a second as though she would revert to the Neila of old and throw up hissy fit worthy of harridan Neila-of-old, but she didn't. Instead, her voice carried a heavy and quiet threat -- blueblood stuff.

'I would like them back. Haven't you been listening to anything when I've phoned?'

Phone calls? Getting my brother and me so mixed up surely meant I just got shot of her just in time. The sex looseness I could understand, but getting to confuse whose ear she'd been bashing was another thing.

I answered the way I knew my brother would have wanted me to -- or, in fact, wanted me to. It was getting a bit confusing, I have to admit. What was I there for anyway? And just how do you get the predications right when your twin is in your head with what he is thinking? I took a guess:

'They're destroyed, don't sweat it.'

'How do they know that?'

'They?'

'Don't come that. They don't think they are destroyed, I can tell you. You refused to tell them face to face and,' the Camefors needed to push a little harder on the training etiquette; she was shedding class like a decomposing butler, 'they've told me they are going to turn the tables on me. They're hassling me. They think I've got something to lose now, and they're right sure as eagles' shit. It's fucking bargain time now, not word time, Johnnie, you buggerlugs. They've agreed to take my word the bloody things are destroyed but not yours. You listening? You gone off again or what?'

I took a punt at relevance: 'I'll have a word with them at the next SLA meeting.'

'There is no next meeting, fellah!'

Neila was on her feet. The Camefors prepollence would have to be wound back to lesson one. 'They don't want anything the fuck to do with you any more, bud.'

111

'My brother, you mean.'

'Sure, sure, your brother'.

'No need to get sarcastic, Neila.'

'Weird ain't the word for you, you know.'

It wasn't too bad, actually. I was getting loads of her quincy breath and loads of flesh under the housecoat. It's really much more look- see when you're not married to it. I guess it's the way the look-see is given.

At least she had confirmed 'they' were the SLA mob. Well, I thought she had or maybe I've just now been thinking she must have.

'So, you going to cooperate or not?'

'Neila, I'm cooperating. Look, I'm quivering to cooperate with the big shots of the world.'

'Kay,' she calmed down enough to manage what had been an impossible thing to do -- getting a real cigarette out of a real pack from somewhere very real under her housecoat, and: 'Kay. Let's just finish this, Johnnie hon, what say? Return the pictures and I'm not talking about the ones you sneakily took of you'n'me and those other blubbery bods, yuk.'

She said it Camefors-wise, as though the subject was beneath her not just the blubberies, whoever those poor saps must have been.

The training in stated class started to come back. A few puffs and she was back into prepollence.

'See, hon, all they want now are those final-phase photos.'

'The final-phase photos.' Can you nod and not know what you're nodding for? And, again, why was I there at all, did I remember?

'Now, you're humming.' The Camefors had added sarcasm to her repertoire. 'The accepting money; the bribe set-ups in the car parks; the hotel lobbies. They had to go along with it, or the naughty vids get trotted out. D'you think they'd forget those?'

'Neila, Neila.' I hoped it sounded charitably dismissive.

'Don't,' she replied confirming it had, 'you try to sweet talk me anymore.'

'How can I give them to you when they're already destroyed? I should've mailed them to you as ashes in urns by way of evidence?'

Hit 'em with logic. She had to fall silent for a moment.

'Tell them,' I gave a strong guttural tone to for some reason, but confident my brother knew what he wanted me to say and how he wanted it a loaded threat, 'I only want to talk to them. Forget what's on tape.'

'They're shitting scared of even seeing you!'

Enough was enough. Now I could even imitate my brother's voice, he was so near to me in exasperation. I heard the tone myself; a haggard, threatening whisper:

'And you tell me why might that be?'

She actually cowered at it. 'The police whatnots. The travel operation busted wide open in Sydney for starters'.

'What police?' My brother was still somehow speaking through me. I had never realised that I could imitate him, perhaps whenever I wanted to. It was a far more of an uncomfortable thought. Those brutal implications in every word. Tiring. Of the *pip*. Sometimes you get to be.

'Not local, hon.'

Now she was trying to appease me and I felt the power... and I have to say, not for the first time... that this twin brother of mine had over other people, 'Some Inspector Gobbledygook ...'

'Charles? Ekanayake? Sri Lanka?'

'You say so. Calling on them. Looking down at some great height, they say. Just routine, he says. They're upstanding citizens, 'kay? They get scared. Right now, you can bet your bottom dollar they are all in need of a word of assurance from you. And so am I. Give me a break, will you? Let me off the hook. I got *duties* now.'

'They're destroyed, Neila.'

It was Tasker, not me, still, as I heard myself. I could see him in my mind's eye literally walking out on her, leaving me behind to pick up the pieces, whatever whole those pieces came from.

She hadn't told me where I could find my brother in reality, but now I knew he must have been somewhere near. For sure, from the urgency with which Neila was talking to me, he was in Canberra some place and he'd have to know about Inspector Bloody-fucking-hell Ekanayake and his request from me for extradition advice by this time, so it was a safe bet he'd be coming to me to learn more about how I was getting involved in all this.

Still, one track had been covered.

I was confident that Neila wasn't going to volunteer any connection. To prevent her from mouthing everything she knew, they'd have to put her on some sort of man starvation diet and, while there were gaolers with any understandably human weakness for her silky corruptions, that just wouldn't be possible.

And I now knew where to keep covering tracks next.

Neila was standing in the doorway, watching me leave. With that afternoon sun and that housecoat not doing much to impede it, the plain-clothes security guys weren't even taking any notice of me. Neither was the Doberman.

And this was supposed to be one of the Governor-General's listed residences. Which goes to show you how Neila was still a bit of a looker even with those new haunches.

She had seen me off with the parting shot with her re-come prepollence out of the Camefors:

'You ever get a knighthood or whatever, do come round again.'

If I was Cary Grant and it was the 1933 film 'She Done Him Wrong' and she was Mae West, you wouldn't have known the difference.

I will always miss her.

After that Neila time, the first of the SLA bigwigs I had to see, I figured, was the brains who was the most likely to have been behind or at least advising the travel-agency scam. Dr Yogendra Nath.

Around town his nickname was Yogi, not because he looked like a bear, but because he looked like the cartoon of a bear.

By now he would be a very nervous cartoon of a bear.

That made him the immediate danger, at least, apparently, to my brother.

I somehow had the impression from Inspector Charles that the policing agencies were sweating on catching the operations in flagrante delicto, which presumably meant they were letting them keep operating while they built up the case against the wider network. After the travel-scam fiasco in Sydney, that meant the chummy little Serendip Lankan Association had a lot of nervous 'principals' walking around its loose circle in loose circles -- and just possibly looking for cover, like rousing on Neila to have destroy some incriminating photographs everyone seemed to know about except me.

Or looking for some law-enforcement shoulder to cry on. Which is why, I was thinking my brother saw that Dr Yogendra Nath as that most immediate threat to him being dragged in to it all. Yeah, and so me.

If for nothing else that gave all the excuse I needed to justify taking off on long-service leave so suddenly.

Somehow my brother knew our Yogi Nath was up to his neck in a far more immediate bucket of poop. Underneath him it was all blown away with the suddenness of a Bangladeshi major flood. He had no time, presumably as the others had, by now, to get the records, the books, the paperworks related to the travel scam disposed of. All these would have been swooped up by the Inspector's merry little band and gleefully seized.

Not that I felt there would be much of a paper trail leading to the man. You don't leave your chop of top-class counterfeit traveller's cheques and the like for public shows of appreciation. Even so, Dr Yogendra Nath would still be feeling decidedly naked. And naked men leave a trail of really tell-tale footprints. And naked men feeling very naked indeed, a big tell-tale trail of droppings.

You would know that I wasn't feeling too unnaked myself, and it wasn't the new crew cut and beard shave I had escaped out of Johnno's office to get as the first thing on the agenda, either. (Lennie the Barber had muttered at the beginning, A bit long in the tooth to be wanting this done, aintcha?' and, afterwards, scrutinising the shape of my jaw line and the contours of my scalp, 'Them's natural misshapennesses, not my blame, okey?')

The Inspector had already interviewed some of the lads of the SLA, Neila had said. That means, in in-parlance, he was on to them just as there was something about how he looked at me which told me he was onto me for some reason too. That might be all well and good for some, but, in order to do so, he must have done so without telling me or Johnno. Yet, he was supposed to be desperate to know about any extradition hiccoughs he might get with those three Tamils he had bagged and the one with the alias of 'Tusker' I just knew he wanted most. You work in the Australian public service you get a feel for people wanting to see you and when you should hide out.

This I knew too: that Inspector had the memory of one of my father's elephants. He would not have idiotically simply forgotten about my report regarding extradition. And if it wasn't important, why did he go to so much trouble to seek me out personally in the first place?

I knew in my bones he was a bit suspicious of me when he met me, but I presumed that was only because he had come

116

to know about my Sri Lankan lost horizons. On the other hand, should I be letting my paranoia have more delicious rein and suspect he suspected my tenuous connection to all this before he came to see me... meaning that he knew or guessed the alias called 'Tusker' was my brother, as I had no doubt? Hadn't he deliberately singled me out from among all the other lawyers he could have theoretically seen? Unless, since he was a cop, I was the slowest to drop out of sight.

Well, this much was sure: the whacker's visit turned me from a bearded, distinguished-hairy lawyer, rightly and occupationally smug with my lot, to a razor-stropped potential felon by alias-association.

You talked about flies, Neila.

There were no flies on me, either, when it comes to a lot that was sorry.

Mind you, in turning towards Yogi Nath, I had no intention trying to break up this network thing my brother had going, maybe even controlling. I was actually trying to keep it from falling apart just because I'd been pulled into it all.

I figured that doing my own confronting of Yogi was my best way of covering my brother's, and hence my own, tracks.

I realised this very soon after her Camefors gates were left open because the plain-clothes minders of Neila were being unhinged by her standing in the doorway in her housecoat-but-nothing-else like she was. I had actually been incredibly stupid in telling her the photographs had been destroyed. I supposed I had wanted her to feel better. Dumb of me. Really very, very dopey.

I mean, I didn't have to know what the hell those pictures showed to know my best bet was to have them in theoretical existence forever. If they were destroyed, pieces of this so-called Tusker's organisation would start flying sparks of clues all over the place, easy traps for a hunter like this Inspector Ekanayake obviously was.

Somehow, I had to get to that silly bloody brother of mine and tell him not to dismantle anything. Hold tight. Whatever criminal hold he had on these SLA characters or Neila had on him, he had to tighten, not loosen, it for the time being.

Which was just wonderful logic, wasn't it? Because then I would be, in principio, not just a withholder of material evidence for which I might have been able to plead a dumber-than-I-look. Or even than bloody Tilly says I look.

I might just *pip* my brother for a change.

Yeah, into the jug.

The names, the names. I was thinking like the dumber-than-I- look-than-I-was. I should have wheedled out of Neila the names of the guys photographed, as I naively presumed, in those various (knowing Neila it would have been many various) incriminating positions with her. I couldn't now go back to her Governor-General's milieu and say I want to talk sense now that you aren't wearing that see-through nightie thing of a housecoat.

No, it had to be Yogi Nath the Nervous. He just had to be one of the administering angels of the Sydney travel-agency rumpus. If I was right, he might appreciate a little training in falling catatonic before the Inspector got fully at him. If I was wrong, I could just go catatonic on him and pretend I didn't know what I was doing there. I had, after all, a public-service medical certificate coming on top of my leave entitlements.

By the time I got to the local office of the Australian Prudential Regulation Authority , or APRA-hours as it is snidely known as. It was around four-thirty, a quarter of an hour before most of the government flexiworkers were due to knock off -- which meant it was already rush to get to the exits and be ready for the real rush hour home.

It took a bit of time. Canberra traffic goes by the year and the model of the other guy's car. The later and/or bigger means you are higher up the winding path of service to the public, which means you have right of way at all time, except for another later model and bigger vehicle. It is the parking order of the pecking order, in which I was way down the list.

Because of the deserted-desk hour, I was able to talk right in to the Authority's offices by mumbling something about the Attorney- General's legal division to a few stranded security ghosts who weren't listening anyway. I found Yogi in as big an office as I had expected by the narrowness of the corridors and the apple-crate size of the elevator. His piece of governmental action obviously didn't rate much in the dynamics of the country, and certainly nowhere near proportionate to his standing in the local Lankan ex-pat circles, obviously.

By then it was after five, and so almost midnight by Canberra's work clock. The offices had the occupancy of six o'clock on a Sunday morning. Nath had the reading light on his desk on, as though to convince himself he was really putting in the overtime, rather than being too conscientious to leave his daily womb prematurely. This time it looked more than that. He was really very, very nervous.

You could tell that because he sat beneath at his desk under a lamp like a taxidermied owl, frozen under his frosty mop, before the impressively few papers on the wide inlay of leather of his desk top. The effect of the owl was from his steel-rimmed glasses, the heaviness of his jaw, and the maroon waistcoat he still had buttoned up despite the way it looked to be crushing his chest.

Here was Yogi Bear being owl at the top of its tree. I hadn't met him before, but had heard of him. The first word on him was that he would gladly tackle the seemingly impossible. The second word was he was pushing for

119

Australia to be the next world's next cultural holiday with all sorts of travel rebates underpinned by luscious government guarantees.

If only for that, it would make the first word on him just about right.

Among the original paintings and artworks upon his wall, the only photograph was of a Japanese couple, standing in the middle of the Outback somewhere and smiling at the limitless horizon.

Bloody Tilly would have said that maybe they were waiting there because they had heard what time the Australian culture was passing through and had been warned beforehand they'd better be prepared to be quick.

As for Nath out of the picture he looked like wishing he was in, he finally managed to get an owl's or bear's eye beaded upon me. He literally leapt to his feet and cried out one of those 'you!'s:

'You!'

'Me.'

'You said no contact', he threw at him as some sort of terrible accusation that should wilt me. He must have realised he had shouted it because, even before I could do any required wilting, he had lowered his voice to that of a very unhappy whisper:

'You shouldn't have come here.'

'Take it easy, you fool.'

That wasn't my voice, but I had said it.

It was more like how my brother would have sounded. No, more than that... it *was* my brother's voice. Again and as suddenly, I could feel him seeing me in his mind's eye, as I so often saw him.

As Tasker had expressed the command, so Nath looked to instantly obey. He flopped back into his chair fully and put his face in his hands. Under the desk lamp there he looked like looked he was just miserably realising he had just confessed under interrogation.

For my part, I sat down and waited, but he kept refusing to look up.

'I'm not here officially,' but I heard myself, not my brother, sound this this time; a much more reasonable tone. 'Nathie old son, but I know your problem. All I want to do is find my brother.'

'You mean there's two of you?' He was surely trying to wax cynical and I must have been showing I didn't appreciate it, because he quickly followed it up with: 'Don't worry. I'll never tell.'

Again, my voice was brother-hard; I could hear it. It was as if he was puppeteering me again, dammit. The *pipping*. The never stopping of it; the never getting away from it.

'Tell who? Inspector Ekanayake?'

He was nodding even before I had finished the sentence, and:

'He's been to see me. That's why you're here, aren't you?, when there was supposed to be no contact.' He was rising to a panic again, and fast: '*I told him shit all!*'

This was getting me about as far as I had got with Neila. I tried putting us both in the same pot.

'Mr Nath, mate, I'm dealing with that policeman.'

'No violence!'

Now he was really about to climb up the wall. That new tack went down like a lead balloon with me. Impatiently -- with me? -- my brother's tone jumped into my voice again: 'Nath, will you shut the fuck up? That Inspector knows nix. So he's closed down the travel operation. So what? You told me you'd already done that anyway.'

'Those two cowboys, Premachandra and Ponnambalam, I told to get out a month ago, but, no, they were having too good a time in the clubs of Kings Cross, weren't they? The money rolling in.'

'It's not worth their families back in Chennai to talk, Nath.'

Now, this tone I didn't like.

121

This was me made to sound deadly serious.

Yet Yogi removed off his glasses. It was a sign of some relief. The poor sap sighed such a sigh. He obviously needed to feel muscle behind him. A bully.

I couldn't help glancing up at the Japanese still waiting hopefully for a glimpse of that Australian culture -- better they wait for the next tsunami -- while we both listened to my brother: 'There's a worldwide structure behind you and it doesn't break down when a little piece of it gets lobbed off. It closes around. It protects its own. Inspector Ekanayake has proceeded as far as he can go, get that into your head.'

Nath was nodding now. Still miserable. But at least nodding.

'Now,' and I now knew it was Tusker putting the hard grit in my voice because I personally didn't believe a word of the nonsense I just heard myself spout, 'where's Tusker?'

Nath looked at me in brotherly join. I could have sworn he almost winked: 'You think if I say it just once, it's going to start spilling out all over under some spotlight they put on me? You think I'll start squawking? Do me a favour.'

I stood up. I seemed heavier than when I arrived, and wondered whether he had the same effect on wayward travel agents he carpeted.

'Ekanayake will go and see the others,' I grunted.

Again, the guy seemed to think he was granting me medals by telling me nothing: 'I'll tell them you said so at the meeting on Thursday. Don't show up. Do I have your word?'

Unwittingly, I lost my own temper.

'What meeting?'

Why was I losing my temper over that?

He was just shaking his head. Now he was Uncle Remus Nath: 'We'll be driving out to Queanbeyan as usual. Nehru, Selverajah, Duraiswamy and Professor Josephs.'

I guessed: 'All of that SLA of yours?'

He was almost chirpy at the thought of being able to get into an agreement.

'The meeting's just driving?'

'Like Tusker always says: what better cover than a moving car?'

'Who's Tusker?', I said amazed at how be-very-careful it sounded.

But Yogi immediately dropped his chin to his chest as though nothing would make him open his mouth on that subject, never. I had to try again, shot out with:

'A meeting, driving... in that white Mercedes of yours?'

He gave a small nod to that after considering whether it was safe to give that out having got so far. But, for my own self, I was wondering how come I knew what car he drove anyway; he could have been a Volkswagen junkie for all I knew?

Anyway, it was all we were going to say to each other, quite obviously. I had cheered him up, and that added fortitude, after all, was why I had come. It all had to hold together. Now Yogi was even switching off the desk lamp with a decisive gusto as much as to say bugger this overtime for a lark.

He had waved me away by then. The way he then swivelled his back on me, preferring the cheap framed print of a Kandy perahera kitted-out elephant on the bland off-green wall to my mug, I knew Dr Yogendra Nath had recovered his composure senses enough to have returned to naturally controlling the exchange. I was going to get nothing more.

As I was leaving, I couldn't help registering the fact that our Yogi spoke with no accent at all. Not even an Australian nasality, let alone with a rubbery Subcontinent tongue trilling the sounds at the lips. No wonder Sri Lankans make wonderful migrants. They assimilate so well, right down to the cavities. You could say they keep their tongues further back, not poke them further out.

The world should give them entry priority to anywhere.

From there I was on my way to the Canberra Inn to see if I could flirt with reappearing to the Inspector after disappearing on him. It was precisely against the reason why I went all catatonic all over my boss and bloody Tilly, yet for some reason I felt thrilled to be, yes, flirting with the risk.

My second wife and I used to stay at the Canberra Inn often, in order to avoid having to be at my house together.

New item: second wife.

Neila introduced my second wife. It pains me to remember that.

After a year of marital hell and six months of blissful separation, you'd think I would have been lost to Neila as a lost cause.

Not so fast. With Neila, once a lost cause, always a lost cause. She couldn't help herself. I think it was how she could keep up a pretence of self-esteem in the face of overwhelming odds of all the lost cause 'out there'.

Neila really was the pits. As in cess. For example, she liked, she said, to breathe into my face in bed over unscrubbed teeth. I mean her unscrubbed teeth. But that was Neila: all *tastes* that first gave you the creeps but you kept coming back for. They should have named her durian.

Anyway, it was on a Friday afternoon, when ex-wifey Neila sashayed into my office, turning heads by turning her own and winking at whole roomfuls of lost causes among my colleagues... more lost-cause I suppose that anything she could ever dream of because they all knew they were lost causes, working there. And when Neila's eyes light up, watch out, World!

She was flapping air tickets in each hand in some imitation of a bird flying. A freebie, an all-inclusive weekend trip to Melbourne, bub, she screeled; I could pay her later. For now, just get it in a sling and swing.

At three-fifteen on a Friday, there was no problem with slinging and swinging. At that time, she was lucky to find anyone, let alone me or Tilly, who must have forgotten time on account of something like mulling over the poisons she concocted over some weekend barbecue she couldn't be kept away from. No gate or dog squad strong enough.

Bloody Tilly was as perspicacious as ever and thought Neila had returned to her former cleaning duties, the true status of any wife of mine, she explained later. Even before Neila had gotten over the treasury of lost causes she found herself in and could get out about the air tickets she was flapping, bloody Tilly was loudly complaining about the unwiped state of the indoor plants (even though they'd died long ago, even though they were plastic imitations) and how it wasn't her place to have to do a scrubber's job. Neila told her why not; she wiped her arse, didn't she?

Neila and Tilly. A charming combination.

And so Melbourne it was to be. It never goes amiss to occasionally look up what they've done lately to drive an Australian city underground, so why not, I said.

I sorely wish I hadn't.

At the airport, Neila seemed to know every politician from the floating around the place wishing they didn't have to float around something common as voters, even down to the Leader of the Opposition, whom she chatted with over the chewing-gum section of the kiosk. And I had imagined that during out hitched time she'd been a stay-at-home wife. Why should I have been surprised? This was Canberra and she was the queen of lost causes.

It was much the same thing on the flight. She sat on political laps that not even babies in the hustings have watered. She was as happy as I had ever seen her -- and, with her raucous pre-Governor-General-escort southern yankee accent of the time, that meant a little on the hem side of hysterics.

125

There would not have been a moment on that flight that the cabin crew didn't have a finger on the emergency button for internal turbulence.

Did Neila care? Did even the pilot Captain after she ended up sitting on *his* lap too?

All this suited me. The weekend had started out promising, in that since I was able to ignore her all the way there, maybe I could ignore here while in Melbourne and even ignore her all the way back, without it falling to me to wonder why I'd been called to even be there. It almost turned out that way too.

I hit the bar at the Melbourne Holiday Inn immediately, since she was paying and hadn't even got me in a tooth brush or toothpaste so being in a hotel room without scrubbing implements wasn't suitable for a government lawyer when there was a bar around to compensate nicely. And there, some guy with a thick and incomprehensible accent was talking drunkenly, I think, to me, I think, about the country being ruined by allowing in, I think, millions of people who couldn't tell their l's from their 'r's -- neither of which he was in any state to be phonetically demonstrate -- when Neila came back down sleeked out in a surprisingly prim outfit in soft pink.

I was literally dumbfounded. Every button was safely through a button-hole, and the correct button-hole at that. She wore flat shoes. Even her mouth was mutely lipsticked to false thin'n'prim proper.

I should have suspected something right then.

She gave this other fellow with the drunken obsession over the word 'roll', I think, a woefully disapproving look, before informing me in a most bloody-Tilly-type tone of dirt-bag-you-are: 'She is waiting, you know.'

I didn't care in the slightest who might be waiting; there was the matter of getting me tooth brush and paste, but she took this as being precisely why she'd ditched me, going:

'Think, dumbo. Even on our honeymoon, you wouldn't stop talking about her.'

'We didn't have a honeymoon, Neila.'

'And you're telling me that didn't make it worse?'

Somehow that exchange had taken all the time needed to get me out into some hire car and get me halfway across Melbourne city. We had pulled up at a house, not to call it a substantial house, I knew very well indeed.

In the fifteen years or more since I had been there, the outside had changed with the same affluence as I would find upgraded inside -- and, in my book, that's rich-rich. So etched in my mind had this house been since my youth -- and undoubtedly for my brother too -- I immediately noticed that instead of the once waist-high cyclone-wire fence, now there was an iron-grill fence of height and substance, with a really nasty looking bit of security in the form of arrow tips at the top so turned out that only a eunuch protected by a cast-iron chastity belt would even think of trying to climb over. The wrought-iron gates were positively medieval castle. The old place was still set back from there, but now among a lot of tall timber and shrouded anyway by spotlights which made the garden itself mere plant-like shapes patterned to a wall of blinding light.

The Ramaswarmys had obviously done very well for themselves since the days they welcomed my brother from a bloody and bruising Adelaide and had entered into some pact or other to support him from then on.

And me. I have to admit that. Through uni and things.

What more can I say than we were actually 'shown' in.

Who showed us in was some dude-type of guy who spoke and acted like a concierge but who could have been into the pastime of lifting cars. Physically he was like Jeeves on steroids. With his teeth alone you'd think he could pull container trucks.

The other curious thing was that the Ramaswarmy tribe met me at the front door. Unlike my brother, I wouldn't have exactly been their prodigal son since, as much as I guess I owed them, I had always kept out of their way, and by their

127

disappearing Christmas and birthday cards, they knew it and agreed to it. I had gladly left it to be Tasker as our occasional contact, that's all.

The old man, Appa Ramaswarmy, had hardly changed at all, but then I hardly ever look at people in that way to notice. Still, it did surprise me; he was always so badly bodily bloated that I always imagined something had to change or Nature stood still, having given up. His face still had that incongruously angular look for such fob-watch rotundity; his cheekbones remained high, delicate and shaped down towards a long and thin nose that could have belonged to an Indian bharatnatyam dancer... at once flashing for your attention, at once comic.

He should never have lived past Sydney Greenstreet, the actor, who to my mind reached his heyday in 'The Maltese Falcon'. That was in 1941 with Humphrey Bogart playing exquisitively, to my mind, the part of Sam Spade from the 1929 <u>detective novel</u> by <u>Dashiell Hammett</u>, originally serialized in the magazine *Black Mask* beginning with the September 1929 issue. If you must know.

Anyway, that Appa Ramaswarmy's son, whose name I remembered as the weird one of Joycie, was still Peter Lorre to his father (Peter Lorre playing the role of Cairo opposite to Sydney Greenstreet). He -- Joycie Ramaswarmy -- had the same cheekbones, the same acumen or menace, whatever, of his father.

But somehow his scarecrow point-counterpoint made him just seem dangerous rather than interesting, as though being a smaller version made him a sharp splinter to the barrel of his father.

Mrs Ramaswarmy still wore the traditional saree, and this made me nervous because it was a formal saree by the way it fell probably exactly two feet down her back after passing over her left shoulder.

Surely someone had died, perhaps even my brother Tasker. I felt a slither of alarm dig at me, until Neila took me maternally by the arm and would not be surreptitiously shaken off. On second thoughts, I noticed Rehana, their daughter and my brother's puppy love, wasn't there, so perhaps it was she who had rung heaven's bell not my twin. Or the other son, Kara somethingorother; he certainly wasn't there.

I'd better sober up fast.

I remember that despite the solemnity of the greeting on the threshold of the front door and all that hand-holding, Neila wasn't helping the weird atmosphere. She was unnerving me by being the first to push inside the house and then by sitting there with her knees together primly, for chrissakes, and the hem of her dress pulled down to cover them. Her hands were clasped in her lap without secretly doing something lewd by way of signal to someone, and she had that artificially primmed-up mouth drawn even more nunnishly tighter.

Tea and *petit fours* were wheeled in on a silver serving trolley by Mr Hulk of the gate himself.

Tea and *petits fours* from the Ramaswarmys I used to know, for crying out aloud.

Finally, Neila leaned over to me and purred in a leering sort of way I definitely did not like -- but then she knew that which is why she did it: 'Something wonderful is going to happen to Rehana.'

Just to do something, I sort of leapt to my feet with pretend joy, pumped Appa Ramaswarmy's huge pudgy hand, and hugely ringed too, then gave a son's sort of peck on a surprised Mrs Ramaswarmy's forehead, where resided her brown polka dot of Hindu devotion still as to nothing really ever changes despite all the changes. I turned to shake the solemn son's hand. He lifted his—I thought to take mine—and plucked his mother's Hindu blob from off my lower lip.

Technology. One time, they used to paint them on. Now, they stick them on with spit.

The Ramaswarmys and Neila were crowding around her trying to get it back on, as though I had disrobed her and was a combined disgraced public which shouldn't be watching,

129

when she pushed their hands away, stood in rapture and announced that here she was.

The pottu blob thing somehow ended up just about over her right eyebrow instead of in the centre of her forehead. But this was small beer compared to Rehana now standing in the doorway. She too was a-saree'd like her mother, but that's where the comparison ended.

Gold embroidery on a rich puce silk. It bound her body in that half-naked, hip-elegant glyptic form that only a saree can do. Her eyes were widely, juicily expectant with purple eye shadow; her lips bright and full over sparkling lips. All this I still remember clearly. The blouse top cut low over her breasts, heavy to the transparency of the silk and to the welterweight of high-carat chains and clumps around her swan-same neck. All over her hair, to swell down around her ears, were gold-linked bangs, not made of glass beads, but real sapphires, moonstones, emeralds, garnets. Against the purple sway of her skin, the rows of golden bangles, the hand chains reining rings to wrists sparkled with rubies and tourmalines, as though they lay on Damask velvet.

And her feet, as clear to the exotic as the 1600s Dutch painter Johannes Vermeer would have ever crystal-light rendered it, were flowered in golden-strand slippers, golden anklets with tiny gold bells that were almost perfumery to the air when she moved. The toenails painted red, one, gold, the other, and so on.

She was gorgeous.

National Geographic High Definition TV should have been on the camera lens trail right here instead of somewhere else extreme.

This was no teenager any longer. This was ermine. This was sable. She was the jewel that the Ramaswarmys had rightly built a crown around.

I was almost enying her future bridegroom, which had to be my brother, otherwise Neila wouldn't have dragged me all the way down here. The sudden surliness of being *pipped* again was soon countered by realising the freebie was on him. When it came to another marriage, I'd take the money any day.

I tried to launch myself forward on behalf of the bridegroom's family, plus get in a bit of closer ogling, when I was literally tackled by Neila and dragged back to my seat. She had the gall to keep her hand on my chest to anchor me there while she leant forward to Appa Ramaswarmy and I heard the business in her voice:

'We were last talking about the dowry, hon.'

'We are in Australia where we don't have dowries, fair crack of the old whip.' And Appa Ramaswarmy rolled his thickish eyes getting out his thickish Aussie tongue.

'We are not doing this the Aussie way, hon. This is arranged.'

He shrugged as though he had got used to the pain in any case and had it already to trot out:

'Her jewellery and pots and pans.'

'He doesn't wear jewellery and he doesn't wash up.'

'Who?', I butted in uselessly for the bridegroom's family. I mean, after all.

'We throw in the motorbike she goes shopping on.' Appa Ramaswarmy spread his hugely fat arms in crucified suffering.

'He doesn't do shopping either, believe me.'

'Don't put the acid on, Miss.' Appa R. had certainly been working at the vernacular of his second citizenship. 'No coming the bullsh. Her life insurance. My last flamin' offer. Burns me up to say it. Two years' Medicare, top cover, fully paid up in advance. My second last offer, stone the crows.'

'He's not planning on causing her damage, hon.'

'Who?' Me. Again. I was the bridegrooms nearest relative after all.

'Okay, okay,' Appa answered, as though Neila had laid a Buster Crabbe hold on him, 'you wouldn't flamin' read about it, but I am chucking in one hundred thou. Am I having a hernia or going blind as a mullet, or what?'

Neila considered this as though she was reluctant to release out of the Buster Crabbe leg-breaker, before she finally nodded, then put low cunning into her voice: 'The broker's fee, hon, as agreed, huh?'

'Agreed, although it's killin' me. But it comes,' and the father of the bride swept his mightily wobbling arm towards me, 'out of him, don't argue the toss like a whingeing Pom, orright?'

'Who's "him"?' But they still ignored me.

'A deal, hon', Neila exclaimed, clapping her hands as though we were in a bazaar and she was calling for Turkish delights all round.

She wheeled around, clasped me under the armpits frontally, clapped me on the back, and then pushed me towards those stunning Rehana eyes, splendorous with all of India's glory, and went going:

'Congratulations, Johnnie Tasker!'

'*Who*?'

'You, you dumbo. You heard the man. You owe me ten grand for the marriage-broking fee. And don't forget my expenses this weekend.'

'I'm still married to you, Neila!'

Goes to show how desperate I was.

As if that mattered to the sudden full weight of Mrs Ramaswarmy in delighted banshee right in my lughole, and Joycie Ramaswarmy assisting me to stand on my own feet by shaking my hand and saying he'd kill me if I make his sister unhappy, and I saw he had a knife clipped in his inside jacket pocket, and then felt the defeat of gravity when Appa Ramaswarmy took up the swoop and had me in a room-swirling bear hug saying he'd waited fifteen years for this and I should have kept my word instead of marrying that there American slut who I could point out and he'd whistle, and you don't have to be stiff to be dead.

And all the while I was trying to break away to get a groin kick into the quoit of Neila and only heard her cudding an answer to the small married-already problem I had raised:

'Well, very few of us are unsoiled goods, Johnnie.'

Neila should never have lived past the moment of birth. With her, it would have just happened along anyway.

Before I got back to the Melbourne Holiday Inn, I did manage to get a good belt of good whisky with the *petits fours* under the look of sheer hatred from Mr Hulk of the gate who had to serve me as, obviously, the Ramaswarmys' butler inside when he wasn't outside minding the gates.

I also got more than I probably wanted to know about my once gravy train, now in-laws-to-be, the Ramaswarmys.

For one thing, I got to know more about them because I suddenly decided I should start to listen. For another thing -- and if I can be forgiven for rolling a few items in together as the 'another thing': the floodlights, the knife-packing, the twenty-first century's equivalent of kick-sanded Mister Atlas of Bondi of the 1960s ads serving *petit fours* off the silver service; the Ramaswarmy residence becoming a consular residence for here was where the registered address of the TGTE, or Transnational Government of Tamil Eelam, by far the major Tamil international 'community' said to be mighty close to being on the outlawed list of many countries but registered quite legally in Australia as a political organisation. And there, from out of the mouth of my upcoming brother-in-law Joycie, was the mouthpiece of that organisation... and the silly fellow with the silly name was proudly pointing to his father.

One of the capos, I guessed (because I wasn't my brother who'd *know*), of them Tamil'd Aussie all which, given Neila's presence again, had to have its nails into the Serendip Lankan Association as well.

I asked Joycie, because Appa Ramaswarmy seemed to want him to be forefront of any answer, and I asked dumbly I know, but maybe it was my way of batting a cliché back across the net:

'How long has this been going on?'

'My father told you years ago we could use a lawyer in the family like a country house is needing an outside dunny.'

Joycie obviously wasn't adept at the Aussie slings as his Dad. Though a real tryer.

Meanwhile I noticed how Appa was looking at his fob watch as his son answered and then repeated the same answer word-for-word even though I hadn't said anything. The business of the old man's only daughter seemed now to be forgotten; he was looking at the time like it was going to tell him how the New York stock market had ended the day if he could concentrate on communicating with it hard enough.

'I can't remember you ever telling me that. You must have told Tusker,' I ventured using my brother's supposed alias for some reason they would understand since I didn't. Hell, I wasn't even convinced that the old man Ramaswarmy could even tell the difference between me and my brother. If he ever had.

He reached across and gave my cheek the bloodiest of tweaks, and Joycie the spokesman the widest of winks: 'You've done good, Johnnie, but do not being trying to confuse your own family as well as the outsiders. What's past is the bowyang era.'

He had me there. What's the bowyang era without looking it up?

I wasn't so uncaring about Neila, though. At the bar, back at the Holiday Inn, her exposed leg resting in stake-out across the lap of the now barely conscious guy who had been complaining to me about the lack of l's for 'r's coming into

134

the country, we had some sort of conversation that went like mud would on mud, going:

'Neila, what the hell are you doing?'

'I'm getting married, hon.'

'You've got your leg over some guy at a bar, Neila.'

'Yeah, well, I won't ask him his name so nobody can accuse me of getting too intimate. How's that?'

'To surfboard shorts with the one leg, you're getting married to?'

'Don't call him that.'

'What do you call him?'

'Hopalong.'

'Jesus, Neila, you're hopeless.'

'I just wanted to see you settled down before I get shot of you, Johnnie. Anyway, all you guys from that Indian joint...'

'Sri Lanka, Neila, and I'm not from it.'

'... Yeah, and eat this. You all arrange your marriages, like them gals're just hog hides. You oughta be ashamed of yourself.'

'You arranged this trip, Neila.'

'That's the way, slip out of all responsibility. And you owe me ten thousand round dollars. You heard the fat man.'

'That's all John Wesley Hyatt got from Phelan & Collander for saving the elephants of the world, you know.'

'Judas only got thirty pieces of silver and look where it got him, starting out so cheapskate.'

'Australia Then', back to the earlier item I put down.

When I finally got to the Canberra Inn after seeing Yogi Owl Nath, the Inspector was moving towards the pool.

I didn't call him. I watched him.

He was wearing a terry-towelling robe from his room, the type they put there in the bland surety that all humans either fit into the one for short men or the one for tall women.

He had got collared with the short option. It did not come down to his knees, even. Despite his appearance of being gangly, his legs were actually bolt-right with hard muscle, so that he looked like an ageing drag queen from the waist down. The trouble was those bandy legs of his would have definitely let him down on stage.

I took a lounger at the far end of the pool so I wouldn't interrupt his swim. I don't know why. I always equate everything to do with Sri Lanka with elephants, and he somehow looked like he wanted to mud bath alone.

Elephants do not purr. Nobody said they did. But they can, and sometimes do, blow lazy strings of bubbles into the water, and these I used to fancy trailed away from them like happy thoughts, especially when they were being scrubbed slowly behind the ears.

I watched him emerge from the dressing room. The hotel must have lent him the bathing togs. From somewhere archival they had dredged up one of those woollen types that I hadn't seen since I was a kid, with a flap at the front that was supposed to be the skein of modesty, but which always rode up above the genitals to outline in every detail what they were supposed to be covering up. Woolly bulls indeed. And he rated too on that scale; the big hands and big feet type. He might as well have gone in there and changed into a royal blue see-through.

Nor did it take any time for him to spring into action. As he stepped up to the pool side, a blonde little girl, maybe three years old and joyously quite nude and tanned down to the dimples in her tiny bum, came hurtling past his right to throw herself into the pool. The deep end of the pool.

The snag there before his eyes was she obviously had no idea how to swim. She sank like the proverbial stone, managed to come spluttering up to the surface frantically throwing her arms and legs about, then sank again.

The Inspector was stopped by surprise only for a fraction of the moment at seeing a tiny tot Aussie gone lemming before he flung himself in after her. It was incredibly awkward and must have been an incredibly painful bellyflop and probably was more dangerous to the child than the fact that she couldn't swim for nuts.

I was not watching the greatest swimmer on the globe. Nor the smoothest rescue of all time by water police.

For some slipshod of flotation, he seemed not to be able to grab her, and she seemed, with her down two-three, up two-three, to be in danger of eluding him before she or he or both drowned.

I realised a lot of my problems would be solved if she did take him with her.

I started rooting for the kid.

Finally, but, he managed to heave her up the ladder, and broke out in a grin that shone magnificently, until the kid kicked him off, gurgled happily and took another flying leap backwards back into the deep end again.

She still looked like she was drowning, but she was having a whale of a time perfecting her perfectly safe sink two-three, stroke two-three, sink two-three.

The Inspector stood there aghast, took a look at his bellyflop welts, and gave up on her before someone called for the police.

It was only then that I got up and went to greet him. He quickly retreated behind his welts and dignity, and his only words on what had happened were: 'Bloody fucking hell, there should be being a law against drowning them at that age. In my country, it's at birth or not at all.'

He sat down with a sheepish grin while I took the time to realise he could, and had, cracked a joke, sort of.

Maybe this wouldn't turn out as badly as I feared. I parked on the plastic opposite him.

Why didn't he, I inquired, as though we were on the same side of the fence, let me know he was coming back into town?

'That muscly woman in your office is saying you are coming, you are going, who knows where?'

He shrugged.

Bloody Tilly. If she kept dogs, her dogs would walk her on a leash.

I looked at the kid swimming or drowning and tried to see Tilly in there with lead flippers on, and decided to try a little conversational tone to my voice: 'I hear you're now interested in something local and wider and Tamil called the Serendip Lankan Association?'

He nodded shortly, without giving anything away.

'Hey, Inspector, we're on the same side, remember?'

He gazed at me like a bloodhound might, upwards and lugubriously, and the impression was fairly helped by his eyes being bloodshot from the rescue attempt.

'So why all the secrecy?', I asked the mist he must have been looking at me through.

'No secrecy, Mr Tasker.'

'Those two travel agency characters you've got locked away blabbed?'

'Blabbed?'

'Talked.'

He took a long time to answer this one: 'A little, perhaps. We are being told Canberra might be 'Tusker' country. You remember the name 'Tusker', Mr Tasker?'

'Sure. The charge sheet. So what?'

'A word here and a word there, *nae,* bloody fucking hell sorry?'

'Hey, it's a free country, Inspector.'

'*Oh.*' Yes.

Time to get aggressive as a government lawyer made to get off his bum and take time out from his long-service leave with catatonia should get angry. Beneath that, I needed no reminder to myself that the reason I was there was because I hadn't gotten far with Yogi Nath and needed answers from someone if I was to protect my brother.

'Inspector, if there's going to be any extradition situation here, I have to know what form your ... uncredentialed?, if that's an okay word... barely legal anyway, right?... investigations on Australian soil are taking. I don't know who you're reporting to but, if it's not fully authorised, like my Department seems to feel it is not, then,' the fellow, along with that patrician nose making it worse, just would not stop gazing steadily at me, 'I don't want to be reporting to the Attorney-General one thing, when you might be planning to spring something else on us. You came to me for help. No making me look a fool, okay?'

'*Oh.*' Yes, again, meaning, presumably, he understood. Infuriating.

'That your answer?'

Apparently, it was. Charles Ekanayake eased himself back into the lounger with a sigh. He pulled out dripping sun glasses from the robe, put them on while squinting into the sun, and seemed to go all dead lizard. And that, apparently, was that, when there I had been thinking he'd would have had all the stops out looking for me.

It seemed the only uptight thing about him was that bellyflop branding across his guts.

I felt like pouring raw alcohol over it.

I got to my feet hoping my exasperation showed but knowing he wouldn't even be looking. What I must have done was stay staring down at him long enough for him to suddenly wave his arm concessionally and to concede to pipe up with:

'Mr Tasker, tell me about your Sri Lanka.'

This was more like it. I sat back down. Even if he was trying to slip in a surreptitious interview, I was confident Aussie nerve would take the points from Sri Lankan obduracy anytime.

'You're talking a long time ago, Inspector. Gampola, in the uplands, where there's not too many elephants left if you want to know.'

'I know Gampola.'

'We were running one of the tea estates there before the government took the tea business over. Good time and old

139

times. A set of ebony elephants on our mantelpiece at home in Adelaide after we landed here was about all we had left of it. Talking about elephants, did you ever hear about a man called John Wesley Hyatt?'

He hadn't and apparently didn't care that he hadn't, certainly not to any extent of making it look like there was any life behind those shades. Not an elephant man, obviously. But yet, he was finally retorting:

'Any family still in Gampola, Mr Tasker?'

I'd never fall for that. Hey, a lawyer, remember?

'So why not close down all the Tamil operations here, Inspector? You did it with the travel agency.'

'They would be only starting up somewhere else, isn't it? You catch the principals, they cannot, *nae*? Gampola? *Oh,* yes, I know the estates around there, bloody fucking hell, sorry. Yours?'

'Monegala.'

'Ah, high, high up. Not Gampola. Near Gampola. And where were you coming to, Mr Tasker? Sydney, is it? Melbourne, is it?'

I knew he knew already but played along: 'I told you, Adelaide. The hole they dropped me into.'

I couldn't help the feeling that came into that. The scorched earth. It was still with me, and bitterly, bitterly.

'Your parents and you? A little half us, a little half Aussie, isn't it? Any other family?'

No. No alias called 'Tusker', thank you, bloody Inspector. No brother, no pack drill for you. Here is a law graduate from Melbourne Uni, not some dummy or even one of Neila's dumbos.

'Just me.'

Not a question of foolishly lying, either. I knew very well that after my brother migrated with my name pinned to him, after my mother sighed and died and left me, after those noodled aunts went the way of all fired-up glory, and after that

140

hellhole at West Beach where nobody gave a stuff about anybody, my brother was untraceable. Literally.

Heavy black holes litter my life, you know. Any tracker would just fall into one of them and disappear. This tracker of a bloody-fucking-hell-sorry had moved on, however, to something else:

'Mother and father?'

'My father was never able to get away from his elephants. He was famous for them.'

'For *aetha*, tuskers, Mr Tasker?'

I didn't like the insinuation, and glibbed it out with a shrug and a turn of the head to watch the three-year-old still going through her drowning pace in the deep end. Some mummy must have given up on her.

Inspector Ekanayake looked out from beneath the towel he had now flopped over his face and lifted his sun glasses. Both his eyes were still bloodshot from the pool's chlorine. Must be a weak condition. Funnily enough, I saw sympathy in those eyes too. He understood white mother, Sri Lankan father and all the niggles in life that would have come from that.

'Do you,' he asked, with no change of bloodshot sympathy, 'still keep up with your yachtings?'

'Yachtings?'

Now the sun, not just the three-year-old, must have been getting at him. Whatever I wasn't going to fall for that either. I went:

'Inspector, I walk past a boat and they bring up the vomit bucket.'

'I heard you are big on admirable ocean-goings, Mr Tasker.'

'Do me a favour. Can you see me in something that goes along by means of washing on the line?'

And this was my brother again. And I knew it. And I suspect he suspected it by the change of tone. Still, apart from the scaffolding that was his body, he didn't go flat out. Rather, I think he was being amused.

141

'And you are married, Mr Tasker?'

'Divorcing, divorcing. She's gone back to Melbourne.'

'A second marriage, nae? My commisseries. She was the Miss Ramaswarmy, is it?'

'She will be again.'

'And are we not talking about the sister of the spokesman of the Tamil agitators in many countries including here?'

I lied like a cur, fiercely: 'I didn't know that.'

'How would you not be knowing your wife is his sister bloody fucking hell, sorry, Mr Tasker?'

'Hey, I've only met them a couple of times, him, Joycie I suppose you mean. An arranged marriage. Sri Lankan old style. It turned out not to be, as they say.'

At least he had the good grace of not watching me go through that little performance. Momentarily on my heels and rocking, but at least there were still those black holes, those lovely black holes. There was no way of tracing me to the Ramaswarmys during my uni days. It was my brother who was the one always around the Ramaswarmys, not me.

'They tell me she is a beautiful woman, Mr Tasker', he went.

'Like Greta Garbo, she shouldn't have lived past the silent-movie era, especially 1927. I've read that her best was 'Flesh and the Devil' of that year.'

'You don't seem to be having much love for your fellow man, Mr Tasker.'

'They've got the brains of elephants but ain't so cuddly.'

'I see.'

I moved to go. As with Yogi Nath, I could see I didn't have the knack of extracting what I wanted from out of the fellow man I didn't, no, have much love for. This had almost been the same waste of time. I cheer them up; they depress me. As a private eye, I'd never make a twin brother obviously.

But I couldn't part leaving things as though they were all-me and on the wrong foot:

'So, that's me done over, right? What about you? Any friends here?'

'My childhood cobber,' *cobber*, his Aussie English, with its bloodyfuckinghellsorrys, was either going to make him a wonder or totally unintelligible back home, 'lives up in Cairns, isn't it? His name is Garel Swensen. He is being a great writer.'

Said so proudly. I actually knew the name of this 'great writer' who was nothing more than a newspaper columnist. No wonder he lived in Cairns which I'd read somewhere could well explain why his tripe always looked like diatribe off-centre. A bit unkind. If I wasn't mistaken, he was involved in some Aboriginal murder trial going on at the moment in which my department was advising.

I grasped at the straw that could maybe let me put the boot back in:

'Can't keep away from it, Inspector, is that it?'

'And what is that, Mr Tasker?'

'Murder. Murder trials.'

'My friend is only a witness.'

'So am I, pal. So am I.'

'I will be remembering that, Mr Tusker, sorry Tasker.'

I could see he was now too comfortably ensconced under the sun to rise to too many more barbs, so I let that one pass and got for my impertinence as I was leaving:

'Do be watching out when you are always admirably ocean sailing, Mr Tasker.'

Bloody sailing and yachts again. What was with him?

And Neila had the cheek to call me weird.

By the time I got home from being grilled by at the poolside -- and I still don't know how he turned it around and was pumping me rather than me him -- my thoughts were doing what that three-year-old kid in the pool undoubtedly had graduated into: tumble turns.

I sat there on the bench at the sunset side of the wreck of a shed-my-home, but do you think I could concentrate on scams?

Inspector Bloody-fucking-hell-sorry again had my marbles rolling around my father, my elephants, Gampola, Rehana -- almost everything of my old Lanka, except how I was going to be able to find my brother and cover his tracks and so ensure I professionally survived myself.

You know, speaking of elephants, a rogue beast will smash down a house to get to a poor cowering human it knows is hiding from it and then wham, bam, thank you mammal.

In the bush, it'll actually wait in ambush along a human track and will probably choose to squash the *pip* of the first poor loser who comes along. Just because it can't find a willing female. Like, welcome to the world, elephant head! We humans have glands too, but who promised you a living?

Mind you, rogue elephants don't do anything disgusting or anything that God didn't equip an elephant to do. They stick to the mangle-press-trample to a pulp business, and then they generally leave well alone. Gentle, tis said. I bet my father would say. He'd have to be kidding. You fall foul of any one of the dozens of noble and ancient Ceylonese kings, you wouldn't get bothered by anything mundane like the chopping block. That would be too quick and not much fun for the invited masses. I've read mano-on-mano to the death is never very artistic when it all boils down to it, no matter how much I know my brother claims he artistically is.

No, but instead you'd get bothered by the royal elephant. With one of the royal mahouts to guide things along, they could run their tusks right through your upper parts of its choosing. That, they could do probably too easily though.

To make it more entertaining for the king and the invited masses and to flesh out those boring late afternoons in the tropics, three-edged and very sharp sheaves were slid over the royal tusker's right royal teeth first. Then the beast would push you to the ground, cut and thrust you a bit with those nicely extended swords, do the elephant equivalent of a pirouette for the delight of the cheering crowd, put a languid foreleg on your torso for a bit of leverage, wrap its trunk around, say, your leg or arm and start the real proceedings off by simply tearing that arm or that leg right off. Or maybe it's the other way around and your torso gets torn off. Not the legs off a fly but a Christmas bon-bon sort of thing.

That would be just the sampler. By the time it had finished with you you'd be sans arms, sans legs, sans head—sans, as a froggy Shakespeare would have it, toutes.

It was only then that humans became directly involved with your miscreancy... when they staked out your torso and head on a crossroad for the good villagers to titter over and the crows to titbit.

On the other hand, elephants do enjoy a bit of light relief on the little bipeds that prod and boss them around. It is true that they squirt water at people, like you see in comics. But it isn't true they do this naturally. They have to be taught this trick.

My father did that to me one time.

One day he got huge Majah to squirt water at me. It knocked me clean head over heels and I came up bawling.

Did my father and my mother laugh together then? Do you think they might have ever laughed much? I don't think so; at least not in front of me.

But I do hope they did. He owed her that.

I would guess my mother never got much of a giggle up at the big house from those sourpusses of parents of hers. Being my grandparents didn't make their pusses any less sour, either. And she never got much rib-tickling by being landed in Adelaide as Australia's first stop. And I know I wasn't capable of making her laugh. My brother wasn't exactly a bundle of joy to behold, either. And those burnt-out, hipped-done Adelaide aunts would have only been able to drive her to tears.

145

You had to be an eligible male and three parts cut to get a laugh out of them.

So, if my father never gave her anything to laugh at, she never had anything to laugh at. When I think about that, I find that sad.

My mother.

She sighed and died and left me.

Those slow thoughts of slow deaths in that sunset, after returning from the swimming pool and bloody lifeguard Ekanayake. A wonderful effect he had on people himself. If they were young enough they kept attempting to drown themselves. If they were old enough they'd be keeping away from swimming pools.

If he was an early Charlie Chaplin, he'd be playing to graveyards.

I'm talking about the Charlie Chaplin of the immediate post First World War before he was allowed onto any film set to meet such people as those real oldies Greta Garbo and Mary Pickford.

Now, my wreck of a tin shed-as-house was built on the rise towards the northeast corner of my property, about fifteen kilometres westward of Canberra. It's not so good when the south-easterlies are blowing and it isn't too good there when it comes to the westerlies and the northerlies either. It isn't much good in that corner when the southerlies and the south-westerlies come, come to think of it. It probably wasn't the possie you'd lay the foundations of your dream home, either for the killing sun for half the year and the blistering winter easterlies that used to whistle through the other half of the year.

But I liked it there. It was as far from the road, which means as far from people, as I could get. Besides, cropped out like that, it gave me the fairest of warnings of anybody's approach --say, wives -- which suited me even better.

You try to tell me, then, how I didn't hear whoever it was who tried to kill me.

Whether they were already in the place as I sat there doing my own (mental) tumble turns in front of the sunset and before the spectre of Ekanayake, or whether they were waiting in the scrub for the right moment to go for 'go', they had to be somewhere very, very near.

The strange thing is, normally, I would have been able to sense someone coming a mile off.

That Inspector Charles Ekanayake, then, nearly got me shattered in body as he had me going to mental pieces.

Thank you, Inspector Charles Bloody-fucking-hell-sorry Ekanayake. You're a real pull-through.

It may be ignoble to say my bladder saved me, but it did.

Your senses may flop on their backs like dead fish; you might have catatonia come upon you; you mightn't be able to get one thought through to the broken nail on your big toe. But the bladder still works. It's just a little workaholic, is all. Sucks it in, strains it, squeezes it out; sucks it in, strains it, squeezes it out. They say your workaholic bladder gives such relief that that relief is better than a feed, better than a nookie, better than winning a lottery.

Mine was better than a bomb.

I didn't wish to go. I was set fast in misery before that sunset and was quite happy there. But I did go. I was propped upon the port-a-loo in its own nifty tin outhouse down the rise, when it all fell in on me. Just collapsed in on me like a pack of cards before I heard the rush-then-roar and the crack of the second shock wave that seemed to be dragging hell's chains along with it.

I had the impression of first being flattened, then being lifted and flung high, high into a pitch-black sky that was opening up specially to receive me. I settled up into it feeling that it was me-special, as though my time of disaster had shown me a flattering attention that was time, however fleeting, which belonged solely to me.

Perhaps the man trying to kill me was wrong only in his locale. Each of us will have his famous moment all right, but maybe not in some village. It might be, rather, in the transit lounge between life and death; a special mini-accolade, a momentary darkening of the sky at noon, for your passing through, for finally facing it, for encouraging you to make it through.

But I didn't need to make it through, although I wasn't returned so nicely, either. Pain woke me up. My head seemed to want to drum up another explosion. When I opened my eyes as painfully as if they had been stitched to every nerve in my brain, I found I was hugging the side of a sheet of iron that had once been the roof of my outside loo.

Perhaps I had flown through the air with it as Sir Knight and the Shield of Evergood, because it had sliced me as neatly as a scalpel down my face, down my torso and down to my crotch. It must have slashed my pullover and shirt and flung them to the wind. I had one slipper on, as pantomime as the rags on me that used to be trousers.

My ears were thunder-bells.

I pulled myself stickily away from the razor's edge of that iron sheet. There was blood in my mouth. Internal bleeding? Well, at least my tongue could feel my teeth were still in place. Such are small mercies. I moved, finally, under what seemed to be a heavy rain of dust. It proved to be smoke. Electrical black smoke. In that once corrugated-iron environment, it would have needed a bomb, and a whopper of a bomb at that, to set anything alight.

I looked down; somehow my foot was stuck in the bowl of the actual port-a-loo itself. I can recommend them if you're going to get bombed; real feet protectors. There was only a small dent in its side; it must have followed me dutifully as I sailed high and sailed back to low and obviously couldn't feel it should let go entirely until my bladder, and my bladder only, gave the signal. The only thunder.

I gave myself up to the leadening weariness again.

When I woke the second time, I could see now that my place had been totally levelled. There were corrugated sheets

148

flung about everywhere, some charred on one side, some buckled, but most of them lying apart in a wide circle.

I managed it to my feet. It only changed the direction of the booming-away in my ears to pulsing from on top of my head. It pile-drove me to the ground again.

Whoever it had been had blown me into the reptilian.

I still recall slithering across the debris not knowing I was trying to make the utility shed I had down over the other rise until I rolled downhill to it.

There was something there and it was suddenly important for me to know it was still there.

But I decided to go back to sleep anyway.

When I woke up again, the brumm-brumm in my ears had turned stormy with rolling modulations that encouraged me to think the storm was breaking up. Despite this I knew there was silence all around me.

There was one other thing all this brought home to me, too, and that was I was still ever alone.

So much for emergency services. Neighbours, helpers coming to the rescue, drivers-by, anybody, phoning in for the police, ambulance, the fire brigade.

Not a thing, not a body.

I found what I had been sensing I should be looking for at the shed.

It was my brother's motorbike. You should not ask me what it was doing there.

How I knew it might have been there is beyond me to this day. In my blackouts, I just knew he would have come. I called out for him. I think I called out for him. I crawled back up the ridge to the wreckage of my house; how many stops and how many blackouts to get there? I remember I stood in the centre of what had been my home, wobbling on the thudded-up concrete that had once been my living-room floor.

I called him again.

I was the boy on the burning deck.

But still not a thing, not a body.

149

My brother, even with his alias maybe of Tusker, was not there.

I staggered and crawled around as best I could. I could find no other trace of him but the motorbike. Finally, I got myself back to the utility shed and sat down against his motorbike. I needed to feel him.

Whatever time after, it struck me that they had got him.

He must have arrived, didn't realise I was out on the port-a-loo, waited in the house and had it explode around him. I groaned for my brother. I felt for him for the first time in my existence.

Stupid, stupid. I should have known he would hear I had been asking around for him and would come out into the open to find out why I had suddenly taken any interest in him. I had made it easy for someone to just follow me, knowing all they had to do was bide their time until he showed up, so very easy for the killing.

It was groaning stuff. I rolled over and pushed at the door of that utility shed. I don't know if I was pushing it in or out; all I knew was this was where I should have been looking for him.

What he had dug up there I had had no idea he had buried there.

It was a regular cache of arms. Even in my bleary condition, it was somehow still shocking to see in Australia. I know that sounds feeble, given the scale of things. But I had been in law all those years. Oh, you hear of the occasional .22 ending some domestic argument or the odd shotgun robbery gone wrong or the semi-automatic some lunatic wants to use on anyone so he can show his mates he's not afraid to use it. But hardly ever caches full.

That makes them weapons of war. These weapons of choice.

There were a couple of automatic rifles, which I now know to be British AS80s; a self-loading Browning 9 mm Mark 1 that I likewise now know to be called the Hi-Power with a thirteen clip; a drum- loaded automatic shotgun; ammunition steel boxes; a box of plastic moulding material that could only have been an explosive base; and lots of other things. He had dug a trench there for them and lined it with black waterproof sheeting.

These weapons of war, yes.

If I had been thinking straight, I wouldn't have needed to be second-guessing where he had secured them. The whole journey's end of this mess he had gotten himself into, and me through that alias notification, were weapons of war like this had to be to wrest some initiative in the perennial Tamil homeland obsession.

Even given all of that, there was one thing I simply knew was glaringly missing. As if it was truly there in front of me, I could see in my mind how it was a Japanese samurai sword, the kind I suppose they used to commit seppuku. Its scabbard was gold-plated and its ornamental carvings inlaid with silver and bronze. It would have been a magnificent cutting instrument, forged by some master blacksmith in the time-honoured way of repeated drawings-out, foldings, re-weldings of the finest steel on the heaviest of forges under the rhythm of the sledge hammers.

It would have been, oh yes, and you know that. But it was not there. Don't ask me how I knew it should have been there in the first place. Whatever else my brother had taken when he had escaped... and now through the clear-set image of the sword being missing I just knew he had.... he had also taken the sword.

I lay down with my face against the edge of the trench he had dug for the weapons of war with the not-so-silly idea that it might serve as a resting place touched and secured by my own.

Of the violence I could feel, I could do nothing to help prevent.

I could only lie and sleep and wait for help to come.

I lay there for two days, healing.

No help came.

I dreamt, though. No, more. I *saw*.

Oh yes, I saw what he was doing in my mind's eye.

Twins, twins.

Talking about disasters: another one was Rehana.

My second wife didn't say one word during the affiancing occasion in the Ramaswarmys' living room, looking there like the reincarnated Parvati but something you could definitely put your hands on without too much urging.

What agony that must have been for her. I mean obviously having been instructed beforehand she shouldn't say a word.

In the nine months we cohabitated as man and wife -- and there was certainly no cohabitation in any stretch of a conjugal sense -- she never stopped to think in case she missed a mouthful of whine.

They could call it logorrhoea, but I don't think they have ever invented a specific term for what Rehana had. I couldn't believe it. Neila's was a mightily dirty and sometimes erythrismal mouth, but Rehana's was a torrent of waterfalling sounds, sometimes intelligible as words, but always on shattering cascade of whine like squeezing out through the nostrils.

She sometimes whined in her sleep all night. But what she did every night bar none, whine-talking or not whine-talking, was managing to grind her teeth with or without the whine. I mean, really gnash and do a millstone job on them. All those long nights through.

I came to think it was the grinding of frustration that she couldn't stay awake twenty-four hours a day to keep whining.

She could whine the back legs off a rogue elephant.

She pitched those whines high; she pitched them low. She modulated them at you like jabs from my brother's samurai sword. You were near, you risked verbal seppuku. Five minutes of her whining would have used up a two-hour recording tape.

I didn't realise it at the time, but she whined through the hand-tying ceremony in the Hindu kovil down there in Melbourne. I thought she was just humming the Hindu equivalent of hymns to all that clanging of cymbals and crashing of drums and gongs in the middle of Brunswick, but no. She whined through the reception afterwards, but I thought she was just over-excited or someone hadn't told the bands to stop.

I have to admit that, during the wedding, I was too busy still looking at her. She was exquisitively dressed traditionally again. Change the saree's deep puce silk with a warm and loving vermilion, but with the same lavish gold finery, and you still have sheer beauty out of the mist of the ever-changing swirling hues of some ancient harem.

And her large eyes were still as imperial as obsidian, still as arresting as unlimited innocence.

It's also hard not to take your eyes off the money you're marrying into.

The trouble was no one saree, even a saree like that as worn by her, could forever stay bound majestically to the hips and thighs where, lurking to shock, snaking up her legs, were terrible varicose veins in, as they say, one so young. Talk about me having the reason to do the whining, not her.

It wasn't that she couldn't carry on a conversation occasionally either. If you got her cornered with something she couldn't understand, there might be enough dull pauses out of her for you to wedge in responses that, taken together, might constitute a conversation technically.

Of the two 'conversations' I can now remember, the one just before I decided to go down to the corner store to buy a figurative packet of fags and not non-figuratively never to return home, one can still spring to mind. It was after months of Melbourne Ramaswarmy pressure, bullying, cajoling about

153

where's the evidence of the first grandchild, sonnyjim, like what the ferg's going flamin' on up there Rehana?; public servants all impotent after all, stone the crows?

There was no way I was going to figure in any baby.

What was good enough for Onan had always served yours truly quite satisfactorily, thank you.

Yet I actually came to hear her whine something about being pregnant; whine through, even, a couple of morning upchucks; whine through the beginnings of a wobble while she walked; whine as her belly got bigger and bigger. Suddenly, it seemed, she had got so big with child that she was legitimately whining about it.

I could stand it no longer. I had to waste the energy to ask her if she was pregnant and I'd reluctantly admit she might be, how come?

The conversation I remember went something like this:
Me. 'Wind'

'Of course, wind. Daddy said what do you expect? Gas?'

'Gas?' Me, thinking of natural gas. Getting confused by her whining sincerity.

'Not gas, wind. If you know anything, you should know you cannot get babies from gas.' Rehana. No Rehana, she. That whining, that whining.

'You think you get babies from wind?'

'If I keep up the prenatal exercises, sure.'

The girl hadn't turned out to be brightest migrant from Sri Lanka.

I just went to the shop for fags and, yes, simply fell into the joke of taking the opportunity of not coming back.

It was pointless giving any reason other than the joke was impossible to resist.

It was easier just to nod about her getting on with the prenatal exercises regarding wind behind that constant and happy whine of her complaining how hard it was to touch toes when pregnant via the wind route, and never have to set eyes on her again. Not that we ever come anywhere near to living together anyway. That's why I had jumped in with: pregnant?, how come?

After the wedding Mrs Ramaswarmy had flown back with us to help with the settling in as Indian mothers will do if there are no in-laws. Or even if there are. She and her daughter took one look inside my Nissen shed-you'd-have-to-say-was-home and screamed so that the cab actually turned around and came back, even though it must have been halfway back to Canberra's airport by then.

They packed themselves back into it and got off to an apartment in Belconnen that cunning old Appa Ramaswarmy had apparently bought years before as an investment, even though it turned out to be more of a safe house for his push for some Tamil-homeland shenanigans while trying to drag me and my brother into it. I'll come to that later.

After seeing my home and dismissing my home, what we did was to come to a whining compromise that Rehana would treat my home as a weekender when she hated the countryside, and I would treat her city apartment with contempt.

She actually tried the weekender idea out on a few Fridays, Saturdays and Sundays, but I don't know about her, but they were sheer hell for me. Whining all night and the damn crows trying to compete with her all day. I'll give her credit for turning me off that cohabitation caper.

After that, we would meet halfway at that roadside motel, where the walls were pretty thin and the manager pulled his braces pompously when he asked if we could keep it down, newly-weds or no newly-weds, although he was obviously mixing arguments with passion when it came to the higher decibels. Her constant whining through those walls wouldn't have helped either.

It was enough having weekends with Rehana whining, let alone having the motel manager's whining thrown in as well. I soon tossed that meeting halfway compromise in.

Mind you, there was one other conversation I remember having with her during our nine months of being hitched. I

155

distinctly remember it on account of that apartment in Belconnen and my brother in his absence.

She had been whining that I should go to the Belconnen apartment instead of expecting her to come to me, going:

'Daddy only bought it for you.'

'Leave off. He bought it years ago, your mother said.'

'But for you. Neila says how weird you get.'

'You stop seeing Neila.'

'How can I,' (how can you whine even saying that?) 'when she's always at the apartment with one or other of those friends or acquaintances of yours.'

That was from when I was able to gather where my brother or Neila or both must have photographed all that blackmail stuff that even Neila started whining about wanting back, or for assurance that they'd been destroyed. My own brother, my own ex-wife, my own then-current wife. In an apartment Rehana's whining on about having been bought for me. Apart from anything else, no wife of yours should be mixing you up with your brother. And even if that was excusable, what's the going all sly and crafty when she mentions it, whine-wise?

She shouldn't have lived past Uriah Heep who I read about as coming from Charles Dickens's novel 'David Copperfield' of 1850 or thereabouts and the guy's hand-wringing, and he going:

'Who am I to complain? Daddy bought it for your use, didn't he?'

'How would I know? Ask my brother.'

'There you go going all weird again', and she was actually *giggling* a whine at me, 'You're all so secretive.'

'I hope I never remember having this conversation, but are you whining on about my brother being around lately?'

'Oh, you!' Pinching me. I *hated* that. Then she wriggled her gaseous belly at me, which she would have called windy, in some sort of parody of sexual play, going: 'How come you never used all that camera equipment there on me, like Neila.

That was kinky. You never tried to' (whine, whine) 'go kinky on *me*.'

'You're telling me face to face that you stay in the apartment even when Tusker comes to town?'

'Weird, Neila says, weird.'

Her chortle and the underlying whine was a rattlesnake snorting.

You can see what was going on, can't you?

My brother was having more of my two wives that I was.

It was more than likely his wind in her belly, not mine. He might have even got the wind up Neila for all I know.

Anyway, not long after this whine-upon came the inevitable phone call at my office from Appa Ramaswarmy. Who else?

'Listen, you mongrel's dog, you, I can be as obstinate as a bulldog's bum leech, too. My daughter's staying in that apartment where she'll be living and breathing Tusker and keeping any eye on Tusker.'

It was the one and only time I had heard Tusker used to mean my brother. That's why I wasn't so ready for it when Inspector Ekanayake fronted up with those charge sheets.

But right then all I was hearing was Appa Ramaswarmy not missing a beat so that you knew where Rehana got her whine from:

'... She ain't there to keep an eye on that shaggin' civilian thing, you mug, you get off on being. Cripes, I am thinking you are having turned out as weird as a bromide tea at a wedding, ya mug'.

Yes, Rehana.

I should've got around to divorcing her sooner.

Very strictly speaking, maybe I should tell Father Thumbayaserni that I never got around to sort of getting officially shot of her.

But then he might decide I'm not free to marry Virathni, whom God has sent me. Virginally. He can think some things really through. Maybe going to the seminary teaches you how to worm-work through things like that.

On the other hand, God not only forgot the importance of John Wesley Hyatt's invention of plastic on the celluloid influence upon the whole development thing of Hollywood, not to mention Greta Garbo and Charlie Chaplin et al, but also, with a little divine help of His own, the fact that He might have prevented the elephants of the world being in such a parlous state as they are in to this day.

He also overlooked the importance of the invention of forgery, especially when it comes to, say, divorce papers.

And, after all, I'm trying to marry my own aunt who's younger than me, so why should Christian theologies even want to be obstructive when it should be quite beyond them?

I feel another item coming on.

'Their Lanka now.'

In this now-time, it has changed now, this upland town of Gampola. They tell me that, when I was a lad running after my father over that mountain there, it was mainly a Tamil place, then a Singhalese place. Now it's mostly Muslim. I like that. They don't blackball you if you give your women a hard time. That's comforting. What's also comforting is you can hit the bottle without worrying too many out there are hitting the bottle. That's order. That's control and order and comforting.

Peace here in Gampola.

But, yes, peace here, curiously enough only because there is no such thing as privacy. The human sounds that are constantly with you are warming, enveloping, bathing as wet goo to an elephant in a drought.

It's because in Gampola you don't have to be involved. It's because the constant sounds at you are anonymous. Since it's mostly Tamil or Singhalese or Muslim or who cares, you don't have to worry about it being wholly one thing or the other or bother what other human beings are ratting on about.

Anonymous is fine by me.

I have my church; there could only be one Father Thumbayaserni; I have my leper hostel and Hansen; I have my lovely virginal Virathni, my aunt younger than me; I have the family with whom I sleep on the floor mats. And daily I turn the other cheek. Maybe the Gospels were right.

The peace is living out of your time, like it was for me back home before they blew it up. It's like no fluorescent light or neon has been invented yet; only the single bulb or the candle at night, warming and soft-sun beacons that invite the amble. The time where there used to be electric cuts all the time; water rationings. Smell the spices and the roasting cashews and the curries and the oil lamps of the street carts at nights. The Morris Minors still kept going on lick and spittle and now worth a fortune. The flies. Living with fucking flies... 'mama, tonight we're having fly curry'.... before anyone thought of the cagey little dung beetle as they did for the Australian Dung Beetle Project of 1965 to 1985. The hand-made furniture, like you handmade it, but out of hardwoods, made to last forever and forever polished, not Ikea pasty pines shamelessly begun by the Swede Ingvar Kamprad around 1956 out of his own warehouse. I can buy one cigarette at a time. I can squat to void, even peeing like a woman. I don't even have to bother looking at books in bookshops; there are no real books. Bookshops still mean exercise books, stationery. Picture parlour means pictures of weddings in frames for the sideboards. No ice. Thank God, no ice. You need refrigerators to make ice. In the fifties in Adelaide, my mother had the ice box. Here in Gampola, it's a double-door fridge or nothing at all. Here a lot still buy what's wanted for the day in the morning, just enough; who needs the expensive fridge? Here in Gampola you can get back to what you basically are: an animal that only needs a slight lowering of the outside temperature to be refreshed. The drinks, the water, just less than room temperature are delicious again. The wetness, not the coldnesses.

In the morning on the radio, they still play Johnny Reeves, Mantovani, Dwane Eddy and his electric guitar, and it sounds like the sita.

It's all wonderful.

The pressure's off.

It's living in the fifties again.

But if you are thinking I must have had a good day today, forget it.

It was marred.

I was coming back from boiling Hansen's bandages, and others', from the hostel when I thought I spotted Inspector Charles Ekanayake.

There were four of them in that bottle-green police four-wheel-drive that pulled up at the local police station next door to the courts. I only got a glimpse of his face, but I am sure it was him. You don't mistake lanky that lanky like that.

I didn't wait around to get his autograph.

What is he doing up here in the uplands, so far away from his southern port city of Galle or if he had some good excuse, why so near me?

I am sitting here waiting, I think, for him to come for me. Why, I don't know. But no one has come knocking yet. My protectors are the five little girls sitting in regal solemnity around me. They are dutifully doing their homework because I am here, and they love me being here.

I haven't worked up enough head of hate, so Mister Bloody-fucking-hell-sorry Inspector's coming for me now would be premature.

What has to be done is none of his business, anyway. It's between my father and me.

But, knowing him, he'll claim that weak copper's excuse that we both are on the wanted list.

Oil.

It must have been the lubricating oil on the assault rifles my head was lying next to.

My brother seemed to be coming into my head on the heavy waves of the oil of machines. The machines were entering my head and the presence of him was greasy as a mechanic, grim and grease- crusted.

I could not move my head away from him.

I could not talk to him in my mind and say you're too heavy. You are too dark and grim for me right now. I ache and I am burnt and I am cut and I need to sleep here to forget these things you want me to be doing with you. My tin-shed-as-home has just been bombed out of existence while I was sitting on the port-a-loo.

Just leave me sleeping here next to your weapons of war in this utility shed here. I need sleep but you stand there in the doorway of some room in my eye, ominous and oily black with the headlights from somewhere outlining that samurai sword you are holding at your side. I have just thought: so that's where it's gone, even though I didn't know it was with all this weaponry I didn't know you have stashed on my property.

Cool and refreshingly metal against my brumming head just now.

Where am I going to go? Hey, leave me out of it. Let my being here damn near busted up be as much as I need to know. It is enough that you let me lie here, if you insist on taking me with you.

And then the oil that was fuming my head became a road at night. A flat black strip escorted by the roadside reflectors, arched by the lacings of the dark gums, and everything seeping

161

oil, even the oncoming headlights. One after another, emblazoning filmed by the coloured smears of the oil. In the nostrils. On the road back into the city. Going to where people are again.

Everywhere.

What do I want to know of any of this? I hurt still.

I knew it was the Queanbeyan Road and it was on the Thursday and my brother was travelling me out from Canberra. Oil from the front wheel of his motorbike tearing at the puckered surface of the night road. Oil and grease and petrol, the tank a heavy bulb between his knees. As cold and oil-cut as the tail lights up ahead of him.

He was closing easily, matching only a little over its speed. This car up ahead.

This white Mercedes.

Yogi Nath had a white Mercedes. This, I can arrive at.

The oncoming headlights no trouble at all. All is in oil; all lubricated.

The white Mercedes, yes. My brother drew slowly up alongside the back bumper, I see, then moved as smoothly as in oil alongside opposite the back seat, from where I see, we can see, J. R. Nehru, N. A. Selverajah and Mahinder Duraiswamy not bothering to look out at him. From where the freight king, the jewellery king and the publishing king did not bother to glance at my brother matching their pace out here. Then, in glissade, alongside of the driver, the front seat, from where Professor R. E. Josephs and Dr Yogendra Yogi Bear Nath did not, do not, bother to turn their heads to look out at him either. At us.

No, the oncoming headlights no trouble for him riding on the outside of the white Mercedes like that; all is viscous; all slow and smooth moving through the oil. All oil.

My brother has matched his speed to that of the white Mercedes when he has reached the driver's level, and now they are just starting to wonder, to look at who this crazy fool outside might be. Hard in the dark, in the oncoming headlights, through the oil-black clothing my brother is wearing.

The oil-black night of his colouring. The oil-black colouring of his intention.

Except for the smile; the slippery white teeth, teeth smiling at Nath now.

And Nath can only make furtive sidelong glances back, yes, in the oil of the night; the coloured smears of the oncoming headlights through his windscreen; the dash reflections on the door window at his side, while we seem to reach easily over. Does my brother. It is all so smooth a luge. My brother, yes, reaches over and raps on the driver's window. He is smiling. Nath is frowning, trying to keep control; the annoyance is making him swerve; he seems to be driving on oil. He cannot take his hands off the wheel; it seems to slip frictionless between his hands.

Oil, oil. An item.

My brother has seen the Professor say something to Nath in anger, then reach across from the passenger's seat and push the button that winds down the driver's window. The sudden rush of lubric'd air into the car. Yogi Bear Nath not hearing the warning from the Professor. He has steadied the car and turns to shout at the crazy keeping pace with him outside. He screams when he recognises who it is. It is a scream of disbelief.

He is still screaming when the samurai sword, the satiny sheen of oil on its perfect blade and how it sloops through the window and slides globulously right through both cheeks of his face.

And then is gone. The sword, the motorbike, both in oil.

Only the interior of the car heaving and juddering. The night lights, the blinding lights, the heavy oncoming traffic.

Yogi Nath hears the screams of the others in his car, not his own, until all and all explodes.

The night. The dream I was surely having from the utility shed.

163

This is what I witnessed in my mind's eye, only half-conscious and needing to go back into the night where I could move away from the fumes of the oil. Needing to move away from my brother's light of actually doing what I didn't even dare to think should be done.

Total carnage everywhere or not, it was still my home.

I had a right to sit there, right bang in the middle of it. If I wanted to spend my long-service leave right there in the utility shed next to where I just knew the samurai sword was missing, I would spend my long-service leave right there in the utility shed where the samurai sword had gone missing. And I would do so right smack bang in the middle of it, too.

The view across my property was better without walls anyway.

There is only two and a half hectares of it, but it is as wide to me and as broad to me as the whole of the Southland. In winter, the dried old gash that struggles its way across my land was actually a creek. It never much more than trickled, but in those times it could have been the River Ganges for all I cared. Maybe sometimes in summer it got like that as well, and then the galahs and the parakeets and the cockatiel or two would latch on to the tortuous branches of the gums and the kurrajongs and play me merry songs, and the kookaburras I fed with my leftovers would break into raucous chuckles about the small pleasures of transients.

My alarm clocks, the laughing kookaburras, the kingfishers, my tawny frogmouth, my robins and whistlers. Clock-clock go the alarms.

My property.

When I bought that property, I bought with it the ants, the termites, the black-bellieds, the red-bellieds, the blue-tongues, the long-nosed, the pouched rufuses, the bandies, the night fruiters, a koala that I only saw twice, the rock roos that could come in summer or might come in winter, the birds, the gums and wattles and scrub and the wild wheats and the snake grasses.

164

I bought that icing of pathetically-thin clayey soil that supported beautifully that which it was supposed to support: the scrub of the southeast open forest.

My forest.

I bought the birds. I bought the mosquitoes, the bluebottles, the domestics, the lone wasps, the possums, the wild cats.

I bought them all, and I tried ever since not to harm one single hair on their revolting legs or nightmares of scaly trunks. They were my part of Australia I had won at long, long last from my own sweat, from my own brow, from all of the lands and all of the seas in all the damn world outside of the land of my father's elephants. And with all my might I would keep that a sacred trust.

I mightn't have won any medals for how I carried out the trust. Okay, no doubt a host of black, red and bull ants did go the way of all annihilation under these great clodhoppers of mine, and I didn't care whether they were native mosquitoes or imported by some mad scientist, I did battle with the mosquitoes. And, probably the greatest failure of all, a few human beings were allowed to step on my place over the years. But not so many. Take out Neila, who wouldn't be prised loose from where she wanted to be with a crowbar and who never stepped much outside anyway, and take out Rehana that once or twice with her whine to beat the mosquitos dead, and there was precious damn few, thank God.

Every right, you know, to sit there and stew in my own misery about what they had done to my tiny piece of the world.

I fixed up a lean-to from a few of the iron sheets and stakes and wire. I still had the indestructible port-a-loo. Now there was plenty of kindling for firewood; that was for sure. You hunt around, if it happens to you, and you'll find the cans of food maybe a long blasted way off but still edible. And somewhere else you'll even find the can opener and all the eating utensils you need.

I might just spend my long-service leave there, after all, bruised and battered and really-and-truly bombed-out.

The fact was that my misery guts were telling me I might as well go back to work now. I had taken the leave to cover my brother's tracks but I now sensed that, in one fell jab of a Jap sword, or whatever, he had covered all the tracks that needed to be covered. Or uncovered them. I couldn't really care just about then.

Maybe I should never have thought of doing what I think he had done with the samurai sword and the SLA hotshots, now really shot, in the white Mercedes.

The trouble was I had, hadn't I?

I had hoped it was just a dream, but I knew in my heart it was the seeing of it just like all the other times of my brother's violence I suspected seeing too. Tasker does; I see? Do I see what he does?

Was I only some amanuensis to him?

When he's accorded the alias of 'Tusker', do I get accorded the alias of 'Tusker' too?

Or can it be *he* does what *I* see?

No, it can't be anything to do with me. It's being twins. It's some sort of state of interconnected dreaming. Some sort of sleep-wake premonition. It has to be something like that. I never had the nerve to do the things I saw him do.

From the age of six or seven, with the explosion up at the great estate house, he's been at it. Chrissakes, who knows what after that? Who can even remember?

For all I know now, Tasker could have been the Mozart of the criminal world, the child prodigy who should have been playing the world's equivalent wurlitzers at the age of three around 1760 in Salzburg, while whole theatres burnt down as far as anyone knows.

Chrissakes, what did it matter what it was? It wasn't my brother who had brought the one place I owned in this sorry existence down around my port-a-loo. It was me somehow.

It had to be my dim-witted amateur sleuthing around, asking dim-witted questions.

I should have given the extradition advice to that ham-fisted copper from Sri Lanka and not batted an eyelid. Then I should have just gone back to trying to bust Tilly's balls and take as my one ambition in life winning the office jackpot betting on whoever could prove she really did sport balls and was the office's phantom impregnator.

Hell, I couldn't even remember seeing my brother for years -- nor did I have that wrong too? Had I heard from him, cared desperately to keep in touch with him? No way. He hardly existed anymore. Do you have a family? Who, me? It had been like that.

It was the way I preferred it.

Damn it, I was happy in my misery. I was really starting to relish what I was officially encouraged to do in the public service, and that was to shy off other human beings who didn't have official passes.

Well, it was over, anyway. Perhaps I had been lucky just to lose only my home, my car and the go-anywhere usefulness of my port-a-loo. I don't know which hurt the most.

Could I take it that the Serendip Lankan Association, the SLA, was now a dead duck, a spent force sent flying, and that the only blessed thing that Inspector Bloody-fucking-hell-sorry Ekanayake would now discover from them was that dead meat doesn't talk, even if it's not in home waters?

Any members left would close it down quicksmart due to the fact if murdering fingers could reach out to the top five of its leading lights in one horrifying tree-head-on ceremony, then what chance did they themselves have of seeing any tomorrow out to pick up any of the pieces?

And me and life? Well, I'll tell you this much: that bomb from nowhere and my brother had both demonstrated to me how the fly can get out of the bottle before you can put the lid back on.

167

I mean, how could those poor sluggers in the white Mercedes know what my brother was really capable of under threat of being exposed along with them?

They probably figured a little untraceable bomb that kept their hands clean and Tasker's brother property in scatters would point the authorities to where he could be found. Or where they, like Ekanayake was a 'they', could start looking. Or where Tasker himself could take the warning of look what happened to your twin. As in the SLA wouldn't be crossed.

Well, the SLA, or most of it at least, crossed the line where the road into Canberra met the tree line.

What they couldn't have known, either, was that nobody cared a flea's tit about me. And maybe I have to include Tasker in that. They could have nuked the place, and all they'd probably have gotten was a letter to the *Canberra Times* complaining about the noise.

I didn't need Tusker to tell me it was my own damn fault either. I had barged into Nath's office, not to mention Neila's charm circle because of that, and I had demanded answers to questions that not only told them I knew all about the scams, but also that it looked like my brother had panicked and gone on loose-cannon. Either that, or they thought I was about to buzz away in the ear of the Inspector from their old home so that he would turn up the international and killing heat on them.

Either one of those would have made them feel very secure, wouldn't it?

The worrying thing about it all was that I had this strong sense of already being convinced Tasker was planning to go after them in the Mercedes on the motorbike like I imagined him or me or us doing. It had to be the concussion I was obviously suffering from. Yet there was the weird... yes, that word again... premonition of it all.

Why else did I query Nath so closely about the meeting in the car and what his car was still, and who was to be there?

I tell you what not even the concussion could stop from being self-evident. It had to be because *he* wanted to know. Tasker. Brother of mine. Alias 'Tusker' of his.

And didn't that mean he had developed some sort of power over me which he could use me when and how he wanted to?

The stuffer had to be *pipping* me again, but this time in the mind-meet, as in those mind-eyes of his were *pipping* these mind-eyes of mine.

We had become the monster Cyclops with the one round eye in the middle of our forehead.

Nevertheless, I'm positive I was sitting there, like I am now in Sri Lanka, waiting for the 'him' to show up.

Then, it was Tasker to come back with the missing samurai sword.

Now, the 'him' is Inspector Charles to come with, what?, handcuffs?, and his bloody-fucking-hell-sorry's.

So here in this now-time Lanka waiting and then in that then-time once-what-was-shed-as-home waiting, it's another little irony to report that who do I get?

Not my brother. Oh, no. I get, would you believe, Inspector Charles bloody-effing-hells Ekanayake. If you please.

Back in Canberra way with my concussion and only bombed-out shards of my port-a-loo, it's my only piece of the whole world -- and suddenly there he is, on it.

This time he wasn't alone. He had an Australian rozzer with him. I never did get around looking up the constabulary powers and jurisdiction of officers of the Australian Crimes Commission which he said he was from. Anyone who can walk into a bank and demand to see your financial dealings ... that are clout. But I didn't try to fret it out then. I hadn't been left with much stuffing left in the old carcass just at that time.

And Ekanayake knew it. I think I've told you how you could tell he was a real hunter.

This other one with Ekanayake wasn't a large man, but he had bulk. A grey suit with deep and wide lapels which could have been Sydney mod or Anywhere op shop and snapped up for its period pieceness; black socks and maroon slip-ons with leather sides, which definitely made him out of town in lace-up Canberra.... all of which was fine except his shirt and tie. The tie was askance, not by much, but aggravatingly so if you're on the peeved-by-anything trail with concussion. There was no way in the world you could keep looking at it and head-throbbingly happy. But that was nothing compared to the shirt.

The shirt was either dead filthy or he had slept in it while it got mangled in the wash. On his bloat of a chest and guts matching bloat better, it could never sit comfortable on such narrow shoulders. It hung skew-whiff -- over the trousers, partly over the tie, around the small of the back, under the armpits in puckers -- far more annoying to the concussed eye than the tie.

His name was Baybe. Martin Baybe.

Don't get tempted with rhyming slang: he was no baby. He gave smirks and stares from a lipless mouth and muddy eyes. And when I came to know him better, I saw he could hoist his forehead, under thinning hair, towards the back of his elongated head whenever he didn't believe what he was hearing. For all of that, he spoke with a menacing softness, not natural but practised. Hours before a tape practising that; it had to be. That would be Martin Baybe, detective sergeant.

And this Baybe guy was to dog my brother's heels right up to Hong Kong. This I know.

But I didn't know then. Then, it was first and foremost, Inspector Charles Ekanayake at my heels, barking a load of attempted cynicism my way just because he found me not far from my own bomb crater.

I only knew they were there when he tapped my shoulder with one sharp finger while indicating the wreckage with the scaring-crow index of his other hand.

'Bloody fucking hell, are you reporting this, Mr Tasker?'

170

'I should report it, Inspector?', I said up through a lot of stars.

'I would say you should be thinking insurance, *nae*?'

I shook my head; it seemed appropriate to seem more miserable than I really was. He wouldn't understand about the lean-to and the port-a-loo being losses nothing could ever compensate me for, least of all reporting any of this to the cops or insurance, not even by his attempt at being cynical.

I could barely watch him stroll around for a while, but wariness of him forced me to. He finally came back full circle, and languidly kicked over a few traces, which was about all one could do, given the what was left of my home. At least he had the decency to be clucking his tongue at the carnage.

But Baybe. Not Baybe. He just stood back unintroduced at that stage, and kept his eye on me as though he expected I would make a break for Ned Kelly country afore the telegraph wire got mended.

'I would say,' the Inspector turned back to Baybe, 'people with Sri Lankan connections are coming and going with wreckages all over Canberra, isn't it?'

Whatever that meant. Or maybe I'd gotten it concussion wrong.

Instead of waiting for an answer, Ekanayake contented himself by bending to pick up a leg of a chair, practised a few straight drives with it in the cavalier fashion of his country's professionals, threw it away back to smoking junk land all around and then rose to his giant needle-shaped height, going:

'How would this have been happening, Mr Tasker?'

Apparently, I had that story ready enough, concussion or no brumming-bams in my head. Leastways, it came out easily:

'Gas bottles. I prefer gas bottles. Also insist on pilot lights on the stove. Few realise the importance of pilot lights, Inspector. I recommend them if you ever settle in Australia, especially around these or other parts of the continent. Must have been a loose fitting. Surmising here, Inspector; maybe the kitchen filled up slowly like a bathtub until the gas reached the pilot light. This is the big bang theory. Me?, I was port-a-looing at the time. I must have been watching my pees and not my pilot lights. That sounded like I was being funny, but I don't feel like being funny. Where was I again?'

'Y'know, if I were you,' came the new voice of Baybe with that annoying affectation of jolly speech I would come to know too well, 'I'd be on the look-out, matey. You're a bit dangerous to be around.'

'This is...' Ekanayake hesitated over the title, 'Detective-Sergeant Baybe, Mr Tasker. You will be finding he is being from the Australian Crimes Commission. He will be taking over after I am regretfully having to leave your shores.'

So, I didn't bother with a come-back as I undoubtedly would have for someone I liked. But this Baybe character I would have to deal with in the future with a bit of rotten bad luck... I wasn't going to let him get so easily on top of me; I ignored him therefore and therefore had to talk a bit music-hall-ly to the Inspector, going:

'This Detective-sergeant here, what'd he mean coming out with "dangerous"?'

The Inspector sat down eye-to-eye to me on a very filthy metal frame that, for the life of me, I couldn't recognise; it was a shocking thing to do even to his already kakky trousers but it was obvious such things never entered his mind. Must have always had someone to do his laundry. And I was hearing him bouncing back at me:

'The men I have been interviewing killed in one tragic road accident, Mr Tasker, isn't it?, and now I find you in all of... *this*.'

'I wouldn't know about that.'

'About what, Mr Tasker?'

'About any of your *'this'.*'

'But all members of the SLA, *nae*?'

I shrugged and sighed. How did he expect me to know? My mind's-eye might have become my brother's, but it hadn't become Ekanayake's too. It wasn't about to, either.

'You have trouble with gas bottles, do you, matey?' Baybe butted in jollily. He was calling out from beside the stricken remains of the port-a-loo as though he expected it to deny I was in or on it at the time of the explosion. Still, it had saved my live so I didn't grudge him too much for wanting a closer look at the eighth wonder of the world. They should sell tickets to it.

'He is meaning it is something similar to a house of two elderly ladies in Adelaide in September 1959, bloody fucking hell sorry, isn't it, Mr Tasker?'

'You've been burrowing around on me behind my back, Inspector?'

I tried to put high dudgeon into it, but it was difficult to make the shift with a brain that was still lapping around its pan from side to side. The Inspector opened his hands as though imploring understanding if that's what I want but it wasn't come from him:

'Migrated to Adelaide. One woman, English national, Eileen Mary Tasker. A child, plain old John no middle name Tasker, aged nine. Rumoured to be two, as you yourself have sworn to, isn't it?, but not verified. Mother is being deceased February 1959. Thirteen, and you are being an orphan. It was good, *nae*?, you had your brother.'

I was miserable but not so dumb miserable to fall for that one.

If they knew about my brother, they would have mentioned him having to migrate alone those years after my mother and me. They still had nothing. Bloody-fucking-hell-sorry Ekanayake therefore had nothing. I could get very annoyed now.

'What's this brother nonsense?'

'No, no. Let us be assuming something, Mr Tasker, before I leave. Let us be saying you know *all* the people on the charge sheets I showed you, as it is appearing the people in the SLA are claiming they know you very well. Well, they *did*, past times, isn't it? But let us say for the sake of argument you are even knowing this *hora*, rogue, with the alias known as 'Tusker'. I think he would be being dangerous for you, too, *nae*? He is wanted for being a director of the travel agencies, not just here in Australia. He has his name also with Corporate Affairs as being part-owner of the building in Chennai where we are knowing the forgeries were being printed. A man called Tusker was talking to an Australian gem dealer in Thailand last year and taped talking about geuda stones going into Thailand illegally. His name is also being mentioned in extortion and standover tactics for the getting of monies out of Tamils in this country and others. People are talking all over, Mr Tasker, and the name Tusker is being popped up, pop pop pop, isn't it? He has recently being hiring a yacht using a real name...'

Here there was a loud cluck from Baybe, obviously satisfied with his examination of the port-a-loo and now scratching around where my kitchen used to be, while Ekanayake kept up the pressure, or though he was:

'Well, in being short, we are having a pretty good profile of this person. He is Tamil, erratic, neurotic, isn't it? Alienated. Let us say too perhaps he is never wanting to take anything from you by force. Maybe he is trying slyness instead. Being cheery. Smiling all the time, pretending to be mates, bloody fucking hell sorry. Wanting to show emotion...'

He had left that hang in the air and I couldn't help but rise to it:

'Like for what?'

'Like for a father figure, Mr Tasker. Are you wanting your father, Mr Tasker?'

'Oh, do me a favour.'

'No, like to tracking down sense. Maybe this Tusker does too, or tells you he does, *nae*? Haven't you got a famous father like we know he is claiming more than once to have a famous father, Mr Tasker?'

174

He didn't wait for my reply; this time he would have had to wait a long time. By now that Baybe had returned to almost be pressing him on from behind:

'Careful, I am telling you, bloody fucking hell sorry. Careful, Mr Tasker. He is suddenly brutal often, this we know. But always detached, *nae*? A killer who is not caring about anything at all, isn't it?'

Now it was Baybe's turn. He let his jolly atrocious shirt and tie push at my sensibilities again, going: 'In respect of that, matey, we are not talking about the Sugar Plum Fairy. This Tusker's bad news all round, get it?'

'So,' I was getting the old one-two from them, it being the Inspector's turn: 'you should be watching out for things that are happening around you, Mr Tasker, isn't it? There was that boy beaten nearly to death at West Beach migrant camp. Don't think it was so long again, *nae*? And there were being those elderly Australian ladies looking after you.'

'Not so long ago, either, matey.' Baybe.

'At Melbourne University, isn't it?', the Inspector pretending annoyance for his interruption, 'your roommate was being found drowned in the River Yarra, isn't it?, beaten and burnt just like the boy in the camp.'

'I wasn't in any migrant camp.'

'But next door, *nae*?, at the Our Boys Home? There was also the fire at your mother's people's house of the old plantation, so I am hearing. Perhaps I can be learning more about that when I return home, *nae*?'

'You're digging around where I grew up, too?' I was not thinking anything now, but about him getting to my father before I could.

'Pure curiosity, matey. Nothing to worry about, eh?'

'So,' and I tried to be as laconic as the manual to being Aussie said I should aim for, despite Baybe's continued shirt fronting, 'what happened to my father?'

'Your famous father?', the Inspector shrugged. A long, tantalising, deliberately so, shrug, while Baybe nodded yet frowned approval.

'Come on, Inspector. If you know something about my father, I'd like to know. Forget this Tusker guy.'

'Okay.'

'That your answer?'

'Oh.' *Yes.*

Anybody knows there's something's very wrong when a cop like him goes supercilious. Only try to be patient -- and laconic -- the manual says and I might have even achieved it:

'My father still there on the estate?'

That was obviously a clue for both of them to peer at me even closer, if that was possible.

'But your father left the estate around November 1975, isn't it?'

'I don't know. I'm asking you. I'm more worried about all his elephants, anyway.'

'But aren't you knowing, bloody fucking hell sorry, Mr Tasker, the upland elephant is almost being extinct?'

No, I didn't know that then.

I do now.

How could that be? I could feel how it would almost kill my old man. The pain of the slow deaths, and, despite putting everything into them, his breeding programme not working, obviously.

As they say: extinction is forever, give or take a day.

Or did he just walk away from his herd too, like he did my mother and me? And not forgetting the man with the alias of Tusker who was only a lad there too.

I suddenly didn't want to talk much anymore. I said so in so many words.

'That is all right. Goodbye to you, Mr John Tasker.'

Who cared how he and Baybe left? I had closed my mind's-eye to them.

176

They should've been made to sit through 'Separate Tables' with David Niven and Deborah Kerr in the original 1958 print with my personal favourite being Burt Lancaster. And, if that didn't improve their sympathy quotients, they shouldn't have been allowed to live past the ending when the neurotic daughter decides to defy her mother and talk to Major Pollock.

Bon voyage, Inspector Charles Bloody-fucking-hell-sorry Ekanayake. May your plane develop Australian termites in its fuel lines and very high up.

'Their Lanka Now';

Okay, I'll buy thinking about that.

You know, about that not sort of being divorced from Rehana and sort of fibbing all that stuff to Father Thumbayaserni about it. It worries me with regards to another minor point that comes up, too.

Perhaps I shouldn't have told the good Father I'd never been baptised so I'm not really anything, let alone Roman Catholic.

It might make it a little more difficult for him to make the right decision and marry us in Church.

Surely, it's enough for me to gaze up at the Cross and feel the need for baptism as much as I do? The horror. I feel the bleeding. If I was Christ, it'd be good enough for me.

Here in Sri Lanka I have found the Christ where He feels most happy. Among the poor. He'll have to keep holding down the burgeoning GNP though. Over here and the exchange rate, don't tell me the Aussie dollar's shot to pieces!

But I have to find out whether they pass out certificates for baptism or not. Maybe I can get my brother to forge one.

If I don't get to know that for sure, how am I going to justify getting my brother to show himself?

Sisters Lima, Margaret, Sriyani, Camilla and Fathers Thumbayaserni and Jayakody -- not to mention my lovely old leper man Hansen whom you couldn't expect it from -- haven't thanked me for the work and the money I've put into Hansen House. They don't have to.

But the Sisters give me their strange little secretive smiles as I sail in and out past their poor-and-destitutes, and the good Fathers go on nodding and quietly clapping me on the shoulders.

My poor old Hansen still greets me at the door each morning and each afternoon when I arrive there for my usual stints. He is able to stand for quite long whiles now. The multi-drug therapy I paid to be flown in from Germany seems to be drying out his lower face and hands no end.

Not that they will ever do anything more than arrest the eating away. A face like a half-eaten pasty my Hansen would always have, and that pained me. Hands like two pieces of Hollywood special effects he would always have. In these, he has no feelings, due to the thickening of the peripheral nerves. I should manage him on the TV wrestling circuits. The Mauler from Gampola. They could beat the hell out of him and he wouldn't feel a thing. Hell, those hulks would break down and cry at the sight of him.

My poor Handsome Hansen. He gurgles at me, but we make good conversation. We touch a lot. I read the English papers to him. He doesn't understand a word, but he gurgles happily along while I do it. 1 feed him. It is like pushing food down the rubber inlet of a dish-washing machine. His eyes are watery with the efforts of swallowing. The thing is he is eating a few solids, sort of, rather than existing on warm tea and clumpless soups.

The warm teas of the good Sisters would eat away a cast-iron boiler.

For all of the patients, not just my Hansen, I clean, make the beds, make sure they get and do the basics, keep them in magazines with pictures. I boil up stinking broths of dirty

178

bandages and hang them out on the lines alongside of the poor shreds of the Sisters' women and children off the streets.

So many women, so many children.

The Sisters seem to know them all by name.

But then perhaps there aren't so many of them after all. I'm not talking about the lepers, but the street poor here. I'm getting pretty sure it's mostly the same ones coming in, getting softly spoken to, getting scrubbed and clean clothes and fed and promised they can stay until they are on their feet again, providing they pitch in a bit. They are so downcast and mangled-haired that it's hard to get a handle on their individual looks.

They leave just about the next day when I think of it. Then a week later, bruised and battered by either man or the monsoon... if I'm right about it being the same ones... they're there drooped near the main door again and painfully allow themselves and their children to be led back into Hansen House.

But I try to keep away from that destitutes' area as much as I can. That's the Mother Teresa stuff, not the leprosy to my mind. That's the hard road of charity, not just giving it as I do my lepers, but having to give it time after time when it is thrown back in your face time after time.

And for what?

Just so one part of it might stick, so you can say some part of all that work you put in on your fellow human beings has stuck. But it doesn't stick, except in so far as they walk out with thanks and wind up coming back in a few weeks without thanks. Hell's bells, the Sisters are worked so ragged, they're going to need their own charity.

I keep away from that destitutes' area when I can for another reason, too.

It just seems a bit close to the bone to me.

Oh, I can see myself as a leper. Maybe I've always been a leper of sorts in that mind's-eye of mine. But to be ditch-homed, drain-bound...

I couldn't face being that pitiable.

Tomorrow, and this is why I am thinking of the Sisters and such, we are sending my poor Hansen away to the capital Colombo for advanced treatment.

When he understood that he was finally going, he started doing that number of falling down before me at the door again. He cannot hold my hands enough. He runs his inner wrists up and down the sides of my face.

If he gets it into his head to kiss me, I'll throw up.

All this is because I happened to meet the right brother or something of the right man in the main Gampola mosque one Friday afternoon.

No, I am not having six-of-one, half-a-dozen of the other when it comes to the right connections in the hereafter. It's just that I like to get shot of my sandals occasionally and sit in the mosque for a bit of quiet from females. I don't mean that in any bad way, but it's nice to do it in a place where as a reason it doesn't need explaining.

It's the coolest spot in town anyway, with the breeze tingling off their little pool for your beetle crushers, and the tiles on the floor and walls. Soft pink and creams. Somewhat feminine, ironically. The Muslims don't mind me being there. Amazingly, I've found they have a long acceptance that goes beyond patience. A bit stern, perhaps. Something like the Founding Fathers would have been if you'd been around Virginia in the early 1600s and kept away from witch hunts, but look where that got America.

I knew Joe from over a few bottles of arrack here and there. I think he must be the only Muslim in town who drinks enough to drown a duck, and defiantly openly, and hardly ever goes to prayers. So, I took it providentially that I met him in the atrium of the mosque, and found out he was there because his eldest brother was back from the UK on a holiday back to his native home.

And what did the brother do?

He was a plastic surgeon, of course.

He was a darkly handsome man, with alabaster skin and gossamer black hair. Not large. What they call trim. They must do stretching or diminishing exercises in order to be able to walk trimly up and down Harley Street.

He turned to me after examining Hansen.

Of course, something could be done, perhaps in two sittings, and of course he'd have a go at it while he was here, bearing in mind Mother Teresa practises her good work up near where the Muslim part of the world really begins (I presume he knew she was in Calcutta and left it at that). He was going down to Colombo the next day to see his wife's family and, of course, providing the hospital he well, sort of, partly owned had the theatre free, would, say, a week from today be all right?

Of course.

Would I guarantee the necessary spondulicks; special rates, of course.

Of course.

He took another look at Hansen's face and: 'No need to bring a toothbrush, of course,' and presumably laughed his way out back into his annual Sri Lankan holiday.

It was at that time, too, that Father Thumbayaserni blessed me. I would not kid you. As we were getting up from Hansen's bedside, he put a hand on my shoulder again and held me there. He stood over me and solemnly made the sign of the Cross. And he said: 'John, if you do not watch out, you might fall into grace.'

I hope that didn't mean I'd have to go to confession.

I'd hate to have to lie during confession.

But to get the money for the operation, I had to get more telegraphically transferred urgently. There was nothing else for it. It was a gamble I just had to take. I was well aware that all foreign currency brought into the country is registered, and therefore another avenue by which Inspector Charles could come to know I was back in Sri Lanka. And where else but back to this district?

181

The other thing is, with that Inspector Charles nosing around the area and if I can't get a line on my father soon, Father Thumbayaserni will be a little off the mark.

Grace won't be the only thing I'll fall into. It might be otherwise called the boob.

Item. 'Family.'

I'll give me family for thinking about 'family'.

They call it of a bacilliferous family, leprosy. They shouldn't even put energy into calling those scaly, fungus-faced, scrawny-dicked germs something as mellifluous as bacilliferous.

Doc Hansen was only thirty years old when he discovered the rotten little fungus-faced, scrawny-dicked turds swimming around in spittle as merrily as the Inspector's three-year-old kid in the Canberra Inn's swimming pool's deep end that time.

For two-and-a-half thousand years, those scaly little buggers had been gold medallists of gob and spittle.

I'm only guessing two-and-a-half thousand years, as well.

And talking of gold medals -- and I'm thinking here of the whining of it -- I didn't do that Rehana Ramaswarmy of a second wife full justice.

Her other string to the bow was that she was also the archdeaconess of starch.

What can I tell you? She took starching things to a new height of the concrete. She starched sheets, pillowcases, shirts, singlets, socks, all her own outer and inner gumpfs as far as I wanted to see, towels, table cloths, my ties, my handkerchiefs, my drip-dries including those intimate, curtains.

She starched the cleaning rags.

You try wearing starched underps, socks and singlets and tell me that nine months with her wasn't a long enough marriage trial. It wasn't a trial of being in metaphoric stitches; I *was* in stitches. Most of the time I remember, I wore stitches.

182

You might be thinking now he's becoming nit-picking. But all that starching became a big gripe with for me. If I was Rehana, a big, big whine.

It wasn't only the clothes.

There wasn't one night, whenever she had a night when she got around to do some cooking, that she did not dish up mashed potatoes.

Some domestic-science teacher at Lauriston High School must have mentioned that mashed potatoes had plenty of starch in them.

She said she served mashed potatoes because they kept clean and didn't need special folding.

You think I'm trying to pull your leg?

The washing machine got more concrete-mixer miles on it than the television she never turned off. I looked in that washing machine one day. It was all blanched inside. It had become enstarched. It looked sicker than the Great Barrier Reef under a load of crowns-of-thorns.

So, I rang her family in Melbourne, because, in marriage, so they say, you have to at least try, right? And I had a genuine grievance. Papa Ramaswarmy had lumbered me with this lemon and hadn't ever come through with the $100,000 dowry like I had had to come through with the $10,000 broker's fee to Neila. In advance.

I shouted at Papa Ramaswarmy, 'Alright, you want, call it compensation not dowry!'

But he still didn't pay up.

That phone call, I first got through to brother-in-law Joycie, just after he had started to make a few air waves about being the spokesman for that Transnational Government of Tamil Eelam cause, or self-profiting fund-raising ruse, or whatever. When he deigned to come on the line, it seemed only courtesy to comment on something topical.

'I notice,' I put in knowledgably, 'that a couple of your charming boys in Chennai beat an old flower lady to death in broad daylight because she accidentally spilt some water on the photograph of your dearly-departed leader when they bumped into her.'

'Carrying a what, cob?'

'A photo of your dearly-departed leader, bullet through his third eye, like.'

He didn't even have to pause. This guy was good.

'Oh, I can explain that, cob. It could never happen again in a million years.'

'Why's that?'

'There's only two photographs of him in existence where he'd be recognisable. We don't like to spill the beans, we don't.'

I was hoping Appa Ramaswarmy might be a little more up to the mark, so went at him when *he* deigned to come on the line to me, but all he started in with was:

'Starch, you great big dork? My baby's star-studded, not starched, stone the crows that are flamin'. For you, isn't it?, I have been star-studding her hair, her ears, her nose and feet? You should have seen her once upon a time; she was spit. Have I not even being star-studding even her belly button for you, you drong? Starched? Star-sapphired, ya mug.'

I could see that probably her mother doing their underwear like she was doing mine was the reason those Ramaswarmys walked around with the dignity of ducks.

Two wives in two years and all I had to show for it were lost-causes bunions from the first and starch boils from the second.

Don't tell me about 'family'.

They tried to start more families, too, the upland elephants, but you can easily see where they went wrong.

The basic family unit comprised a couple of cows and their young 'uns. So far, so good if you got that through your head.

The bulls aren't allowed into this unit. They are given the old heave-ho when they get to graduate to be young bulls. Not that they would wait for an invitation when the cows got into oestrum; they'd just get right in there among the family unit and start playing pyramids. So far, so good, too.

The bulls' family was the wider clan. They wouldn't know what a clan was, but clans they were in. A clan might consist of two, three, four herds and some outer groups of males, and even a loner or two wandering around the fringes.

So, all right. Nothing much wrong with so-far-so-good there, either.

The trouble began right at the natural-selection start. Leaving the herds to the females only made the structure matriarchal.

You put that sort of power in female hands and see how quickly they start sighing and dying on you when the going gets tough.

Major trophy-hanger Major T. W. Rogers, with his bag of thousands, was just shooting at a large fundamental flaw in their character.

I give the basic structure of an elephant's family as a metaphor of me.

If I was an elephant, Major T. W. Rogers would have shot me. Probably wouldn't have even bothered getting off his planter's chair on the old veranda to do so.

Back in Australia, and the fact was it wasn't much of a compliment to have my tin-shed-as-house blown up beneath me and nobody take a blind bit of notice was much the same.

But now I see I'm back in Canberra. Okay. Make it an insert-item.

And despite the alarums of Ekanayake and that Baybe about the sociopathy of my brother, I did decide to return to work. I figured I might as well be licking the wounds in front of bloody Tilly who would at least enjoy the sight, and keep my remaining sick leave due to going all catatonic on Johnno for days off when I was well enough... meaning not so bombed-out concussed... to enjoy them.

In the public service, they appreciate that. You can't be bringing too much contagion into work if you are still thinking

185

as logically as that, quite apart from demonstrating a mind that was thinking ahead.

Even Johnno displayed extreme sympathy for me. He didn't let me into his office, but jumped up quickly and cut me off at the door to it.

He declared with an avuncular concern that anything I would want, anything I felt I needed to do, was perfectly fine by him, providing I returned to the troops and never tried to enter his office again until I had a doctor's letter to say I was over the catatonic black-plague stage.

Bloody Tilly was sitting at her desk staring at her spreadsheet, her hands clasped in her spread lap, maybe attempting to look beatific, as if the news of my catatonia had worked its way around to her as being a marvellous idea. She had on the pink sleeveless shift, the second of the two dresses she had ever worn in the two years.

When she saw me re-enter, she looked up in the manner that the appearance of a blood-spun apparition might effect, sighed, and dropped her head onto the desk with a self-mortification that made me wince.

I hurried to her, registering someone somewhere calling over to her: 'Here he is, Till. You'll be all right now.'

As soon as I got within range, her rubbery upper arms rocketed out to grab me, avaricious as a magnetic device that's found a magnet, to haul me close with a clutch that would only be reserved for those drowning at sea. Her voice suddenly took on the energy she usually reserved for sarcasm; it lit the whole section up to listen, going:

'Goes away and stays away, doesn't he? Do I get a card or anything? I do not. Then he thinks he can just waltz back in to someone's life as though nothing has happened.'

I think I heard clucks of disapproval from those piss-ant colleagues of mine; but those hardly dug their nails in because now she had my hand, the back of it, against her lips, and those lips were going:

'I love you, you fool. I want to do right by you.'

186

'Your marriage, Tilly,' I begged to mention.

'See,' now she was playing to the claque for the piteous thing of it all, 'the callousness that I have to put up with?'

'Where's your,' a little sympathy of my own for the demented needed here, 'husband, Tilly?'

'I have to boot my husband out of his own home because of him and the kids won't even show how pleased he is for me.'

At least her tears upon my hand were lubrication enough for me to be able to slither out of her clutches and retreat to my desk, from which sanctuary I had to hear a multitude of shames which 'Pull your socks up, Tasker' would just about summarise without the invective.

And bloody Tilly not leaving well alone, going even before I could get seated:

'I will not say a word more', and announced with a huge moral superiority, 'until he corrects this terrible predicament he has put me and my husband and poor little defenceless children into.'

You could say this much for her: she was always as good as her word. Oh, she would come to answer the phone, since that was her duty, but would not speak into it, and would replace the receiver when the caller got to realise he was calling the public service and hadn't done too badly at all by getting that far. Quit while ahead/

And I was doing quite nicely in that utter, blessed, total and irrevocable Tilly glumness, until the tenth of the last ten working days I will probably ever have, in which I insisted on coming into the office and greeting her surly silence with my own tortoise-shell back to insults far and wide.

It was on that tenth morning, rather late in its morning if I don't stand corrected, I heard Tilly break her vow disapproval at my rejection with a loud petulance that was the epitome of a cautionary note:

'He's not seeing anyone until he's made the right decision!'

I looked up slowly, dreading to think who it might be, and was somewhat startled to find Neila's one-legged and apparently new other-half standing fretfully before my desk. A bit on the slant but understandably.

Boardshorts looked as rough as I had ever seen him. Over his missing leg, the kaleidoscope of the American flag hung in folded limpness. On the other leg, the shorts were hoisted up to crutch-level. He looked as bedraggled as he ever would have bombed out on a dumper. His grey-streaked hair was stuck about his cranium in greasy strands, just as if the brine had claimed him for its depths. The T-shirt, with its iridescent 'Aloha', seemed to have shrunk miserably over his hunched shoulders.

Except for the crooked grin on his face, he looked the picture of misery.

Here we had the only child of the Governor-General of Australia. Still Elect, so maybe Poseidon fashioned our leaders from seaweed.

That would explain a lot.

I hope I was looking urbane. I wasn't feeling it. This could only be about Neila and that could only mean those damn photographs I had decided to forget all about lying to her about having destroyed them.

I mean, looking back, those pictures constituted the one track my brother had not covered. The one track I had not covered for him.

It would take bad-penny Neila to turn up again to rake them up again.

And despite his miserable sight, Broadshort's grin widened and he actually giggled. Then he slid a chair around to the side of my desk, and reached across to hold the bottom of my tie in two trembling fingers. I had the mad thought he thought it was his board's ankle strap between us which, given the rough going, would be madness to let go. Still, his eyes were bloodshot. He looked terrible. But again, he sniggered or giggled or whatever, while he hissed:

188

'Neila...'

He obviously wanted to go on but equally as obviously couldn't finish what he wanted to say. He choked on a gurgling chuckle or a chuckling gurgle if it was more like that, as though he had copped a mouthful of wave.

'Neila who?', I lied fast and freely.

'She's bad, man. Really bad.'

Now he was tugging on my tie like I was the R-and-R patient in a surf carnival. This was getting unnerving. I could only commiserate with him having gone through Neila myself:

'I know she's bad. Bloody terrible actually.'

'No, man, bad *hurt*. Help me!'

And he tugged and tugged on what might well actually turn up to be a surfboard's ankle strap, until I got to my feet. He tugged me across the room, snickering me away, past bloody Tilly, who was also snickering away even more.

For a start, I was eloigned from my only paying livelihood.

In his car on the way to somewhere, he kept snorting with a sort of ribald rhythm, which finally got on my nerves.

'Shissakes, will you stop laughing?'

'Who's laughing, man?', he sobbed between a chortle and a sigh, or vice versa.

And there weren't any guards on the gate of the Governor-General-Elect's residence, and this surprised me because it was silly to think guards only turned up when Neila was running around in a see-through housecoat in the middle of the day. Remember? Anyway, to the lack of security of this time, I raised an eyebrow at just being able to drive through open gates of an official residence, kinda, and Boardshorts giggled that they were all away on holiday at the --where else for Camefors? -- beach villa in Batemans Bay.

Neila, he chokingly said, had received some phone call and had jumped in her car and left. That was yesterday. Today, he had hopped it back here -- I presumed he was speaking figuratively -- to find out where she was.

I, too, found where she was.

She was in the swimming pool out back on the surfboard.

The trouble was the poor love was on the wrong side of the surfboard.

More particularly, she was bound arms, waist and legs to the wrong side of the surfboard.

Whether they had launched her topside up, knowing that she would eventually upset it by struggling, or whether they just flopped her in upside down like that, didn't matter a real lot. As she always said about the lost causes she took to her bed and thereabouts: 'Hey, you always end up the same way'.

She and the board were nudging gently against the side of the shallow end, otherwise only as deep as her mid-thighs and otherwise a finger grip to life. But with no way of standing against the board's buoyancy and no finger loose to gain a purchase that would have been small consolation.

Neila. That was no way for her to go.

My poor lost cause. A surfboard in a swimming pool, and the shallow end at that.

Her head hung down in the water, hair strewn across her features, as though it itself was tied to an invisible anchor. Her struggles, if I may say from this distance of time, had been washed away. There was not a ripple on the surface, and the swirling reflections from the bottom of the pool seem to sway her into lolling around in a lazy, lullabying rhythm.

Some of the photographs floated near her, too. The laziness of their drifts gave to them a slow motion, such as Neila and the various SLA guys she was romping within them were in no hurry to complete their entanglements and shorten their shame.

What I took to be the rest of the photographs were stuck around the poolside like Pompeian tiles. They must have landed in the wetness of the struggle or had been blown from one of the tables.

If they were Pompeian tiles, it would have been a sad frieze.

Boardshorts himself had dropped down onto the edge of the pool, his one leg dangling in the water, as if he was fishing for a nibble from her. His demonical giggling had blessedly stopped by now. The man was weeping into his own swimming pool.

Me? I have to confess that it was as though I was on a movie set. I felt no pity whatsoever. I seemed to be outside my body and could feel that this might be a pitiable scene if I didn't feel so completely opposite. The fact was I felt businesslike, as if I'd been there and done this. It was therefore no surprise to me to feel it was my brother's voice in my mind's-eye again, rising up from his violent alley, calming me, entering for a job to be done by the Tasker boys.

And I felt the power in his volatility once more, and how different he was from me. Appa Ramaswarmy had told me to go back to my civilian life, and I knew then what he had meant. He was comparing me to the wild side of my brother. The alias. The Tusker. The great teeth, the ivory gorers.

These, I heard my twin say about the madnesses I felt about him, are what you have to have, or you don't bother leaving the buffer of your desk.

I felt unbewildered by violence, the power of being accustomed to making a decision before it, in spite of it, against it, for more of it.

It was frankly exhilarating.

I stripped down not too hurriedly and slipped into the pool. My brother could tell me why Boardshorts had sought my help, too, as the unlikely first order of things. Ex-husband, lawyer, perhaps the only friend Neila had. Perhaps, too, because she might've been the only friend *I* had. Certainly because, overall, he knew this couldn't be a police matter, no straight off.

And whether he was thinking of his Governor-General of a father or Neila, for the love of her, I wouldn't know. What

191

was sure, he had the nous to know he didn't want the scandal. It wasn't so much the murder of his darling-or-otherwise wife. It was the photographs with the murder of his darling-or-otherwise wife. It was being the son of his top-grade father.

I'll give him genuine motives around caring, but these things I was sure of. Why would he come and drag me out of the office otherwise?

And I was thinking, as I gently peeled the photographs off the meniscus of the water and waded gently back to the poolside with them that, finding your wife strapped to your lost-cause obsession surrounded by dirty-linen images of her with others, some very compromising, that it might well be enough to make you want to be laughing with Neila's sense of the ironical right then. Maybe that would explain his chuckling type of gagging-gurgling too.

I waded back to the surfboard. It seemed to want to buck away from me and only allowed itself to be pulled in as if I was the first suction of the next coming wave.

I tried to untie the poor love but the water gripped the knots too tightly. Finally, I worked the ropes forward to the pointy end; not easy when the torso of Neila started to swing free after I managed to get her arms uncoupled.

There seemed now to be no dignified way I could balance her to stay in union with the board and get the rope that was around her knees to slide down over the front of the board too.

Boardshorts was no help. His mock turtle weeping or giggling or whatever it was had turned into a repeated sniffle, but he stayed helplessly where he was, glued on watching me struggle with her, as though I was trying to demonstrate to him some new surfing manoeuvre.

Excuse me, Neila pie; the only way I could manage it without his help was to jump astride the very toe of the board and make it sink like the last moments of the Titanic. This pinned her head rudely against the bottom of the pool. It might have been an insult added to the injury, but at least it gave a

192

slope downward by which I could work the last rope over the bulbed middles of her and the board.

From then it was all restoration of dignity for Neila. The ropes slid from her body. I threw them onto the poolside, and gave the board a push towards the deep end where it belonged seemed fitted.

Neila herself seemed reluctant to leave indignity behind. She neither wanted to float nor to sink to the bottom, but to remain suspended in between. In my giving the board that irritated shove, she was also evidently more of a mind to shoot off in the other direction. I managed to grab her by the ankle just as her head was about to collide with the wall and to hail her back. The rest, so to say, was easy. I mean, it was very easy. It wasn't that I was enjoying it; it was just that I seemed to be going about a business I just knew instinctively how to do very well. My brother and mind's-eye mounted, I have no doubt.

And so, I managed to hoist her to the surface as one would hold up a baby to be taken for christening and examined her for rope burns. I didn't expect any and had no idea why I bothered. It was like I was going through a well-worn routine.

And then, instead of trying to land her on the side, I found myself walking her out to where the deep end began, like a child I was trying to teach to float little by little. And there, I gave her an underwater shove to send her on her deepwater way.

No, I did.

I launched my Neila out of my life, God help me.

I then re-emerged to confront Boardshorts with the ropes and the pile of photographs, and heaved him by the T-shirt collar up into one of those very solid white plastic poolside chair only the well-off have. He sank into it a miserable snivelling heap. I forced one of my knuckles into his temple so that he would listen. For the ropes, fellah, throw them into the dankest corner of the garage you can find. For the photographs, did he have a barbecue? Then burn them all now, and I mean now and I mean all.

He understood and stood. He was surprisingly nimble on his one leg, could balance immediately and seemed like a one-legged seagull as he quite adroitly moved forward purposefully without a cane to do what he'd been told.

Here's what else I'm sure I told him. He wouldn't have to spin many lies to the police. All it needed was: he had had no idea why his wife wanted to return home on her own from the beachsider at Batemans Bay. When he got worried not hearing from her, he called for help from his good friend Johnny Tasker. We had a few laughs in the office, and a few laughs in the car. He never dreamt we would find her just where you see her now, give or take a few circles of the pool maybe... or maybe not since she couldn't swim for nuts.

But before I went inside to telephone Martin Baybe, the Australian Crimes Commission character who had come out to my place with our returned-home Inspector Charles, there was something I should know as his longtime buddy and first friend he would call on:

'You think you'd like to tell me your moniker?'

He looked at me reproachfully and with inbred Camefors pity-the-poor at the same time:

'I'm the up'n'coming Governor-General's son.'

'I know that.'

'Well, what did you want to know exactly?', he went, genuinely confused.

Jesus.

'Maybe as surfing buddies or whatever we are, you could try a Christian name.'

'Marvin.'

Marvin. With a lost-cause name like that, no wonder poor Neila's knees went to jelly at the sight'n'sound of him.

'You got a thing about being a board rider, Marvin?'

'I have', he said proudly and very inappropriately given the situation by that swimming pool.

194

'Okay, Marvin, you just do what I've told you and you'll be around to day-dream again one day, you'll see.'

'No day-dream. I meant I was. Junior World titles in 81, 82, 83.'

I stopped to take another look at him. That was achievement. And I could see in his eyes that he had been up there at the top and had had the grit, in his own metier, to stay there. A bit humbled, I could only nod a question towards his missing leg. He was not maudlin at all... Neila might have just been off taking a quick dip... but simple-fact in his reply:

'Shark.'

'Jesus.'

'Jesus in the form of a shark.'

Neila had picked a good one, after all. The lady had been genuinely on her way to respectability. Whoever had done this to her had cut short one of the great reforms of all time. Respectability, her innateness for lost causes, a bit of afternoon naughtiness on the side, and, as the full-on Governor-General's consort, she might have become the American-Australian answer to what ails us.

There I was sinking deeper into criminality, and all around me everybody else was working their ways up towards horizons of probity. Terrific.

I wait around to watch Marvin turn the photographs to burnt sausages. I could see him through the french windows while I phoned for Martin Baybe at the ACC in Sydney. I was told by an adenoidal voice which hadn't exactly been put on this earth to exploit technology to its fullest, that I should ring the following Canberra number. The guy was still in Canberra. Then was told immediately to belay that. Belay it. The ACC must have sunk to the bottom of the recruitment barrel and gone in for off-the-hook Wrens. So, it was belayed for me, until I was finally commanded, in a way that made it clear that I was unauthorised to be making this call from any traceable number, to give my number and just belay it where I was.

I belayed it as I was told. I needed to belay it only five minutes watching a bonfire of pornography concerning Neila and incriminating association concerning my brother before Baybe returned the call. As a sworn lifelong friend of Marvin, the son of the Governor-General to-be, I told him about finding his wife at the bottom of their pool.

Detective-sergeant jolly-old Baybe arrived alone in a surprisingly discreet white Toyota. If Neila deserved a bit of fuss, I had picked the wrong man to ring. He wasn't exactly yawning, but he squatted like a contented toad at the poolside while Marvin hopped around him like the same disabled seagull and told him pretty much down pat our agreed story. Even from the living room, to which as an innocent friend of the family I had withdrawn, I could see Baybe's scalp shifting back and forth with annoyance. He obviously wasn't a man who believed in simple lies being treated simply.

At the completion of Boardshorts tale of woe, Baybe nodded, then clicked his heels together in a strange confirmation of that's-it-then. Suddenly he had the agility of a now-jumping toad and scrawled notes with a flourish that could only be fitting ten words to the page of his notebook.

All through Marvin's talk, he had been eyeing poor Neila in there as one would a gold fish in a ceremonial pool. Now, finished apparently with the notebook, he clapped down on Marvin's shoulder by way of concluding with him and turned to come in to me. He didn't seem or care to notice at all that he had clapped the poor fellow on the shoulder above his missing leg and had collapsed him to the decking like a sand hill.

'That tawny Inspector matey, matey, was right,' he announced unceremoniously as soon as he came through the french windows, 'you are definitely a piece of walking chaos.'

'My dear friend's wife is out there in a position she would no way want to prolong for chrissakes, Baybe, and you're on about *me*?'

'She always swim in the nude?'

196

'Get your mind off that, will you? But, if you must know, a little menstruation never bothered her.'

He settled himself in an easy chair and casually surveyed the room. His eyebrows gave it the thumbs up as not half bad at all. He had one leg slung over the side of the chair; one arm crooked over its head rest. He looked like he had changed his suit but had persisted in skew-whiffing the same shirt and tie as he had on at my property a week ago. 'You don't,' he finally got up the jolliness to put out: 'You two don't expect me to believe that claptrap he told me, do you?'

Fortunately for that shirt and tie of his, he had chosen the easy chair by the phone and didn't have to ruckle them further when, in the face of my refusal to even answer that, he called in the troops. I was surprised how he did so with such an easy confidence from his usual facetiousness. I could see he had his mental compartments too, like Inspector Charles, like my brother. He was obviously part of the big league I was flirting with. He had, he told the phone, what would be a DOA for them with an excess consumption of chlorinated water; nothing much for anybody but better bring in a few cars, ambulance, whoever's on duty at the coroner's. He had the statement. Didn't seem they needed to kick up too much dust around the Governor-General feet, even if it was tempting to. Try to keep the sirens down; keep it low low-key. Keep off the two-way.

'Been meaning to have a little pow-wow with you, matey,' he crooned to me as he put the phone down. 'Helpful this happened.'

'Neila was always obliging.'

I tried to kick back with the caustic but Baybe was either above it or contentedly beneath it: 'So the word goes.'

'That mean?'

I couldn't pass up the only occasion I ever had of defending Neila's virtue, and had put as much outrage as I could into jutting my jaw out at the fellow.

'Am I talking to gimpy's lawyer, now?'

197

'It shouldn't come down to him needing a lawyer. Forget the 'gimpy' shit too, Baybe. I'm an old friend.'

'Sure, and look where that's got him.' I didn't deign to reply. 'Rang your office and got some female who said, until you saw sense, you were locked out and she wasn't talking to me. You all strange in that legal beehive?'

'We call it weird, but you'd have to be in the know. Anyway, what did you want?'

He didn't answer immediately but, instead, got up and took down an impressive silver trophy from a lot of other trophies in a display cabinet. I could see now it was one of Marvin's teenage surfing championships. Curious how I didn't notice it or the other with it them when I was here last month with Neila. Had to say something for that housecoat of hers.

Baybe returned to the chair with it, inspected it musedly, and did not say a word for all that time until the men in plainclothes and the men in uniform and the men in white and the coroner's man with the white overalls and cameras began to appear, as on a video screen we were watching through the french windows. In their silent show, they went about their businesses. A quick look of appraisal and then roping off the pool area. Usual procedures followed. I watched while two detectives began their preliminary perusal of the scene; they lingered halfway along the pool where Neila must have been floating by then and would have been less than human if they weren't adding curiosity to their eyefuls of her nudity.

Show woman to the last was my Neila.

I was somehow proud of her. Even in Baybe's presence:

'So, matey, tell me about this brother of yours, that Inspector kept calling Tusker just to annoy you.'

I was cool. I was still amazing myself with my brother's mind's-eye accustomness of being able to handle any, and more, of all this.

'Tusker. A name, an alias. Inspector Ekanayake showed me a few charge sheets. One had this alias Tusker. Nothing to do with me, why should it? Something in his Sri Lankan head. Might be all the elephants. They affect you, you know.'

He nodded, and with pleasure too.

'So, the Inspector drops the Tusker sheet in your lap. You're right in respect of that. As a shock tactic, a bit of a joke. He saw some reaction and took a note of it. More of a whiff in the nose, I think. Maybe even elephant shit, like you say. Personally, I don't go on whiffs in the nose like that. Wouldn't know elephant shit from my dog's.'

He stood and returned the trophy to the cabinet. We were both taking our time.

That was fine by me. Nobody should live past the superb timing of Edward G. Robinson and the silences of sheer bloody-mindedness he brought to the silver screen. You take his Rico in 'Little Caesar' or his Rocco in 'Key Largo'. I wasn't alive in 1931 and too young in 1948 to see them, but if I wasn't I would've been in the front stalls with my feet up on the seat in front, you betcha.

Behind Baybe, as I contemplated telling him about Edward G. Robinson, the camera people had moved in. Two of them, looking like the sorcerer and his apprentice, were taking plenty of shots of Neila's nakedness. Baybe was seated again and strapped down to speak again with that irritating superciliousness:

'I erased old Eka's report about your reaction from the files. Who cares what's a whiff of elephant dung and what's not a whiff? In respect of that, you can take it you owe me a favour.'

And I felt my brother's pleasure at being able to play, not by instinct but by knowing, the games of men like Baybe. In their world, 'favour' didn't rate a reply. Baybe nodded with almost appreciation for my professionalism.

'Awkward for your mother. Mixing with the natives like that.' I could feel the hardness come into my eyes from, oh sure, my brother's eyes. But this guy wasn't stopping: 'Something about you, matey, jumped out of two different set

199

of loins on the ethnic scale, so to speak, always hanging around with your father's native crowd. So, let's say this Tusker isn't your bro, but became near and dear to you. Maybe you're thinking of some boy of the village who covered for Mummsy's hanky-panky and is owed an everlasting debt in respect of it. What say?'

The feeling that Baybe was going to die then and there for mentioning what he shouldn't only slowly, very slowly, subsided in me. I didn't even want it to.

Baybe seemed to wait for it to, then spread open his arms like a redeemer now ready to start redeeming:

'So, who's Tusker, matey? I need to know what I dealing with in respect of all this.... unexpected stuff like drowning and boom-booming going on.'

They were trying to fish Neila out without getting wet by using the pool scoop. When they did manage to get some part of her in its frail net, she made the handle bow hopelessly before she seemed to get irritated and floated away. Gradually, though, the agitation of the water got her pool-side and into a wrist lock and an ankle loch and an old heave-ho.

I hoped her out-of-body experience was over; it'd be no fun watching herself being scooped out like an overnight leaf.

'Okay,' Baybe was continuing, 'your way, matey. Just that, if I were you, I'd be starting to give that brother of yours or that Tusker a few warning signals.'

'Why would that be?'

'We wouldn't want this Tamil question thing getting like AIDS before anybody's immuned to it. Australia's small fry, like that poor sheila out there.' Neila would have hated the way he cocked his thumb over his shoulder towards her. 'We intend to keep it like that. So, you tell this bro or Tusker that he's now a nasty chap to his own mob, in respect of that. That bomb. Now this. I don't know him, but if I was close I'd be worrying about him, matey mine.'

200

If he cocked his fingers at her one more time, she'd come back from the dead and, when she returned, she would be wearing garters made from his guts.

'I'd say anyone like you're describing would have worked all that out for himself.'

'You betcha. And who was really pointing the bone at him? Well, you tell him it's nobody around Canberra here and tell him good. So no more five-man pile-ups on my doorstep, ever.'

It was a warning, but incredibly he seemed to be on our side:

'Mad keen on yachts, you or him?

Now this was annoying. I didn't like these loaded hints I couldn't understand. Nor the way they were now so roughly examining Neila, nor the way Marvin was weeping and giggling or both again.

'The Inspector got to rave on about yachts, too.'

'Hire yachts in the name of Tasker all around Southeast Asia, do you? Or is it this Tusker? Grape vines, matey. So we paid for the Inspector to go home via Hong Kong. In respect of that, I see you're a wee surprised. Word all over the place has it these yachts aren't for the joy of the lonely sea and the sky, but for cruising where they know where to pick up naughty packages from the sea. Could be this Tusker character doesn't know everybody suddenly seems to know his business. Know his arse from his elbow, does he?'

That my brother was now being set up. Understood.

'Don't you love it when thieves fall out?', Baybe twisted the knife with.

'If I knew him, why would you be telling him this?'

He made the skin of his scalp move with impatience again, just as they were covering Neila's stretcher with a heavy blue plastic. I regretted ever telling her she was just a lump.

'Now, don't go shirty, matey. In respect of that, old nose-whiffing Ekanayake's already got up to your old estate.

Sketchy after so long, he faxes, but your Dad's been a bit of a villain too. He's wanted as well. His alias is 'Aetha'; am I wrong? Old Eke tells me 'Aetha' is the local lingo for elephant with tusks, right? Tusker. So over there, Daddy is Tusker. Down here is Tusker. You're Tasker. All a bit strange and foreign for the likes of us Aussies. French stock me; a bit thick.'

I didn't know how I was looking at him now. My father. Still alive, and trackable. The old estate. My mother sighing and dying. This Detective-sergeant Baybe smirking over it all. He had the audacity of breathing on me; his ember eyes hot; his scalp twitching back and forth.

I wanted to tear him apart bit by bit. But I also felt sick and vertiginous. Still, I felt my brother barely holding me back from him, or was I barely holding him back?

I have to tell you, either way. Martin Baybe was in very real danger of dying right there and then. I don't know how, but he was.

'You tell him down here we like to keep it all unstrange and unforeign and you tell him: no more shenanigans not-around-here. See you, Mr Tasker. Don't get your ivories knocked out.'

I should have been more alert and told him to tell this Tusker character all that, not me. But Baybe had gone.

And the plain truth was that I knew where I was going, too.

And the plain truth was that I knew where my brother was going, as well.

Me, I was going to get to my father before Ekanayake did.

Tusker would have to look after himself -- first in Melbourne, and then in Hong Kong.

But my father.

But my father had a reckoning to me before he had any reckoning to any Sri Lankan Tamils.

Still alive and he had spat me out like I should never have been born in the first place.

1 think I smashed Marvin's trophy cabinet before I left. Yes, I think I am sure I did.

They used to think elephants that rocked their heads up and down, to and from, and swung their bodies to some internal rhythm were neurotic and would probably become man killers.

They still think it. Why not? They're probably right. They're only supposed to do that when they're in heat. The elephants not the human 'they'.

An elephant doing that goes to show that the elephant is not all lovely and lovable beast.

The ones that keep carrying sticks, or want to suck on stones constantly, they're not likely to be the full dollar, either.

I'm not only talking about the tuskers, either. You get your aggressive tush elephant, the one that doesn't have tusks as such... well, short tusks but no pulp inside them... it's still has plenty to do you in with, and he or she will throw a tusker-type tantrum now and then, too. You'd think a fight between a tusker and a tush would be an uneven fight, but old tush ain't always mush.

Tush can charge and smash heads just as effectively. If tush can beat tusker to the punch and get in close without being gored, he'll get under the tusks and push upwards against the curve of the tusks. The tusks are curved upwards so that the animal can lower its head and use them against great weights by shoving forward or hooking them under whatever it is and heaving upwards. The upward curve's probably mainly been developed in order to resist breaking better. The tusker can never push down on anything, not really. It never tries to push anything over, by throwing its head back and shoving; it always lowers its head and uses its forehead.

So, this fellow tush gets in under tusker's guard and heaves upwards against the tusks. If it can get tusker's head back and keep it locked in close like any good fighter with inferior reach, then more often than not those tusks will snap like the pieces of bone they are.

Then, bingo, you've got a new herd-master and one less magnificent tusker. And there's might not even be a poacher in sight.

They also used to say an elephant cries like a baby when it's done something wrong. Like tread all over some human being who found his or her way under those cloppers of it. Poor loveable giants, shedding tears of remorse for how it can flatten you. What a shame for it.

Not tears, though.

No way near tears.

This is musth calling.

What musth is, is an oily discharge secreted by the temporal glands, situated in the temporal hollow which is that dish-like dent between the ears and those neanderthal frontal ridges that any Australian politician needs to get ahead.

This oily muck only seems to come from the eyes because the glands are near the eyes and it streams down the cheek in weep-streams that keep the anthropomorphologists happy.

Both bulls and cows get musth. Mostly they get musth when he's got the hots or she's got the itches. He's on heat and she's in oestrum.

They used to say the only reason musth flowed was because of the hots. Don't be fooled, though. They can get musth substitute when they're not even interested in rooty tooty.

The only conclusion you can make from that is that elephants get to musth when they just plain get the shits about something.

Any damn fool knows you keep well away when your dearly beloved elephant starts 'crying'. The mahouts will whip it away somewhere where it can't do much damage and normally try tying one of its back legs to the biggest tree they can find.

And any fool mahout knows, too, that you hoist not yourself upon said animal even when there's a hint, a soupcon of a doubt, that those cheeks aren't a nice healthy leathery texture.

So, you tell me, then, why my father put me upon that animal that day.

That Rajah. That biggest and finest.

The archduke of the whole herd.

Forget that he had some mahout up there with me. What did he say to the guy in Tamil or Sinhala? Take the little squirt for a quick whizz around the estate? Forget that, too. That animal was either in musth at the time or at least showing some of the greasy tell-tale signs, like swaying crazily or those rills down its greasy chops. Someone of my father's experience doesn't notice that?

Give me a break.

Did he see the great rills down those cheeks and those mad eyes and not give a diddly-squat about any of it or, worse, cast around to see if my mother was anywhere near so he could laugh her up there too and get both of us out of his hair in one fell swoop?

Some maintain you can never tell about what state an elephant's in with any accuracy. But I can tell you, you can tell even by the little rebellious jerks an animal gives beforehand. I don't care what way it is. That father of mine was supposed to be the top nut with elephants. There wasn't anything he wasn't supposed to know about aliya, elephants. He was supposed to be famous for it.

It seems to me now not to have been more than a few minutes down the estate track before the brute just dug in its heels and started to do a mock turtle even worse than poor Neila's Marvin-by-the-poolside.

You know what makes me think about this now?: because of some poor whacker with one leg sort of giggling or gurgling over Neila when he really meant to be bawling his eyes out, when I wasn't man enough to do either giggling or gurgling

205

over one of the world's great women and one of my only lifetime friends of a few minutes ago... and this was most probably due to remembering how I was told my father was still alive and kicking, and then realising how much I hated this native who dismissed me like I was a piece of fly shit on his sarong...

And because of my mother more likely never hearing even that bit of news, and because of the reckoning due to her, to my brother, to me from that heartless, that bastardful, that self-centred, that wicked shithead of a father of mine...

And because he tried to kill me on his biggest brute when I must have only been five or six years old. Yes, five or six years old.

That brute of a beast Rajah was a quivering mountain to a five- or six-year-old. You didn't have to be Einstein at the top of his game when he proposed $E=mc2$ in his wonder year of 1905 or an officer in the Bern patents office to realise you don't do that to a five- or six-year-old kid When my father and that mahout hoisted me up, I can remember thinking they were never going to stop hauling me towards the sky.

And it stopped dead in its tracks just at the edge of the estate where the gorge started down through the gallery paddy fields and the upland rainforest. And it would have had that rilling down those cheeks and a mad eye and would have been giving rebellious jerks an animal will give in musth just before it cracks.

And let me also tell you about that upland rainforest, because now I am seeing it in my mind's eye -- or my brother's mind's eye and I don't care -- for what it really was. Most of it had already been cut down for the great hardwoods. What had, and always will, come up in its place? I'll tell you: maybe something that looks a bit like rainforests to the eye of a dummy, but it's all really only the quick-growing species -- what they call the 'secondary' woody species: and that is just a euphemism mainly for the climbing vines.

206

How do these charming vines climb? I'll tell you that free, too. They mostly climb with thorns that are needle-sharp, knife-slicing, and they smother and entangle and woe betide you if you're stupid enough to try to bully your way through them. You will end up as shreds. You'll end up in a parlous state like some poor five- or six-year-old on the back of a crazed bull elephant.

That was what the rainforest around the estate really was, and getting back to this giant of a brute called Rajah, it refused to move any further.

At my back, the mahout started grunting away at it, started reaching around me and beating it on the crown of its head. He began to kick it behind the ears. He was prodding it with that ankus of his, that brute of a hook, digging it into the shoulders, hooking at the top part of the trunk and trying to pull the beast's head up.

Jamming me up there, the guy was hurting me more than the beast. But still that Rajah wouldn't move. It stood there terrifying silent, as silent as those rills that were running down its forehead and smelling of *male*.

What can I really remember from so long ago?

Plenty enough.

For one thing, the mahout was suddenly somehow not up there with me anymore, but down on the ground, way down there, crying up at the animal. I thought he might have been shouting at me because he was bleeding terribly from the temple for some reason I couldn't understand until I got to know what trunks can do.

And then he was gone.

I remember very clearly looking down at that mahout from that height, from Rajah's line of sight, and I can see him still. As a human, he didn't look so puny as much as craven, a gangly scuttler. That impression has never left me.

He also looked to be at the bottom of a ten-storey building.

I remember, too, doing the one thing that saved my life. I grabbed hold of that chain around the brute's neck -- my hands were so tiny I could only grip one side of the links -- and I held on for all the tea in Sri Lanka. And I might have been just in time.

I can still remember the frightening speed with which the bugger finally burst into action. One moment that deathly silent swaying, then next an exploding swirl to the right. I was flung upwards as if I was a matchstick. I held on. The chain held on to me. I was dangling behind its ear. My head was bouncing against its hide in numbing punches. Its great ear thrashing my back in a strangely evil rhythm.

Even today, I can smell the drenching heat from its body.

And then it suddenly stopped again. I don't know whether it had heard my screams. A slow swaying. The humming of its blood, its heart, beneath the skin at my ear. I scrambled back on top of it; what more could I do? The chain wouldn't let go of me anyway.

That chain wouldn't let me go.

And at the top of that gorge it seems to me now that I could see across the tops of the trees; so high, so far down, so far down below.

Then it started for real.

The beast ran straight at the bush and kept going. We hit that so- called rainforest, thick walls of cutting and jagging edges, and it ploughed us both straight through them all. I buried my face. I buried my face into its terrible hide. I felt my shirt tear. I felt my back becoming hot, then on fire.

We burst out into the gallery paddy fields only finally. From there my height above the valley floor was even more terrifying. At least we were free of the forest. It slowed. That Rajah did. The irrigation banks were crumbling just as terrifying beneath us and it stumbled, it seemed, in the mud.

That chain, that chain, it still wouldn't let me go.

Now it was grunting with rage at the mud but for all of that it seemed clever enough to be trying to keep to those crumbling levees and to zigzag with them down and down the mountain side.

About half way down it literally leapt one of the banks and cut straight into the forest again. Now was the real pain. My poor little body was just now plainly being whipped, flogged by all the world of fathers and grandparents. The thorns of the debased rainforest.

What could I know otherwise at that age?

I don't know how long that lasted in itself. Some time. Sometime. The animal got itself onto a track and then really went hell for leather again. I looked up once to see the earth opening up for me with a huge enveloping rush, rising to swallow. Terrifying. A boy, for Christ's sake. Five or six years old.

Yes, some time. Sometime. It just halted after some time.

And then that silence again, which I shall never forget either.

The humming of its heart. The steam from it.

Was it thinking? Did it have any thoughts at all? Was it even aware I was still on its back?

The chain, that chain, it held me with, yes. When I looked I could only see the blood of my hands welding me to it.

I lay back again and must have slept in the musth, the mustiness of the beast.

I think perhaps we moved a few times after that. Short bursts, charging phantoms, maybe monkeys or snakes. I wouldn't know for sure.

I think I fancy it charged my father and his men. It might've. I was too tired by then.

I had been up there ten hours.

A boy. Five or six years old.

I have to this day scars along my back and butt on which Neila used to love to trace famous American train journeys.

Some sightseeing, she used to say.

I have no top to the little finger of my right hand anymore.

On my left hand, the little finger will always now be bowed from the multiple breaking that chain gave it like the parody of fingers at a tea digit on the grounds of Buckingham Palace.

I woke as I was being carried in his arms. I see his biceps with their cording veins, the skin like dark molasses. I see the hairs on his chest, mulberry to the evening light.

I woke as we came back into the compound to hear my mother scream with fright.

I think I woke to hear my brother cry for the first and last time in his life. I pretty sure I really did, although if you told me it was, now, a memory of our entwining mind's eyes then I'd have to think about that too. What I do know it was as if he was crying within me, so bitterly was he doing so. So furiously. And I can still how he had his fists bunched in anger. He had his fists bunched in anger within me, just like, too. Oh, yes.

So Baybe says Inspector Ekanayake maintains he calls himself, or is called, Aetha—Sinhala for Tusker—does this father of mine?

I didn't know that.

But I do now.

What sort of monster would do that to his own child? Five or six years old.

Inspector Ekanayake and Baybe and someone else I nor, I think, my brother knew at the time were hunting my brother whom they insisted on calling by that alias of Tusker, who could be called Aetha.

At the same time, I am hunting Aetha, my father who could be called Tusker.

Here's another thing: should my father be hunted and trapped down like a rogue elephant for what he did to me, or should he be hunted and trapped down like a rogue elephant for what he didn't do?

Either way, he has lived too long past the bolt of lightning which gave despatch to that Major T. W. Rogers, hot-shot tusker bagger, who should not have died before him, certainly not smoking his pipe peacefully near his veranda and being struck by lightning in 1845 while Assistant Government Agent and District Judge of Badulla up in the highlands.

'Their Lanka now and Virathni'...

... a fair-enough item, and it's a relief to be able to think about it again. Anyway, I met her in church, and Father Thumbayaserni can deny me a lot of things but he can't deny that.

She did not just kneel there and pray in the conventional manner. Hers was a pose of such submission that God must have been having a private word in her ear.

She had her head bent right down to the pew in front of her and her hands were touching palm to palm, thumb to thumb, fingertip to fingertip, perfectly union'd, and held as a steeple above her bowed head.

The fall of her jet-black hair draped down her back as if it was the very veil of Mother Teresa herself, smooth and untarnished by some saintly ironing... unlike Mother Teresa's, come to think of it, which always looked a bit scrappy.

At the small parting of the bodice and skirt of her saree, a few vertebrae were picked out smoothly, scintillant by the overhead lights. From there the curve of her nates were bold in a way that suggested she would not easily be budged from her cherishing.

Her face I could not see. I watched her body move away from me; it was petite and perhaps maned too much by all that wonderful hair, but there was a straightness, a worthy play of hip sway and a smooth shape to her that made her thinness not an insufficiency but a perfect smallness, her size a perfect miniature.

I took the Fall.

You get lumbered with someone like Neila, then followed up by someone like Rehana, and you drift into a celibacy as unforgiving as one of Rehana's starched bed sheets, I can tell you.

Besides, I will confess to never enjoying even the thought of the act. Making double humps with one of the species you have always pretty well detested wasn't lighting any candles to creation, as far as yours truly was concerned.

But the next Sunday, I got behind her and slightly to her right, knowing that, in the part of the Mass where you bestow your blessings on those around you, she would turn to bow.

She did, and I had her face to face.

It was as thin as it should have been proportion-wise. It was her eyes which mainly bowled me over. They were as almond-shaped as I remember my mother's to have been, but amethystine as a late sunset, as early sunrise.

Her lips were full, yet it was not a wide flat mouth, oh no. Her lips pressed forward elliptically as with the line of her jaw, so that they were both joined to a winning pout that gave firmness to her profile.

But.

With women, I have found there is always a but.

But, in the side of her left nostril was a gold stud, and in the middle of her forehead a blob, a dark brown equals-Tamil pottu.

I have never been able to stand even looking at either. The nose thing looks like a snot catcher, and the blob like they have been shot dead centre and the wound had dried.

Nevertheless.

I have found that there is always a nevertheless with women, too.

Nevertheless, let's just say you're not the most likeable, the most sinless, the most endearing character the world has ever seen. In fact, let's say you've travelled along life's bloodied highway pretty much wrapped in the scum bag you ought to be in.

212

You've virtually become a bum. You certainly have become a criminal with a record, a person who is going to kill his own father.

You've got no friends, no family, a full-on head of detestation for all other human beings. You have wished multiple murders as they have happened by having a psychotic twin who carried out those wishes like he was doing you a bob-for-a-job. No job anymore, no prospects. Looks, you're in no final or even quarter-final with. Personality, to be truthful, like a flat tyre.

And there you are, nevertheless, in church one fine day, where in theory you shouldn't be because you are also a liar about your atheism, and you look up, and, by God, you take the Fall.

Never mind you immediately recognise her as your aunt.

The little girl who used to stand in the corner of my father's hut when my mother and I had our lunch there.

How's a little impediment like aunt going to make any difference to the likes of you?

You take the Fall and double it up by even realising it's your aunt right at the time as in who-cares.

I'll say one thing for you, though:

Well, bless me.

Don't ask me what love is. I never thought I was capable of it, so I never thought about it much.

Neila and Rehana you didn't love. You controlled the fire damage and made sure your lungs didn't get too much of how they smoked.

They say love is loving someone greater than you love yourself.

I have to admit I find that totally indefensible.

But and nevertheless... there they go again... even I could see that the sort of love we're talking about was in her eyes when she turned in church and maybe recognised or maybe didn't the son of her brother from the hut of her childhood.

The following Sunday, a real drag of seven days away, I went right over and sat down next to her. A pew seemed as good a place as any to get the incest I had in mind to get going.

'I think you're my aunt,' I whispered behind praying mitts.

It was too hard. Said with an Australian accent I had completely forgotten about and therefore like a rugged magpie.

'I am not.'

Her voice was so waifish, so feminine, yet her body language was heavily dismissive of the impropriety.

But and yet again nevertheless, she did finally stop at the chaplet and waited until I had the nerve to approach her again. She didn't look any the less stern, yet:

There is always a yet when it comes to women, even those who surprise you with top-notch English, you know.

Yet:

'Would you,' she asked, 'like to be coming to tea?'

'Then you are my aunt.' I felt terrific and terrible.

'Do you want me to be?'

'Nup.'

'I was your father's house-girl. My family was being poor, *nae*?' She shrugged what can you do. 'One day your Auntie Jayalitha adopted me when my parents are dying.'

'That still sort of makes you my aunt.'

'I suppose, *atcha*.'

'Do you know where my father is now?'

It was disconcerting to notice how she could change so quickly to be so inconsolably sad.

'I am not knowing.'

'Virathni.'

'Yes?'

'Call me John or Johnnie or the guy who just took the Big Fall.'

When she takes my arm, in this now-time, it is not just taking an arm like you'd know it. It's running her arm up mine

214

to hold lightly onto my biceps, more in the way of gently guiding you.

You got any idea how that feels, the dead beat that I am, to be leg to something good?

Bestowed upon.

Am I ever getting the runs on the board here.

Little things like that.

And how's the little thing, for example, that she looks late teens and not the early forties she really is.

One little thing that's a bit of a problem, however, is that she is a virgin.

I said it. A virgin.

And on our wedding night, when Father Thumbayaserni listens to his heart and not reason and marries us, she will open her hands towards the light of my face and she will set her palms out to me and she will offer unto me a maidenhead, going:

'This is my gift to you'.

After all that I've done in life, a maidenhead.

I was thinking: may I have the grace to remember how virginity's valued here.

Being Australian, I'll have to try to dredge up some long-lost racial memory.

Sweet Jesus, Lord, You know that if there is to be any grace for me, it'd would have to be an open drain on a rainy night for me to get stumble into it.

Actually, and probably more to the point of you listening to this Virathni could or would tell me very little about my father, even after the time my mother and I were dismissed from the estate after the great house's fire like a couple of clerks caught with their fingers in the till.

She seemed to remember the anger my father had with what she thought was an Australian immigration official who stayed up at the great estate house for a few days, and seemed to be laughing with my grandparents in my father's face quite a lot about his chances of a new life given his colouring.

Going back into the present tense, she cannot at all remember my brother, even though I kept pressing her about him.

But she did recall this: my father and my Aunt Jayalitha moved to another estate upside of Badulla (yes, Major T. W. Rogers's bailiwick!, bang bang!). That was when she was about eleven and just after her own parents had died. It was then she came to know what the English term of being adopted meant.

Something like ten years ago, around midnight and when my father was away from home, a gang came bashing at the walls of their hut with their machetes and rifles.

They wanted my father. Bring out the counter-revolutionary, they called. They would not believe my Aunt Jayalitha. They pushed her side and searched the house, while she, Virathni and an old man, who slept on the kitchen floor and 'minded' the house, were kept under guard. They slapped the old man around because he could answer in the only language he knew: Tamil. It marked those goons as obviously Sinhalese. When my Aunt Jayalitha, too, could only answer in Tamil too, one of them punched her in the mouth. They shouted at her: speak correctly, speak Sinhala, the only language of this country, you Tamil dogshit from a dog back-ending your own damn mother.

They had left Virathni alone. She could speak Sinhala. Their leader turned to her and said, whore bitch you tell Aetha what has happened here.

Aetha, my father. Even then, they all knew what name he went by.

And then he shot and his men hacked my Aunt Jayalitha and that old man to death. They did so knowing that nobody who mattered would give a rat's arse.

These charmers were the resurgent JVPers, the People Liberation Army, who had tried to lead a popular uprising for Sri Lanka for Singhalese way back in 1971, but had been put down at the time. Then, in the early new century in the last

216

years of the civil war and the avenging years just after, they reared their nationalistic heads again and nearly achieved the mob rule they were after. They succeeded in setting the dogs of anarchy loose upon the communities of Sri Lanka, especially in the northeast and the uplands.

You can put them down as part of the worldwide Tamil question too -- and think of Papa Ramaswarmy and his TGTE, *and* the Serendip Lankan Association of Canberra *and* poor sucked-in Neila and her Boardshorts, *and* my brother in the same breath. Then throw in the over 60 million Tamils worldwide if you like.

You can also put them down under the items of busting the lid on the simmering racial and religious intolerances of Sri Lanka that had been bubbling away for yonks, *and* renewed their terrors against non-Singhalese *and* Sri Lanka for Buddhist Singhalese and all that, *and* no Indians, no Hindus, no Christian, no foreigners, *and* no running-dog bleeding-heart liberals out of the various diseased parts of the UN.

The new JVPers soon had the northeast and the lower uplands of the island hunkered into a level of atrocity that was maniacal. Where law was Wild West, mornings saw raped women and children left hanging on lamp posts or policemen floating in the rivers. Members of unsympathetic political parties, even those Singhalese, were dragged from their homes, placarded as traitors or cowards and publicly shot.

The special JVP modus operandi doesn't bother fighting the enemy himself; just get his family. Fewer comrades get hurt that way.

They came at night and went for the lambs. In the small hours of the morning, they would simply shoot or hack to death your loved ones in front of you. They might let you live to tell the tale, to spread the terror. If you were really lucky, they shot you in front of your women and children and left it at that.

217

That's how you whip up terror. Forget beheadings on video.

Tarquin abroad with his ravaging strides. Right out of William Shakespeare's fifteenth or sixteen hundred and something play 'Macbeth' where the forests came to the castle.

That forest should have come to the new JVPers.

My Virathni had been taken away by neighbours before my father arrived home.

She only heard much later that Aetha roared revenge like one of his bull tusker's and left, making for the forest and not waiting for it to come to him.

She never saw, or heard of, him again. The Convent brought her up after that.

My charming father does it again. Up and disappeared when the going got tough. But maybe this time it might've been for the best.

If he had stayed on to look after her, he probably would have been made to adopt her properly. So, maybe, you know, not my Aunt Virathni, maybe my *sister* Virathni.

Now, *that* I wouldn't have been able to slip past Father Thumbayaserni.

Can you believe the absolute bastard abandoning her too?

When it came to sticking and looking after his family, the man has a wonderful record, right?

I'll say it: what a prick.

So, when you get life's happy happenstance of boy elephant in musth and girl elephant in oestrum, they'll slip off into the bush and dally around with each other for about a week.

There is much binding in the marsh during that week, although what the poor dear thinks about the chosen one not only being the heaviest lover alive, but also the champeen of praecox ejaculato.

Most of the time, she has to sink down on her hind legs to support him or go under three tonnes of bull not knowing what the hell it is doing.

Meanwhile, he's mounting her bit by bit, inching his front legs up along her back until he's got, or thinks he's got, her in the right position.

You've heard women talk about men crawling all over them; well, this is it.

He's certainly got the right equipment, though, to make it worth the eye-rolling patience. At least theoretically. It can be almost a metre and a half, and that's a mighty lot of equivalent inches to be swinging around.

Incidentally, 'tis said that he is the only animal that doesn't grip the female around the girth. He lays his legs along her back. Lazy sod. But, with her collapsed onto those stout, pretty unsexy back legs of hers, and with the size of that bridging apparatus of his no longer swinging in the breeze, there doesn't seem much opportunity for gravity to get in the act anyway.

All this probably takes well over a whole ten minutes to get set up.

It is a slow, exactly and carefully orchestrated manoeuvre.

So, what does he do?

He lasts for a minute, max.

One lousy minute.

This is the character who, when he is in heat, you watch out for, right? He's the world's great wrecker. The guy's a berserker. He will simply kill anything thing that comes between him and a her. If he has to, he'll run right over a whole village like the worst drunken moron. Get in his way, and he'll show no mercy to king or country.

In short, he is so led by the short and curlies that he would tear the world apart for a week in the bush with her.

And what for?

For a lousy minute.

Figure that.

Shows that there's a lot of human qualities in elephants.

Not that he doesn't make up for her disappointment. He does this by just plainly exhausting her. In that week, he goes through the whole exhausting performance, with its lightning denouement, more times than her back legs can stand up to, or not stand up to.

Or if she manages that would have to be where the term the constitution of an elephant comes from.

Their bundle of joy she might deliver in about twenty months' time. But that can be up to two years if it's a male. Twins are very rare, perhaps only legendary. One at a time is the go.

What she'll then have tottering around her feet will be a hairy little thing -- if being something in the region of 180 to 115 kilograms without an ounce more in the US and already standing about a metre high can be said to be little.

But there it is: wire-hairy with black hoof nails and using the latter to balance itself within only a few minutes of birth.

In an hour, it's not tottering, but walking already.

It is sheerly beautiful. It is in perfect proportion of the great beast it is destined to be, but it is now cuddly and adorable, and it's not going to go berserker on you any time soon or make any human's life a living hell, so that makes it even better. You can even get it as a him or a her to suck milk from a baby bottle while you go ah.

Give it another five years and it already has its shoulder higher than the top of your head; by then it's well over six feet, two yards, two metres, or any yardstick you want and all at the same time.

Meantime, there is debate about whether mum voluntarily putting stress back on her back legs in some secluded bush love nest after six months or after ten months. There is a lot of confusion about regarding when a female is ready to have him or some other great oaf worth a minute of bliss testing out gravity on her again.

Again, it shows the human qualities in elephants.

It's a dirty shame they're almost extinct in the uplands now, because elephants actually prefer rocky and uneven ground despite what you'd think.

They love the mountains.

Visions of them falling bum-over-boobs over cliffs because of their size and fictional clumsiness are totally wrong. Their huge feet with those ivory toes make them excellent hill hikers.

More particularly, it is said elephants like to breed in the higher country. What they mean they like the higher altitudes while lying on or being laid on other of their breed.

World champeen tusk merchant, our old Major T. W. Rogers of the Ceylon Rifle Regiment used to always look for the herds in the higher hills because he knew where they were best distracted. If he was hunting on the plains, he'd always lead his merry native troopers towards the nearest foothills, no doubt beating the bush as he went. That was, of course, before that bit of lightning got him at the age of forty-one. As I said, 1845, that was.

Food? Well might you ask. I bet John Wesley Hyatt and Dr Armauer Hansen -- if you remember those two gentlemen maybe linked by the brand-new technology of the bunsen burner invented by the German chemist Robert Wilhelm Bunsen in 1855 probably out of the then equivalent of his garage -- they would have been tickled pink to watch how littl'un elephant can put the nosh away. You watch them and you can see how they grow so fast.

Elephants eat for about sixteen hours out of every twenty-four, which doesn't leave much time for working, wallowing, foraging, sleeping, getting off into the bush for that long week's recreation, or doing the everyday little things we all have to do.

No wonder they've only got a minute to spare on the how's-your-mother.

A tame elephant will stash away around 500 kilograms of food a day, and won't give a stuff if that comes in at a thousand pounds weight in US terms. It'll eat any shoot whatever, except something called the 'shoot-of-flame' which I can't help you with. Google it, if you've got electricity. Here in Gampola, in this now-time, it's more off than not.

It's also into leaves, barks, sugar cane, paddy, manioc, coconuts, oranges. And wood. It eats wood like it's gone out of fashion.

I couldn't believe my father throwing them logs. They'd be attacking these things by tearing strips from them with their trunks while holding one end firm with a foot.

What it is is actually the wood from their favourite kittul palm tree. It has a sweet core. It was all wood to me in those days.

But that's not all they will shovel down.

If it gets the chance, it is said to be partial to digging up human graves and, if the flesh has rotted away, chewing up the bones.

Apparently one of the things we contribute back to the good earth is the mineral salts in our bones.

It'll be a shame to cremate all that nourishment, when it comes around to your turn as an average healthy-appetited elephant.

Elephants positively slurp away on any of your remains.

Save the cremations; instead give the produce to the elephants.

While I'm both willing away and whiling away the time, next item:

Virgin.

Good God.

What a solid body is that flimsy wall of skin!

You're kidding yourself if you think it's a shrinking violet.

A hymen grows more tyrannical the older it gets.

What it is is an unhearty chaperone.

If it could speak it would only tut-tut. And that would be when it was feeling polite.

With it as chaperone, Virathni and I cannot even walk arm-in-arm in public, because that might make it look like a wanton missing friend, instead of an unhearty chaperone.

We talk too animatedly, banter too intimately, sip tea too familiarly, laugh too closely, and everybody gets to presume it has slipped out of the window, that hymen, and taken flight with the dawn light.

Even so, as far as I'm concerned, it can remain our sour-pussed companion, our unhearty chaperone, as long as it likes.

That's one area I can manufacture a bit of my own grace, rather than stumbling into it like I seem to be doing lately.

'Australia Then' comes back to mind and, yes, I heard my brother had gone to Melbourne, but for the life of me I can't remember how I heard.

The attempt on my life, then what happened to poor Neila.

He must have known it wasn't on behalf the poor SLA whackers who had ended up, anyway, mangled in the white Mercedes by his samurai sword.

No. they were just the business guys, Inspector Ekanayake's 'principals'.

As far as I was concerned, what did I know? All I was certain was they might have arranged the attempt to blow me and my port-a-loo to smithereens, but they could never have inner fortitudes, not even combined, to make the original decision. The same went when it came to poor Neila. No way, as I just felt my brother would be thinking too, would they have dared to lay their hands all over Neila in that way. Whoever had done it already had the photographs before strapping her to the surfboard but still went through with using her as some lesson of some sort. The SLA boys would have grabbed the piccies with glee and run off home. So not them, no way.

I did not have to ask why Melbourne, either, even though I had the feeling that he operated out of Sydney whenever he could. I figured I would come to know soon enough.

It might have been the thorough rattling of the old brain pan I had got from the bomb, or it might've just been the heightened awareness you get from suddenly being in danger, but I now found myself with even a higher level of re-awakening of him. That mind's-eye, our mind's-eyes, fully awake.

Now, I could actually see what he was doing and, instead of being passive to it, could understand just why he was doing it. It wasn't just what I sort of sneakily wanted doing; it was full-on endorsement of what he was doing and getting right in there mentally with him.

It was like, draped at the back of my mind, a wide screen starring my brother, such an easy viewing, as if it was 1953 or 1954 and the old silver 35-mm screen burst into full Cinemascope wide screen courtesy of 20th Century Fox and especially its President Spyros P. Skouras, even with a name like that. Talk about eye opening. I was playing the part with him, a sort of *pipped* understudy again, and for once I didn't care.

I witness in my mind's eye how my brother knew the dark spots around the floodlights of the house in Melbourne and used them to his advantage by force of habit. His was the nature of breaching the wall. The frilled gate with its pushbutton bell offended him.

The dog didn't hear him until he had reached the lighting of the actual front door. It howled out of shock or violation, charged, then stopped short to a meek crouch when it recognised him. He could remember it since a pup.

He didn't like it then; it doted on him from then. He didn't mind its killing instinct; he just detested the unnecessary noise it made at the mercy of it.

There was no need for the door knocker now. He let the dog sniff and lick the back of his hand, while he waited for the bodyguard to come heavily from around the side to see what the dog was on about.

My brother merely counted the seconds. Twenty. It had taken twenty seconds for the man to make an appearance, plus the seconds to see who it was, plus those few to take his hand reluctantly out of his breast pocket. Too slack; too much time for any emergency.

Apparently, we knew the so-called bodyguard's name as Graddle. It was all my brother wanted to know. He would not even have to know that when the time he had in mind came.

This Graddle was all brute force. He was not a Tamil, but Irish Australian-going way back which, to my brother's mind, was dangerous in all circumstances.

They had never spoken, I could sense, in the two or three years the man had guarded the Ramaswarmys there, when my brother, it seemed, was a regular visitor if not actually staying there. It was another weakness in the bodyguard that he obviously thought his size advantage would be diminished by conversation.

My brother obviously had always liked that sort of information, too.

Graddle knocked once and hard on the front door then ungraciously unlocked it for him. Behind it, and standing enough off-centre to be clever about such things was the elder son Joycie Ramaswarmy, that inner seed to his Appa's full fruit of a body.

The snub-nosed Smith & Wesson he held lowered when he saw who it was, yet my brother noticed how reluctantly that was done. There was no welcome in it. Still the sharpness of his cheekbones and the elongated point of his chin giving him the predator's look. But a sharply-cunning predator's look. Joycie Ramaswarmy was a carrion eater in another reincarnation, always had been from teenager up when he and my brother, maybe even with both of us although I can't recall that cut their teeth on threats and extortions for funds for the Tamil homeland cause from the wealthier resident Tamils of Melbourne.

As he followed Joycie Ramaswarmy and Graddle further inside, I could feel how my brother was more watching out for the younger son, Karavai as being far more dangerous than either of these two at a time like this. He sensed the Karavai was not in, and was mildly relieved to realise it, and then mildly amused at himself for being mildly relieved about it. What would it have mattered?

Yet that one had been sent for four years to study at Harvard by his father who was not alone amongst the tinpot capos of this world in realising Business Administration would be more useful for family survival than the flexing of bigger muscles. It seemed that the youngest son didn't agree, such that when he returned fully qualified he had also trained himself to be also the most dangerous and volatile of all the Ramaswarmy ilk. Years of being safely tucked away in America, not allowed to return for the many crises, asking himself if he was a protected species during the dangers his family was constantly under, returning determined to prove otherwise.

I could feel how my brother had always been true to the covenant, in return for helping Appa Ramaswarmy taking us under his wing and teaching us survive... well, my brother anyway... but I also clearly knew, as I watched him enter that Toorak house again these so-many years later, that he had long ago lost his belief not just in the homeland cause but, more contemptuously, in the people backing the homeland cause.

He had been the network's axial for years, the field manager, yet nothing more than my father ever was in the tea estate... the equivalent: a herdsman, a foreman living down below the great house of the estate. And that's about all. A noted presence but not that important.

He was not Ramaswarmy, not family, and never could have been. He was just a worker.

I think my brother had only remained for his own satisfaction, for the opportunities to inflict pain from his own inner pain, for the smiling while detesting.

And I was shocked to realise it as he was moving back through that Ramaswarmy house.

My own brother had become a rogue elephant, just as they now brand my father a rogue elephant.

You can see how the alias Tusker had come about. You can see how the nickname Aetha had come about.

At least I could.

And my brother was not in the least surprised to find Appa Ramaswarmy not home either. There was no way Joycie would have been in shirt sleeves in the house if his parents were around.

But he was surprised when the little man moved so bullishly, so this-is-mine, into the studio and sat behind his father's desk.

Presumption had always been the Ramaswarmys' weak spot.

This bodyguard, this Graddle, is staying in the room, even though there is presumably network business to talk over which has to be why my brother has come. My brother lets this ride for a moment.

'Good to see your ugly bugle, Task old bitzer.' All these years in the country and still the whole family seeming to feel the need to flog the idiomatic. 'How's that blister of mine?'

My brother said he thought she was all right.

'She could be happier, is what I turd.'

My brother reiterated she was doing okay.

'Bit surprised to spree you, but. Heard you're in more strife than Ned Kelly's dog.'

My brother said he had come to talk to Appa about that.

'Dad's not in the Smoke. I heard you're supposed to be up in Hong Kong.'

'That right?'

'That's right, cob. Where're you camped?'

We let them know we have hired Hertz from the airport, just planning to keep on the move, kip in the car.

'That's the ticket. Sound as a nun's chastity belt. While you're down here, I say you might's well make yourself more useful than a flea with a dog with an itch, and check out the handover, nice little pile of fifties I hear, what's going down tonight. Save me the diddly-ouble, 'kay? 'S settled. That all?'

My brother nodded at the framed photograph on Appa's desk. There used to be one of the family and him. He wasn't in the frame anymore. He was almost bored in asking did bodyguard here know about the night's handover, usually meaning an extortion collection on the front doorstep of some sap well-to-do Sri Lankan, too?

'Sure as a goog's egg, Tasker the Basker. He's family, almost, no? And you know how easy it is to worm your way into this family with Appa, right?'

At least the dog had been friendly enough.

It is easy for me to see my brother waiting on the shoreline of Crib Point, just as the two who are stalking him through the bush will soon see him.

His squatting on a small plot of sand wedged up for this tide's time between the plopping, croaking, clicking stands of mangroves to either side of it. This is here, yes, in Crib Point on the eastern side of the Mornington Peninsula which, on its good side, borders the outer reaches of magnificent Port Phillip Bay, that watery funnel to Melbourne. But the Peninsula's eastern side seems lost to man and lost to the

228

softness of Nature. On this eastern side, the countryside seems unhurried to meet the shallow and unlovely waters of Western Port Bay, with its stringency of wispy, crackling open forest of tea trees and box thorns and a forest floor of sloughed barks and native grasses as sparse and seemingly unfructive as an aged Mandarin's goatee.

This I can see clearly.

Only the navy, with magnificent foresight, could have any use for this lost bay. To Tusker's right somewhere, lost among the sapless vegetation in mats of spindly tangles, is the Cerebus Naval Base, but from which are hardly any sea-going efforts across the shallow, sand-barred and seedy-seeming waters. The naval base has wharves that have been left to decay even while it was in the heyday of its use as a basic-training centre. Make that lack of magnificent foresight.

And I see them, as surely as Tasker senses them, these two men comically camouflaged in dark clothing and with mud actually smeared on their foreheads and cheeks, instead of where it perhaps should be -- on their teeth -- since they are already naturally south- Indian camouflaged.

They are very uncomfortable. They are not used to the bush dangers of Australia. The venom everywhere, they have heard. They are only city cobbers, but, venomous themselves in overcrowded streets in slums. Their survival routes are along the dark alleys and the fetid canals, not here in this alien scrub.

But they have been assigned this task, simply because they were in town at this time. These are part of the Tamil flying squads out of Chennai you've heard about, a potent weapon of untraceable retribution against those citizens who might be refusing to pay the extortion demands of the local network... potent because of their mobility and the blithe indifference they have to any degree of violence towards man, woman or child they don't know, couldn't care less about, and detest for their good lives.

If you could spot them, like my brother and I can see them, you'd spot them all over the world in loose teams, or busily on their scavenging own.

They are not so much trained to be careful killers as trained to be unbelievably vicious, almost berserker, unseen -- and if seen, totally unknown. They cannot be tracked down and certainly cannot be linked, except by circumstantial evidence, to the wide-boys of the local Tamil-question organisations in most well-heeled countries.

They have their orders beforehand. They fly in; they do what they paid to do. They fly out. They don't look behind.

But even I am seeing through my brother how they are not so hotshot, no. Their effectiveness is in not being known, in often being in and out of the country before the authorities even begin to investigate.

No ninjas these two, either. My brother hears their approach as easily as if they were fanning separate breezes for him with large branches.

It is early night. I think around nine o'clock, but I am not getting this exactly from him. He continues to search the moon-smacked waters for the shallow-bottomed runabout.

Beside him he has dug an open grave.

He is smiling. I cannot believe it. My brother is smiling because of the thrill of all this. It is an intellectualise thrill, not merely an emotional high. And I come to know he has never stopped experimenting as to whether, in violence, human nature still conforms to a pattern of predictability. Over the years, he has apparently found it so, at least with himself, such that the very violence itself can be toyed with, experimented with, can be refined beyond the sheer brutish. And therefore, an amusing art in and for itself -- and, even if the game is ever lost, still given some sense, rather than the violence of the meaningless.

How is he able to do this? These men are going to kill me. I can feel this clearly. It is frightening. I can feel the panic mounting my back.

Now they have crept to the sand ledge's edge. They have these weapons of war again, these AK47 automatic assault rifles, that will shred us fearsomely.

These men look across at each other. Their teeth show in a grim amusement that is more relief, because a quarry like this who is so thick-headed as to be micturating out to sea with his back towards them, is pathetic. Let him finish; we're all human that way.

This is what my brother is choosing to experiment with, this predictability. I cannot believe it. Peeing.

They wait, even so, but when the hard bubo of cloud passes to them from the moon, they find they have lost sight of him. It is a small moment my brother has been waiting for apparently for he is no longer at void nor any longer on the sand ledge when the cloud passes.

They look at each other from across the opposite sides of the sand ledge, and they do so wildly because something has happened that is not predictable to them. The quarry had not dashed back into the bush; he would have had to pass one of them. If he had cut along the shore they would have heard him scuttling through the water.

Yet, truly, he is not there now.

I sense them guess individually that he must be trying to swim for it. They break cover almost simultaneously, automatics ready, and scuttle across the ledge, one to each side of where Tasker had been.

The bigger of the two chooses to move into the sea up to his ankles before primordial pangs make him feel vulnerable in the mud. He casts around the water surface, searching for the break when my brother has to come up for air. It is all too shallow for him to get very far, he is thinking. It should be easy. Just wait.

But nothing.

But dares not to take his eyes from the water.

Without moving his head, he calls out of the side of his mouth to his partner.

231

But only the mosquitoes are in annoyance.

He looks across the sand ledge, where there is now no other companion.

He calls again, clearly this time, then starts to feel the fear of being alone in a strange land, of strange night sounds, out of the side alleys, in heavy mud.

Now he edges towards where his offsider should have been. It is difficult getting back in the swim of things as training would have it. All's too slippery; all's too thick and out of thwack.

The man feels the tap on his calf rather than feels the violation. At the tap on his knee, he has looked down and has had the impression that his offsider is laid out in some sort of grave and some grave digger or something is grimacing toothfully up at him.

My brother's kukri, the short and curved small sword of the Ghurkhas, has come up from the grave and is passing through his sac into his lower stomach.

I see him falling and my brother instantly above him, hand on his mouth, heaving on the knife like a butcher gutting.

The grave is shallowly fit enough for the two of them.

Now my mind's eye is having him taking his time barely filling in the hole. He uses only his feet. The fiddler crabs will soon be at the bodies anyway; it is pointless doing too good a job. He does so with a great deal of intellectual satisfaction which I found, find, quite sickening.

He is looking out to sea again as he does this. But he is not looking out for the runabout. He is sensing the surroundings for the third man.

It is as he expects. The other man has not come with these two. But I see how my brother knows pretty well where he is, and that the weakness of over-confidence has had him stay where he would be expected to be.

That bodyguard of the Ramaswarmys, that Graddle, shouldn't have lived past these two poor itinerant strong-armers.

My brother turns and begins to make his way through the mangroves, following the sorry shoreline.

It isn't as hard going as I would have expected it to be, the mud not sucking as I would imagine. His feet are wading through a waving carpet of fiddler crabs, skippers and mud fleas. We see once the imperious slither of a white-bellied mangrove snake. Our boots crack the whelks and the mangrove snails, kick over the mounds of the mud prawns.

Above it all, and most of all, are the constant Rehana whines of the constant mosquitoes. All is constant.

My brother has been in this place many times before, it seems. We are feeling the pleasure of being prepared for this new platform of thrill; I feel it as a sickly feeling. But he does not, and, knowing him, will not analyse why the Ramaswarmys had suddenly decided it was perilous to let us live. He smiles only grimly when he remembers the photograph on the fat father's desk, the one in which he was cut from. Appa Ramaswarmy is so fatly monomaniac that he must have actually thought to remove the image was to remove the man, and merely on his say-so. It is probably that which my brother finds so foolish.

Mind you, I've thought about it myself from time to time. What caused the Australasian operation of the otherwise upfront Transnational Government of Tamil Eelam to be breaking up like that? Had Appa Ramaswarmy gone senile, sloppy, stale with over confidence to match his physical grossness?

Sure, my brother would have appreciated the need for continuous regrowth to keep the network vigorous. Okay. So, lop a bit. But why did they decide to attack him, their general in the field, as my brother seems to be allowing me to know? That's no lopping; that's ripping strips off your own skin.

My brother remains silent on this. I think that is because there might be more to it than that, and perhaps the Ramaswarmys weren't feeling safe with the Tusker any more for no other reason than his deadliness made them just getting plain edgy.

If it is or was plain edginess, then the change they didn't like must have been coming from my brother himself, and that could only mean one thing: that he, as their main and most competent operator in the field-or-planning, was making a push for the leadership.

If that's the case, then these killings are on his head, not mine.

And therefore, shag you, brother of mine. If you were making a power bid, you should have protected me better.

Not that I'm still mad at him, sitting here in this now-time in Gampola and thinking. The crazy thing is I feel I've grown closer to him than at any time in our lives. It's this quietus in my life right now that's doing it. Sure. It's the minor miracle of the little lady in the church called aunt called Virathni and Hansen House and my own poor old leper man Hansen and the goodly Fathers and the merciful Sisters of Charity. And the five little girls. Sure and sure and sure.

Yet what of that?

When should I live if not now?

But that's the 'if' I was thinking about then... the if about doubting my brother. Lately, I've been having doubts about that too. There's this growing feeling, you see, as if my brother was whispering it, that there was more likely the reason for the Ramaswarmys' panic came from someone higher up actually manipulating what was going on between them and him.

If that's more correct, then my money is now on fucking Inspector Charles Bloody-fucking-hell-sorry Ekanayake.

That long tall streak of poop did me for a start. One moment he's there in my face asking advice about extradition, the next I find myself privy to a conspiracy for withholding information, then party to a cover up in poor Neila's murder.

Not to mention my job, my house, any prospects I might have ever had for a halfway decent life in Australia.

Now, in this now-time, the long tall sod is turned up here in Gampola and officially on my hammer.

And they talk about justice. Where's the justice in that?

Mangroves.

Mind wandering is what *I'm* good at, never mind what Ekanayake's opening the batting for.

Mangroves, mangroves. Sure. My brother working his way out of those mangroves now, doubling back to where he knows the other man will be waiting. My mind's eye. Ours.

I now know this too: there would be no so-called handover of any extortion money from anyone that night, no runabout belting in with its waterproof bags. It was just a set-up. And a set-up means the whole international TGTE operation had been warned about the man with the alias of Tusker.

This is only what he has expected this night to be. He has gone along anyway. I now know why that is, at least. It's that challenge he so willingly takes up which scares me so.

Now we are clearly in sight of Appa's Volvo. It is parked behind our rented Toyota so that it would be hard for us to get out in a hurry.

The third man is a silhouette in the Volvo. He is just a smudge to me.

Appa Ramaswarmy's best Volvo. He isn't going to like this.

The way I feel him, my brother is, though. He is in thrall once more.

Up against the boot of the car, we are near enough to hear the man tapping out a rhythm on the steering wheel. He could be humming.

I feel myself wondering at my brother's sure hands. He has already unscrewed the petrol cap, inserted the material one end, then the other end, until he is calmly satisfied that it is a true wick. His lighter he leaves on the ground there.

What the man can see from inside there I do not know, except that he is not so edgy. The diffusion of the moon must be giving him an adequate sighting of the track leading off to the shoreline and a confidence that his goons will do the job. We know that it is towards there he is keeping his head turned.

Humming, he is definitely humming.

Further along the far side of the vehicle, my brother tightly wedges another slice of his shirt around the spring-loaded front-door handle, then does the same with the other end around the back-door handle.

He is on his back as he does this, and I can feel how practised he is at keeping our breathing wedded to the exertions of being in such an awkward position.

The shirt piece won't hold as a tie between the two doors with too much sustained pressure, but my brother is in thrill that it will do well enough with the shoving of panic.

We are smiling now. We are experimenting in extremis again. I feel it.

Now my brother works his way on his back towards the front of the vehicle. Beneath the front bumper bar, he takes out these damn weapons of war again. I just cannot get used to them. The Browning, the MK1, the kukri.

And then, with his heel, he kicks the front tyre hard the instant before he stands up in full view of the man inside.

He should be brandishing one of those weapons of war, surely. Aiming, for the love of God. But he is momentarily just standing defenceless there. The weapons of war are dangling at his side.

I know for certain that my brother is grinning at the guy!

It must be the sheer fury that the man swings the blunt-nosed shotgun up from the seat and, comically cramped, fires straight through the windscreen at the man he was sent to kill but who isn't there anymore.

I hear him curse and shove at the door. The rag tie holds enough so that he can get only his lower leg out. Where my brother is now to cut his Achilles tendon viciously with the kukri. The man cries out and slams the door back shut and throws himself low to the front seat.

There is no hurry now. We are scratching tauntingly on the boot of the Volvo. I know the man is slowing moving the shotgun towards the rear window. Again, my brother stands and grins at him. And again, the stupidity, it seems, of a blast blowing out the back window for a target that is again not there anymore.

It has become comical, yes. We can sense the fear from inside the car. The man is, crazily, crazily, trapped and is having difficulty thinking how he should not move but shoot his way out of it.

He panics as one who can no longer breathe and tries to throw the door open again, yet his knee this time, and then his hand, are so blithely open to the kukri. The screams, all that there is in the world you know, as the man slams the door closed again.

Silence. At least until I am hearing the poor fellow either whimpering in fear or swearing softly with rage.

I know my brother is surer than me, is confident it is whimpering, and I can feel how he is almost at the point of laughing out loud.

I do not like any of this. This going too far.

My brother shoots the MK1 through the back-passenger window, straight across the back seat so that both these windows are exploding hideously. The man has wedged himself as much as his bulk will allow between the front seat and the floor. There is now no earthly way he can really use that shotgun of his down there.

No, no hurry whatsoever.

237

My brother shoots out the two front side windows as he did the two side back ones. It must be terrifying in there; the showering of shattered glass; the thunder above.

Even I know the man is surely whimpering now.

This giant of a man and the smirk of his over-confidence with which he had treated us only a few hours before, knowing he was coming out to this place to ambush and kill us.

And even I am remembering this and feeling now only murder in my heart for this low life cowering in there, as my brother walks casually back to the petrol the long way round, to the lighter back there, to the wick ready there.

Where we light it and trot away. But not too far.

There is little to worry about.

There is the explosion. I feel it tug at our hair.

We are sitting on my brother's heels and watching. We will shoot him out of his misery if he somehow manages to emerge from all that.

John Wesley Hyatt would have been mighty proud of that heat treatment. If he had known, he could have bypassed the Phelan & Collander competition and gone in for yellow or blue sapphire alchemy from geuda stones.

John Wesley wouldn't have got much change out of Appa Ramaswarmy even for doing that, though. Appa definitely would not have appreciated what happened to his Volvo.

But then, you never send the hired help out in the best car. Anyone should know that's just asking for maintenance trouble.

Somehow, I just knew where my brother needed to go next. It was not more than an hour's drive along Mornington Peninsula.

Yet he still drives the slightly scorched Toyota all the other way back to the Ramaswarmys' Toorak home first.

The revolting thing is that the body of the bodyguard Graddle smoulders in the boot.

I do not and did not agree with what my brother did back there, but eventually the dog didn't seem to mind.

Graddle was hired as muscle to keep unwanted people away from the house, so my brother has strung up his carcase on the Ramaswarmys' otherwise impressive gates.

Once the dog had been pacified, as I have said, it did a bit of sniffing and presumably a lot of canine thinking, then, when it thought our back was turned, obviously came to the conclusion of what the hell; it's not every day they serve up charcoaled beef hanging tastefully on grill-iron gates. It was as much a slurper as its master's daughter was a whiner.

Though it is night, I can see the rows of strutted vines hair-pinning the hill between the Ramaswarmys' artificial reservoir and the Harvard son's country house built in the ground out back.

Undoubtedly that is because my brother has been there before and doesn't need anything other than the lights from the dwelling to move undetected towards the rear of the place. The Harvard confidence of the man. He must think being what Harvard told him: its MBA is all the protection he needed in life.

The Joycie smaller Volvo is there too, as it would be, alongside the Harvard prerequisite BMW. Only now to match a comfy trio would be the arrival of Appa's best, his Volvo, and we all know what condition that is in at this particular time, and they would stand out in tomorrow's early morning light as triple beacons to the rise and burnt-to-crisp fall of the immigrant: the Smarmies Dynasty.

In the kitchen, the wife of Harvard is fixing what Harvard would now probably insist on calling *casse croute*, instead of nibblies, for her husband and bro-in-law sitting by the fire with a glass each of Harvard's plonk, which he had recently appellated for the small and pretentious wine holdings of this

Melbourne-Club-held district, the cool climate wines of the Mornington Peninsula.

Harvard is sipping with appreciation of labours ineffable because they are his own. Joycie takes the occasional mandatory gulp and reacts as though it is a mouthful of vinegar, which it mostly probably is. He seems only gratified that a glass of it takes only one of his gulps

It is like strolling around a large doll's house looking in at warm Charles-Dickens Christmas doings, warm and cosy and somehow inviolable to the true light ending just beyond its windows.

I am not surprised to feel as though my brother hesitating for a moment in what he is about to do. I know what it is instantly. It is the book we had when kids on the estate of Charles Dickens's 'A Christmas Carol', an edition of 1937 of the old Chapman & Hall 1843 original, if I'm not wrong and probably meant to be Tiny Tim if I'm not wrong again. More especially it is the illustration on its cover of a half-frozen poor kid looking in through the street window on a room of warm Christmas cheer that was an eternity beyond his reach.

I know what it is for the likes of us who have never had a home. It's calling up, like his experimenting with peeing on the beach, some primitive honour to confront it. Momentarily, the hand lowers. For that moment, the intrusion seems intolerable, violence against the home lights in the windows unimaginable. And you feel the enigma of a mystery greater than disquiet, grief, rage, greater than the murderous revenge you have in your mad heart.

That's what I think anyway. How my brother thought of it, I don't think I'm privy too yet.

If I said it was a hesitation even for a moment, I'd probably be exaggerating. My brother is already at the kitchen door and tapping it lightly to get the attention of Harvard's wife, whom I at least presume to be an innocent as far as it goes.

She turns quickly but seems only slightly startled.

240

Harvard has chosen what probably the famous school has prescribed for a maximally enjoyable business life: a comfortably chubby wife. In a couple of years she will be so fat as not to cause any of his pretty personal assistants any trouble, so Indianly swollen by their cooking ghee that she won't rate a mention as to whether she minds how far the 'personal' goes with the assistants. Now, though, we see, mind's eye wise, she is full-cheeked and pert-mouthed like another of those dolls made of cellulose invented by John Wesley Hyatt. Carefully hair-gelled bands show she is chezelle and therefore working. But her eyes are greedy green and those, and the way she is drawn by fascination to the conspiratorial tapping, shows she adores gossip, yes, but by far prefers the scandal that can be won from gossip.

'Tasker?'

Her surprise tells us they haven't told her we were in town, let alone boast we were nowhere in the land of the living anymore.

My brother has his fingertip to her lips. She nods; she will, yes, honour anything conspiratorial.

For some people the irresistible can only come in whispers.

I hear him using my own voice for its softer quality to ask her if she has enough food in to last for at least a week. Yes. She has. That's good, so now she can go, take the children, and get to her parents' place and say nothing of this to anybody. Tell your parents you had to take a little break from the daily grind.

For one week, you don't put through even a phone call to here.

'Tasker...?' She is excited about the implied danger and wants to make it right by speaking it up as ghostly gossip.

But he motions they cannot dwell to savour it for too long. All he can do for her is tell Appa that she wasn't even here. That she wasn't mixed up in anything of this. When, and he

241

has lowered his own voice to a thrilling conspiracy level, the worst comes to the worst.

And now she is sharp to the nuances. She glances quickly towards the other side of the house where the Ramaswarmy brothers are sitting. In answer, he nods sadly, sagely. Naughty Harvard hubby has to be held until Appa decides what to do with him.

Now her eyes are wide. Forget that hubby might be in danger; if he, then more importantly, so is she.

She sibilates; she has already changed sides: 'Why a whole week? Appa's only in Hong Kong.'

He shrugs the humility of his not to reason why. It is the perfect cover for learning the whereabouts of Appa so easily. Hong Kong. A fat man in fat Hong Kong.

She pretends one last twinge of the marriage vow, then shouts 'kids!' at the top of her considerable voice, then clomps out of the kitchen to upstairs. This is obviously one part of the operation that is not going to take long.

Because of her noise, the heads of the Appa sons are turned towards the doorway as I almost walk in there too with my brother. I can feel the pleasant sensation he is experiencing as they register him, then sit back in rictus as he waves the Browning casually.

These hateful weapons of war.

There is no talk. He stands behind Harvard's chair with the gun impudently resting on the man's head. Its barrel is lined up on Joycie. By the look on the older Ramaswarmy face, we weren't wrong about it being vinegar he was drinking. Maybe it's also because he is looking across at a dirty and mud-caked man out of his own childhood who will be his murderer in a way that is painful for me to have to remember. That sounds ridiculous, but I am feeling so all-present that I'm actually thinking that, I think, and I think then.

The wife, the Harvard children come stumbling, it seems, down the stairs. The children are both grizzling from the rupture of sleep and the confusion of being shoved out of the house in the middle of the night.

When he hears the front door being unbolted, Harvard cries out his wife's name. I can hear it but cannot quite make out what it is. It matters little. Incredibly she calls back:

'We're not here, all right?'

It is as much as that to be deserted by your family. A lesson for us all. Harvard seems to shrink from the realisation and from that the realization of what is going to happen is going to happen.

My brother lifts the gun from the younger Appa son's head and uses it to summon over Joycie. It is as if Moloch had descended and struck the three of them dumb. You know the Moloch I mean; he's the one from Wikipedia associated with child sacrifices, and from my favourite OT book of Leviticus: 'And thou shalt not let any of thy seed pass through the fire to Moloch'. That's Leviticus chapter 18, verse 21 for those who are sticklers for those things. As, meanwhile, I see how the brother Joycie just manages to get across the space between the two chairs. It looks to me as if he was going to fall on his knees, and understandably. With a circular motion of the Browning from my brother he understands he must turn around. He does so. Tusker pulls him by the collar backwards to fall plum back into Harvard's lap.

The Ramaswarmy sons. Sitting on each other, as it were, in one easy chair. If they puffed out their stomachs, they might resemble one Appa Ramaswarmy sitting there.

We tie them like that.

My brother does so sloppily as though there is no danger, even were they loose. It aggravates me from this distance. But I notice he does so with a lot of silly knots that would take time undoing anyway, and he does so around and crisscross and up and down their bodies until they are trussed together like a Christmas gift tied in a crazy kindergarten kind of way.

My brother then puts down the Browning on the occasional table there. He takes a swig of the Harvard cool-climate wine and spits it out into the fire, where it belongs.

Then removes the kukri and slices off, like roasted meat, each ear lobe of each son.

Oh, the silence breaks then, but I am not listening. I cannot stop the mind-settlings with my twin, but I am able to dub here and there to protect my own sanity.

It is as if the tape of my mind's eye starts to break up at this point. I know my brother is out in the workshop in the garage and is returning to the house.

I know the Ramaswarmy sons are pitiable now.

I know he is at Harvard's PC and is typing some letter that annoyingly flashes in my mind to blank now, yet I know it is a letter to Appa Ramaswarmy telling him that this man Tusker, yes, did come to town and was handled as Appa would have expected in such a contingency. But, just in case, he and Joycie are going to vanish for a few days. Whatever Appa hears from Australia, don't, underlined, don't bother to take it seriously. Everything is fine, and all's fixed as Appa would want it.

I see the letter going in one addressed envelope to Hong Kong and put fastidiously by the front door for us to send by courier later.

I see the ear lobes wrapped in kitchen shrink wrap, put in another envelope and then fitted into my brother's side pocket for taking himself to Hong Kong.

I wonder whether life's little ironies will have the letter on the same plane.

All this I don't mind too much: I watched as he takes their wallets and extracts something near enough for the fare to Hong Kong. It seems and seemed only fair.

No, I do not blame my brother.

I do not even judge him.

My brother is my brother. I am me. Sure, that's obvious but the point I'm making is we must have been criss-crossed in the head at birth. That is no fault of his and it is no fault of mine. It was up to someone else to get blamed for that in time.

When they, whoever they are, find the Ramaswarmy sons, they would have discovered them as charcoaled as the family's bodyguard called Graddle on the Toorak house's gate. After the dog, not much Graddle left for the griddle, no.

Had 'they' arrived prior to the blast and the resulting fire, as I had, they would have seen my brother light the oxyacetylene torch he had brought in from the garage, place the bottom of the cylinder in the fire, bend the torch hose into a loose U and tape it like that so that the flame plays against the body of the cylinder, like a snake licking lazily at itself.

The tank could have been only a few feet away from the Ramaswarmy boys.

I have the feeling, too, he had hack-sawed a leak in one of the oil-heating pipes and had turned the outside valve to that on full.

I think he then turned the flame of the oxy torch up high and watched for a moment as its now almost transparent tongue began to lick through the cylinder's wall.

I think. I've gotten used to the mind's eye but how much trust do you put into what you thinking you are seeing from it?

I know he had to wade carefully through something on the polished- wood floor. It must have been the oil spilling everywhere.

But there is not enough clarity left to me to see what happened after he left.

What does amaze me about mind-eyeing all this is that I don't feel he was in any hurry to get out of the country.

If there had been an explosion and raging fire, which you'd have to presume, the bodies would have been discovered in a matter of hours. One of the first things the police would have done is put through a call to wifey's parents' house down the coast from Melbourne at a place called Koroit. As soon as she turned around and got back home

245

there in a day or so -- she sure wouldn't have been hurrying -- my brother's name, even the alias of Tusker, would be as well-known as last week's track winners.

Nevertheless, he did the couriering of the letter at his leisure and he did the ticket-buying only the next day, I know, and there was no hurry in us. None.

There is never ever much thrill to hurrying. I sense that.

But I guess I know overtly why he didn't hurry.

He was confident that that the National Crimes Commission detective, that annoying Baybe, would cover for him at least until Hong Kong.

But I also know neither of us had any idea why. I have a slight feeling maybe Baybe didn't even know.

You'd have to admit this in my brother's life, though: burning them down is a specialty of the house.

'My Lanka Now'.

Okay, back to this item, and to me living back here in the uplands again, the upland elephant might just as well be extinct.

What's fifty or so left in the wild?

What's fifty spread over this once great mythical area, once impregnable to even the invading Portuguese, Dutch and British with their modern weapons of war and their iron carriage wheels they said could get them up and down any mountains. And that's not even throwing in the ivory-tooth champeen of all time, Major T. W. Rogers. What a guy.

Where, as they rose out of the mists, the elephants seemed the strength of the ancients, the guardians of the traditional homelands, while all else on the plains around had fallen into the hands of the foreign devils bringing their buck shots.

Up here in the uplands of the island, the elephants were venerated. They were sacred. Malignancy followed any who interfered with them, any who hunted and trapped them. Only the *pannikers*, the traditional Muslim trappers, would risk the ill-fortune that came from their trapping, because they were neither Buddhist Singhalese nor Hindu Tamils. They were Muslims, so you could safely not have to worry about their safety even then.

The elephants' tail hairs were used by the ancestors up here, and would be by many today if possible, against evil and for protection against other wild animals. The most efficacious tail hairs came through sheer guts of whoever was mad enough to gather them and added to their magic properties. You plucked them on the run, while the animal was in the wild, making kinds of matador passes at it while it steamed around and at you in rage. These hairs worked their protection best because they had been untouched by man.

Yes, the upland elephant might just as well be extinct.

Take that one last bull somewhere. He's weary. He has old wounds that are giving him hell. He cannot chew much anymore; no more ripping the sweet core out of the kittul palm. No more crunching on the crisp great palm leaves. Now, only the soft fruits and the soft grains, sweetest and easiest from the human paddy fields and vegetable plots.

He knows he has no herd to call being part of anymore. He knows he is alone now.

He knows he has become easy meat and a pest.

He has become rogue because, for some reason he does not know, he has to go on living while living there is.

When should he live if not now?

And he will be in hiding in some deep overhang, maybe in some dark rift around the bottom reaches of Bible Rock.

All he has going for him now is his cunning and his unspent savagery.

It will be doing him a favour to put him down.

And it will be me who does that.

I vow to you here and now that it won't be Inspector Charles Ekanayake and his band of not-so-merry men.

247

It will be me because it was to me that the last old bull taught the ways of hunting and trapping.

As young as I was then, I have never forgotten the teaching.

Besides, it is in my blood.

I am his son.

He is alone and the last. And I am onto the last hair of his tail.

But all is not gloom and doom.

My Hansen returned from his plastic surgery in Colombo today.

My Hansen can smile!

It's not too much of a smile. But the lips are there, and so is the chin and so are the lower cheeks, and there's not much else you need for a smile, except the will to smile.

My Hansen has the will to smile.

I feel as terrific as he must feel, although I hope I don't look as not-so-terrific as he looks.

You couldn't really call it skin; it's more like scar tissue, a blotchy yellow and blotchy red, but it's alive and it's sucking up all those red corpuscles as hard as it can go. It's just like a tracing of the final picture to come next year when my drinker-of-a-Muslim friend Joe's brother comes back from Harley Street, London, for his annual holiday and completes the job.

My Hansen can not only smile, but he can move his jaw. When he chews, it actually looks like he's chewing. When he's just got it all still, it looks like he's got it all still. If those aren't a combined progress I don't know what is.

Oh, sure, you wouldn't want to be presenting him to any fair maid's family as the catch of the century. But, you look closely and you can see he's even younger than I thought, not much more than thirty really, when before you would have thought he had walked out of the Middle Ages wearing rags from the early Christian era.

There wasn't much Joe's brother could do with my Hansen's hands. Yet there are now extremities that you can look at and see where hands would once have been. He has a combined six fingers now that sort of work, and when the new skin has properly taken and stretched, you can already see how he will be able to bunch and stretch those, even point at things maybe. Maybe one day soon be able to pick things up.

We are talking here about my Hansen soon being able to feed himself.

There could even come a time when he might be able to dine out.

The people with him will admittedly have to have pretty strong stomachs, but he won't give a stuff. He's a gutsy little bugger. He'll put it away in those hollow legs with the best of them.

He would have been verging on handsome once, too. Even Father Thumbayaserni has no idea why he came in for treatment so late, after those fungus-faced, scrawny microscopic turds of Dr Armauer Hansen had eaten so much of him. He must have had the disease, with its loss of sensation and those white numb spots, many years before he started to go the way of Dorian Grey.

All we know is he came from some village deep in the southeast of the island and was probably kept hidden for fear that the village would ostracise the whole family. There are fiercely malefic deities in those villages. When my Hansen walked out of that village, it's fair to say he really did walk out of the Middle Ages.

There was sheer joy and anxiety in Hansen House on his return from the surgery, too. Remember that, even with modern drugs, all of the others must have had great fear that they would end up like him. He was their hope.

So, when he turned around to face them with that smile sort of thing and the radiance in his brimming eyes, there were gasps. Of joy, of relief. How unusual was that for Hansen House? They were the expressions of paths of dignity still open in the world, if only you kept on searching for them.

Sisters Lima, Margaret, Sriyani, Camilla and Fathers Thumbayaserni and Jayakody ... they were all present when my Hansen insisted I have the honour of removing the bandages he had worn up from Colombo. And so were all the other patients and so were all the other destitutes, and also all the orphans of the latter-day poverty holocaust, and Mrs Hokthar, who helped the Sister with the daily chores, and the two dogs and the many cats.

Mother Teresa wasn't there, but I bet she would have given a bob or two to have been.

I can tell you a hell of a lot of us cried.

He was tired. Oh, he was tired. Soon all he could do was lie on his cot and watch me while I carried on with my usual duties. Even the old lady who keeps farting in my face when I body-wash her didn't seem much interested in farting in my face.

She did anyway. God love her.

When I had finished with my other duties, I covered Hansen with a brand-new sheet. Tired, oh yes, he was tired. He let me stroke his head while he held my other hand as tightly as he could with his two new ones. It was like being held by latex gloves.

I smoothed his head for such a brilliant job well done, the bravery of the man, until he fell asleep.

Then I returned home here with a bottle of arrack and, after the house's little angels had fallen to sleep on their mats, had my own party.

I had not gone down to Colombo with my Hansen. Father Jayakody took him down and returned to bring him back.

I went to the Gampola station to meet them, though. When they got off the train, Father Jayakody hurried ahead of my Hansen so that he could get to me first. Such a serious look on his bulldog of a face with those asthmatic eye pouches. My heart felt like it had been stabbed.

But, you know, instead. Instead, what the good Father did was to slightly bend before me, take my hands and bring them to his lips.

It was only passing and it didn't make him look any happier, but the thing of it was he would have done the same had I been Mother Teresa herself.

I know that's blasphemous to think, let alone say. But it's out now.

Sisters Lima, Margaret, Sriyani, Camilla and Virathni.

Yes, Sister Virathni. As good as.

With that unhearty chaperone of a hymen, God has sent me an odd's-bods nun by measure other than a name.

But then, as I have said of my father, when will I live if not but now?

And where could I go if not stay here?

Shaming, a bit, perhaps, when I think about it as I lie here in the night and a few of them are gently zizzing around me. There are so many sounds of sleep that it seems the very house has begun to ever-patiently throb.

They get so very little grace. Not one of the eleven other people living in this house has ever had what you would call even a small break like, say, a small win in the national lottery.

What harm would that do?

A small win wouldn't change their frugality, wouldn't turn the universal Scheme of Things on its arse-end, would it?

They might buy a few more clothes, splurge out on a bit of meat, buy a gas bottle for cooking instead of having to scrounge wood for a tiny fire three times a day, lash out on a few more blankets for when it gets bitterly cold up here nights for months on end. And maybe, just maybe, they don't like having to squat over a hole in a concrete floor and having to try to flush and clean themselves with a can of water however more hygienic that still is than that disgusting concept of toilet paper.

Joseph Gayetter, that American inventor of toilet paper should have been ashamed to take out a patent on it. No wonder it took from his introduction of it in 1857 to the 1920s when you could first buy it in ordinary shops. He first claimed it treated piles. Then they put a watermark of his name on the first commercial sheets, so you just think about how many bums he wiped half-cockedly given that the average person uses 57 sheets a day at around 8.6 sheets a pop. Yuk.

The kitchen is box-size, black with soot. The chimney is a hole in the tile shards they have up there for a roof.

Roof? You can see the sky through this 'roof'. When the monsoons come, we are reduced to half the usual floor area for our sleeping mats. This is a wartime refugee huddle.

When the rains come really badly, there is no sleep, not even for the five little angels.

But in the mornings, they are still all mostly smiles. Their poverty is not their state of deprivation or their state of quaintness to write home about.

It is simply what state they are in and cannot do a blind thing about.

One half-sized table is where they lay out the food, but pushed up against the walls to make move for passing, which means only seating on two sides of it. The others sit on the floor with their plates in their laps or on the two concrete steps. The old people share the two nedun chairs they keep for visitors in the entrance area.

They remake-do with old cans, old bottles, old wrappers, any plastic, the rare newspaper. Plastic is magic to them, not the horror of the environmentalist. They are true John Wesley Hyatt children. They honour plastic. Plastic means cleanliness and preservation. They can wrap their food in it and it keeps a little longer; they can store their rice in layers of it, resistant for a time from rats. They can put out their rubbish in it rather

252

than, as a few years ago, having to dump it on public stinking, fly-ridden, rat-infested, dog-slathering, disease-ridden piles virtually outside their very front doors. The trouble is they can't afford plastic. Even the cheapest John Wesley Hyatt shit costs a relative fortune here.

My two of the Big 'They' are Geoffrey and wife Dashana. I will name them all here because they would never think to ask to be named.

Geoffrey-and-Dashana's little angels are five girls of names Brenda, Stephanie, Janice, Michaela, Marini in descending order. Thank God, they didn't keep trying for the missing boy. Stephanie doesn't speak much and only sometimes seems to hear; they do not know whether her hearing or her sight or her understanding generally is defective. They have never been able to afford to find out. At school, she has now to sit with the six-year-olds. She is thirteen, and she is crossed in her beautifully inky eyes.

It is hopeless to correct. Not even my Hansen House can help. She needs teaching in an environment this country does not have within reach of people like Geoffrey and Dashana. Or me now, after Joe's plastic-surgery brother insisted on getting his fee for Hansen in advance.

There is also Auntie June with her recurring bouts of malaria. There is Uncle Edgar with his urine problems. There is Grandma and then Grandpop Romesh, who is healthier than a mallee bull and twice as salty at eighty-one.

Grandpop needs no glasses, needs no cane, has his dick mostly flopped out to prove it does not drip like his brother, or so he says, but I'm sure he's still hoping for some lass to leap on him. The silly old codger. No mosquito had given him malaria or dengue or filaria, even though he's never slept under a mosquito net in his life. He eats everything like he doesn't know where his next meal is coming from and he gets to eat it before anyone else because who's to challenge he's still not the head bull around here?

So, I'm up to my neck in people here and, you know something?

For the first time in my life, they're not sending me crazy. For the first time in my life I am not screaming inside, like my brother.

And I think it's because of that I've just realised something very important:

I've returned, truly returned to my Lanka and the roots of it.

I have to tell you!

I have found my father!

The elephants and Aetha; it's him all right.

It was only by chance that I even bought the paper that first started running the story.

On the run from the local heavies was a grim-looking fellow they tagged Palhirana for exposing State terrorism at the highest level.

The guy had made a lot of enemies among very, very scared very, very important people.

He had come out into the open about a vigilante group called a reformed group called the Black Cats once a force for terror among the higher-ups of Lankan society in the 1990s. The Black Cats had reared its head again. Over the last decade dozens of opposition people had been murdered; top brass of the forces car bombed; screen idols suffered fatal accidents and gangland-style killings.... supposedly by the Black Cats then and the Black Cats death squads now. You know the sort of thing. What the new terrorists could do, the Black Cats could do better.

Mostly the Tamil Tigers fighting the war in the north and northeast of the island were originally blamed for the killing of opposition leaders.

It wasn't them then and it isn't anything to do with them now, wrote this Palhirana.

I declare under oath that it was and is me and my Black Cats.

If that's not making yourself a rogue elephant expressing a death wish, I wouldn't know what was.

However, I didn't take much notice of this until the next day the newspaper pieced together what was 'known' about this local Robin Hood, in the course of which it mentioned his code name.

It was Aetha.

I knew my father would have gone rogue. I told you.

In the Sixties, the article said, he disappeared from being an elephant master somewhere in the uplands. The rumour was that, even then, he had been working undercover trying to enrol the tea-estate Tamils into the Tamil-homeland struggle.

My snooty-nosed grandparents had an agent provocateur for a son-in-law. My father was upstaging them for artificiality.

I am so tickled pink about that.

Anyway, he apparently re-appeared in the early seventies in the Jaffna region in the north, openly working with the Tamil militants there. It was certainly known that he subsequently turned up in the Tamil stronghold of Chennai, where it was rumoured he had been put in charge of reorganising the fund-raising efforts from abroad.

Sure, 'efforts'. They had a lot of kiddie's fêtes around the world and gave out funny noses while they gave their parents bloody noses if they didn't meet their extortion demands.

It then skipped a whole period. All it said was that he was next seen around the ruling-party circles in Colombo --people who were supposed to be his sworn enemies.

I didn't need that explaining away. My Aunt Jayalitha and those JVPers who strolled in one night and said say hello to Aetha and bye byes to her life. Remember? And how Virathni

255

had said she had heard that my father had vow revenge for her?

It doesn't take much to guess he was always working for Colombo as a double agent anyway, so he just turned turtle one more time to pop up in Colombo government circles after supposedly running the Tamil's worldwide rackets for all those years.

It would have been simple for a double agent of his double-crossing instincts to convince his new masters that, backed by arms and men of his own choosing, he could turn the resurgent JVP latest tide.

How to do that?

Simply start terrorising them. My brother's mind's eye would have him saying. The JVP squads have the methods of going after the innocents, so we go after their innocents. We pull those damned puppies out of their beds and we make them watch, and we do it at night and we do it scary and we're do it as professionally brutal as they couldn't imagine they, as amateurs, could ever compete with.

He was successful, all right. The threatened new anti-Government uprising lasted only for a few months. By the end of that, the JVP leader found he wasn't any revanched Mao Tze Tsung and his rejuvenated uni students no Red Guard wave. More than 2000 youths were in gaols this time around alone. How many of them killed by the Black Cats under the cover of night, how many of them and members of their families buried in unmarked graves, would have undoubtedly stayed unknown. But now here was this tagline Palhirana, or this code-name Aetha, or my father, coming out as a double or triple agent or number-of-fingers agent, threatening to kiss and tell now.

Aetha would come to corner a dying, poisoned JVP leader in a farm house around here somewhere. How he really died maybe only my brother could imagine.

The self-confessed leader of the Black Cats was admitting he might have been getting out of control then, but he charged that there was absolutely no difference in wartime or peacetime violence when it came to high-up instructions for the Black Cats. Now even minor ruling party officials were using the group's squads to clean out their electorates of a lot of irritants. Why did he do it?, the newspaper pompously asked. Because he couldn't care less, he said.

What other credentials for him being my father would you want?

Why was he exposing all this now?, the newspaper naively asked.

'What fair trial can expect?', he apparently answered as though that was an answer other than a pale excuse of his actions, an evasion.

Again, in even that, what other credentials for him being my father would you need?

This Palhirana or whatever was demanding an independent commission to investigate the Government's crimes against humanity alongside the one being conducted by the UN, and would not give himself up until he was assured that was going to happen and that he would live to see the day.

'They have forced me go into hiding and are at this very moment hunting me down like a rogue elephant.'

Rogue elephant, oh yes. That's him.

And, now, somewhere close around here in this now-time of Gampola, here was another reason for Inspector Bloody-fucking-hell-sorry Ekanayake to be nosing around town.

That's why he said he was hunting an Aetha. He's got some sniff of the leader of the Black Cats.

Or maybe he knows the father, the son, and maybe he reckons he can nab both of us in one go, caught in the same net.

So, it's going to be a race as to who's first to track down and trap the old rogue, is it?

If I were you, I'd put your money on me. Don't forget I've got my brother's mind's eye. Oh, I mightn't have any ideas as yet; and I mightn't know where I could even buy an idea from if it was looking me in the face; and I mightn't have any resources at my beck'n'call like Ekanayake has. But I've got this thing called moral certainty on my side.

That's simply because my father owes me far more than he owes them.

And, I tell you, what he owes me is more than Phelan & Collander came to owe John Wesley Hyatt.

Even if it is slightly less than the game of billiards once owed to the once upland elephant, as I think you'd be justified in saying.

Part Three

I notice that my brother is able to see across the Tung Wan Beach with his small travelling binoculars to the Appa Ramaswarmy apartment.

Sitting out on that little balcony in the heat of the day, a rug around his knees and socks and slippers, the fat man looks like he is rugged up against the cold on the deck of a weight-watcher's cruise. Which hasn't helped his weight much.

His presence, through its sheer corpulence, shines foreign in this skinny place of Hong Kong.

My brother, whom I am now convinced operates with the alias of Tusker (without needing any of the Inspector's snide remarks) doubts that, even back in his native Tamil Nadu, the gross fat man across the bay would look in place. It is a measure of Appa Ramaswarmy that he looks singular and knows he looks singular. It has given him a pompous air all his life, and quite possibly all tee health he ever needed. But, up close though our binoculars, the eyes are still always sliding. It is as though the awareness of always being watched is starting to wear him down.

Tusker guesses the man must be feeling exposed right now. He has come to Hong Kong without his normal protection, removed himself to safety while his sons handle the Tusker problem. The letter which my brother has written on the Harvard son's PC might even be on its way to being delivered right now, or maybe even just delivered.

Coming to Hong Kong, protection or no protection, is rare for the fat man. That apartment, like the one in Canberra supposed for Tusker but of course brought for his Rehana, he has purchased according to his tastes, but not nearly for his own use. It is more of an operational centre, with Appa's imprimatur on it, so that whether it is Tusker himself or one of the hirelings who is staying there to ensure the drug deals go

259

through smoothly, there is always the reminder of who the king pin is.

It is a wonder the man has lived past such vanities. The only person he should be living past is the architect of the New Parliament House in Canberra who is rumoured to have never owned up to it. I wouldn't know about that. I don't think I've ever read anything about that.

An apartment on the tiny, crammed dumb-bell island of Cheung Chau, a ferry choof from Hong Kong island towards the southwest, was pure Appa Ramaswarmy idiosyncrasy. Sure, it is only one of the 235 islands that make up Hong Kong, so in theory securable. For one thing, it has a tourist slogan that few tourists from the west could resist: its streets are so narrow that cars are banned on Cheung Chau. They have a fire, they have to trot down the alleys with a fire cart that looks genuinely eighteenth-century London. Tens of thousands of fishermen, boat builders, commuters to central Hong Kong trading bourses, tradesmen, tourists and thugs are packed into the few squares of whatever type of area measurement you're into.

From the ferry terminal within the anchorage of junks, sampans, yachts and trawlers and rust-gutted coastal traders, it is only a few minutes' walk across the narrow part of the isthmus, through the mad-clamped centre of the town, to the lifeguard-guarded Tung Wan or Morning Beach.

But securable, no. Tusker's innate sense of natural cover was always offended by the fat man's choice of this place for the Hong Kong base of the Australasian Tamil homeland operation.

The only vamoosing you could make was by sea, and, by the time you got around to vamoosing, those from whom you were doing the vamoosing would be bobbing around out at the narrow anchorage's entrance with their eyes gleaming along their gun sights.

260

To Tusker I sense that the need to take that apartment was the ultimate testimony of Appa Ramaswarmys obsession with standing out.

My brother is, in fact, in thrall again, and I feel uneasy realising this in his mind's eye reaching out to me. It means there is danger here in this place he is taking me to, and in what he is going to do.

He turns away from scrutinising the fat Appa across the bay and leaves for his appointment.

At this time of day, Tsi Sui Yuen, or Sunny Rug as the old Chinese boss was affectionately called for no reason my brother could guess except that the man might have cut a mean Bunny Hug in the thirties, would be sleeping off his lunch on his sampan in Cheung Chau anchorage.

The mooring position of being inboard to the harbour wall and halfway along the wharf from the ferry terminus showed the seniority and the respect accorded to the old fisherman and boat builder -- but, to any who knew, that respect was built around legendary exploits of the old crone and his fiercely revengeful extended family over decades of smuggling and not a little outright piracy.

You could say he was the Oriental Major T. W. Rogers. If Hong Kong had elephants, Sunny Rug would have had quite a few heads and trunks hanging around his bulkheads. The ivory, of course, he would have carved and sold. He was no way a sentimentalist.

Tusker has never quite known whether the old man headed up a crime Tong on Cheung Chau island or if his extended family consisted of only members of the Yuen family. The point is, of course, academic. Sunny Rug headed one of the traditional families of Cheung Chau, so that he could call on any number of men, had he need, to take you out to the breakwater, gut and fillet you, and then bring you dressed up fit to sell as shark from the wharf's fish stalls.

Tsi Sui Yuen would be snoozing on the sampan, along with a gaggle of his sons' wives and an array of their bright children, because this was his business office as well as home. He would only have to raise himself on his elbows to see the glass obelisks that shimmered equatorially and beaconed Hong Kong's economic boom to a world of admirers, apart from Tsi Sui Yuen. A few floors amongst them which he surreptitiously owned himself would be more than a mere optical illusion also.

But Sunny Rug prided himself on the continuity his life represented. If this sampan was good enough for his mother to give birth to him on, it is good enough for him to work within the life he owes to it, just as it remains to him the perfect upbringing for as many lives as possible.

As wide as his world has been in one sense, its centre has always been locked on the old craft he is now not really sleeping on, only dozing. For Tsi Sui Yuen is fretfully waiting for Appa Ramaswarmy, who has already caused him incalculable loss of face for not yet paying his respects during the four days the fat *gawloh* has been in the apartment just down the narrow island streets.

The old man will not come to know, as my brother is already sure of, that Appa Ramaswarmy has not paid this required courtesy because he is feeling his age, suddenly, too much.

If not a visit from the fat pig, then it has to be Tusker, who Sunny Rug knows has arrived that very day.

And if Tusker, he is expecting an explanation as to what by all the dogshit gods of the dogshit sea was going on.

Yes, my brother. So clear now, my eyes to his, stepping down the parapet of the hotel, cutting across the messy sand shoal they have perhaps jokingly put down as a tourist beach, and moving along the market-stalled, people-thralled streets towards the wharf in the only way you can when in a Chinese shopping street, certainly as confined as this one: one step forward and two steps sideways. You crab the streets of Hong Kong and you crab the streets of China. It is the natural weight of other people combined. But my brother is too impatient to have ever appreciated that.

Near Sunny Rug's berth, he buys a strip of fried and dried cuttlefish which, in his struggle to get teeth into, will mark him as just another *gawloh* tourist, and waits at the wharf's edge.

Immediately, the usual Sunny Rug grandchildren come trilling up on the salt old wooden rower, leap up the rust-rilled iron ladder in precarious delight of crawling over one another to be the first to get to the top of the wharf, and then to surround him like a long-lost uncle who has a lot of Christmasses to catch up on.

They are as cherubic as all Chinese children, cherubs on the chatter, nifters of the sharp innocence. How do they come to lose it at some sad undetermined age? It seems a rude metamorphosis for such a quality of sheer joy. No one god from any set of religion, of course, will put up his or her hand to say I do it. If any did, the Chinese would wave the claim away; they know one can blame nothing. One can only chastise the childlike perversities of their household gods for the tragicomic acts that sprinkle their mortal road, because it is these they feel they can box the ears of and off in the privacy of the home.

The Yuen grandchildren now have my brother from the wharf, down the iron steps, off that leaking coracle of theirs, and up upon the stern of the sampan by means of mysterious fluttering ministrations. They must have all come from spirit children.

Waiting to greet us is the middle stage of their losing innocence: the gristled jaw, pinched nostrils and narrowed black eyes of middle-age in a face that is still masking youth. He, this Sunny Rug middle son, would be armed, but it would be with the narrow, slithered knife, the rib tickler, of the Hakka sea pirates of his ancestors.

Towards the bow end of the interior, having brushed through three sets of gaudy and musty dividing curtains, harsh with their faded dragons, we now confront the legend himself. In Tsi Sui Yuen's face there is a patience as the flush of dozing sinks back into the ancient earth of his wrinkles. But it is not the patience with the transience of all things, as many would have the oriental inscrutability. It is the patience of accepting this is just the next struggle to bear along the long path that has taken him from humiliating poverty to where his grandchildren can cavort shamelessly without any desperation that makes it imperative they leapfrog over their youth.

The venerable Yuen.

He does not bother to rise to meet us. Chinese ceremony is as Chinese inscrutability, and mainly in the quaint assumption than in the practice. In fact, that the old man does not need to stand at my brother's entrance is salutatory, rather than impertinent. Tusker, not exactly a friend and perhaps never could be, is an old business partner for whom over-niceties would be so unnecessary as to perhaps provoke suspicion.

I have the feeling, as the two men meet that that old business has always been mutually rewarding.

He has nodded to my brother and clapped his hand once and hard in acknowledgement of his arrival. At this, his two other sons, nimble men with springy bandy legs and heavy chests, are then able to stand and short-whoop and shake hands western-style, an indication of the changes to come if they should ever live past their aged, ageless, reverend father.

Tusker waits a moment to give accord to the greetings, then bows from the waist and clasps his hands together, fingertips touching his forehead, in a formal Hindu greeting. This amuses the Yuen mob greatly. At one, my brother has deliberately reaffirmed to them the superiority they have over the barbarian, a darkly-hewn devil as he is, from the uncivilised land of purple gods, mad female gods always with

264

female trouble, monkey and elephant-headed gods. Not a household god to boot around among them.

My brother prefers this pecking order with Yuens. I do not know exactly why but I can sense it maintains his freedom to experiment when dealing with them. It allows him the room to cut closest to the bone, I feel.

So, he laughs widely himself as they chuckle, as ever, at his greeting, and sits down on the low hard stool opposite the old man.

Again, I find it surprising to understand there will be no tea taking as the Chinese gazers would have us think, no slow indulgences of small talk before business can be brought up. Among old business partners, there can be nothing more pleasant than business; to small talk would be inconsiderate, to delay would be unethical. Besides, Sunny Rug is a gutter of fish from his boyhood; and time and his nettings have always been on the tide.

The old man wants to hear apologies, and will not waste time, politeness or not, in getting them or in giving vent to outrage if they are not forthcoming.

'You have come from the fat taipan, Tusker sinsaang?'

The insertion of the adjective for Appa Ramaswarmy is proof he is not happy and wants it known. This is a deliberate breach of etiquette.

'Yuen sinsaang, I have come instead of the fat man.'

Even I hear the return implied insult clearly. It is the first time I hear my brother's voice so ringingly. I think it has something to do with the confidence of now knowing that Appa Ramaswarmy has not visited the old man. It is a sloppy and arrogant oversight.

'Ah.'

The old man returns the glances from his sons. Yes, a sloppy and arrogant oversight which, together with our reply, has convinced them they have indeed lost face, but that my brother is certainly so aware of it that he is even pointing it out openly, and perhaps has even come to correct it.

265

The old man taps the coconut matting on the deck between them with the back of his meaty hand, the elder son there calls sharply, and my brother waits humbly while one of the wives hurries in with mai tai and wooden lacquered cups.

As the old man pours, the sons are now free to light cigarettes, the pungent people's smokes from some mainland government warehouse. They have apparently told us long ago that contraband tastes sweeter, but their smog mixes heavily and conspiratorially with the existing weight of garlic, cooking oil, diesel and impregnated tar already in the air.

My brother stands to toast the longevity of the venerable Tsi Sui Yuen, as do the sons.

The old man remains seated still, his heavy eyes appreciating the small honour being accorded to him, while remaining unsure whether to accept gracefully or impatiently until he hears if and how his loss of face to such coal-coloured hyenas is to be compensated.

Despite knowing the old man is undoubtedly thinking this, I am feeling comfortable enough. I see how Tusker has never been so foolhardy as to think his dark skin has become less abhorrent to the Yuens over the years. He knows, too, that it is only while their dealings continue to proceed smoothly that they will give sway to their quite real admiration of how he operates. It has been that ability, and that alone, which has guaranteed the survival of both parties, and we know the old man grudgingly knows and respects it.

When Tusker drains the aggressive white spirits, he sits down and levels his eyes at old Yuen. There must now be business, or at least talk of it.

He tells Sunny Rug that he has learnt there is to be a run on from Guangzhou tomorrow night in the usual way that it has always been done.

'I have not heard this,' the old man cuts in sharply.

'No, Yuen sinsaang,' we are expressing this with slow gravity it seems, 'as regrettable as it is, it seems whom you call taipan has made the arrangements himself without the prudence of consulting any of us.'

Previously, there would have been careful consultations about auspicious times for all, or the inauspicious time for this one or that.

Previously, we know we must involve only tried and proven friends, those who have benefited over the many years. Our mind's eyes.

Previously, those basics were everyone's guarantee of security.

'Of course.'

'But it seems, venerable Yuen, that the man called Appa Ramaswarmy,' and we see the way the Chinese are sharp to my brother distancing himself from his once-senior, 'has seen fit to do his prudent partners and friends the disservice of contracting another group to carry out the operation.'

'Who?' but the old man is looking angrily at his sons as though their guan-xi, their connections, have put the family in danger for failing to have learnt any of this.

'It is a group from the Hong Kong island, where rats have ears. It is some running dogs from Causeway Bay, I am sorry to say.'

The old man nods grimly at my brother. There are no twinkles in his eyes now; they have grown watery, as though the thought of further dishonour, this time at the hands of this rival and hated community from Causeway Bay of water dwellers, was about to make him cry.

There are many influential people back in Chennai, I hear my brother saying, who consider this a dangerous course of action. It can only be seen, they feel, that the Ramaswarmy family has chosen to forget the safety of the whole international organisation and, to add to the disgrace, the honour of our Hong Kong colleagues.

Yet no one could possibly say the Ramaswarmys were fools. They were showing themselves to be unstable and therefore inherently dangerous if they thought they could accomplish this secretly by contracting strangers without the powerful Cheung Chau people learning of their deception. But fools? No one could think of them as fools.

'I do not think they are fools.' The old man is hunched, as though he is going to spring, sensing all. His sons are nervy.

Fools, no. Therefore, why are they doing something so foolish?

'Well, ha?'

My brother leans forward and the old man knows that now the hard business will be spoken of.

'The consensus among the influential people in Chennai is the Ramaswarmys are taking this action in order to deliberately bring the operation to the attention of the authorities, Yuen sinsaang.'

'So we can be sure they have new friends, ha?' The old man is speaking but more to concentrate better on listening.

'We do not think so. We think they might want no friends at all, Yuen sinsaang.'

'Explain, please.'

My brother shrugs. 'Perhaps it is that the Ramaswarmys want to withdraw into, shall we say?, more mainstream activities. We do not know for certain. We only know this: they have arranged tomorrow's run,' but, he is pausing for emphasis, 'they have taken great pains to divorce themselves from it while at the same time drawing attention to it by organizing it ad hoc.'

One of the sons stifles a cry of fury and swings out his slither knife. The elderly Yuen nods at it with smirking approval of the reaction. He is still a greater pirate than his sons will ever be.

My brother waves his hand in mild reproach.

'It seems the Appa Ramaswarmy has had a yacht leased at the Royal Yacht Club for the exact time of the run. I regret to say he has done this very openly and very loudly.'

This makes the three Yuen sit dumbly with open mouths. This is foxing, surely. To hire a yacht for the operation, as against the usual speedboat of the Yuens', and to hire it for the exact time of the operation are crass enough. But to do it from the Royal Hong Kong Yacht Club, where everyone knows whose panties who is chewing, and to then make a loud thing about it, is sheer madness.

'It is even an open secret with the police in Australia. How would the Hong Kong police not already know of it? There is more.'

'Please.'

'The Appa Ramaswarmy has not hired the yacht in his own name, nor would we expect him to. But neither has he hired it under some fictitious name. The name he has hired it in is mine.'

'And?'

The old man's eyes are twinkling again. We hear him thinking that all he has really heard from all this is that these melanous barbarian devils are at each other's throat. Be wary. Nothing here has been heard which directly threatens him or his family. He will revenge himself for loss of face on the bloated farting hog Appa Ramaswarmy to be sure, but that is far less trouble than if he was stupid enough to become involved in some dung-coloured *gawloh* power struggle. As my brother is continuing:

'He has my address as Cheung Chau island.'

'Aeeia!'

But the old man's wide eyes to his sons are really amused eyes, in crafty twinkle again, to his sons. It means that Appa Ramaswarmy has clearly tied the hiring of the yacht to the Yuen family.

'Tsi Sui Yuen, the influential people in Chennai and many in Australia consider this further proof the Ramaswarmys are planning this run only for the purpose of having its previous partners compromised.'

'It would seem so, Tusker sinsaang.' The old man has gone cagey. He can see it might be no longer a matter of loss of face on the part of Appa not paying respects, but one of actual finger pointing by the Ramaswarmy faction. Yet finger pointing kills no clever cat, and he can deal with that at a later time. Where is the Yuen family involvement? Maybe the fat half of a dog's turd is trying not to involve the family and it's just barbarians at each other's monkey throats. What else can civilised people expect?

'When the yacht is confiscated,' my brother answers instinctively, 'and the Causeway Bay running dogs are caught red-handed holding their dicks waiting on the barge for it, they will be most unhappy. They will know it has all been set-up. Might they think they have had their gullets opened not by the Ramaswarmys, but by some jealous ancient rivals from along the Harbour?'

The old man stiffens with the realisation: 'Those Causeway Bay lovers of rat piss are not even a family. They will leak like their flea- infested boats about us and only think they have gained a year's good joss by doing so.'

'Aeii, we use the knife.'

The oldest son, who has the knife held as though lecturing about its qualities, gutturally interrupts. The old man is understanding about why he has taken the unprecedented step of breaking in over his father so coarsely, and only inclines his head with heavy wisdom. Now it is a question of survival of the Yuen family.

The scars on the son's forearms and the lack of them on his face show, as an artist might, that he has had a good deal of practice in what he is advocating.

But I can see clearly how it is my brother, rather than the old man, though who responds by shaking his head.

'If there is no operation, if the police have nothing, how will we friends know what the Ramaswarmys' intentions are? Are we to sit around and wait for another time when we do not have the advantage of prior knowledge? The influential people in Chennai have thought about this, and recommend a course of action.'

'They want?'

The venerable Yuen can wave away his son's knife. He knows by Tusker's steadiness of reply that we have a plan, a plan that would not just be running like beaten curs for some dishonourable cover. If not...

The influential people think, Tusker is replying, while I sense he is in thrill again with the danger of knowing by the poisonous expression that the old man is already thinking perhaps the safest way is for both the fat toad and this charcoal one here should be put to the knife. I shudder at the realisation. I seem to see the old man looking at us like fish for the slab.

They think, Tusker, yes, is responding despite me and my mind's eye, that if the Yuen family have the connections, then the man who has hired out the yacht could be persuaded to see the wisdom of changing the name against the yacht's hire.

'We perhaps could assure your friends of his cooperation.' It was no out-and-out commitment by any means.

The man should also be wise enough to see the name would be better returned to its true hirer: Mr Suresh Ramaswarmy of the apartment on Tung Wan Beach.

'We can perhaps assure you of his wisdom on this will be sought out and got', whispered Tsi Sui Yuen but narrowing his eyes to his sons without, somehow, looking directly at them.

'My people also think,' my brother -- I see now satisfied and feeling the thrill of that -- continues in this dark moment with too much amusement for me, 'that the operation should be allowed to go ahead as the Ramaswarmys have scheduled.'

'Explain.' It is a very unpleasant command.

'But that the feared Yuen people should take the place of the Causeway Bay sewer muck.'

This is puzzling the venerable Yuen. He leans forward sharply, as though he has suddenly realised his mind has wandered.

'Explain to this tired old man why he should, please.'

271

'We know there will not be a full assignment from Guangzhou, but there must be something to make it authentic. Let us say it has to be at least half-shipment, or the police will smell a fat Ramaswarmy rat. Why let the corrupt ones among the police carve up 'goods' like that?'

'It would be a shame perhaps.'

'Even a half-shipment would still call in a minimum of a two-thirds of a million American dollars wholesale, no?'

'Usually, *hou*.'

This humble half-shipment, my brother purrs, while worth far too little for a worthy enough gift, he has been instructed to offer to the esteemed Yuen family of Cheung Chau as an apology for any dishonour incurred at the hands of the rogue Ramaswarmys and an affiance of even greater business in the future.

There is no hesitation. It is an easy calculation to realise this is at least three times their usual seventeen- and-a-half per cent.

'It is I who am unworthy, Tusker sinsaang. But, tell me how they think we could go about evading the pig police.'

We are being modest again, but not so much as we look like we are talking to unworldly men. The usual time for the barge to get alongside is nightfall. We are suggesting we make the recovery in the usual way but while there is still evening light -- say, an hour earlier.

Furthermore, if the venerable Yuen can assist in that, then my brother guarantees that the police would still gain something from their otherwise failed raid.

'Something that will make them visit the apartment of a fat, filthy black sow guts, ha?'

Oh, surely.

'And for you, Tusker sinsaang?'

The old man will not, cannot, believe my brother wants nothing; even I realise he will go on wheedling for an answer until he can feel sure.

We answer simply: the Australasian operation.

The old man can understand and be content. He sits back and waves his sons to do the same. There is not even *li*, obligation, required of him. It is better than he could have negotiated for himself.

There are perhaps a few favours to be asked by way of tidying up. Momentarily, Sunny Rug sways forward again in an automatic reaction to possible bargaining.

Perhaps the honourable Yuen would see to it that the hotel bill is paid if my brother decides to depart in all of a sudden? Perhaps the manager of the hotel can also be convinced of the virtue of erasing all record of my brother ever staying at his establishment?

The reply is easy, relieved, and quick: 'We can assure the manager's enthusiasm.'

Tsi Sui Yuen glances at the younger son who has barely moved but whose lighter complexion has flushed deeply with emotion throughout the conversation. He nods to the unspoken delegation from his father to handle the manager. No money; it will be done through the back door, or favours owed and to be given.

'And afterwards,' the old man is now full of contentment, 'with the fat dog of a devil bitch?'

My brother had only small requests there of the venerable Tsi Sui Yuen: that he allows to be delivered to the Appa a note from his wife and a tiny package of dim sum. Also, if the esteemed Yuen knows the police who will surely visit the smelling fat swine's apartment to be *yungwo*, or night-time or corrupt, ones who can be bought off, then the fat hog should not go unpunished. But, if the elder Yuen knows them to be good-soup police then, together with the Australian police, they will have enough on the hog who barely pisses to compensate any dishonour or treachery given the honourable Yuen family.

Either way, the Appa Ramaswarmy is not welcome back into Australia and should not ever again be seen in civilised company. Agreed?

Agreed, Tusker sinsaang.'

Now, even I can see from this distance how it has become an out-and-out commitment.

Sunny Rug sits back with satisfaction, with a leer that would upstage Charlie Chan, whom he has certainly lived past but probably only because Charlie Chan was fictional, although a real favourite of mine, especially the films where Number Two Son, Jimmy Chan, kept annoying the old man.

'So, we are to have the pleasure of turning the dead cat towards both the suppurating dogs from Causeway Bay and the fat pork who sits not far from here. So, until tomorrow, *ha*?'

I can see past musing about Charlie Chan's wispier moustache that they all know the usual time and place and what to do. All my brother and the Yuens have to do is take off an hour to, yes, turn the dead cat.

Of course, I wasn't in that nous-speak to understand all the details of the operation or run or whatever they were talking about. I guess there are limits to the mind's eyes.

I guess too it was all pretty simple for my brother to set up if you had the purchasing contacts in the then-Burmese part of the Golden Triangle, and then the organisation to get the poppy pollen across the newly opened southern China route.

There were plenty of Chinese couriers waiting in line to hop, step and a jump it through Mengzi and Miyama in Myanmar-of-now, then hug the North Vietnam border, where the Chinese patrols had loftier international concerns on their minds to worry much about you, until you turned to do a quick lob through Jungxi and Nanning down to the entrepreneurs in Guangzhou, which was fast doing a reverse metamorphosis into its former capitalist state of Canton.

From Guangzhou, there were ways limited only by the imagination to get your harvest of the Golden Triangle to the back alleys of the world. You could wing it to and out of such cities as Shanghai or Beijing; disperse it through any one of thousands of ports and harbours along the way; ship it out to

South Vietnam or Hainan. You could get it there by cart, car, bicycle fleet, plane, sampan, junk, freighter, passenger liner, in bellies, in bowels, in suitcases, in tinned fruits, in dolls' botties.

Out of Guangzhou, the tried and proven way for you was along the Pearl River and down the estuary to the archipelago of those over two hundred islands which comprise Hong Kong.

Oh sure, the Pearl River route had been 'blown' years ago; a few years ago, if you chose this way, you loaded up knowing the only real-percentage chance you had was if you had your fingers crossed in a fashion some passing God might smile upon, while your harvest ran the gauntlet of highly sophisticated, high-speed detection units patrolling the Pearl estuary. But, lately, what with all those other labour-intensive avenues thinning government resources, the Pearl had made a comeback as an avenue in your favour.

All you had to be, as my brother Tusker always ensured, was sure of your details, efficiency, and the security of those details, however minor, and the Pearl offered a lot of advantage. Good old girl as she is and hopefully always will be. You have to look your frilly best when you flow past the Bund in old Shanghai as it hopefully, too, always will be.

I don't think --no, I know – that my brother had anything to do with the deal-making in the Triangle or the source payments, or the courier networks across southern China -- other than doing the initial notifications along the ways, that is. In the worldwide Tamil homeland network, it seems to me, once given a little authorised push, moneys were smoothly transferred among Zurich and other central European banks, and even through the new numbered, Swiss-style accounts you could now open in most revenue-hungry countries if you knew the right person. And Tamils always know the right person.

Chennai coordinated these aspects, as it did the despatch and delivery of the consignments, and simply debited or credited, say, the Australasian contribution through its external account, like any well-run international corporation would.

My brother's preference whenever it came to direct involvement, yes, mostly seemed to be straight to the heart of the main shipping stands of Hong Kong Harbour itself. There was no night-time dropping off of buoys at the termination of the Pearl River and then trying to outrun the radar to Hong Kong. The Hong Kong water police were still well used to nipping off that sort of endeavour for all but the foolhardy or raw-boned or desperate of attempts. They had the technology for the commonsensical criminal.

No, Tusker used simple limpets that held the waterproof bags in place below the waterline of the cargo ships against any current at any speed of knots cargo ships are capable of.

The bags themselves had magnets to their sides and were attached top and bottom on either side. They were not placed so that you needed scuba equipment to retrieve them when the ship arrived in Hong Kong Harbour; scuba diving was just too obvious an activity. A good swimmer slipping over the side of the supply lighters that contracted to the ship at journey's end could do the retrieval quietly and efficiently while other lighter crew bustled around attending legitimately to the ship's needs.

The exact placement of the bags, then, was paramount. I find it amazing how accurately this could be done. All my brother had to know was the heaviest cargo the ship was likely to arrive in Hong Kong with, and then simply have someone consult Lloyds' cargo-loading manual in order to find out the displacement level at which the ship would be sitting in the water.

Depending on the cargo displacement, the magnets were set on the hull at Guangzhou at a depth which would bring them close to the waterline after cargo clearing in Hong Kong. By arrangement with the cargo officer on board, Tusker and the Yuens would know what cargo would be unloaded in what sequence, and so be able to make a quite precise assessment of the time the bags would be convenient for the swimmer.

With the Yuens' humming activities on the lighter, it mattered little even if the ship was berthed right in the middle of the lanes of Hong Kong Harbour. Even careful binocular scrutiny would have an improbable time picking out the swimmer/retriever from among the hustle and bustle of taking the 'gash' or rubbish off, cleaning above and below decks, sending up pre-ordered supplies, caterings, pumping the drinking water, and the loud bartering for the human services that make a Chinese mainland sailor's life, without many Hong Kong dollars for any sort of shore leave, worth the hard cake.

A servicing lighter was the perfect cover for a painter to be hanging innocuously over the side to allow a good man to slip over the side, dislodge the magnets and attach the bags to the underwater end of the rope by clamps.

The Yuens would not pull the rope up. They would continue to service the mother ship in the correct way -- the supply contracts were a profitable legitimate sideline, anyway. Afterwards, Sunny Rug's men would merely pull away and tow the lighter back to its Kowloon-side berth up along Ferry Street, during which the bags would be attached, still under water, to grapple on the Yuens' speedboat which everyone knew came to ferry Tsi Sui Yuen himself or his sons back home on Cheung Chau.

It seems that occasionally, over the years, the Hong Kong Drug Squad had rounded on the particular ship they were 'unloading' and conducted a search of the ship and the lighter, including their hulls. Frogmen had never discovered any of the bags. The old man Yuen always insisted that that was because the bags at the painter's end were easily manipulated out of the frogmen's way in the murky water.

But Tusker seems to know that it was more likely the obligation that Yuen had many of the police under. They got many back-door benefits by cooperating with the Yuens; their families could get into the best clubs, the best schools, the desirous positions. They could, as the Chinese would say, 'live under the shade of the Emperor's favour'.

If ever anything did go wrong, the Yuens -- simple lighter contractors -- the owners, the officers, the crew would simply deny any involvement. Anyone could have attached those bags in any one of the stopovers along the Pearl River.

I can see how my brother's genius or flair, call it what you will, was to always clear with the Ramaswarmys the most obvious routes combined with the simplest methods. But what he is planning this next night I am sharing now is different, in that he and the Yuens have to interfere with the Ramaswarmys' existing scheduling and so deliberately flaunt their 'piracy' of the consignment. The Yuens were not even officially contracted to service the ship.

A lot of satisfactions have to be arranged in this one day. The Sunny Rug eldest son is undoubtedly waving his slither knife under many noses while silkily reminding of many alternative advantages.

Even a dummy like me could see how easily their plan could backfire, leaving their fat and indigestible gut worm from a rabies dog, Appa Ramaswarmy, feeling more than smarmy as the only one left in the clear.

For the charred splinters that were all that was left of my own crap-house-as-home and my life in Australia, I close my eyes and wish it not so, but I know my linked mind's eye is not lying. If only because he is so grossly fat and now sick, I should live past Appa Ramaswarmy.

They have broadcast warnings of a rising typhoon over the South China Sea for the next few days.

Already, I can hear the windows to my brother's hotel room begin their spasmodic rumblings from the strengthening wind across the waters of Tung Wan Bay.

It is not affecting Appa Ramaswarmy, whom we watch over there again through the binoculars. He still sits rugged upon the balcony of his apartment, so perhaps the man is as ill as my brother now thinks he is. He is in the lee of any coming typhoon, and seems to be huddled there in preparation to witness the typhoon show, if and when it arrives.

Yet he does not seem to have any energies to call upon, even for the best wild theatre of Nature.

In better times, he would have paid at least the nominal respects to Sunny Rug, whom he despised because he knew Sunny Rug despised him, even if he was intending to doublecross the old pirate. He would have come armed with a simple story that would have allowed Tsi Sui Yuen to withdraw from the run without loss of face to the Causeway Bay gang. There would have been no sloppy and offensive oversight.

In better times, too, the fat Appa would have his own set of binoculars and would be scanning the town, the small curving beach below him and, especially, this hotel across the bay where enemies, like my brother is now, would have been staying. He would have done so precisely because his latent paranoia would be warning to look out for someone watching him.

But, no, he remains sitting there, decked, and so my brother can confirm how sick and feeble the old man is. It is certain he cannot even entertain the prospect that his sons back in Melbourne could fail him with pushing Tusker out of the way, what with all the resources and precise instructions he has gathered for them.

And while, at that moment of clarity, we are watching him, my brother sees the wife -- in theory, still my mother-in-law if that wasn't enough to starch my gall -- come out onto the balcony with the Skypak envelope we have sent. It is not

279

exactly Skypak's usual efficiency. Nonetheless, it has arrived and is being opened for him by her.

To the news supposedly from the Harvard son that Tusker arrived in town and has been 'diverted', Appa reads also that he should not worry about what he might hear in Hong Kong there because he and Joycie are just going to ground for a while as a precaution. The two Ramaswarmy parents consult urgently. That is, Mrs Ramaswarmy consults Appa urgently, her mouth close to his bobbing ear and undoubtedly on the whine, while the old man sits otherwise immobile, decrepitly. Not even this sham good news looks to be giving him any sort of animation.

Our binocular mind's eyes.

Finally, we see the head of the Ramaswarmys look up as though his wife was at the top of a deep, deep well above him and he smiles wanly. I presume it is a smile. It seems to me more like rictus that has faded out of itself.

The woman pats him on the shoulder and returns inside. Appa Ramaswarmy sits there. It is hard to discern whether he is sitting there with any sense of relief or is already dozing again. Our Skypak letter slips off his lap.

It was a bit of a shock to see, when he looked up at her, that he didn't have his teeth in.

Appa Ramaswarmy has gone gummy.

These visions, as I have been telling you, only really come in clumps. It is almost as if I am connected to what Tusker only wishes me to be connected with --or, perhaps, our perceptions can only link on the level of higher excitements, not for everyday occurrences.

I am starting to worry whether that means I will see, perhaps even experience, my brother's death -- or he mine, and how I feel it.

But, if it does mean one or the other of that, would that also mean, for example, we will each also die a little or, worse, die too, when the time comes for the other?

I will not think about that.

To avoid thoughts like that breaking through was precisely why I made out a list of items to think through in the first place.

I think I've already taken you through most of them.

You know, I've gone into raptures about it, but maybe the quietness, the being left to your own devices, of this now-time in this Gampola isn't all I cracked it up to be.

Anyway, from that hotel room we are now noticing the silent, flushing son of Yuen sinsaang sitting on the beach where the old man Ramaswarmy could not notice him, even if he had the energies left to use binoculars, but he *is* in view of my brother's room. It is what my brother has apparently been waiting for.

From the main entrance of the hotel lobby we too are able to move down the track to the beach where the Yuen son is, without, just in case, being noticed from the other side of the bay.

Sunny Rug's son sits waiting there in the blue serge outfit of the common fisherman, or hawker. His feet dig into the sand, free of his rope sandals. He holds up a few pairs of shorts, wafer-thin designer copies and is urging us to buy. During the bored interest my brother shows in them, he learns that the man from the Royal Hong Kong Yacht Club has seen the honourable way of correcting the bad joss he would bring upon himself if he were not to change the name of his yacht's hirer to that of Mr Suresh Ramaswarmy, temporarily of the Tung Wan Apartments, permanently from Toorak, Melbourne, in Australia.

My brother nods and, while the Yuen son looks earnestly worried he has missed a sale of a pair of shorts on the side, walks along the beach a little, so that he comes into plain view of the Ramaswarmy balcony.

I don't know exactly why he is doing this or what he is looking for. It is something to do with that thrall of the unconventional again, something to do with testing his guess that the Appa is now too sick to be of any danger whatsoever. Surely, this has to be foolhardy of us.

The son of Sunny Rug has leapt up and followed. I do believe his mind is more on having another go at selling the shorts than anything else. As a Chinese, he would ask your fair price for his soul.

Is it the word that the Causeway Bay people have not heard of our plans?

'The afterbirths from a sow's bloated arse are not aware, Tusker sinsaang.'

My brother asks another small favour. The son stops, hesitates and then remembers that his father is not too strict against filial initiative, and gestures a yes expansively with his arms full of clothing.

It is a phone call to the Ramaswarmy apartment. The wife will answer it. You should say merely that the Harvard son has come hurriedly to Hong Kong and needs to talk urgently to her before he sees his father. The news he has is very upsetting. She will answer the father is ill anyway and she does not want him upset, so it will be easy to get her to meet at five o'clock at the Jordon Road ferry pier. She will just have the time to make that.

My brother finds the shorts back in his hands.

'You sure you no like to buy, good price, *ha*?'

But my brother's back is turned now on the son. He must leave, sale-less, and do the small thing that has been requested. We are looking again, even more openly, up at the balcony.

Now it tears at my heart to realise how unhappily my brother is thinking. It is made worse to realise even he can think like me. After all, there were times when Tusker felt and hoped he was part of a, the, family.

Who could deny that that family was the Ramaswarmys, or that the old fat Appa had helped us mostly along all the ways?

When, putting his life on the line so many times for the Tamil homeland question, but really only for the aims of the Appa, he was carrying out duties, surely, only what a dutiful nigh-adopted son was obliged to do.

Wasn't this Appa the father who at least hadn't abandoned us? That, at least, yes.

Yet when there were all the times of all the successes, of all the overseas pleasures expressed through Chennai, that were solely only of my brother's making, the Appa had been the one to take all the accolades. He had pushed us aside for that. From all of the profits too. He had made us yes, but only to keep us where he wanted us.

If that wasn't *usage*, as bad as abandonment, what was?

On that... pretending to be our father and *using*... he was as bad if not worse than our real father. They both deserved the same.

When the shutters of the mind's eyes go, how easily you can see how had not once did my brother begrudge Appa Ramaswarmy any of that manipulation, or even thought about doing so.

It had been his duty, the obligation he was duty bound to pay and repay -- on my behalf too, oh yes -- but for what? A little agreement he had once negotiated with the fat man, once sealed throughout one long night one time when we arrived destitute, young boys only, still children, on that damned old man's doorstep from out of the kids' Home.

But did that fat shit of a man up there, ill and blob-weak and defenceless against us, ever even bother to think something along the lines that he had a third son, more completely servicing to him than either of his other two?

And while my brother might have some tinge of regret as he stands below Appa on Tung Wan Bay, I see that I have none. None of the regret; not even, no, a tinge. In that I see I am stronger than my brother. I never felt duty bound to the gross and disgusting head of the Ramaswarmys; I never acknowledged that I would never have amounted to anything had it not been for me giving unquestioning allegiance to him and to that crazy Tamil homeland dream. For me, even now, the nothing that is the grease ball head of the Ramaswarmy crowd, no matter how decrepit he is, is gloating over our destruction he has ordered his sons to carry out.

Is there one qualm in that gross head about what he cold-bloodedly planned for us? So why are we even slightly hesitating?

I know and my brother shakes his head with fury to know that there was absolutely no answer to that question I know, too, I am posing.

We are already dead in Australia to that man up there.

Appa. Father. We never even existed for him. Why does he for us?

Well, for that, now my brother's hunt is almost closed in on him, just as mine for my father will surely soon start.

If you never asked to belong but gave your all, how can these people just up and try to flush you away and think you would thank them for it?

They should choke like dogs on poisoned meat.

I am so agitated now. This mind's eye and its entwining. I haven't been able to have a good think about my own problems for days.

Even at nights, my thoughts either tumble around or make me so nervous that I actually could be in physical pain.

Or I just drop off into a sleep from which I emerge just as exhausted as when I dropped off.

Tusker's blood staining and my father could be killing me, have you thought of that?

Frankly, everything, every little bit of it, seems like a dream to me now.

Perhaps it's just been that. A dream in fever from go to woe and back again.

Geoffrey, lord and master of this house in this now-time in Gampola, has given me their only bed to get over this bout of malaria they say I have had for the last week.

Or maybe all the days of my life.

Maybe they haven't taken into account my mind's eye.

You've probably had malaria before, the doctor, who kept telling me (I think) about what's wrong with his Mazda, told me. A good-o but not too bad about, the news from the garage, is it? He says. Like the second-hand motor they have been selling me as new, isn't it? He has said. I think. I know he has been grinning over me. He is literally on top of my fever.

I've got to start believing in God and ask Him about these fucking mosquitoes of His. If He's not going to tell me, then at least tell me the year He invented them. And what-the-ferg sort of creature design is it that helps itself to a pint or two of the red stuff from out of one of the only bit of life He was supposed to have made in His own image -- then, as payment, drops a load of parasites in the palm of your hand?

If the doc says it's malaria, there's a fifty-fifty chance it is malaria. But I'm inclined to think that I had the shock of reading about my father around the time my stock of values was running out. I know me; I just got over-excited to be back, finally, finally, in the hunt.

Then again, if it is malaria and he is as right about it as he certainly is about being gypped over his car, then that's interesting.

If I have had malaria before, then I must have got it when I was a kid around here, since no one I know has invented a strain of malaria for Australia yet, certainly south of the divide, wherever that is.

285

And, if so, could that mean that most of what I remember about the elephants and my mother and my father is all only delusion in fever?

I have to admit that, since reading about daddy-o, it all suddenly seems so very long ago, down long sighings and dyings, down the vapours of long wearinesses.

I am tired.

I am tired to think of any of it.

I am tired to think I have come all the way back here and tried to think it out, instead of just getting on with it.

All there seems to be is the mind's eye and eyes.

I am tired of my brother being called Tusker like my father's Aetha, and taking the opportunity of my weakness to get in with these nightmares he is involving me with.

I'm so tired I feel like I've been dragging Neila's board-shorted Marvin's missing leg around with the shark still attached to it.

It can't be malaria.

I've come to the conclusion it's lassitude.

I have the lassitudes, that's all. I am lassitudinous. I am even too lassitudinous to dwell on the lyrics of the word.

I must be delirious with the lassitudes to be letting Tusker take me through what I am seeing now:

It is so easy to follow the ultimate source of while, that podge Mrs Ramaswarmy in the ferry from Cheung Chau to the Kowloon side.

She has discarded her saree either because the Chinese would mockingly keep plucking at it to see whether it was saleable or discarded it because of the urgency that fear engenders when she got the phone call. Some vestige of wanting to be ready to move fast.

Not that there could be any speed in her. This is one woman who was not built for speed. As the Ramaswarmys became more prosperous, she slowed down by virtue of some parody of being stately. There must be still some visions, ludicrous vestiges in her simple mind, of the Indian Raj. Now if she had concentrated on the full-belly of her rising wallowing whines someone *would* have built the Taj Mahal for her.

In western pea-green dress outlining a gargantuan corset, her attempt to hurry makes her look like the lead elephant at Kandy's perahera but lost by itself in one of Kandy's side streets.

She should never have lived a day past that man who would have been riding her.

The blubber of her nates is formless and sucks in behind her lower back as if pulled forward and upward by and towards the engines housed in that swollen gut which has already greedily consumed her breasts and has made her neck a single and massive bubo.

Even I am feeling, like my brother is now, that she has become just a thing of my massive contempt.

I know you won't like me saying that, but I've got the excuse of the malaria and God's not helping.

She pushes and shoves her way without apology or retard. They are not people to her, as she is not person to them, to us. She could well be wading through soft butter. It is somehow clear that, whatever dire tidings Harvard son has come personally up to Hong Kong to bring, she has something to say to him about disturbing her day.

Even in the crush of the Outlying Districts Pier and the taxi ride through the harbour tunnel and then on to the Jordon Street Pier, there would have been no trouble for a blind dog to follow her.

And this is good for another reason. It makes it no trouble at all for my brother to keep track of the Sunny Rug man who is following him and her both.

We let her wait with an annoyed mother's impatience for a good ten minutes at the meeting place -- a lifetime for her. She has grown hot and flustered now in the static and resin'd air; even in just sitting, she would smell mightily to the locals. She has refused to allow anyone to sit down on the wooden bench beside her, probably saying to them in a strange language that the space is reserved for her son who's come such a long way and who's *late*.

So that, when my brother walks up to her and literally stands toe-to-toe, she growls out a whine which would have done her Rehana proud. When the shoes she then hardly dares to look up from do not move, then, and only then, does she look up with agony for herself in her eyes.

I am suddenly realising that this moment is the test and why Tusker has chosen the missus instead of Appa to confront. Up until now he hasn't had proof positive that it was her and not the old dogshit himself who has actually ordered our death. The sons, maybe, a palace revolution, maybe, or just asserting themselves knowing their mother was turning out the strongest, maybe.

Even as I realise this, her expression changes from a slow uptake to a squinging horror at the sight of Tusker. Instinctively, she squeals:

'What have you done to my boys?'

Boys. Not boy. It is the sure knowledge to my brother that she has known there was going to be a bloody business back home. But a 'thing' she is not. At least I notice that her first thoughts are a mother's thoughts and not for her own safety. But what can I do?

And yet I also feel the hot jet of venom sparking through Tusker. For me the feeling is sickly, one of putrescence. It is momentarily the blind frenzy of filicide.

And then he knows the feel of her head in the palms of our hands. And he holds it hard so that she cannot move. These heavy bones of a now-hated head.

He bends over and kisses her on the forehead, on that black third- eye of her many-armed gods, just as I once did when Neila took me to Rehana. He sucks deliberately as I had once only innocently placed my lips there, and the religious spot comes off in his mouth. He is just experimenting again and she is, she is still, using stick-on ones.

You see how he must find out things in these extremis times?

Tusker contemptuously spits it out into her face as he would something disgusting. She bucks as if he has slapped her, then begins drivelling in a near faint.

This woman who might have once been a mother to him.

There is no interference.

In the eternal time for her we have had her waiting, my brother has convinced the Sunny Rug man it is better to do what we tell him than have the venerable Yuen come to know how easy he had been to spot as a tagger. This man is now standing behind Tusker and explaining to the waiting passengers there that the over-puffed powdered peacock from the land of baby-eating monsters has just been told of the death of her only child.

The Hong Kongers hearing him stare at her without sympathy. They see such fate for foreign things as beyond their ken. You need household gods to understand what goes on in life.

Only her gross weight makes it slightly less than easy to get her out of the terminal and waddle down the wharf to the berth of the lighter.

The Yuen man is told to wait on the wharf; this now is officially part of tonight's operation, he is warned, so redeem your failure as a tagging man by being extra wary. The man squats, armed and dangerously hawk-eyed, a powder keg now that he has to undergo this loss of face because he has failed.

I am sure the titular mother of the Ramaswarmys is not feeling anything much anymore or I would be able to decipher it. But perhaps not. Perhaps, as with her sons, there are limits that my mind will venture with my brother.

I only know she is making sounds, and that the movements of her body have now become involuntary, twitching, automatic reflexes only. She is opening and shutting her mouth; in silent screen, it is ugly and distorted as though she is miming an attempt to scream, but I hear nothing, and I can suffer that.

Under that tarpaulin, it is drenching hot down there in the equipment bay of the lighter my brother has brought her to. You cannot miss how much she is sweating, as my brother ensures the working of the hatchway which has been cut at the water's edge there and recessed-hinged inside such that it is all but invisible if you didn't know it was there. It is through here that someone will soon slip in and out in order to retrieve the bags magnetised to the hull of the mother ship.

Now my brother has called in the Sunny Rug man from the wharf. He is instructing this surly fellow to undress her.

The man is a stick to her tree, as near teenage as possible to her late fifties, yet he cannot believe his luck. His skeletal face breaks into a sickly-sweet grin. Obviously, his idea of the erotic is not what you could call normal, and the way he thrusts at her without hesitation shows he is well used to the violence of aberration. He begins as though he actually has the ritual of seduction in mind; her shoes first; then standing over her, his crutch lewdly level with her face, undoing the top buttons of that dress. The breasts that are presumably massive and provoking to him are just the lunge of fat pressed on from below. He has her on her feet, licking at her face as he does so, perhaps crooning unintelligible things to her or perhaps just salivating; then he plucks loose her buttons all the way down.

The dress has difficulty falling away and needs him to tug it roughly. Amma Ramaswarmy rocks before him in her slip. She could be at a public mourning. What can I do but keep watching?

Corset and pantyhose as gross as we envisaged, a question of pressure upon gelatine.

Now black and raven, the man tries but cannot get the pantyhose down, let alone the corset. This is not funny. In irritation, he pushes her back down on the bench and endeavours, at first roughly then with slower relish, to work

290

them off. There can be no way two hands are sufficient for the task with all those ridging puckers of flesh.

Before leaving, I see my brother sigh impatiently. He taps the man on the shoulder and makes exasperated cutting motions, as though to a backward child, while indicating his knife.

It does not matter that Tusker is now sitting up on deck to sit in the shade of the warehouses; I can still x-ray that the man has understood and pulled out his dagger. It is finer than the working one he will need for tonight's operation. This is his street protection. He slits the materials from her hip to her crutch, so that removal is only a matter of tearing them, now, aside. Even in this he is fumbling. No, I do not like this, but closing my eyes is doing no good. I can still *see*, can still sense malarially, how he is even more aroused at that straight trunk of blubber now that it is open to his wants. He teases the knife at her lower belly and leers cruelly.

The Amma seems somehow to awaken, to make an effort to recover. She opens her eyes and doesn't appear in the least surprised of being, for the most part, naked before him. It might be in my brother's imagination, but I could almost say she is seeing hope in being alone with the lewdness of the raven Chinese, for it looks as if she lets her legs open towards him and it looks as though she smiles invitingly as she pushes her hips forward.

But, yes, surely this is in our imagination up on deck there, him, and on this fever-soaked bed here, me.

It is a flash now of black discontinuation, like you might say a change of scene is on film. I find my brother has somehow returned below decks to her and her now fiercely alive eyes. You could swear that it has been she, not the male, who has triumphed in their *danse macabre*. I feel my brother admiring her gender's absolute confidence in the power for survival of its sex, alive and in secretion when a man would have given up all hope.

291

She apparently even thinks it is a hopeful sign when Tusker insists she write a note on a page from his notebook. She cooperates and seems almost happy to be doing so.

The note says simply: 'Try these. Delicious? Shall I bring some home?'

And now my brother is up on deck again, once more enjoying the deep afternoon shade from the warehouses lining the wharf. The

harbour is gilded with the late afternoon sun, burning a melting hole through the ponderous monsoon clouds. The wind whips at his clothes. The typhoon, yes, is still coming.

I feel how good it will be to have the covering of its early howlings of the wind and its impatient scouts of rain this night.

The old freighter from Guangzhou, the rusted cowling over its starboard anchor port particularly catching the sun and glowing now like blood, stands at anchor amid forty or so others. My brother is content with it having to moor there; it is quite accessible yet central enough in the roads for a good measure of obscurity of observation from onshore.

There is some time, I think, or maybe not, before my brother wearily raises himself and reluctantly returns below deck.

The Yuen man, this raven, has finished with Amma Ramaswarmy.

My brother takes an envelope from his pocket, lifts her lolling head by grasping one ear at a time and does the cutting.

Whatever cutting he does will not hurt her anymore. She is not feeling anymore, no.

To the envelope, Tusker adds her ear lobes to those of her sons.

The ear parts of the mother and the brothers who might have been.

To our side, Tsi Sui Yuen's man is now nervous, ready to defend himself, wondering whether it would be safer to despatch Tusker too, wanting to escape, not stand there and have to look down on what he has done. My brother smiles at him invitingly for a dangerous moment and, when the man lowers his eyes, orders him to calm down.

I know he tells the creature that the venerable Yuen need not know any of this or that the white devil did it, we do not care. He gives the vulture money and the note and the envelope. The venerable Yuen, no, need not know, providing two simple things are done as redress for butchering otherwise perfectly good hyena meat.

The man smiles wickedly now. Sir, what things, sir?

He must go to the assistant sous chef at the Hong Kong Hotel, the Filipino called Albert, and give him the envelope. Albert will be expecting it. You wait for as long as necessary for the packet he will come back with and you will then deliver that packet and this note she has written to the fat old pig in the apartment across the Tung Wan Bay.

You will smile and be happy to be of service to the fat man. You tell him you have come from his wife who awaits an answer at the Wharf Restaurant.

If he does not eat, you may force him to. Do whatever you want, as you would any squealing swine, but ensure you do not kill him without the venerable Yuen knowing.

These are left to your scented discretion, providing you do the two things asked. If not, pieces of your disease-ridden fruit will be feeding the crabs by morning's light and not even your foul-breathed ancestors will know where you have got to.

It is over.

I am looking, but the only sign of Amma Ramaswarmy I see now are lazy tugs from the end of the painter which hangs down into the now-inking water of the harbour from the bottom of the truck-tyre bolster just below the hidden access hatch.

Things I have to follow but things I will not.

Brenda, Stephanie, Janice, Michaela, Marini of this now-time. Little fairy godmothers. They are as sick as I am, off their tucker, just because I am ill.

And when I can get my eyes open, there is always one of them waiting for me to do that, and smiling at me a beam of sweet charity that says this is what life can be. Even my Stephanie takes her turn; her deepest smile is cock-eyed and directed to the wall somewhere to my right, but what of that? It is more fully on me because of that.

But, oh, these inextinguishable revenges. Even as my lassitudes wetbag their flames, they continue to itch hotly for spontaneous combustions, the fierce consuming of everything in one shrieking and evil purging.

My brother would understand them. But I am having in this now-time a hard time wanting it anymore.

I must find my father before the Inspector. I know I will. But, by doing it, I'm surely going to lead those who are hunting him too to him. And for what? So that they can quietly extinguish the embarrassments of some crass politicians. The now-unwanted leader of the Black Cats. Now spieling in the newspaper under some tag line of Palhirana.

Spieling the beans, sings the Lieder.

Do I really have the strength to be that sort of beater in the jungle ahead? Perhaps I'll just lie here too lassitudinous to move. And pretend it is malaria.

Oh, I know and you know it's the lassitudes. It will be better when I get well enough to get back to whipping up my anger at him.

If I ever get to get out of this bed.

Item equals no further than my mind's eye.

When the major part of the dung-worm Causeway Bay mob has come to board the lighter, they can do nothing from the wharf side about seeing it already busily alongside of the mother ship out in the harbour.

When the other part of the Causeway Bay dogs tries to come alongside the lighter fifteen minutes later, they are contemptuously told to shove off and return to between their mothers' legs by the Yuen crew working so busily at their tendering duties. They aren't able to shove off, though, despite the realisation they have been betrayed.

Instead, they find themselves wedged against the mother ship's hull by the police launch.

They do not find comfort in being the cause of the only consolation the police have this night. Under the sink of the yacht from the Royal Hong Kong Yacht Club are two packets of pure heroin weighing a piddling one kilo between them.

On the lighter, the Yuen working party are not above swearing foully when they are interrupted in their duties by the searching uniformed men. You find what you find, what do we know? *Aeeia*, is that the first disgusting thing you've ever found at the end of a rutting rope in rutting Hong Kong rutting Harbour?

The police know the yacht as one which is regularly hired. They know where to trace the slobber of a fat man who has hired it.

By that time, too, the venerable Yuen and his sons have already reached the Cheung Chau anchorage. They even feel much the richer for the powder they have escorted home from its long journey from northern Myanmar across southern China. It is ten kilos of two-bags-ful.

It feels richer than usual because it has been won famously richly. In cold nights or during bad times, its story will be told. More than the money, it has become an honourable part of the legend of Sunny Rug.

The police will soon be arriving at the apartment across the Tung Wan Bay.

On that balcony over there, Appa Ramaswarmy waits for news from Causeway Bay just as impatiently as he is for the return of his wife from some eats-house she mentioned in that stupid dingo of a note.

It has been over an hour since he sent back the verbal message if I say they're shithouse what diff would it make to what you want to buy?

But force of habitual gluttony has made him gobble them up anyway.

We have even heard the old man has tipped the sharp raven of a messenger to get her back quickly with more.

My brother sits on the beach wall and we watch the old man Ramaswarmy get up from his deck chair, struggle to keep the rug

around his shoulders so that he staggers precariously towards a fall, lunges for support, then slowly shuffles his way from the balcony to answer the door.

He will be winding up a whine to his Amma about where has she been and he can't be getting up all shaggin' day to answer the door himself.

But it is not his Amma. It is the bitch-bred gangsters from Causeway Bay.

Appa Ramaswarmy does not return to the balcony.

One of the last things Tusker knows the old man would have heard was the only thing the infested police found on those limpets was some fat black dog droppings who they say is his wife.

The last thing, my brother knows positively... and I too undoubtedly simultaneously... will be the ear lobes the greasy glutton has wolfed down; the venerable Yuen would have had the pleasure of half-ordering what was left of the disease-ridden Causeway Bay pigs hit to ensure it was the last thing the traitor heard. That was payment for informing the police on them.

When Appa fails to reappear on the balcony, I sense Tusker move away from the beach wall.

But we feel heavy. I think one of our migraines is coming on.

It must be because of this that my brother is taken by surprise when plainclothes Hong Kong johns take him from behind in the lobby of the hotel.

Will my father be as dark-scowling as I remember him?

Black Cats and on the run.

There will be a force coming out of him I will have to be careful of now. It will be as inextinguishable as revenge, as immutable as the unavid infamy he's brought upon himself and, because of that self-infliction, as tedious as the struggle he has to put in just to survive. Now.

That makes a dangerous rogue.

On the other hand, it might be a force that he will let loose only on me ... a force of a father bailed up by a son. If only because I myself have carried it around, wrapped and life-proofed in my pilgrim's scrip, I know it will be there.

I am having these half nightmares, or are they something from his mind's-eye?, about whether they've put out a reward on his head.

Better we call it a bounty.

You could get two shillings and sixpence a tail in Major T. W. Rogers's time. Before the lightning got him dead-centre, his fortune would have not only been from the ivory of the tusks.

One tail.

You pot-shot all that magnificent animal so you can get two-and-sixpence for the last tiny bit of it?

Mind you, it wasn't to be sneeze at as much as you think. If you pot-shot over 2000 of them like Major Rogers, you'd be sitting on a pretty penny, and it wouldn't even be your tail you'd be sitting on there, sipping on your pink gin on the veranda for the evening. Oh, the all-round balms!

After 1895, the wolf must have really been at the door; they busted the bounty down to two shillings a tail.

Times were getting tough all round.

Not a doubt in the world, though, that all the tails handed into those government clerks would have been hairless. In the local market a bunch of those magical hairs was priceless.

What happened there was you'd strip off the hairs and sell them to the local village mad *rodiya* women to use in potions and creams and other fiery agglomerations to ward off, or herald in, evil.

Those clerks must have puzzled over that, though. Suddenly the elephant population of olde Ceylon had gone hairless of tail. Did they constitute a new species? Should the bounty be raised or lowered because of that?

When they got back to good old England... and I suppose I'm talking of the Royal Society types... I bet they regaled the other members about how the jolly old Ceylonese pachyderm, dontcha know, has got a hairless tail.

So, make that three bob a tail, just for a lark, plus throw in a bit more for any hairy stuff on the side.

It'd all add up.

I bet Major T. W. Rogers was in on the tail-hair market as well.

But the old mind's-eye mind's rambling, isn't it? Somebody should have given me the word.

As I think I was saying: yes, by the arms from behind. My brother.

Plainclothes or not, they know my brother knows immediately who they are. They do not need to do any talking.

For them, it is a good time of weakness to have come. Even my brother feels weary. It could be my malaria.

There is another of them at the reception desk. The manager has his head averted; he will be wondering how he can now honour his debt to old Yuen about erasing our name as having been a guest. The copper at the desk merely holds out Tusker's room key and nods his head towards the lift.

We walk along the passageway to my brother's room. Nobody has bothered to follow him.

In the room, there is Martin Baybe. The Australian National Crimes Commission detective is standing looking across the bay towards the apartment and so has his back to us. The plate glass of the window is beginning to rattle uncomfortably with the rising gusts of the coming typhoon.

All is no bother, and disconcerting so. Not even Baybe bothers to turn when he surely hears the door open, but remains looking out in a very rumpled way as though he had just got off the plane in the only suit his agency will afford and cannot believe where he's ended up.

I find it surprising to sense now that my brother too feels yet again how oddly the man is shaped, like a pear that has already dropped to the ground. Even that atrocious shirt and tie amuses both of us in how, even from the back, they look the same ones dyed or made fitted by some tailor with railing astigmatism.

I say surprising, for how could Tusker have met this man who, with Inspector Ekanayake, has been hounding me to tell who the man with the alias of Tusker is?

At this point, I just know my brother and I must be really cross-wired. For, when Baybe deigns to turn around, working his scalp in that infuriating way, a mockery of really being jolly, his smile might be cold but it is also one of outrageous over-familiarity.

It can't be that my brother and he possibly know each other?

If that were the case, then my lemming-like plunge into criminality had no point to it at all. I would have been trying to cover my brother's, my tracks after everybody has already thundered on through.

It can only be that my malaria or lassitudes is causing my brother's images to be heterodyned with my wavering own.

Even so, I'll be blowed if Baybe isn't now talking to Tusker just as he used to talk to me:

299

'Matey, you looked shagged out. Probably should be, too.'

Again, my brother's reaction amazes me. I would have expected him to make some move against this buffoon-looking agency man. With what he would have to face in court, he surely would not give up so meekly.

I know his nature enough for that. Yet, he moves from the doorway and into the room towards this Baybe and does so quite calmly.

Baybe indicates the apartment across the bay with a thumb flick.

'There'll be a mess over there already, more's the likely, that I just do not want to know about. In respect of that it was enough to catch a Captain's Cook at the fat sort hanging from that ship.'

The man is even testing the springs of the bed!

'Matey, I think you have blown your Hong Kong, is my opinion. My colleagues out there now know how you've been doing it, and who you've been doing it with. And you'd have to suppose Running Log or Sunny Bun or whatisname will never want to know you now. You'd have to be a bit surprised if he was delighted with that piece of unladylike lump you left dangling on his lighter. Velly velly great loss of face, you'd say, Tusker. So,' and he stops bouncing up and down on the mattress to smile up at us, deliberately, comically, working that scalp of his as though he was about to let it take over the talking, 'where to now, matey? Don't tell me. In respect of next destinations, it should not, repeat not, be Australia. One of our dug-down-deeper citizens or not, we don't want you and your Tamil little frenzies anymore. Sorry about that. Too unAustralian if you ask me. Me good maties here in Honkers won't be leaving the welcome mat out either. Pity that, eh?'

The windows shudder again. It disturbs Baybe enough to get up from the bed and return to look out across the bay. Our reflection is clearly there anyway, even if he seems not to be watching Tusker. I see, even so by storm-cloud reflection how much alike my brother and I are.

None of this will stop the detective-sergeant from trying to jolly it all up.

'Don't tell me the great Tusker really got his gander up over the bumbling Ramaswarmys? I would have figured you with too many smarts for that, matey. You'n'me, we know poor old Appa's always only been a lackey for lords of other manors, like Chennai. Were I you, I'd forget India as a stopover, too. So, where? Well, in respect of that, our good woggie Inspector Ekanawhatever tells us what you oughta be doing is taking a flight to that Ceylon or whatever you call it these days and have a shooftie around there.'

My brother speaks a word now. It is a weary why of being wrong. A simple, not-so-simple why.

'Why? Why, the mighty Tusker asks? In respect of the why, we hear tell that is where the order for your goodnight-nurse came from, matey. Not the Ramaswarmys. Not first, see. Not too good that. We no likee foreign persons trying to stir up placid old Oz. You got B.O.? I mean, the closer they are to you, the more they want to get shot of you. Poor Orphan Annie, right?'

My brother speaks again; he asks quietly another why. He means the help.

'All these whys! I'd get your plane before the typhoon if I were you. So why, why. Got enough troubles of our own, you see: Abos, Mafia, Tongs from all sorts of strange places. Did I mention Islam? How could I not mention our little Islamers? With you lot, easier, in respect of that, to let you knock each other over. Small fry, your weird homeland mob, but it saves us a lot of hard yakka. Said this once to your other half.'

Personally, I don't appreciate the smirk on his face when he calls me the 'other half'.

He reaches to the windowsill for a Scotch we have not noticed. This is from my brother's bar fridge! His shirt collar seems so tight that it can only be with the greatest difficulty that he can tilt his head back let alone get the liquid down his gullet. Maybe that is the reason for his shirts; their collars are all too tight that they never come off.

You see how well I am holding my concentration now, don't you? Anyway:

'I hope,' Baybe is gasping as he seems to go through pain gulping, 'you can see why we needed you. We could have sided with the Ramaswarmys, but you got lucky. Don't forget the plane and beating the typhoon, matey.'

Baybe lowers his drink, only so delicately sipped, and comes towards Tusker, but only to leave, but only to have to stop because we are not moving out of the way. I feel the familiar thrall shoot through my brother. There is a moment I think Baybe may never walk out of this door, after all.

Yet, surely sensing this too, still Baybe seems to remain unconcerned: 'Of course, in respect of running, you could do that now and we might give up hunting you down one fine day, give or take a decade or two. On the other hand, if you choose to go back to old Sri Lanka and do what you should do best, we wouldn't forget the favour of you showing your Chennai masters how baddy Tamils aren't welcome anymore anywhere near Australia. Your life, your choice. Now, in respect of me finally able to get out of your sorry existence, you can move aside, matey.'

It might have been my mother who told me my father always refused to look in mirrors.

He would be one, just for the sheer romance of it, who would believe the story that elephants don't like looking at their own reflections because they cry when they see how ugly they turned out. It's said that's why they stir up the water before they drink. Some modern eco-heads maintain they do this so they can get a muddy cocktail containing tiny stones and the like. These, they say, help their digestion.

I'd rather go for the anything-but-a-reflection story. Maybe that's because I take after my father and elephants when it comes to mirrors.

I cannot abide looking into a mirror. Did you, could you, know that?

I don't know whether I'll ever 'see' Tusker again.

I fancy that, somehow, after what happened to me in the last few days of this now-time in the uplands of Sri Lanka, we won't be, you know, networking at the mind's eye level for quite a while from now on.

I'd fancy getting back to normal that way, even if getting back to normal, meaning a normal life, seems decidedly not on my horizon anymore.

I fancy, to be frank about it, he didn't take Baybe's hint-hint and come on to Sri Lanka here.

I fancy I saw him being quietly escorted onto the plane, but getting off at Bangkok and eventually winging his way back into Australia. God knows what he's up to there.

I don't fancy that was any sort of a safe option. But you know that brother of mine.

As the screen I had on that whole ugly Hong Kong affair finally, thank God, went blank, I must have had a kind of premonition to think to ask him what was the purpose of it all. You know, his life and all that.

I fancy I will remember his answer all my life: 'I feel I have come to live a perfect life through imperfect means.'

He said. My brother. Fancy that.

The thing is: now I have a description of what my father looks like. I have a mirror into him.

They gave it out in a small box on page one about a week after they first broke the story about the new Black Cats with his letter.

They have my father down as a tawny-to-dark-brown person, quite fair in a few places (you'll have to work that one out yourself), with pink lips and panda rings around the eyes (I mean, where else?).

For crying out loud. Panda rings round the eyes and pink tender parts.

He has a round face, a slightly elongated head, a long nose that has not quite mended after being broken, and coppery pupils. He stands 168 centimetres (you'll have to work that one out in feet yourself), is of heavy build in the arms and chest, thin hips, muscular legs.

Pink palms and pink soles to go with the panda rings and pink lips.

He walks with a pronounced sway, thought to be from an old hip wound. He is usually clean shaven with a full head of hair gone grey and swept back into a duck's tail.

Pink palms. Pink soles. Pink lips. Panda rings. Now a duck's tail. For crying out loud again.

Distinguishing marks are few. There is a little finger missing from his left hand, it said, and the little finger of his right hand has mended crookedly into a pronounced bow.

I don't call that a few distinguishing marks at all.

I call it distinguished marks, and I can now tell you why:

To his little fingers are my little fingers, but mirror images.

I am not joking.

The little finger on my right one I had lopped off that time by that damn Rajah's neck chain, and the little finger on my left one mended badly into a bow at the same time as well.

Can you beat that!

They talk about the whirling spokes of the great wheel of life. Well, fate must have played the ha-ha joke on my father and me by shoving our hands into those spokes from the opposite sides.

His right missing, my left. My left bowed, his right.

I'll need time to think more about that later. I mean, it's got to be the malaria.

Right now, I just can't work out that 'quite fair in a few places'.

Could that mean he has leprosy like my Hansen?

No, let it be instead plain old pigmentation spots that come with just getting old. That'd be right; it's what elephants get as they get on, looking like they've let too many pigeons roost on them over the years.

But I just can't imagine my father standing still for that long.

So now I know what he looks like. And I know how to track him down, because he taught me that. All I've got to know now is where to start.

So, all's nearly ready. All's nearly in place.

When I get better from being lassitudinous.

Nowadays, if you're a ranger with the Wildlife Department or some official empowered to take an elephant -- that is, take it off somewhere, not take it out -- you'll get back to the Major T. W. Rogers school of no-nonsense shooting.

You will.

But this time it won't be a thunderous explosion of bone and brains and a terrible last trumpeting. This time it'll be a quietish sort of sssphhfffftt. And there won't be much trumpeting, if at all. The big E probably won't even feel the one, possibly two, foot long tranquillising darts you have fired into its lower rump. Sneaky.

Big E will probably run a bit, might stroll a bit, more likely just stay where it is *a.* because it's used to whopping great marsh flies or whatever sinking their snozzles through that hide, and *b.* because it would be there in the first place if it hadn't heard you sneaking up. Nor would you.

You'll have to wait a while. Let's say ten or fifteen minutes. All will be strangely peaceful; it might get even more peaceful.

If it's been swaying, then its swaying will gradually slow down to dreamy. If it's been twitching its ears, then the flies and the horseflies get a good go, because its ears will stop twitching.

But what you can be sure of seeing, if it's a male, of course, in real technicolour is one of Nature's wonders.

It's what all that dreadful white stuff my brother used to get from the then-called Burmese Golden Triangle is supposed to do with men -- get them going all dreamy but, with elephant, with far greater results.

You'll see the biggest hard-on, surely, that Nature has to offer.

It is one totally envious thing.

It would put the god Priapus back on the divine drawing board.

Fairy tales have nothing on it, either. It grows and grows. It will continue to grow and then hang, but not hang, flaccid but not flaccid, bent but not bowed, like your arm is when you loosely put it out at forty-five degrees from your body.

That's a puny simile.

It will arc right down, yes, to the ground.

It would have to be an average minimum of a metre in length, and no American's measurement will take an eighth of an inch off that.

It is maybe at least thirty centimetres in diameter. Ditto about the American doing the measurement too.

And it will swing, exactly like a second trunk, in syncopation with the dreamy mood of its thoughts and to the sway of its body in point counterpoint.

It is an anchor chain adrift from its anchor in a lazy swell.

It is loose plastic hose lazily snaking with pulsing water on the slow jazz.

The metaphors within it; the eternal visions of it!

With your drug dart, you have given Big E the ball-tearer high of all highs.

They should sell whatever you've shoved into that dart throughout Amcal Chemists.

Then you can happily waltz away with your elephant.

That's if you have a vet surgeon's degree or a ranger's certification.

If you are a traditional trapper, you're most certainly a Moor, one of the early Muslim seafarers who pitched tent and stayed in Taprobane or Ceylon years ago. As a Moor, you're not into the Buddhist/Hindu superstition about a life of bad karma if you go around catching the noblest of beasts and doing the dirty on your future prospects.

You're called a panniker, actually.

You might have the legendary Pakir Mohammed up front leading you. He's already a legend. He'll go on loping along all day and night if need be, and he's sixteen stone, because Pakir Mohammed weighs himself in pounds and stones, and well over fifty.

This day you might have been delegated to carry the great rope made of deer hide. It's a whopping twenty-one metres in length, is curled around your torso like a Mexican banditto's bullet belt. At one end is a large knot and at the other is a slip noose.

Suddenly Pakir Mohammed grinds to a halt. He has spotted a herd. You fall down, then follow him, slithering if need be... although there's no way he can do any slithering with his size... to get upwind. Where you wait, while Pakir does the reconnoitring. Probably you'll camp there overnight, then at dawn you'll do a little ambushing of your own by sneaking up to the herd and throwing large crackers and shouting like hell or waving lighted torches of dried coconut leaves with a fury that might indicate you believe all that about bad luck Pakir Mohammed says this is all balls.

If it's any sort of herd, it'll panic and take off. Pakir, yelling like he was about to lead you over a hundred-foot cliff, will press you on after one of the younger baby elephants. Sooner or later, perhaps even on the run if he gets lucky, Pakir will get that slip noose around one of the little squirt's hind legs and not too long after that he'll get the faintest of chances, which of course he will take, of dashing madly around a stout tree trunk with the other end of the rope.

Whenupon you and your mates fling yourselves onto that tree end and hold on for dear life, providing the tree holds.

Twenty-five paces away, by any measure, Jumbo will come to a disagreeable halt with that amazing ability young bones have of not breaking. Hopefully.

It's been a hard one this time. Quite often, the little guy will have the smarts enough just to give up the ghost after a few turns around the mad cap. This one goes on thrashing about and hurts itself. But then, you're a panniker, and know you can't win them all. Especially if you're Pakir Mohammed and really in the know.

Only he really knows which one's going to turn out to be a tusker.

And that's that.

Your panniker's livelihood.

It's getting harder by the year, and you're not getting any younger. Though the legendary Pakir Mohammed seems to be.

That might be all right for you because you live in the flatlands of the north and northeast.

But, in the uplands my father had to develop his own method.

Up here were, then, the thick rainforests, the mountains and sharp gorges, the elephants being vicious climbers I told you about to my own cost and have remembered every time I look at my little fingers. Up here, a chase like yours would be as killing to a man as to the bubba elephant. Where could you possibly hoof it at breakneck speed without breaking your neck literally?

When my father went out to catch, he'd take a couple of experienced mahouts with him -- and me once, and I was so proud of that!

He'd locate a herd that contained a youngster he liked the look of. This would be about a four-year-old, not much younger, and, if with tusks, then that would be a bonus.

This herd, this one I remember as clearly as if it were yesterday -- or as clear as it will become in practice, surely, in the next few weeks -- did have a four-year-old, but not a tusker.

It was the one that became his gift to me, the one I called Little Majah, which he then took away and gave to another boy.

Bastard.

My father had us meandering with the herd, not trying to run it down or scare the seven bells of hell out of the herd with fire crackers like Pakir Mohammed did. We meandered along downwind careful not to do anything to make them edgy, and we did this for days.

We even really, really camped near them -- not at the Pakir's safe distance -- so that they got used to our presence. At night, my father would sit a little apart from them, and it seemed to me that he was crooning lullabies, like a flow of calming thoughts or non-thoughts you try to give to babies with the most futile optimism in the world.

Each day, the herd would eat heavily in early afternoon and, with

their bellies full, they'd go to the river of one of the watering holes just to lie around in a shady bath.

Even during those four or five days usually, I think they were, the herd allowed us to sit quite close on the bank to watch them while they siesta'd on the slosh as if they were laying around the poolside in the Costa Del Sol.

It was, let's say, on the fifth day that my father decided the time was ripe.

He would bring out this mighty rope. It must have been far more than the Pakir's twenty-one or so metres one. To me, then, it just seemed to go on and on. It too was made out of deer hide with all that stretchability yet virtually impossible to break if plaited correctly which it always was, of course.

There was the same type of slip noose that you used with Pakir Mohammed, but the difference came at the other end.

At the other end of my father's was not just a knot that you used for keeping hold as you blustered around with your little E. We couldn't go dashing around any tree trunk or anything, not in these harder terrains.

No, on the other end of ours was a sort of bundle that looked like a hobo's post-nuclear scavenged humpy. I had watched my father build this up with great care.

At the core of it was the skull and antlers of a Sambhur buck.

This was tied to the other end of the great hide rope. Then he built this up into a bundle by using twigs and dried leaves carefully tied with a very thin, loosely-twilled string, layer by layer, until it was a full bundle with just the actual top of the antlers poking out.

So, on this designated day, while even the tots were snoozing, my father crept up and slipped the slip noose around his four-year-old's back leg, backed away unwinding the rope, while letting this bundle of antlers and gunk get well and truly water-and-mud soaked.

At the end of the rope he put the bundle carefully on the ground and just simply walked away.

Even to my young mind, this was surprising. He had let go of the only thing that could keep a tag on the Baby E.

Then at a wave of his arm, the other mahouts, whom I now realise had moved off to be deliberately upwind of the herd, started the same sort of wild screaming, shrieking, cracker works, as you pannikers with Pakir Mohammed did.

What a terrible way to be dragged out of a siesta!

I was amazed how quickly such huge hulks could virtually leap to their feet and take off into the heavy forests. Poor little four-year-old began having a hard time of it right from the start. The lead cow had taken them straight across the stream, which is fine if you haven't got lumbered with something that for all the world could be a hobo's post-nuclear scavenged humpy which, after you're almost across, starts to drag you down, and how.

The more the baby elephant struggled and tugged, the more the bundle began to disintegrate -- and the more the bundle disintegrated, the more of the Sambhur antlers got exposed.

The result is you have a bundle that is getting increasingly jagged, and is increasingly digging in, or snagging on this then that, and just getting more bloody-minded by the minute, much as it would be if you wrapped an iron anchor in ordinary paper and started dragging it over a gravel path.

Of course, there came a time when the twigs and leaves and strings had all but been stripped off and we had only the skull and the antlers left.

It looked to me as though the devil himself had popped up out of nowhere and had hitched a ride. But then wasn't I just a lad still?

When this happened, Baby E's game was almost up. There was no way that skull-and-antler was going far before it snagged completely on some root or tree or rock. That time it was a buttress root.

The little guy was exhausted by then anyhow.

By then, too, we were actually walking faster than little E was scrambling. There was no hurry now, it seemed. My father casually strolled up to the Sambhur skull and tied that end around the main tree trunk of the root there.

By this time, by some signal I did not notice, the mahouts had returned to join us and, while Jumbo had got his annoyance fixed on what was holding his back leg back there, one of them neatly slipped another noose around one of its front forelegs on the opposite side. The end of this he hooked around another tree out in front.

We waited there for only a few minutes, while my father crooned and talked little E into relative calmness before he made sure the little guy wasn't injured in any way.

When he was satisfied, he nodded, tapped me on the shoulder without looking at me, in the way he used to, and we walked back to the estate.

I couldn't work out why he wanted to leave the little fellow tied back and front like that. It looked awful.

I found out that the mahouts had to stay out there in order to get Baby E used to humans... used to their body odours, used to their touching, used to the cane rod they gently stroked and scratched him with, used to eating in their presence.

Five days later they brought the little fellow in. He was so docile I could feed him from a bottle within two days.

And that was my father's own special way.

My only problem now is where am I going to get a Sambhur buck's skull and antlers to use on *him*?

Those things don't grow on trees, you know.

The other problem I have is I'm just getting weaker.

I don't know what it is with me.

I'm near to the end of the journey and I just can't seem to muster the energy to get on with it.

It's me who feels Baby-E-tied to the Devil's horny bundle.

I know I am sleeping but half the time I'm doing that I also know I'm not sleeping like I should be sleeping. Vague ghosts, in high disquiet, come at me like rugby forwards. They have no story to tell, no snatch scenario played out for my edification.

They just swirl, tackle, beat me hot and cold, make me dizzy and make me bilious. Not that they aren't vaguely familiar. I sometimes think I see my brother's face but, if it is, it seems to be in some sort of melt-down. I think, too, I see and hear my mother sighing and coming at me as though she wanted to force herself to stick to me, yet her form is gauzy and her sighing is the first whisperings of a coming wind and anyway she sighs and cries and leaves me.

Most times I think I am awake. I lie here at those times and think that I will swing my legs out of bed and start on my hunt. Yet where is my voice, where is the energy? I seem to be sick to vomiting in my own kernel that is in the eye of a storm, and all the velocities of life are those beyond, around, above and below me, not with me.

Yesterday, I think I remember taking soup. Today I am sickened by the thought that I might have.

Yet I do have times when I am conscious, if semi-conscious is what the other times are. I emerge to find the ghosts sitting by my bed, then they become real people, and, if I hold down the sickening dizziness by really gritting my teeth hard and concentrate on focus by knitting my brow and screwing up my eyes, I can talk a little with my visitors.

But mainly there is an indefinable, malapert shape sitting on a rock or something way down the perspective of my inner landscape, back beyond the apparitions which come at me.

There is no mind's eye here now.

Though I cannot quite make it out, I know it is my father out there, beyond my inner reach, yet, too, within this landscape within the eye of the storm. And I realise that he is waiting for me, just as I realise I cannot rise to go to him. Not just yet.

I can't make out whether he sits there challenging me or is sitting there with eternal patience while I just happen to be in the picture.

I am surprised that there is no retribution, none of the screams that my brother caused so much and about which I feel myself just as causal as he because 1 felt and watched and experienced them in my head. My mind's eye, yes. I thought, he did experience them in his head. But none of those inextinguishable revenges come flying back.

Perhaps 1 am not yet ill enough for the promise of chastisements-to-come to come.

Perhaps all this is just the lassitudes.

Hansen has visited!

How many years would it have been for him when he could go out into the street and go visiting without the visitee jumping up and bolting the door before he got there?

He did. He did, though. My Hansen came out into the street and he came out alone and he came out without being swathed in bandages like the Invisible Man, which I prefer thinking I read in book form rather than that disappointing 1933 effort for the John Wesley Hyatt's celluloid in film stocks, starring Claude Raines, which I definitely didn't see. Not in premiere, anyway, if I did since I was way too young.

The skin on my Hansen's lower face has started the process of flaking after satisfying itself that on this part of his anatomy it wanted to belong. It is liverish. Unless Joe's surgeon brother can get some pigment going on in there the next time around, he's going to look like a black-and- white minstrel who'd put on make-up and then decided to shave.

His poor mutilated fingers, the whole six of them in all, are paucy as though they had just started to be born. Yet he has them working a little, and he has his jaw working a bit.

And oh, even how ill I feel, how good it is to hear him talking again.

I wouldn't know whether his few grunted words to me are Sinhala, Tamil or English. Somehow, though, in sickness, there is a sluggish mutual tide of understanding that comprehends what belongs to the ether, where no feet are touching any sort of ground.

And the cheeky little bugger is doing a reverse on me. He strokes my hair, washes down my face, cools down my chest and back. He won't let anybody else do it while he is at my side. He straightens my pillows and remakes the bed.

Despite how he looks, his hand movements tell me he is as fit as a mallee bull. It is the life within him that he has really regained.

The Dallas Cowboys should have him in their starting line-up. With his looks, no one would twig the difference if the helmet stays on.

Fathers Thumbayaserni and Jayakody and Sisters Lima, Margaret, Sriyani and Camilla visit me in this now-time. The whole shebang of Hansen House too. Along with them they have brought the eleven other lepers, except the old lady who could never help farting in my face.

If she did that now, it'd probably knock me flat or maybe if it was a big enough one I might appreciate the fanning.

There are also the more visitable poor women and children from out back of Hansen House, so, all in all, there must be thirty people stuffed into this small room. That includes my five little guardian angels, their chins on the mattress at various places, looking wide- eyed at so many visitors, as well as trying to keep their loving eyes on me and the stick-on religious pictures Father Thumbayaserni has brought for the wall above me.

In glitter and shocking primary colours, there are a Cross, Jesus with a lamb, and St Mary with someone swimming around her head.

My Hansen is not there in the throng, would not deign. His is the permission of the one-on-one.

That I should have come through such a solitary, unfamilied, detesting existence to arrive at this wonderful family, mine in all their assortments! Each heart there has been laid upon mine. Each gentleness and each silent suffering far greater than mine serving me.

The spade, the worm, the wheel ... they are all turning, and I see through eyes that just will not stop watering the coronas of humility that are possible, the rainbows and washes and auroras of attendings that are possible.

I just hope I'm looking sickly enough to warrant all this.

I have a lump in my throat that I cannot swallow. I near choke until Father T. says something and gives me a sip of communal wine.

You see what they're doing, don't you?

It must be Sunday and they've all come to give me my own Mass.

It's not the last rites after all.

I can see now they have festooned this bed with rosaries and unlit candles. They seemed to have come along expressly so that they can be smiling and giggling at what they are doing.

No, not the last rites.

If it was back in Australia, and they were smiling and giggling, you'd have to worry about it being the last rites.

I think I feel little Stephanie's hand in mine.

Or it might be my Virathni's hand.

My Virathni visits, and she visits every morning before work and each evening after work.

I know what the neighbours will be thinking.

That, yes, that unhearty chaperone of a hymen of hers did fly out of the window before anyone blinked.

Some chance, in my condition.

It is when she comes that I am most afraid to die. This dark and mysterious and shining woman.

She sits at my side without guile, shining a plain insistence of our future together through her powerful eyes.

It is she, not me, who has been through a life of deaths, through the malarias, through the dysenteries, and lived with the deformities, the amputations, the untreated birth defects of the living poor. But in the single-minded badinage about the girls at work or last night's teledrama, she is saying to me that this, this illness of mine, she will not live with.

And in this deepening atmosphere of this inner room, she becomes a Shade, a dark echo of how I used to sit in the dark myself with my sickly mother, feeling in the same way that I should show how I wasn't going to live with any sighing and dying.

But she cannot help my brain becoming centrifugal again, it is a pond of unstable jelly and I know it is for me to fever for again. And then the long-away, shapeless form that I have thought as my father comes again to begin again to infuriate me with its distance beyond me.

He is mocking me again.

Oh, how I want to kill him.

And then it is surely Virathni's voice coming through to me as near choking as if I had actually mumbled the murder in my heart out aloud:

'No, no, Johnnie. All the time your father and your Aunt Jayalitha argued. He is keeping us poor, she is always shouting, sending more to Australia for you than we have to live on.'

I wave this rush of unsavoury wind away from my presence for being irritatingly ridiculous.

'Please, don't let this hurt us, nae? When he has heard your mother has died, he started selling the elephants of the estate for money for you and was being made to leave. After that he was never the same man, but he made lots of money, but he and your aunt still argued and argued.'

I am sure I get my eyes open to find she is holding out to me what might be my newspaper cuttings in abject supplication, as though in them lies some indestructible truth if only I had eyes to see.

'One day your father is coming home and oh he hugs and hugs us. He is crying, isn't it? He told us you have passed. You are going to be a great attorney-at-law. And he laughs at your aunt always arguing about the money he is always sending you that is keeping us poor.'

And that bunged-up arsehole Ramaswarmy. And all those bunged-up arsehole Ramaswarmys. That fat-greasy overflow of slug's blubber Appa so righteous, so I-make-this-covenant-with-you, so I-am-your-saviour, so come-to-me, so do-your-duty-as-I-did-to-you, so it-was-all-me... such a filthy swollen pig of a bloated leech who tried to murder my brother, my me.... all the time getting my father's money for us and claiming it was from himself, of his own sacrifice.

I am packed with revenge about to explode.

Now I fancy my Virathni might have been sobbing, but I have no idea how long she has stopped it. Her nose is cold; she has her face to the back of my hand. She sniffs it gently, as they do here, sweeter than any kiss.

I think she is completing some story that has taken her a long time trying to tell me, but all I can take in is:

'He is an old man now and alone.'

It is as though, as soon as those words come to me, I am overwhelmed with hot fury at that hellish form sitting safely back there and daring to mock me. I have the need to tongue-lash it with her words. I spit them out at the creature and they seem to turn into whips: *he is an old man now and alone*.

The words strike my tormentor as knives devolved from whips and thud it backwards in punctuation of the hits; yet, at the same time, its mouth somehow correspondingly becomes propelled towards me, jerkingly, synched in time with the one thudding word after the other until it is closed in to be defined and pucker formed and forces me to quiver with the mouthings it is urging on me and which I must repeat from it. And so I do here as I couldn't help doing then:

318

'Where would he go? You must think.'

They are not said, but I am crying them out. They are mine, but I am the mouth.

They are my reaching, but are the arms of her own Morpheus, not mine, revealing her own voice from out of her own dream, perhaps, but mine real or not real:

'He was always talking of a cave and a waterfall, Johnnie. The place he called Kiruwita.'

I know it and where it is. In the hushed sways of my memory, I am released to remember him telling me. I must have already remembered. I can even remember having looked up a place called Kiruwita only a few weeks ago -- remembering, too, not knowing why I had done so.

I can even see the cave, its mouth opening halfway up one of the last sheered drops of the upcountry plateau to the gem streams of the plains of Ratnapura below. Up around there they had to prise my poor hands from that great chain of the great Rajah.

Up there he would have a view far to the west around to the east.

And he would be waiting.

That last rogue.

The last tusker of the uplands, wanting to make a mad crushing dash for it, but deathly afraid to leave his beloved upland for the dry and killing steps of the open forests of the plains.

The mouth of the cave, the mouth, yes, that could have been talking to me, seems to suddenly sweep me away too as though I was its comet tail, and I feel the weight of my Virathni gradually lighten.

When I wake up, I am on my feet yelling for my Hansen.

My little guardian angels are crowded into a corner of the room, not knowing whether to laugh or cry. They have the sense of, but not the knowledge of, the climacteric. They don't know whether they are seeing Lazarus rising or the last burst of the last Gadarene swine.

I could have told them just maybe it could be either.

Must have only been kidding you all about the malaria. Sorry about that.

Just the lassitudes, after all.

Hansen! Get that Phantom of the Opera to get his leprous butt here. Now.

No time, no inclination and no patience to draw water from the communal tank to wash. I just climb in to the tank, something not socially done, and do a few vigorous turns, like it was just a two-hundred warm-up of once upon a time training session, spring out.

Never mind the nudies, my angels; you'll see plenty of that in your grafting lives to come. And this shivering body, my babes, is just full of rushing blood, which is what makes all those white bodies that amaze you so go all pink and flushed and look like over-boiled rhubarb. It's called energy, my clucks, energy, summoned up, geared up, unnerved. It's also called the water in your tank is bloody freezing.

I have slipped into my bushie's gear: long trousers, tucked into socks, imitation Adidas runners you can get here.

Goes to show God does have reprieves in that bag of tricks of His.

Now I have even got through the front door and ploughed out into the daylight for the first time, I think, in my living memory.

And plough is right.

Right outside the front door, I plough straight into my enemy of late, Inspector Bloody-fucking-hell-sorry Charles Ekanayake.

He's obviously in the process of doing a constitutional Sunday stroll around the town, and I have to fall literally into the prick's arms after hiding out from him all these months.

320

One of us – and guess who? -- turning the wrong corner at the wrong time on the innocence of a sudden impulse

Thanks, God. Some reprieve.

But, fired up so that there're no flies on me, I get back into the house even before he recovers and calls me to stop. For a moment, I think about trying for an unhappy break out through that tiny back yard out there, but realise it doesn't go anywhere anyway.

So, I sit and wait for him to come to me.

He comes, and cautiously enough. He has his baton on the parry. His long face looks decidedly unhappy, giving his features an ancient forlornness, as though all this mucking about was far more disappointing for him than for me. I realise I have sort of missed his nearness. As much as a hunter he is, I hadn't realised how much of a comfort he projects.

He doesn't bother to sit, which is just as well. Poor people's chairs are not made for his size. He just points that baton at my heart. Outrage or disappointment makes it quiver at me. I could have been the water and he could have been the diviner.

'I don't suppose you'd think you need a search warrant to walk right in, Inspector?'

Apparently, this is not even worth thinking about.

'Bloody fucking hell sorry, we are looking for you in Kandy. Cheeky bugger, is it?' And now it's my turn to get something not worth thinking about: 'Up you get and you are coming and going with me.'

Now, my lawyer's nose told me the way he said that he didn't have half a moral right, and knew it.

'What charge, Inspector?'

I watched him flush with anger. This is his neck of the woods, after all, not some secondment in a country strewn of many Australian eggs underfoot.

'Agent Baybe does not protect you here!'

His jerkish body language told me, too, that that Detective-sergeant Martin Baybe probably did protect me. I can feel instantly how my brother always suspected the man with the atrocious shirt and tie and annoying mannerisms is working for a far greater policing agent than just the National Crimes Commission -- and that he has been literally protecting us from the Ramaswarmys' treachery as a way of eventually getting far better results.

Not that I had any idea why he would think Baybe would want to protect me. Rave on, Inspector.

'Baybe? Baybe? Baybeling brook? 'Fraid you've lost me.'

'I could be putting you away and pitching the key, bloody fucking hell. You might be doing what Baybe told you to do in Hong Kong and come back here, but you must be telling me where your father is.'

'Sorry, never been to Hong Kong, Inspector. Never spoke to the Detective-sergeant about here or anywhere either.'

I was in no way lying. I had our mind's eye. My brother had our mind's eye. Baybe didn't. This bloody-fucking-hell of an Inspector certainly didn't. What would they know?

'We have this thing of detention we are calling here the Prevention of Terrorism Act here, Mr Tasker.'

'I'm a terrorist – not even a suspected one -- for coming back to visit my birthplace? For sweating up the sheets equals subversive?'

His shrug might as well have been a yes.

'Inspector, I ain't talking to you anymore.'

'*You will die, Mr Tasker.*'

The man was truly, truly intimidating. He gave me one last and long stare which was articulate in every way you wouldn't want it to be.

Then he turned and walked out.

Being stifled in being able to arrest me on the spot seemed to induce stiffness in his legs.

But I knew he'd be back, all loosened up for all the wrong reasons for me, and in a very short time.

But, to say how Inspector Ekanayake would say it, I am also knowing that a Sunday stroll is a Sunday stroll, and even a terrorist suspect is allowed one.

Once locked into a Sunday stroll, hell or high water cannot break it off. You try it sometimes.

It gave me the breathing space I needed.

I dash off notes to Virathni and to the father of my little guardian angels, and then my Hansen arrives.

His poor flaky face, while at least blessedly recognised as one, is making him puff grotesquely. I hand him the note to Virathni, and urge him to get it to her immediately, *Virathnite hayemma*, and then to meet me at the railway station.

The other note I entrust to my little angels for their Daddy.

There wasn't anything momentous in what I wrote, only that they must protect themselves when the Inspector's heavies came around -- and very heavily they would come around too -- by telling quite freely I have taken off to Kiruwita to find my father.

My Hansen was at the railway station before I was, but that wasn't surprising. I had something to do myself before that.

What I do is walk around the town anticlockwise to the Inspector's clockwise. I have to do something to defy him. I don't try to make a melodrama out of it; all I want him to see is that I am cool enough to be going on my own Sunday stroll around the town too.

I merely stroll-veer towards him as we transect in opposite directions and pass close.

I scowl haughtily and he scowls heightfully back.

But the point is I get my scowl in first and it is, yes, a Sunday stroll that few can or should break into.

The purpose of the exercise, though, is to find out whether he really was on a Sunday stroll *he* could not seemingly break off from. Confirming that has given me the knowledge that he hasn't got all the pieces he needs yet to come after me and gives me just enough time to hoof it out of town before he has.

323

When my Hansen finally spies me among what has to be a third of the country's population that always seem to be waiting for any train any time of the day or night, he grunts that I must show my ticket.

I do so.

He is suddenly all up-and-down movement, which I take for excitement, and he is prodding the name Kiruwita on the ticket and extruding from all the willpower he can muster the word:

'*Dannawa*'.

He is saying he knows. That he knows Kiruwita. And then proceeds to raid my pocket for more money, which he would never do.

It gets him a wide circle of the curious and the admiring. They wouldn't often see a local with seeming little face left trying to effect a pickpocketing of a foreigner in a public place with hands that have the stealth of pile drivers.

Finally, I give in and hand him the money for the fare to join me. My good old boy Hansen.

Nor was the darling man kidding with his 'I am knowing'. He did know the place. More, he really knows the place, even down to some relatives and distant friends of the family. Where a young man like him, locked away out of family shame for so any years in some devil-wracked, superstitious village tens of kilometres away ever got to know the very town I need, I didn't ask. He will never cease to amaze me.

But then, this is Sri Lanka, after all.

The land of the human thread.

Nobody follows us onto the train. Despite the mob launching into its habitual shark's feeding frenzy at the very rumour of a train approaching, I could see through my brother's eyes there is no special interest in us.

Still, just before it is about to leave, I heave my Hansen back to the carriage door on the other side of the train, step gingerly over those already packing themselves onto the outside steps for the best ventilated seats in the house, and climb down to make it to the road on the other side of the station. I know I have done so not to be seen, and have succeeded. How could I know that?

I just do. My brother's entwining mind's eye has returned. Out of the malaria, this is all clear now.

By the bus depot there, we negotiate the best fare a betel-chewing, bloody-mouth-palated taxi driver will have had since he went into hock over some dream of making millions taking tourists around tea estates who never came and never would.

Once the guy's taxi might have been relatively new as a Morris Minor, but there would be few around to remember it. And to look at it would beggar the imagination of it newly rolling off some assembly line; it would have had to be *bashed* off. But that man and that old bomb is my immediate choice to get us started right now. To get us to Kiruwita will take him a wide-berthed round trip of two days, and those two days will be two days out of range of Ekanayake's big ears maybe -- or they would get sick'n'tired of waiting and given up on me and gone home.

As I said, this is Sri Lanka, after all.

It is no surprise, given me springing into action, that my brother has 'come' to be there for me again.

Wherever he is, he might be feeling the family might be crashing together again.

Except for my mother having to be the one sighing and dying and leaving me.

What I do know is he is watching me more than the normal thing of me watching him now.

I cannot go on in the present tense. These last couple of weeks have seemed too much like a dream where I have only been a dumb witness to its present moments. I don't want that.

This was no dream. This happened:

At, yes, Kiruwita.

I stepped carefully to where my poor muddy Hansen was. By boggy gloop he had found a track and my brother knew it was the right track. It pushed away from the back road under a canopy that was closed for some way with a child's nightmare of creepers, surface roots and sharp flints still dripping from the light overnight drizzle.

The crows, the coucals, the Indian mynhers became loud and confidently echoing in their calling of our way. The flies and the mosquitoes paraded along with us. Only the plaintive calls of the cuckoos did anything to lift my spirits in this place that was becoming more bald-pated, more inferno'd as we went on in. I felt I must be walking back in time, backtracking to the deathly earth of my Adelaide scorched-earth time.

The air seemed to smell of bat colonies, jackal offal, urinations of jungle cats. Even my brother had become wary.

But this was not the Australian scrub. This was not any nightmare of the old Adelaide sand hills. I'm not saying it was much better. There was an added spirited disturbance to it. Too many chants upon it. Too many mournful and dispirited passings down through the ages through it. It had monkeys on its back, gargoyling. It had the country's mischievous devils, the imps, forever lodged in it.

Yes, monkeyed. Too tormenting and all eyes. Too many dire passages through this land.

We stopped and rested. I could see nothing ahead but the charnel belt of boulders and the emergent trees across the other side. I went to sit down, but had my shirt tugged sharply by Hansen. He was looking downstream, along that pallid trickle of water as though it, too, was only surlily given. Even the vegetation seemed to shrink back from its meanness.

At first, I could see nothing that should be worrying him. Then I noticed a slight and careful movement. Their bodies down there were almost perfectly camouflaged against the chocolate dense shoals of the creek, their tawn bandannas similar to the bleach works of the boulders. I saw at least three heavily darkened men down there.

They were a few hundred metres away and had stopped stock still when they noticed us. They must have been panning for the famed gems of the region, like thieves or perhaps as thieves, like malevolent emergents from the sinister layers of the forest. My brother could literally feel the murder in their hearts, and I guess the movements I saw were for hatchets or worse.

At least they made no move towards us. Perhaps, even, they might not have been real, but unfancying spirits, trapped to appear within the enmity of the land there. Too much the weight of past civilisations and their bloody suppressions of anything new.

There was a rise on the other side of the stream. We had to heave ourselves up it by over-handing up the vines, testing the tensile strengths of the young bamboos, gaining footholds against the few buttress roots of the few immature hardwood species still left standing.

Yet, when we clambered to the top of the rise, there it was. It amazed me we hadn't been able to see it from further down.

It rose above us as if it would take up the entire seeable world, a huge crag of rock. It looked like it had once been a pinnacle of one of the mountains behind it but had sheared off by a mighty and angry chop to slide down, lopped, to the plain at the foot of the escarpment. And there was no welcoming in it, either.

Nothing but a few ferns and grass outgrowths seem to be able to survive on its sheer face. To me, it was utterly black, as black as ebony, the ebony of the elephant set my mother once kept on the mantelpiece in Adelaide to tease me. It seemed brittle, dangerous, unstable, as intrinsically and slicingly fickle as obsidian.

As consuming as hot pitch.

How could my father be hiding up there? It seemed impossible that anything could live on it, could abide to live within it.

But, to my hesitation, to my doubts, my brother was still with me. I even felt he had lost patience and gone on ahead. Mind's eye, there was no track to it.

I tried my hardest to overcome my terrible lethargy and catch up. I could see my Hansen up there with him, me, but I just couldn't seem to believe enough that I was capable of ever drawing close to them, to, yes, somehow me. It seemed I was just slipping back into the hopeless mists of malaria or the dreaded lassitudinouses again.

Yet, blessedly, I was somehow suddenly standing alongside my Hansen and looking down at his feet with a stupefied curiosity that actually blunts clear thought.

There, on the track that suddenly seemed much more defined as though a mist in my mind had lifted, was the skull and antlers of a Sambhur buck.

It was mine to pick up.

And then I knew I only had to climb to trap my father.

'It is used,' I said as softly as I could to Hansen's mute quizzing, 'to hunt elephants in a very special way known only to my father and the few he showed'.

I moved on with it in my arms, remembering the thin cords abrading, the bundle unravelling, the baby elephant becoming weary; the now-exposed skull snagging on the bush and the hide rope gradually slowing to a halt. Buttress'd. Rooted.

No further to go, ahead the exhausted beast would be waiting.

I hoped my father wouldn't be too exhausted for me.

It should be a fair game after all those years.

The stream proved to lie about half a kilometre below the great rock through refugia rainforest that had survived because of its inaccessibility to the wood-gatherers of the villages.

The distance constantly changed in illusion. From where I started with the Sambhur skull, the monolith seemed to be only a few hundred paces away but, as we swung, and often beat, our ways along the vine and fern trails which had become only discernible by now through the practised instincts of my brother's eye, which I could sense again on the move again, we often seemed to be getting further away from it.

I was again having trouble distinguishing reality from delusion. Malarially. Becoming a misted way.

When I registered that I had really heard it, I found myself detoured towards it. It was the trickling and ffllatt of water off to our left.

I came to a clearing, where an old emergent tree, I think a rosewood, had sown its last seed and had taken a lot of puppy stuff with it as it fell.

There, high up on the escarpment joined to the monolith by what looked like a saving arm, in the tipping sun, was the shining necklace of a waterfall. It did not seem to be actually falling, but rather draped there as a single pearl strand.

I stood there straining my eyes to study its vertical course, straining my ears. For I thought I had heard a calling to me -- a murmuring, particular somehow to me from up ahead.

I turned to my now-nervous Hansen. He must have been sensing we were walking into danger. Not that I would have been a comforting sight, violently stopping and starting and carrying forward the offering of the skull and antlers like some demented ascetic being made to wander forever in this nether land in self-immolating penance.

Even if it had been only half a kilometre, I found myself once more emotionally and physically exhausted by the time we reached the great rock.

From there, the track was easier to follow and, under normal trekking, would have been an easy hike around its winding contours and levels as you climbed. Yet I just seemed not able to gain any breath with each step. Frequently, my Hansen had to wait for me while I gathered the strength to carry on. I could do nothing about Tusker's impatience. If he wanted me to do something about it, he should have been showing himself.

There was nothing above us, no sound other than the cry of the birds and the howlings of the monkeys now cavalcading on the tree tops below us. It wasn't until I thought that I would never reach the summit above us that we arrived. My brother seemed to be half-carrying, half-dragging me. You could say, might say, I could hardly keep my mind's eye open. A corner of the track had narrowed dangerously through a rock fall. We had to grip the handholds of the great rock itself to edge our way around the corner to find we were standing on a wide ledge -- a gallery to the magnificent view carpeted before it all the way down -- surely, on a fine day -- to the southern sea; the patches of refugia rainforest desperately hanging onto existence; the sunned sveltes of disturbance where all the great hardwoods had been removed and the coconut palms, the kittuls, the rubber trees, the wild bananas and the ferns and the vines had taken over in their ever-wrestling entanglements; the plantations; the from-there toy-sized home vegetable plots as far as the eye could see; the glading greens of the sweeping paddy fields.

From here the cries of the animals went out across the land; more than man, more than the plants, these webbed their stout assertions to the living connection of all who and all what lived in this land.

Only then did I have the nerve to turn around and face the entrance to the cave. I saw how it was not the perfect spot. Indeed, there was no consecration to this ground for all of its elevation. I felt strongly, and I could sense my brother sniffing the air (either then or before or afterwards) to try to define it, that something at some time had happened to corrupt it.

The few stunted trees and thorn bushes around its entrance were leafless and blackened as if they had been burnt by my brother's hand and, as soon as I had turned to face it, the air had exploded with the dry and joyless cawings of hundreds of black crows that somehow seemed to have materialised on those fruitless branches around the cave's entrance. It felt like life had departed and they were there, in litany, to ensure it would never return. The ground at the entrance was a black bog with their droppings.

Here, surely, was Golgotha. Surely nothing that was of my father could be living there. I felt the claws of malaria want to drag me down again.

It must have only been my brother's nudging impatience that kicked me to my feet and got me moving forward through the stubbing sound barrier of the crows, dragging, literally, my Hansen after me.

It was dark.

Of course it was dark in there. But it put fear into me, and I felt how it was all-time Mankind's.

For some reason, I had expected that all would be light, lit, illuminating. Yet the air had the sweet coolness of earth, and it was as if, by entering, we had shut a great temple door on the morbid warnings of the crows.

As at a temple's first chamber, we stood and listened, expectant that its secrets would open slowly to us, as images come with prayers.

And they did.

Behind us, the devolving sun must have come level to the eye of the cave. At first, cyan, then copper, then tangerine sun streams crept past our feet, slowly groped across the floor and then suddenly burst upon the whole area with the bright revelation of a new dawn.

The chamber must have been upwards of ten metres as high, as it was broad. Around its floor was a profusion of concrete slabs and large boulders, discoloured with what I thought must have been bats' droppings, yet the patina'd granite roof revealed no bats' roost, no colony.

There were before us three large Buddha statues in the lying, sitting and standing positions. They were regarding us timelessly, with a sort of fatigue of the ever-changing, yet ever-renewing. It could have been they had known all along what it was going to be like changing from living essences to stone. That I was coming to hunt.

Around the walls were huge frescoes, now so faded and calcified that they looked like sinopia only, baseline beginnings, not finishes. Their once blues and greens and golds now only evident splashings, sorry forms of neglect from the too-many human waves, the too- many overwhelming imploring eyes.

Over or under these frescoes were others, plainly Hindu. The temple must have been used by the ascetics of both Hinduism and Buddhism, the one supplanting the other as the outside imperatives swung backwards and forwards. I could see the image of a Vel cart, the vehicle of the Hindu god, Lord Skanda, who I always thought the Hindus had overstated. But that's just me.

Anyway, the image of the god rose in faded spirituality from the floor to almost the ceiling, larger than life. The god of chastity and also of war. The god of the quality of semen flow and the non-semen flow of the south, of the symphony of beauty and truth and love, yet he of the sacrifices to the power of righteous anger. An often sitter under a tree.

He sat on his gold-carved cart, at the entrance to his own thovil, with his consorts Theivanei and Vali, and the two white chargers held in his reins, in his thrall, reining in human passions, driving them to where the eye of the great Siva wanted them to be.

The third eye. The all-seeing eye.

Isn't that the mind's eye?

I called out for my father.

I just whispered: 'Are you here, Father?'

Off to the right of this main chamber, there was another opening. I moved into it, slowly and laden with a sorrowful respect I was trying to fight back. This was an antechamber. Here, water seeped out of the tourmaline wall of rock and was collected in a concrete well, around which were concrete bathing positions. The water was pure and crystalline, biting with coldness. My Hansen drank at it as though it was a cure.

Here the monks must have washed or purified themselves. Here, too, they would have delivered *bana* or performed *poojah* or, if Hindu, prepared the sacred milky jismic unguents.

I returned to the main chamber. My Hansen still stood with grotesque piety at its threshold. He was Christian, but the gods and the nether world's interferences would never have been driven out of the village part of him. He was pointing something out to me.

On the slabs, of what would have been the altar pieces, were open tins of food. I went to them quickly.

They were recent; they were still alive with ants. My father was here somewhere near.

I think I heard it before Hansen.

It was a croak, a sound pushed out before coughing might swamp it:

'I knew they couldn't kill you'

I heard it as saying.

And then the choking coughing. It hacked as roughly and as deathly as the crows outside.

We both leapt up and ran like lunatics looking in all the nooks and crannies there. There had to be another chamber somewhere.

My Hansen found it. It was no more than a slit in the rock folds that would remain in shadow even in full light.

I squeezed through edgeways into what must have been the devale, or monks' quarters. I heard his stentorian breathing, but my eyes could only pick out the concrete slabs that would have passed for their beds once. There was dim light coming in from up high, but it was cathedral, shafting, chiaroscuro to sight.

And I heard:

'Let me look at you.'

I had him then. I put down the Sambhur skull.

Over by the far wall, he lay on a slab. It seemed all he could manage was to roll his head my way. My father was staring at me!

I moved over to him and knelt beside him.

It was the last thing I had imagined I would have done.

Thin, oh, thin. He lay as nothing much on the slab. I could smell the hot sweat, the roast, of him. I reached out and touched his arm. This was drenched in sweat; the heat from him was fierce.

I called to my Hansen for fire.

I was left exploring my father with only my hands. I could only see his teeth set in what must have been a small, painful smile and through this knew he had his head lolled my way. He must have been looking through almost-closed eyes; there was only the small shine of the teeth.

He was naked except for a draped loin cloth. I tore off my shirt and began to rub him down. What a thing reduced his body was to my imagination of what he would be like!

All my life I had continued to regard him from the standpoint of a child; the height of him according to the way he commanded. Now I was rubbing down outlined ribs, protuberant hip bones, arms and legs skeletal not to large. Not very large at all.

In the flare of my Hansen's first match, I actually saw him as a skeleton. Yet, when the flames began to win, he became a figure, and I was able to see the substance that would have been on him once. He opened his eyes fully then. There was

334

in them a fierce light of possession, of some sort of triumph, such that I stopped rubbing him down.

'Stand,' he said painfully.

As I did so, I knocked something like a pack of cards from the slab where his hand lay. I bent to retrieve them, but he waved me away.

'Let me look at you.'

A voice that was still forceful, and so resonant to me that there might not have been any years in between. My mother might walk in, sighing, and we would have lunch in the soft, auburn light of his hut down by the estate's elephant enclosure.

His hair had greyed out and, even though sickness had made it masonry to his scalp, I could see he still wore it long. Illness had so pinched his features that he looked like he was withdrawing into the shelter of his form where he would finally achieve becoming unreachable. Yet it was the face of my father; I had no other; I had only ever remembered the sound and shape of him, never the features.

Of what he saw of me, he nodded only gravely.

I bent down to pick up what I had knocked off the slab. I saw they were old 35 mm photographs. I glanced at him and he nodded: look, look.

There must have been twenty of them. Photographs of us. Of my mother. Of the three of us together. Of me alone. They ranged from battered and yellowing Box Brownie black-and-whites to Kodachromes badly developed.

I won't go into what I've read about the state of George Eastman with regard to Kodak movie film and the development of the modern cinema was around then.

Photographs, yes. That I never dreamt my father would have, let alone keeping by his side preciously. And, even though the light was dim and flickering, I still somehow felt that I had no right in scrutinising them and, in feeling that, realised my father's possessions were not my possessions -- that, for all of how I had always thought he should be living only for me, his life and the possessions of it were quite separate.

Yet still he nodded smally: look, look.

Sepia'd, my mother stood before the great house of the tea estate with her hand on my shoulder.

I hadn't remembered she was as tall as she seemed there. She was taller than him.

He stood on the other side of me, his hand on my other shoulder.

Between them there was a noticeably formal space, as though, whoever had taken the shot -- my grandmother, perhaps, during a time my blunt-headed grandfather was absent -- had only agreed to do so, provided a family-photograph decorum was maintained.

The light, the smallness of the print. I couldn't make out her features clearly, and I no longer remembered them. The waves of her shoulder- length hair, though, clawed my sense of hopelessness with their vague familiarity.

She looked to have a high and pert bosom under that printed cotton frock with its wide darker-coloured belt. And petticoat; some part of it showed below the left hem of the frock. It confirmed my feeling that she didn't ever have a great feeling for clothes; she always seemed to me to be in too much of a hurry, always ahead of me and shooing. I have the sneaking suspicion she might have been a bit untidy.

My father had on a white button-and-collar shirt. He stood comfortably, with sleeves buttoned down and his white sarong long and smooth; it could have been starched by my second wife Rehana perhaps, whined over to inflexibility. His large Mexicano moustache gave him a look that you could interpret as scowling or smiling, depending on your instant reaction to his image.

A few days ago, I would have assumed it was scowling. Now, under my care, I assumed he was smiling.

Other than noting the knee-length shorts and the short-sleeved shirt buttoned right to the top, I could not take any notice of myself. I didn't want to. I was feeling unworthy, and I couldn't understand why.

You wonder where my twin brother was? If you looked very closely you can just discern, or at least I can, there is a tell-tale half space between both my mother and father and me. I can only presume he was there and taking the photograph at the time. Even in that, even then, *pipping* me. Probably smiling over there, I'm here and you have to be stuck over there. Then I didn't look like I minded that. Now, I certainly don't either.

That was the only family shot anyway. The others were ranged over the next twenty or so years of my mother and me, I would guess. They had no sequence to them; it was as though they had come from Australia at someone's, undoubtedly my brother's, afterthought: a photo taken, my father remembered, and, if convenient, posted off to him.

Yet I suppose for him they had enough continuity to be a family album. His wife. His family. My mother and I about to board the ship and taken, I guess, with the same Box Brownie, undoubtedly my mother's, and taken of us by him.

My mother would have taken one of him and me, but that was not there. Lost? Or perhaps, like me, he too had not felt worthy.

The sighing and the dying and the leaving can do that.

And then only two others of my mother: one of the two of us outside the Sturt Street house in Adelaide when she looked like she had just come off shift from the shoe factory -- and another on, what I would take to have been, Henley Beach where we were sticky with the wet sand of a sandcastle in the centre of sand-dune hell. Each so small, so blacked-and-sepia'd, that she had lived on featureless.

There was not a single one of my brother.

I bet he felt all smug, *pipping* me to the shutter, leaving me to the lens. Probably keeping the rolls of film for when he wanted.

337

The rest were coloured and of me, taken randomly, carelessly, during the Melbourne and university days. The last was of my graduation.

They could only have been taken, could only have been sent, by the Ramaswarmys. Those father-cheats. Those dung-gutted liars. None of them should have lived past Hong Kong's latest rare delicacy of fried human ears looking like dim sims.

From where he lay, my father continued to watch my face carefully.

It was as if he was straining to seek the discovery. I nodded that I now understood.

I was under no delusion now, no delirium, that Virathni had urged me to understand how it had been. These latter photographs of me confirmed my father had maintained contact with the Ramaswarmys.

If that were so, then she had told me the truth -- no, no malarial or lassitudinous delirium, no dream of mine -- about the money he always sent on for us, despite the deprivations Aunt Jayalitha had to live through, had to die for.

I hadn't believed it.

Could you have? Magwitch, with *his* alias of Provis, is for Dickens, and that money had always got through. Pip mightn't have known that Magwitch was always sending him the wherewithal and Miss Havisham might have tried a con around it, but no one was like that maggot Appa Ramaswarmy and hid the fact to exploit the fact. What sort of animal?! You look up 'Great Expectations' if you don't believe me. It was the second novel that Charles Dickens wrote in the first person, if you must know. I actually like the early Marcus Stone woodcuts so much that one day I'm going to get around to reading the whole thing.

Neither my brother nor I ever saw a red cent that wasn't supposed to be payment by Appa Ramaswarmy for services rendered to the bloody cause he had bound us hook, line and sinker to.

338

Can I ever tell you how rare even those red cents were that came from those pigshit Ramaswarmys as much as they trumpeted their 'largesse' to my brother and me? We won the scholarships; we worked our way through in a thousand shitty jobs, mornings and nights, even after my degree and my brother's sudden disappearances and appearances. Nothing came regularly. Occasionally, a few dollars appeared.

The Ramaswarmys.

That pack of blood-slurping hyenas that got what they deserved.

All those years, all my father's money intended for me, they must have pocketed for themselves.

I'm going on about it, sure, but remember in the old days those filthy dogshits were just as hard-up as we were. Or just as down-at-the-heels as my mother and me. My father's money... my money!... my mother's-and-my money!... my mother's-and-our money!... it would have been used by those shitheaded Ramaswarmys in the early days to buy decency, to buy their way up, after they drove away and left us to wallow on that baked and killing Adelaide earth of purgatory.

Instead of giving it to us.

And I bet now that when my mother sighed and died and left me, they didn't even bother to tell my father.

I bet he was left thinking through their lying mouths she was alive all these years.

Oh.

And then, when my brother and I escaped that boys' Home and struggled to Melbourne to sit wide-eyed and hungry at their doorstep, the fat pig Appa didn't even ask us in, but cunningly extracted Tusker, talking through the night to lay down the so-called rules of some sham covenant and how we had to give our lives up to the cause, which turned out to be only his fat-blubbered cause, in order to pay him back for the crumbs he threw us. Our own crumbs.

And worse, when you think of it. It was for that sham covenant to the fucking Tamil homeland question that my

339

brother had to set on the path of becoming a killer for the greasy Appa swine.

Can't you see, too, it was more than just the money?

It was my father's way of keeping in touch; the letters he could never write, the feelings he couldn't express, while he too sold himself, fought and killed too under the pay of those murderers-in-their-hearts who funded the Black Cats, outlawed himself too.

That bunch of swollen, maggot-ridden Ramaswarmy swine of an Appa.

If I was my brother I would have made that sous chef at the Hong Kong Hotel that time steam his sons' and bitch wife's steaming guts to shove down his fat throat, not just their ears.

No, no, it was even more than that too. With me at least. I don't know about my brother, but just think of it. It was plunging me into all those years of inextinguishable revenges on my father for abandoning my mother and us. And see how he never had. See how this dying man here at my feet, like, he never would. See how, with these photographs his treasured keepsakes, he would have fallen for every lie and half-truth the bloated suckhole Ramaswarmy would have fed him.

How can you measure that? What can I say to him to change all the lies he lived with, to compensate for the hopelessness when he found out the truth? This man, my father, a victim too.

For, find out he must have, mustn't he?

It must have been around the time he decided to expose those Black Cats death squads in the newspaper those, what?, weeks ago. Was that not a type of giving-up? A type of suicide?

Sniff, sniff the steaming trail, Inspector Charles Bloody-fucking-hell-sorry Ekanayake. Come get me now.

Palhirana, the code name the paper gave him or he gave it.

Another alias. All is alias.

340

And then you hold in your hands a single totem -- a bunch of old photographs -- and you are left with what? The tease of yourself. The teasing you did to yourself all those years, until it became diseased.

And at last with nothing to say.

I could only nod that I had finally discovered and that I had finally understood.

And my father half-rolled over onto his side and, quivering with the exertion, held out both his hands to receive the photos back, in the manner that would have made only one hand an irreverence.

It was then that I noticed his hands.

The description has been correct. On his left hand, he had no little finger. On his right, the little finger was bowed.

I badly wanted to hold out my own to show him how mine too was almost missing there and mine too was bowed there, but then he started choking and shaking violently with fever, so that both Hansen and I had to hold him down.

And the only thing I had to say to my father after all those years was:

'It's all right.'

He did nod then, and smally. And then he slept.

I don't know what I expected, going there so late in the day.

It had been just to keep ahead of Inspector Ekanayake, mainly. I hadn't even imagined we would have to spend the night up there, or that my father might be in need of food, clothing, supplies.

Too stupid even to bring along a bottle of arrack.

Water from the other cave gallery we had. And palm leaves to cover us which Hansen went out to gather back down the track.

At about nine it started to pour down and wouldn't stop until the early greying hours of the morning. It gave a flat drumming to the cave, as though a procession was coming up the hill and was announcing its overbearing intention.

I've got no idea how long it had been since it had rained in the area, but that night it pelted down -- and, if it hadn't, the next day might have turned out entirely differently.

My father slept pretty well at first. His snoring was phlegmy and unhealthy with the huff'n'puff of a heart working with that it's got left, but regular enough and, for that time, the fever seemed minor.

The first I noticed the arsenal was when Hansen got bored and started clattering metal behind the concrete slab right next to my father's. I looked up and saw Hansen pointing something grotesque at me, which Tusker knew was a grenade launcher.

As I had found that time in my utility shed with my brother, my father literally had an arsenal with him in there. These weapons of war, yes. With so little food, I could understand how he felt he would need the weapons very, very soon for Ekanayake's people. But for me, too?

He had been waiting for me, he said.

Had he understood me so well, so all along?

How? Who could have told him how I only wanted to hunt him down like a rogue elephant?

Yes, those weapons of war again. I looked them over with Tusker's appreciation. A bit out-of-fashion... but the single American anti-tank, anti-missile Dragon with its 114-millimetre warheads, infrared guidance, light and portable enough for one man, and accurate to 1000 metres, although I bet the Yanks had it in yards. British LAW80s, not long ago the modern form of bazooka, accurate to half that distance, which was pretty good for an oldtime bazooka. The grenade launcher that Hansen was fiddling with was a Soviet RPG7, which my brother knew was traditionally one of the most indispensable of all terrorist weapons, a hollow-charge grenade launcher of deadly accuracy at 300 metres. At least a dozen assault automatic rifles; a miscellany of the British SA80; the Soviet AK47; the Chinese AT56. The TEC machine pistols. Boxes of the plastic explosives Semtex, micro-receivers, detonators, batteries, electrical kits, ammunitions. The Black Cats arsenal. More than just urban death squads.

These weapons of war and, yes, these men: my father and my brother.

These men of war.

How, in God's name, had some vague dream of a Tamil homeland become our concern?

I am now thinking that maybe it was because we were a broken family, refugees at the core, with no homeland of our own. And maybe that is as much as is ever needed for it all to start... with the fractures and the frustrations that only a mirage mistaken for a dream could ever partly emolliate.

None of us. Not my father. Not my brother. Not me. None of us should have lived a day past our woman so sighing and dying. Not one of us.

Because, without her, it would all come around again, and did, and will yet.

Later that morning, my father's fever mounted him again. I have never heard teeth chatter so much. We had no medicine.

Most of his grinding mutterings I could not understand. What he came to cry out was in Sinhala at first, a street dialect that even my Hansen could not understand. Neither of us could discern the Tamil that then came pouring out, nor when it seemed he was only grunting the language his elephants would recognise.

When it came to English for the times, it was then I heard him speak my mother's name, Eileen.

Eileen. I had only heard it a few times in my whole life.

He said it with such anguish.

He seemed wracked by the very demons that fired their commissions from the Tower of Babel. Such gobbed mixtures. And beneath the rain upon that drummed-upon place, under the huge wavering shadows fire-flung around us, he seemed to call upon unearthly witnesses of the things he had seen and the things he had done to say their names and speak their final dues of him.

For a moment, his face took on an expression of undeniable pride, of gaiting triumphs where others had failed, before some other torment seemed to wrench from him as being unworthy, for he lay instantly back humbled and began to croon softly and echoingly into that night and into a night of long ago:

'Aliya, aliya! Cheeutt, aliya! Hupptt, aliya!'

as if he was seeing and was calling his great herd back to him.

'Aliya, heiiy!'

The fire glow we had up, reflected in the dark jaggedness of the cave's shell, painted his damp face for all his seeming moods, but wildly and coarsely, like a torch shone from under his chin, And, in this crooning to his beloved herd, in finally man-beast gibberish neither Hansen nor I could ever be party to, he would have seemed to have found some peace for a time.

There was a compassion in that voice that probably only my mother and his elephants had heard.

I thought the fever might be passing, but at the dawn of the following morning it pulled him sharply back as if it was furious at beginning to lose him.

He shook himself like a wet dog and then began to babble again, this time so violently that his body rose and fell as though it might have been gulping water through an unquenchable thirst. And in this new burst of semi-consciousness he seemed to be striving for an accumulation of the individuality of his life and the indivisibility of its sum parts.

There was rage, that pumped pride again, that gaiting triumph again, a sung haughtiness, the horror of being alone, pain and the inflicting of it, some tenderness in sup and purr until, seemingly, it was being wrenched brutally away. Always the losses. Ever them.

'Fire! Fire!', he began to rage, then shook his head sorrowfully, 'but don't blame the boy, Eileen. Don't you know there are always really the two of him?'

He must have been seeing my brother burning down the great house on the estate, and my grandparents in panic, remembering that time.

And before my own feelings could take hold of me from this, he had already gone into a reverie in Sinhala. I could feel Hansen straining to pick it up, yet I heard my mother's name over and over again. He was reaching forward, it seemed, then hanging back, and then he shouted her name with such desolation while struggling to sit up that I could only apprehend she was drawing away from him, slipping through the now-petering firelight off into the rain shrouds teeming down outside.

He had heaved himself up on his elbows despite our efforts to keep him down, so slippery with sweat, and then swung his head from side to side, looking, searching, craning out, but not seeing us.

Stopped, then stared straight ahead into the dark corner there, and groaned in the deepest of griefs.

Losings. Leavings. Always those.

As I have said.

After that, he fell back and on his face was a look of such aghastness that I could not see how, with the losses he was re-experiencing, how he could survive much longer.

After a time, he then began to weep soundlessly. The tears rilled across his cheeks and down around his ears and it seemed a sacrilege to wipe them away. Whatever image he was now seeing went so deep as a wounding that his own voice pronounced there could be neither absolution nor renouncement possible for him, going:

'I will not, ever, have anything to do with such burnt flesh again.'

345

Now there was a grinding blabber, yet lucid and reasoning, without much muscular effort. At least it sounded lucid, for it was in English mixed with Tamil now and emerged with only slight emphases on certain words. He could have been around a negotiating table, a priest, a cajoler, a mentor endeavouring to instil common- sense into his listeners.

But slowly even this lenition began to grow harsher again according to the energies fired by each feverish memory. The reasonable voice became more desperate, louder; he began shaking violently again and calling names I could barely distinguish, and probably not have even known.

Not even my own brother could follow all this; Tusker could only give me the sense that our father was arguing with someone not to attack some Muslim village, not to butcher and burn and rape dozens of ordinary people just for being given the allowance to do so if the occasion arose.

Whatever image or images he was seeing was filling him with a flammable anger and a flammable grief, both -- a wounding in guilt from which he was determined never to have to turn back to, never to have to go through again;

'Never. Ever. Never again, you hear?'

It seemed to my brother and me, both, that this was signalling for him the final straw for him for what he had always fought for to protect. He grunted but clearly now:

'Never to do with such burning flesh again'

and appeared for all the world to be just walking away.

Then it was some sort of mixture of all three languages: times and images and illusions to giving commands, expecting to see them obeyed instantly. A humourless imperiousness clearly directed to lives being at stake and lives being taken. This was spoken as best he could from one elbow to the other, pulling either myself or Hansen into the reach of his fiery eyes, commanding us to take orders and forcing himself to give them.

346

And then the phantoms must have come at him in climax again. He fought and struggled, grunted and shrieked from a barbarity that he found within his own self. There came the fluorescence of raw power onto his features, ugly and merciless until he trumpeted, the last rogue of the uplands, in the triumph of having utterly trampled down someone or something.

I found that I was shivering with the fits with him; it was all I could do with what I was seeing of what was my father. I was becoming the useless, helpless watcher of a fatality. Again, it seemed. Always through my life.

And you can see, can't you?, how Hansen was better at this than me, and could keep soothing his hair with heavy and long strokes; perhaps it was the torment of his own life which gave him the patience for someone else's suffering. I don't think I would know.

My father lay still for how long?

I don't know. A few minutes. Much, much longer.

We could not stem the flow of the now icy sweat that poured out of him. Like musth it was. Like the holy oil. I had in my hands the unguents of my father, while he slowly rocked his head back and forth.

Whatever was in cauldron now he seemed to know to be coming and would not have it visit him without a fierce inner struggle.

'Aliya, aliya'. Elephant, elephant; the whispered crooning again, perhaps trying to calm himself, until he could no longer hold back a scream that came from the very depths of all he could express, and with such an irrepressible spasm of sitting up that we finally had to allow him to do so for fear of hurting him by holding him back.

'Jayalitha!', he screeched, and I knew that what had been coming at him was the butchered form of my aunt, hacked by the mad youths simply because they could not find him where they had expected to.

And then the quietus of deep mourning.

He lay still then.

It had nearly passed.

The fire had died to give nothing more than the occasional splutter of illumination now. The gods, the spirits of the cave-temple, could have been waning from the night now that their nocturnal dancings on those earthly walls had almost finished.

I tried to lift his head to a better position. I don't think I have ever felt something so surprisingly heavy. It was the same with his shoulders. He seemed to have become as dense as the cement slab itself and I knew from the groan that clawed its way out of him that this bout was ending for him with the heavy loss of love again.

His hand came up and gripped my shirt front and he pulled me down to whisper hoarsely to me:

'Eileen, you'll see. Take the boy to the falling water.'

With his greater knowledge of pain and suffering, my Hansen left his side of the slab and went to lie on one of his own. I stayed where I was, my back against the side of my father's slab.

It was past midnight, but the rain hadn't let up, the distant drumming still processionally coming. Underpinning that was the sweet dripping of the spring from the other chamber.

As I dozed, I fancied that the bodies of the murals in the main chamber had taken on their ancient substances, and that my father's soul had spoken from out of their darkness, deeper than consciousness.

I had heard the hot ramblings of my father, and had heard him speak from the depths of his being. And I realised that, as long as I lived, I would know my father now more deeply from these moments than if we'd had a whole lifetime together.

I sat there with a coming grief of my own I knew that I would have to render up to one day.

I sat there in grace.

The grace keeps coming.

348

You can get to feel that, you know.

I woke to his voice.

The chamber was all darkness now, flashed upon only by the occasional strike of lightning outside.

The rain might have passed, but there were still the drum rolls of thunder giving a nearing procession to the coming storm.

I comprehended his hand lightly resting on my shoulder, and his voice talking to me again in undertones, as though I might have slept but hadn't stopped listening at any time and was only re-awakening to it, the darkness a confessional screen.

He was speaking to me as I had always imagined he would: something floating down to me in unfolding continuations that never discontinued, blending with the tones of my brother, soothing and known.

While he continued speaking, his hand, still trembling with effort, explored my face, my hair, the back of my neck.

'I knew they couldn't kill you.'

I think he must have been repeating over and over. And this too:

'They found me to be a leader,' he rasped on, sounding without emotion, just the dry recanting of a life he might just have heard of. 'They found me to be a leader, they said. I said yes I will and they said yes you would. But they came to start burning the flesh like those they told me to chase. Those whole people. All of them, many you see and when I heard of you I said no more of that. They found me, they said, to be a leader.'

He said he had come to hear about Tusker from the 'soldiers' he had sent out to Australia or New Zealand or the Pacific or Hong Kong. Everywhere was the same; in the Tamil organization and in his own, they spoke with softly when they spoke of this Tusker.

The man who finally gave him an accurate description of this Tusker was a Tamil in Canberra, called Nath. (Yogi Nath! I saw the economist again behind his desk under lamp light, owl-like and fearful, yes, and I saw him, through my brother's eyes, with the Japanese sword through his neck and his white Mercedes sliding, without traction, out of control, oil lubricated -- and I seemed to feel the gods of that cave move with prurient excitement.)

When he got Nath's description, he knew he had caught up with us again after all those years. That, if the Ramaswarmys had avoided telling him about his own flesh and blood, they must have avoided doing so for years and, if so, they had to have been doing so deliberately, for their own advantages.

He didn't have to it burned into him to understand out what those advantages might be.

How many years before they tried to avoid telling him about my mother sighing and dying?

At least in that I was wrong. At least in that he knew she had passed away.

Tell me, he hardly had the breath to ask, about how she did that?

I spoke for a long time. The dawn light wall shimmering with rain shadows. I could speak at length to my father at last.

I told him all I could remember about the sighing and the dying and her leaving me. And me not being there. That my mother simply disappeared from my life. It's how it goes in our mind's eyes.

I could hear the reverberations of the cave of him half sobbing, half quietly choking in the darkness as though my words were clawing his throat.

I whispered… and I was bitter, yes, why not?… that he could have come, and she would not have done that, and so how was that?

He answered simply: 'I was too black.'

350

And I knew he was he was right at that time, and that it was out of his own fear as much as he cared.

1 had no anger at that moment.

But that moment didn't last long.

Sitting in that enervating temple between night and day, in the dark legacies of this templed land, its peoples and its devil-dancing sways of the mind, it was as if I could use my brother's mind's eye to feel how weary it all was... that this Lankan land seemed impossibly won, impossible to reach except by wading through purgatories that had, it was said, to bleach the soul. How you were tied to it, to its trunks.

And I was going:

'Then why didn't you do anything about the Ramaswarmys trying to have us killed, old man?'

'Ah', he sighed as though the question or its known answer was becoming too long, 'still the two of you?

Yes, we've stayed together; who else stayed with us?

But I had this other thing to say:

'You knew the Ramaswarmys were going to turn on us. Why did you let that happen if you knew it was your son and you knew about those pigshits?

'Did a Detective Baybe of an intelligence agency tell you that?', he half rose, heavily managing it, to ask and weakly add, 'It was not true'.

'He told Tusker. But you knew that, didn't you? You knew everything and said everything, didn't you?

'Perhaps.'

'No "perhaps", old man!' and I let it come -- all the venom I had built up for him: 'Why was it you, not the Ramaswarmys, who ordered us killed?'

I imagine you wondering why I could possibly say that.

Well, you see, all along, wasn't it?, I never had any doubt that our own father had wanted us dead.

You can see how he nodded and turned away.

'You tell me why.'

I could tell I was snarling and I only just saw him turning back to me but I did feel his relief. That and those mind's eye and eyes. That relief-to-tell rising off him as he gave husk to:

'I ordered the Ramaswarmys to kill Tusker because I knew they could never kill Tusker. I knew he would kill them instead. Easier. And... and what they did to me... it was like taking the revenge myself, isn't it?'

But what if they had got lucky? What if they got in first?

'No, never', and now my father sounded, yes, like he was letting off steam, 'I paid Baybe too well to keep you protected. Melbourne. Hong Kong'.

At the last, that Martin Baybe was to send you back.

My father said.

And then I felt him pull on my ear lobe, in the way I suddenly remembered he would do when I was a child and I had the pleasure of knowing I was somehow making him happy at that moment, despite all. And then, we were father and son as you would recognise:

Did I like Australia?

I liked Australia, father, but I am here with you now.

Will you marry the little girl?

I'll marry Virathni, yes.

Can you ever be happy?

We'll see, we'll see. There is just a little matter of an unseen chaperone, but, yes, father, I will see that fly out of the window.

Her aunt, your Aunt Jayalitha...

Yes, father, Virathni told me.

She was your aunt who you should never stop loving. She taught you that. That love.

Yes, father, I think we know.

Well, I think it was like that. I'm sure it was like that. But I could have been dozing, yes, and then sunk back into sleep. The heaviness of the coming morning and the way he could only whisper crooningly; it was like being cradled. There was the drug of light of the early dawn powdering outside.

I fancied I could hear the rain sweeping in then, easing again in rat-tat-tat rhythms and the restlessness of the cave temple deities, so thirsty in the night for the whispered secrets from the world below, begin finally to quieten.

In that light, I jolted myself to look back up at the body that carried his voice to me.

There was nothing left of him, as though the last spark of his telling had used the body tissues as fuel.

I heard then the other drumming above the storm.

The beating of the steel crow's rotor blades.

The thrum-thrumming procession was nearing.

'They are coming now', I said to him as obviously as I could.

'Then you must do what you came here to do.'

His voice seemed to be the only thing alive, so barely.

'Not,' I gave in to, 'now.'

'Then you must leave me.'

'No.'

His fingers searched for my earlobes. A boy once, the gesture of my father being contented.

It was what it only ever had to be.

'Then you must take me to the waterfall.'

I didn't understand.

When I took him to the waterfall, he said, I might perhaps understand. You see, it was there it first happened between your mother and me, it was there your mother and I came to you, he said, and had expended all the energy he had for staying conscious, maybe even alive.

When I woke up, Hansen was not there, my father lame to unconsciousness, not even sweating anymore.

In the half light of the morning chamber, he at least looked soft, as if the hard edginess of the struggle had passed from him.

I don't know how long I stood and looked down at him. I was looking at a mirror that had shrunk me. The nose, the eyebrows, the jut of the chin. In his rib cage I could see mine.

In his hips, mine. I could see him striding, running, bellowing, touching my mother's arms for enough of the rice she was spooning out in the mellow light of lunchtimes so long ago. My father, my brother, my me.

Hansen had come back. He had pain in his eyes I had never seen before for all the times I had sat with him. I knew we had to move quickly.

He had gone back as far as the river below the falls and found the hunters down there signalling to the helicopter

He looked meaningfully at those weapons of war, and then back to me, trying to read what was in my mind. He had no panic, only an indivisible loyalty he might have been starved of in life.

But no more weapons of war. No more of those. My brother was not with me anymore. I had felt his departure during the night. One day I would tell him, but for now I had to do this alone.

I lifted my father easily. Hansen did not have to help at any time along the path, nor show me the way we had to go. The lifting and the carrying were as familiar as the way to the head of the waterfall suddenly seemed to be.

The thrum-thrumming procession of the helicopter kept coming on, but there was, for me, just the journey's end.

I held my father high against my chest so that he could hear me better. I told him of the things I remembered. The things he had taught me that I could never forget.

So light he was, or seemed to be.

I told him about the ebony elephants on my mother's mantelpiece, the ivory pieces about the house, the scarred relics of him. I had told him Adelaide and how the earth was hellish and scorched. I had told him Melbourne. I had told him about the man with the alias Tusker and how he had survived with me, too, only because of what he, our father, had taught us both.

I told him that, while I had been listening to him last night, I had come to remember now how it really had been during that king tusker bolting ride. Now I remembered how the great tusker called Rajah had just tossed off the mahout and left me dangling behind its ear like a flea; then your shout, father, and you seemingly falling from the sky to haul me back up on its back with you as it started to charge forward into the forest; you gripping the chain around me so that if one of us was thrown we would both be thrown; and the feeling I still have of the animal's juddering spine beneath my chest and of your own chest heavily covering my back from the whippings, from the thorns; crooning above the beast into my ear, brave, be brave, it is going to be all right as I love my son.

This I told him I knew.

And then, after those long, long hours, what they had found the chains had done to our hands. Both our hands and the same.

And that was how it really was.

On the way up to his waterfall.

'Eileen, take him to the water and then you will see', he had told me how he had told my mother.

From the single pearl strand as I had seen it the day before, Bopath Ella Falls had become a torrential plunge because of the storm.

It was how I hoped it had been when my father and my mother had come together for the first time at last. Those two strange and exotic bodies to each other. I hope erotic, too.

I hope they tore down those foreign clothing with the best of lusts, with all the grit and all the obstinacy of changing what they'd been told could never be, to what they decided they would insist on being.

I hope their bodies clashed, like ebonite and white mink, and created such electricity that I and my brother were sparked into life, not waiting, then and there. Great crackles of sparks. That, yes, did move the magnetic needles of the earth. That danced and spat around this sacrificial rock so high above the living temple and its ancient gods with all their monstrous prejudices.

I held that light old man, my father, in my arms there, where he and she had made born our spirit. I felt returned to a wanted place at last.

I did. I feel I have to say that.

And, yes, I held my father at my lodging place and I offered to my forever place of becoming and beginning the spirit of my father and the spirit of my mother, and there was no shame in it.

Yes and yes, at the opening just before the fall, the waters stretched into translucency that looked painful, but sexual, a rue'd and ruthless tension just before the huge and triumphal release. It sucked and gushed and then roared to a sweeping depth below that seemed to curl in and under itself in thrashing deliverance.

Where my family had begun while the rains.

Where it would end while the rains.

The helicopter could see us plainly now. Ekanayake might well be in it himself, the only passenger possibly needed.

Somewhere below us, whatever men with their weapons of war he had brought with him would be coming up, too. The procession. The drumming. The beating of the rotors. The humming of the rain that had begun falling again below us and marching up, up-thrummings.

Yes, father, the procession was coming.

But the hunt, the trapping was over. You had showed me so successfully how.

I had brought the last rogue tusker back to the uplands.

There was just now the journey's end.

Then I lowered him to his feet.

He had to try a few times before he could will his legs to lock enough to stand against me.

It seemed to me that we stood at the eye of the world, stationary at the quiet heart of a huge swirling, the whirrings.

He gripped my shirt tightly to pull my ear down to his mouth. I think I felt impatience in him. Perhaps he felt how lodged I was content to be, and wasn't comfortable with that lack of will.

My father's voice gasped out to me, as if these sounds were the last compressions his body could give.

'In all of it. There was only hope.'

And then he pushed himself away from me with all his strength. I can understand how those in the helicopter said I had pushed him.

My Hansen sits beside me, defiantly.

In this church, my church really, back here in Gampola in this now-time, God of there will surely embrace him.

I doubt whether they will accept my claim to the sanctuary of the Church as one likely to be persecuted purely on political grounds. Tilly wouldn't buy that.

But at least yesterday it stopped Inspector Ekanayake and his unmerry band at the door.

Rather, it was Father Thumbayaserni who had stopped them at the door to inform them I had appealed to the protection of the Church.

No doubt he believes it even less likely than I do.

Even though priests are not above the law of the land, still he stood there with his hand raised in warning to approach no further.

From down here at the altar, he looked like Moses at the edge of the Red Sea with me the only one left in the closing's path.

I hope they take a year to decide he can't as any priest do that.

Out of all the swim it is passing strange that here in this church I have found material sanctuary, even if I've got Buckley's hope of being extended any spiritual sanctuary. With his buying the whole of future Melbourne for a few blankets from the Aussie Aborigines, Buckley's ruined it for us all. 1803; a hundred and twelve or so long years ago of some with the seedy Christian names of Frederick Ludowyk getting all the luck.

Gampola St Joseph's, where the goodness that follows you all your life, as the hymn would have it, caught up with me.

And, do you know?, the goodness proved to be people.

Those objects I have always so detested.

People. You wouldn't believe it.

It proved simple after all. People. All you have to do is not keep thinking about what you're doing and what they're doing. You know you're always doing something rotten to them, and they're always doing something terrible to you. But, over all of that, they're just peopling away. Just leave it as that.

To do that, what you've got to do, too, is put on the blinkers to reduce their bombardments, put your head down and bum up and get on with the peopling as if they were actually worth the trouble.

What you should get to know of them should be simple.

What they should get to know of you should be simple.

It's simple.

In my book, complexity only complicates the wonders of peopling.

I'm not trying to kid you peopling is easy to sustain. Who would I be kidding. You know from all this I haven't had to sustain it for long enough to know what figs and what figures.

Perhaps that's the nub of it: make life short and sweet. And fall in love.

Somehow fall in love.

Fall in love anyhow you can.

Fool yourself, fraud yourself, keep hammering it into yourself that you're in love, and what you have, that love you are insisting you're in, is all that there is of hope and grace.

And that hope and grace is all there is of it.

Fall in love like John Wesley Hyatt did with cellulose. Fall in love like Phelan & Collander did with making billiard balls out of substitute ivory. Fall in love with fungus-faced, scrawny little turds of bacilli like Dr Armauer Hansen.

And don't live a day past it.

She came and sat with me yesterday.

Beneath the crucified Christ stuck to the wall with paint directly above us, Virathni came and sat with me and cried for me.

We will never get married in this place now, probably. But the darling one has surely re-sanctified this altar. Aren't altars only tables for tears of love?

I am glad I have chained myself to it.

I see my Hansen still has more than hope. I can see the outline of what can only be wire cutters in his trouser pocket. They must be in case I need a quick get-away.

With the pen and paper Father T. allowed me to have yesterday, I have made out my will. It won't make Virathni happy, but it might make her secure. It might compensate for all those years she and my Aunt Jayalitha had to suffer while my father fed the coffers of the insatiable Ramaswarmys, thinking all they had was going for me, was going for my brother.

And while she cried, I cooed to her that it was going to be all right. I bet her we would be married before this very altar almost as soon as I got unchained from it.

Unchained from it; hitched up to her.

Yes, and while she continued to cry -- a sobbing so deep that it was rendered humbly -- I told her about our father. I told her, even though she looked so unreconciled to hear about him haltered literally by the hind leg and trapped in such condition.

359

More than I could ever know, she knew the hopeless struggle he had had, and the hope, as all, he clung to. And she wept upon this altar for my father too, because she did not have the English to say to me what was really in her heart for him, nor did I have the Sinhala or the Tamil to understand what she could have expressed at last about him.

Because we were the only two who could want to talk of him.

Yet finally incomprehending.

I think my father might have preferred it that way.

He had spoken of her almost at the last. He had blessed us to me.

She took my free hand and bent low to kiss or sniff it, and stayed down there until she could control the tears, and then she looked up at me with such bright and large quickening eyes, and smiled a smile that this altar would never have seen despite the fact that a smile like that was precisely what it is here for.

I know why she did so.

Orphan, she thought, she. Orphan, I had thought, me.

But our own father had blessed us. Orphans we weren't any longer.

As to that, she could even bring her unhearty chaperone along when the time came, and I wouldn't be struck dumb.

For a few years there might have to be a few adjustments to our plans, though.

If the Church does come through for me, I wouldn't be able to leave the Church premises here for many a year, maybe never.

I could end up my days doddering over a broom in here or over a pair of hand grass-cutters outside.

If they give me my own *sanctus sanctorum* in which to throw down my bluey, how the blazes are we going to be able to give Madam Hymen the bullet?

Virathni squeezed my thigh and laughed as only virgins gynaeco-paradoxically can when sex is mentioned. Madam Hymen or not, she said, she would think of something.

I watched her straight back as she left me, the curve of her hips, those unbent and fine legs, the spillways of her spraying sheens of hair. She was pint pot in perfect form, factory mint, delicate and strong and loving.

The grace.

She has gone off with Father Thumbayaserni to plead my case with the Bishop of Kandy.

On the other hand, if the Church doesn't accede to my appeal for

its protection and I get slung in court, providing Inspector Bloody-fucking-hell-sorry Ekanayake's crew hasn't arranged a little 'accident' for me on the way there, it'll all come out about me.

That's the trouble about being hauled before a judge. According to everything I have stood for, the professional vows I have taken, I'd be under oath to tell the truth about myself in there.

Fortunately, I know I'm not quite that stupid.

No, my Hansen refuses to leave my side, although he does accord my right to be chained to the altar table while he must be content with leaning back against the side pillar on the steps.

While Father Thumbayaserni and Virathni are in Kandy, there is nothing to do now but wait.

Something is happening.

Father Thumbayaserni has come in. He is standing there in his white cassock with the black belt and is regarding me from the far end of the nave, but is too far away for me to see the expression on his face.

He is beckoning to my Hansen, who is now hurrying up to him.

It must be the hum of peopling I can hear outside. At least it isn't the drumming.

Virathni has followed the good Father, but she is not waiting. She runs down the aisle and flings herself around my neck. Sobbing again. I don't know whether this comes out of success or failure; for either possibility, her arms holding me so unprisingly possessively would be fitting.

Now, as others enter beside Father Thumbayaserni, my Hansen is hurrying around to close all side doors to the nave. He is doing so as fast and furiously banging as he can, until there is now only the main entrance open, as I see it over Virathni's shoulder.

The wholesome scent of watered earth of her.

Yes, and the others are coming hurrying in, too. Not in confusion, I can see, but determinedly, knowing where to go. They are forming a barrier across the aisle, through the few top rows of pews.

First, there is Geoffrey, that good man who is my landlord of sorts, and his ever-silent wife Dashana. And there are my five little guardian angels: Brenda, Stephanie, Janice, Michaela, little Marini. They are not even stealing glances at me; as poor children, they are so used to facing together, with highly concentrated passive obduracy, the things that are coming at them. In this, they need no instructions.

And there is Father Jayakody, as truly flustering as his smock in the wind, arriving just in time with his patients from the leprosarium.

And comes Sisters Lima, Margaret, Sriyani and Camilla, with their pitiable ragtags of destitute women and children.

Hansen has finished his door closing and even now is carrying in the old lady who could never help farting in my face, to lay her on one of the far pews.

And there have come many people of the general congregation to add to the human wall. They must have left their houses. They must have closed their businesses.

People peopling.

I have up there a wall of people built just for me. People, yes. The often-grace of them.

And I hold now my Virathni back as tightly as she is holding on to me. With my one free arm I hold her in gratitude. For all of them in her.

They are starting to chant No No No now.

I have to presume the news is not good.

Pity about that.

Ah yes, there's the cap of the Inspector Charles Ekanayake, his height.

The man will always stand out in a crowd for someone I suspect doesn't ever want to.

The cap jerks like a sea buoy as he mounts the last few steps to the entrance. It is still all I can see, until he and his gang push unworriedly through my human barrier.

When they pass, the chanting of the meek inheritors of the earth dies quickly. They know the limits of their influence, and know it meekly.

So, the Inspector and his party merely brush the people aside. They are and mean nothing when the State is about itself.

I see Hansen reach into his pocket for that thing I had taken as a pair of wire cutters and move a few paces towards the Inspector. I call out:

'No, Hansen!'

and he stops in his tracks, and then, in hot ineffectual shame, turns and flees the church. As much as my poor friend can flee anything.

Yes, I said friend.

There is no hurry for them to come down the aisle. Charles Ekanayake, instead, stands down there deliberately to give me a good once-over.

363

He feels no need whatsoever of removing his cap in my church.

I see he has the Bishop of Kandy with him. And what looks like military personnel. These weapons of war, still.

So this is it.

The thrum-thrumming procession has come, Father.

Oh, this sturdy man hanging on His cross above me. This man with the carpenter's muscles. This user of those muscular legs, day and night, across deserts, and hard lands, and bad lands, to reach people. Yes, peopling. He had only one procession, too. They hosanna'd Him at the last into the place of His death.

Have mercy on me and I'll try real hard without promising anything to forgive that damn Inspector Bloody-fucking-hell-sorry Ekanayake.

And your damn Bishop of Kandy giving him the nod.

At least they have come in time to witness Gampola's first miracle.

They have opened my eyes and I can see clearly now.

My hands.

You see my hands?

There is nothing at all now wrong with my little fingers.

They are both now perfectly normal.

This day I should not really live one second past.

I am all whole again.

Sequel

Brenton D. Johns didn't feel easy about what was going on because he had no idea about what was going on.

Here he was, with full tenure as head of the Attorney-General's Department, yet it had started to happen that, whenever he entered the general area to check that at least some of his legal beavers were working oftimes, all he was copping was that Tilly female crying out to all and sundry things like:

'There he goes, and not even a blow-me-a-kiss or a kiss-my-bum.'

Johnno was a worried man.

He knew when some Tilly onus was about to descend upon him. He had the instinct for that. He hadn't risen to the top of the public- service branchlets to cop onuses.

Johnno decided on the recourse of hiding his head in work. He would win the 'in' tray and not emerge until it had been scoured. He knew he would win no medals for doing so, but at least by then the Tilly storm might have drifted away to darken someone else's existence.

About halfway down the in-pile -- archaeologically datable at around one month; exceedingly recent -- he came across the last few pages of the Interpol report that he could vaguely remember starting a long time ago before some lunchtime or other had come upon him with much greater priority.

He had no memory of what the thing was actually about anymore, but then that did not necessarily preclude going through it, since most of what he felt obliged to wade through lit up few, if any, memory synapses anyway.

He presumed his secretary had returned the main part of the file to ASIO, the Government's intelligence organisation. But it didn't matter if he was left with the psychological assessment part which came free as an addendum to the *file-propre* (if his French wasn't mistaken which it always was and it made him proud). What looked like something to immerse oneself in from Tilly wasn't to be sneezed at, even if it looked like it had many times over.

When he would be finished with it, he would, as his wont, initial it and pen 'Any comments?' with a mighty flourish before sending it on down the chain of similar non-read and therefore uncommentated-upon comments until there was one junior somewhere left who couldn't escape reading it. That one would know to add 'No comments', even though he or she had plenty, and that would be that.

Few, anyway, would remember the grade eleven lawyer called John Tasker who used to work there. Tilly did, but she would, wouldn't she? It was said he mug shot was one of the mug shots she kept on her mobile to torment her husband with.

As to the loose addendum to the ASIO-related file that Johnno didn't really read continued to read even as he pretended to be reading:

'... is fundamentally because of the amount of time being consumed by the Agency in endeavouring to secure the extradition of our subject from Sri Lanka to face counts of multiple (if not, technically by motive and/or intention, serial) murder, extortion with intent, multifarious drug traffickings - - to name a few of the possible arraignments so far.

'Even with the Hong Kong Government joining our own Government's representations, the Sri Lankan authorities continue to maintain their hands are tied by the local Catholic Church hierarchy, which apparently refuses to be convinced that the man they continue to shelter is the same man as our subject.

'For example, if you take this, your author... on my own fact-finding mission to Colombo, I was informed by an extremely frustrated Inspector Charles Ekanayake that when he tried to emerge from the church with our subject in tow, the same Bishop of Kandy who had initially given him permission in the first place was suddenly blocking his exit.

'According to Inspector Ekanayake, the churchman had declared (and I quote my shorthand): "Inspector, it is appearing I should be asking you and your men to leave. Can you believe the size of this congregation? Happy days!"'

'We have irrefutable evidence that, with the subject John Tasker, we are dealing not with an uncommon, however usual, sociopathy, but a form of aberrant psychopathy arising out of a split personality that borders on the sociopathy but has a fence but not gate between.

'We reasonably expected, then, that all we had to establish were facts that proved a prima facie duality of personality in the man John Tasker and the objections of the Sri Lankan authorities to the extradition and the size of the church's congregation would fall away sharply.

'It will be a regret to all here who have tried to rub themselves off on John Tasker that this hasn't happened, at least when it has come to the size of the congregation as witnessed by your truly on his said trip.

'For the record, the Sri Lankan Government and the Catholic authorities there have had the following inalienable facts laid before them, given here without the italicised numbered bullets:

'All our depositions from witnesses who knew John Tasker well related how he had this compulsion to talk about an identical twin brother, someone who was a shadowy figure even unto himself as John Tasker would have it.

'He always referred to this so-called twin brother as Tusker. If he didn't, he always mostly referred, then, to this so-called twin brother as Tusker.

'These witnesses (*see main file para 148 a. iv. line 15*) were also in total agreement about how John Tasker would use disparaging remarks about his twin's very dark complexion, and if he didn't it was, it seems, always on the tip of his tongue, not so very light-from-dark itself.

'This skin tone of his supposed twin brother seems to have been highly embarrassing to John Tasker, who apparently saw himself as having a skin colour as white as the driven snow, and not at all tinted by the Sri Lankan side of his parentage.

'In point of fact his skin was of the darkest, not just darker, pigmentation. I venture to say this addendum should leave it at that and merely refer to the same witnesses with the same main-file paragraph reference plus sundry *see-alsos*

'Furthermore, we had documented the following findings from our investigations -- and these are number-bulleted to distinguish from the above:

'**1.**

John Tasker himself, and no other Tasker, of any sort of colour or nationality, during either the weeks before or the weeks after, was in Hong Kong at the time of the bloody incidents that occurred there, and about which the Hong Kong Government has issued a strongly worded complaint at ministerial level to the Australian Government. *See under Ramaswarmy.*

'It was his own passport, and no "twin's", that was checked both ways through Hong Kong Passport Control. Furthermore, ex-field-agent Detective-sergeant Martin Baybe, *q.v.*, whose own conduct is currently the subject of an internal inquiry, has confirmed under interrogation by peers that he spoke to John Tasker as Tusker in Hong Kong at that time.

'Additionally, a highly respected local businessman of the island of Cheung Chau, a Mr Tsi Sui Yuen, has signed a notarised statement at the Hong Kong Central Police Station that a photograph of John Tasker was a business acquaintance through buying the occasional short pants from his eldest son on the local tourist beach on the island. He has sworn he knew John Tasker as Tusker, even as to any skin colour whatsoever, even if he had no skin left, to quote, "as he should have".

'Yet John Tasker maintains to the Church authorities in Sri Lanka that he flew straight there from Melbourne and has never been to Hong Kong like his brother Tusker. This is nonsense, see the ticketing and hotel-receipts evidence, he is sticking to.

'2.

Only one John Tasker attended Melbourne University according to the university's Registrar. Nor was there any other Tasker enrolled in any other course or in any other of our universities or in any other surrounding year that he studied law.

'3.

Members of the now-defunct SLA, the Serendip Lankan Association, affirm from photographs of John Tasker himself that this was indeed the man known to them as Tusker. They remember him distinctly because of the many social contacts he had with a few, now- deceased rotten-apple members of the association's old executive.

'4.

Regarding the supposed quintuple murder of the two sons of the Ramaswarmy family, together with their bodyguard and two unnamed illegal (it seems) immigrants, it appears that John Tasker remains equally adamant that he was never in Melbourne at that time or any other time since his marriage to the Ramaswarmys' daughter some years prior. Yet, the car rental forms and the AMEX coupons show his signature and his driver's licence.

'5.

In the collaborative evidence given by the two Tamils, S. Premachandra and K. Ponnambalam, who were convicted for the Sydney travel agency fraud early last year, both were insistent that they had heard that the most powerful figure in the Transnational Government of Tamil Eelam, or TGTE, *q.v.*, in Australia was a lawyer working in a legal government department in Canberra, and whose code name was Tusker. The man not the department, name withheld. They had informed Inspector Charles Ekanayake of this early in the investigations.

'6.

There is one further curiosity about the indisputable split personality of John Tasker.

'It revolves around a common sociopath's trait of being obsessed with how he appeared to the world -- or how he thought he appeared to the world -- in what is often referred to as the "manly stakes". It seems he would often break out into an account about some childhood accident with a run-amok bull elephant. In this story, he would recount how his hands were permanently damaged.

'Even as he was speaking, he would blandly hold up his hands to show how his right little finger had been torn right off and how his left little finger had been badly bowed for life.

'But anybody could see that both his little fingers were perfectly normal.

'7.

Recently unearthed Sri Lankan records show that his mother gave birth to only one son. Furthermore, Australian Immigration archives reveal that she arrived in Australia from Sri Lanka alone -- and that it wasn't until two years later that she agreed to accept the application for a son, called John Tasker, to migrate from Sri Lanka to join her. Apparently, it had been made out by the boy's grandparents who were still existing in Sri Lanka then and living badly-burnt lives.

'Yet John Tasker always insisted he migrated to Australia with her and that it was his twin brother who had arrived those two years later. He maintained his twin's arrival at that time was too much for his mother and was the primary cause of her early demise.

'More likely, rudely rooted out of his beloved Sri Lanka as a mere lad and dropped into the then White Australia, for him her eyes could well have suddenly mirrored his true colour of extreme melanous appearance -- and, for her, and probably more traumatically, remembering those days, the realisation she would now never be able to hide her coloured past with a child looking like that hanging onto her bootstraps.

'Just maybe that was when the split personality began to break out in the boy. Might one appeal to the South Australian that runs through our veins and venture to express it as "The Adelaide Syndrome of The Time"? One can imagine the look of horror the lad saw on his own mother's face when she met him off the wharf.

Brenton D. John's attention gently swayed away from the addendum he would from thence forget to the nice piece of scrimshaw he had picked up last Saturday from Nighs Antiques. As the persona of his nickname of Johnno, he was always looking for fleas in flea markets and, failing that, was never really satisfied with his purchases.

He mightn't have been aware of it, but he always expressed that latent disappointment by bringing them back to the office rather than leaving them at home.

This time they wanted him to believe the ivory tusk carving depicted the Maharajah, king tusker of the famous annual Kandy parade in Sri Lanka.

Pull this one.

Still, it would do nicely for the trophy cabinet if he had a trophy cabinet -- providing he replaced that awful plastic base it was mounted upon.

They should shoot whoever invented plastic.

About the author

Bill Reed is an award-winning Australian novelist, playwright and short-story writer with national awards in those categories. He has worked as editor and journalist both in Australia and overseas. His credits include, for long fiction, the Fellowship of Australian Writers' ANA award; for drama, the Critics' Choice Award and the Alexander Theatre Award; and, for short fiction, the National Short Story Award, plus four other first-places in national short-story competitions. He now divides his time between Australia and Sri Lanka.